AT 8:35 A.M. PACIFIC TIME, THE GROUND BENEATH THE MOTOR HOME BEGAN TO SHAKE.

At first it was a sharp rattle, then the ground seemed to turn into an ocean, the vehicle rocking like a ship drifting atop soft swells. The motor home creaked and groaned, the sound of it mixed with a low rumble coming from the outside as if some unseen freight train was passing by. Another series of sharp rattles sent dishes flying.

And then . . . it stopped.

Dr. Wickshire sat down on the sofa in awe. "It's just as they predicted," she said. "No one could guess five earthquakes in a row. And yet . . . they've done it."

Then her face took on a new expression. Gone was the awe. In its place was something akin to terror.

"We've got to do something!" she said. "There's no longer any doubt in my mind. Los Angeles is about to be destroyed. *Totally!*"

THE BIG ONE

A NOVEL BY

HARRISON ARNSTON

ZEBRA BOOKS
KENSINGTON PUBLISHING CORP.

This is a work of fiction. All references to places, people, or events is made for dramatic purposes only and is intended purely for the entertainment of the reader. Any similarity between actual people or events is purely coincidental.

ZEBRA BOOKS

are published by

Kensington Publishing Corp.
475 Park Avenue South
New York, NY 10016

Copyright © 1990 by Harrison Arnston

First printing: February 1990

Printed in the United States of America

For my sister Margaret Landry, an author in her own right, and my brother Donald. Both have encouraged me from the beginning. For that, I thank them and express my love. To my brother Len — who thought I was nuts — I love you anyway. And a special thank you to Don Rhoades.

AUTHOR'S NOTE

On October 17, 1989, an earthquake measuring 7.1 on the Richter scale struck the San Francisco Bay area, causing considerable death and destruction. Most experts agree that this earthquake was *not* the much-feared Big One.

No one knows exactly when the Big One will strike, where it will strike, or how strong it will be. They are sure of only one thing—it *will* come.

Prologue

Two cars, one closely following the other, parked at a promontory adjacent to a tight curve in the snakelike road that wound its way through the Santa Cruz mountain range. The spot was less than forty miles south of the venerable city of San Francisco, less than ten miles west of the parvenu affluence of Silicon Valley. The air was clear and crisp, the reflected light from the moon casting a soft, yellow glow over the heavily wooded area.

The drivers of both cars exited their vehicles, leaving the engines running. For a moment, the two men, tall, muscular, dressed in almost identical business suits, looked around and listened, saying nothing. All was quiet, save for the sound of crickets and the occasional owl. Satisfied, the driver of the first car said, "Okay, I'll take care of him. You get the gas."

As his companion removed two plastic gas cans from the trunk of one car, the man opened the door to the first car and struggled to transfer a lifeless form slumped in the passenger's seat to a position behind the steering wheel. It took some effort, as the car, a Nissan 280Z, was a low-slung sports car, and the body of the man was heavy and difficult to move.

Finally, after much grunting and cursing, it was done.

The hands of the dead man were placed upon the steering wheel and the seat belt was snapped into position.

Before proceeding further with their task, both men stood motionless. Once again, they scanned the surrounding area and listened for the sound of any approaching vehicle. From the promontory, which jutted out over a deep ravine, the men could see anything coming up the road within five hundred yards in either direction.

There was nothing.

Quickly, they went back to work. While one of them poured fuel over the exterior of the 280Z, the other doused the interior. Then, the gas cap was removed and a long, thin wick was inserted into the neck of the gas tank. The other end of the wick was carefully wrapped around the door post.

As one man took the now-empty fuel cans back to the other car, his partner removed a book of matches from his pocket. Holding the matches in one hand, he reached in with the other and shifted the automatic transmission lever into "drive."

As the car began to inch forward, he lit two matches, flung them through the open window, and ran toward the parked car as the moving vehicle burst into flames. In seconds, the car carrying the dead man rolled over the edge. It rattled down the side of the ravine, smashing violently against the rocks until finally settling upside down at the bottom, still aflame, with two of its tires spinning crookedly.

A dull thud reverberated through the ravine as the

gas tank exploded, sending fresh flames shooting twenty feet in the air.

For a moment, the men stood at the edge of the ravine and stared into the flames. One of them grinned and gave a little wave. "Bye, Tommy," he said. Then, he slapped his companion on the shoulder. "We better get the hell out of here."

"Right."

The two got into the parked car. As they drove away from the scene of their handiwork, the flames from the wreck cast an eerie glow on the leaves of the bushes bordering the gorge. Leaves that rustled gently in the breeze, as though in counterpoint to the violence that had just visited this place.

Chapter One

They both noticed the noise first. Ted Kowalczyk looked up from the insurance policy in his hands to his secretary, who stopped explaining the details of the claim and locked eyes with Ted.

It was as though someone were throwing pebbles at the window, even though that was impossible, since the office was on the fifteenth floor of the Los Angeles high-rise. Then, the sound changed from a light crackling to a deep rumble. Ted and Shirley looked at the window.

The building was swaying.

An earthquake!

"Quick!" Ted yelled. "Go stand in the doorway!"

Shirley ran to the doorway and braced herself. Ted squeezed his massive frame beneath the desk.

The noise intensified. Ted could feel the floor vibrating. The desk seemed to be bouncing up and down. He gritted his teeth as he felt the building continue to move. If this was a bad one, the really *big* one, hiding under a desk or bracing oneself in a doorway wouldn't make much difference.

It wasn't Ted's first experience with an earthquake, and no doubt, it wouldn't be his last. To live in California was to live with the knowledge that an earthquake could strike at any time. Usually, at least with the moderate ones, they lasted for only a few seconds. But those seconds could be terrifying. The earth trembled, walls shook, dust flew, and there was the sound of things falling from shelves and crashing to the floor. For those inside the tall buildings, there were additional concerns, as the buildings had a tendency to sway. It was a feature that was engineered into the structures by architects who claimed it helped relieve the stress on the buildings.

The quake had lasted ten seconds so far. In other parts of the city, supermarket aisles became cluttered with all manner of bottles and cans, lighting fixtures swayed, and some storefront windows shattered. Outdoors, a few highways developed small cracks in the road surface, rivers temporarily overflowed their banks, and freeway drivers wondered if their tires had suddenly gone flat.

In the residential areas, swimming pools came alive and water slopped over onto lawns and patios. Tall trees swayed back and forth as though caught in some unseen wind.

And almost everywhere, ears were assailed by a combination of creaks and groans as walls tried to pull away from studs and heavy beams writhed. The air itself seemed to generate a low rumble that struck fear in the hearts of even the bravest souls.

And as they sought shelter in a doorway, or under a table, or simply fell to the ground, those experiencing the quake would notice a slight uneasiness in their stomachs and become aware of an almost subliminal message creeping along their nervous systems, trying to find its way to their brains. The message was one that repeated itself every time an earthquake struck — more a question than anything else. It was probably the only time that the entire population of a large area was thinking exactly the same thing at the same time.

"Is this the *big* one?" they would ask themselves. The Big One. The quake that the scientists had been predicting for years. The quake that would, as the jokes went, make most Californians instant owners of waterfront property.

The question resounded in Ted's mind as the quake continued.

For a few seconds more, the intensity increased; the shaking became more serious, almost violent.

And then it stopped.

Small puffs of dust filtered down from the acoustic ceiling in Ted's office in the Metro Trust building, just one of a new forest of high-rise buildings located in downtown Los Angeles. On the far wall, a drinking glass that had been teetering on the edge of a shelf lost its balance and fell to the ground. The sound of it smashing into a hundred fragments was all the more shocking now that the quake had stopped.

Ted crawled out from underneath the desk and walked gingerly around his office, checking the minor damage, his confidence slightly shaken. But he knew that in a couple of days, he'd forget all about it.

Until the next one.

This one wasn't all that big, as earthquakes went. A 5.3 on the Richter scale, they would say later. At least the early reports marked it as being a 5.3. Still later, they would upgrade it, or downgrade it, depending on how you wanted to look at it, to a 5.4. Nothing unusual there. The magnitude reports of earthquakes were often changed once additional data was received and calibrated. But it was enough to rattle windows and make tall buildings sway gently. And drive a small nail into the wall of confidence that Californians try to build around their conscious fear of earthquakes.

Ted, like most people fortunate enough to live in California, accepted earthquakes as something to be lived with. It was a fatalistic attitude that seemed to serve him well until . . . the earth began to move and the ground behaved more like a slightly choppy sea than immobile clay.

In Los Angeles, there were minor earthquakes several times a year, but they were usually so small that no one was even aware they'd occurred. But every so often, maybe once every other year, an earthquake big enough to be felt shook things up.

Ted stood in the center of the office and stared out the window. Luckily, it was still in one piece. From his vantage point, one hundred and fifty feet above the ground, nothing seemed amiss. Traffic continued to wind its tortuous way along the two freeways visible from the window. No buildings lay in ruins. No fires glowed.

A white-faced Shirley Baker stood in the doorway, one hand firmly gripping the frame, the other covering her mouth. The attractive brunette looked as though she expected another quake to occur any second. "Did you feel that?" she asked, the words muffled by her hand, the terror making her voice quaver.

It was a silly question, the kind of question people ask when they aren't thinking clearly. When they're gripped tightly by fear that comes from something they know they can't control.

Ted turned and faced her, smiling understandingly. "Yeah, I sure did," he said. "Musta been at least a six. The building shook pretty good."

The hand covering her mouth dropped slowly to her side, the arm hanging limply. She let out a deep sigh and said, "I don't know if I can take this, Ted. I really don't."

Seeing how truly frightened she was, Ted walked

over and put an arm around her. "You'll get used to them, Shirley," he said, with as much conviction as he could muster. As a former FBI agent, he'd been trained to deal with fear, to handle crisis situations. This was far from a crisis situation, and yet he could feel a certain emptiness in his own gut. Earthquakes did that to people. At least for a few hours, they did.

"I've lived in L.A. almost all my life," he said, "and it's just something that happens from time to time." He pointed to the window. "Look, I'll bet half the people out there weren't even aware there was a quake."

He started to walk her back to her office. She was still shaky, her face pale, her breathing coming in short bursts. "One time," he continued, a smile on his face as he covered one of her small, cold hands with his own big, paw-like hand, "I was playing golf at Riviera with some honchos from Chicago. There were four of us, two to a cart. We were driving along and both carts started vibrating. We stopped and the four of us got out and started looking at both carts, figuring the wheels were coming off. Can you imagine? Four grown men actually thinking that two golf carts had decided to come apart at the same time?

"Well . . . it wasn't too long before I realized what had happened. By the time we got back to the club-house, it was confirmed. We'd just had an earthquake. I think that one was a 4.9. No big deal."

She looked at him with disbelieving eyes. "You told me that story the last time, Ted. You also said I'd get used to them. But I haven't. They still scare the devil out of me. My heart's pounding so hard I can hardly breathe."

"I told you that story before?"

"Yes, you did."

"Oh."

Ted started to say something but stopped when the foyer started filling up with people from other offices on the floor, all wanting to compare notes.

For the next half-hour, the quake was topic "A" in the building. Then, as always, people drifted back to their offices to pick up where they left off.

The next day, things seemed back to normal. In Los Angeles, damage had been slight, no one had been seriously hurt, and everyone seemed to want it forgotten. There were reports that some small aftershocks had rumbled throughout the area during the preceding twenty-four hours, but they measured less than 3 and nobody had really felt them.

Ted's morning mail was usually heavy with claims that had to be checked out. Most were legitimate but some, especially the disability ones, required extensive investigation.

This morning's mail was no exception, except for the parcel addressed to Ted and marked Personal and Confidential. It had been mailed from Menlo Park four days earlier and the return address was that of Tommy Wilson, an old college buddy Ted had kept in touch with over the years, albeit loosely.

What made the package especially interesting for Ted was the fact that Tommy was a well-respected seismologist. The last time they'd talked to each other had been two years ago, not long after Tommy's divorce. Coming, as it had, on the heels of a moderate earthquake only made the package all the more interesting.

Ted tore off the brown wrapper, covered with a colorful array of stamps, and looked at what Tommy had sent him. There were two items. An official report of some sort, sealed in opaque, blue plastic, and a covering letter. The letter read:

Dear Ted:
Please don't look at the enclosed until you call me. If I'm

all right, I'll tell you what I want done next. If I'm not all right, I want you to open the package. I realize how strange this must seem, but I don't know what else to do.

I would have put this on overnight delivery, but I just haven't got the time. I slapped enough stamps on it so they'll be sure to deliver it.

Again, I apologize for sounding like a complete idiot, but when I have the chance to talk to you, I'll be able to explain. I know I can count on you.

Other than list his office and home telephone numbers, that was it. Cryptic as hell. Especially when you considered the fact that Tommy wasn't a mysterious kind of guy. He was a very serious scientist whose work was his life.

Ted turned the sealed report over in his hands, then set it on the desk. He picked up the phone and called Tommy's home number. There was no answer.

No surprise there. Tommy was hardly ever home. He almost lived at his lab, obsessed as he was with learning more and more about the very thing that had shaken them all up the day before, earthquakes. His dedication to his work had been the critical factor in the termination of a seemingly solid twelve-year marriage.

Ted called the office number. A little-girl voice answered and said, "Dalton Research."

"Tommy Wilson, please."

"May I ask who's calling?"

"Sure. My name is Ted Kowalczyk. I'm a friend of Tommy's."

There was a pause at the other end and then the little-girl voice asked, "May I ask what this is concerning, Mr. Kowal . . . sick?"

"Kowal . . . sis . . . ick," he corrected. "It's a personal matter, nothing serious. If he's busy, perhaps you could leave a note asking him to return the call."

Her voice lowered an octave and became downright

17

conspiratorial. "Mr. Kowal . . . sack . . . I'm afraid that would be impossible. I'm very sorry to have to tell you this, but Mr. Wilson . . . was killed in an automobile accident three days ago."

Ted felt as though he'd been struck in the stomach with a heavy pipe. For a moment, his mouth refused to work. Finally, he was able to say a single word.

"What?" he asked.

While the stunned insurance investigator listened, she told him what little she knew, including the fact that the body had been cremated yesterday. There'd been no funeral service at the behest of Tommy himself, his wishes expressly spelled out in a will that had been drawn shortly after the divorce.

After a few more moments of conversation, Ted hung up the phone and leaned back in the chair, his body shivering as though he'd suddenly been deposited at the North Pole.

It was strange. He hadn't shivered like that since . . .

He pushed the thought out of his mind and grabbed the sealed report. Inside the blue plastic cover was a thick scientific report and another letter from Tommy. This letter was longer.

Much longer.

"Dear Ted," it began. "If you're reading this, something must have happened to me. I'm sorry to drag you into this, but as I said in the other note, I don't know where else to turn.

"The report you have in your hands is a copy of one I am submitting this afternoon to a secret government agency called NADAT, which means National Disaster Alert Team. This agency is part of a Pentagon task force whose function is to assess the effects certain natural disasters, such as volcanoes, hurricanes, tornadoes, and earthquakes, would have on national security. They are a secret agency that appears to be working independent of either the Federal Emergency

18

Management Agency, or the Geological Survey division of the Interior Department. I'm not sure I'm right about that, but it certainly seems like it. Why, I don't know.

"My report concerns some new research having to do with earthquake prediction. Actually, it's really the reworking of another report that was prepared by a former colleague of mine, a geophysicist named Vance Gifford.

"For the last ten years, Vance had been trying to develop a reliable method for predicting the location and magnitude of earthquakes. Two years ago, he made a major, major breakthrough. As soon as he reported his find, he was contacted by this NADAT outfit and told his work was classified Top Secret. Then, two months ago, he died suddenly of a stroke. Just like that.

"I was immediately contacted by NADAT and asked to review Vance's work and make a report of my own. Like Vance, I was told that everything was hush-hush and I was to discuss this with no one. It didn't take me long to understand the concern. You see, Vance had been successful beyond anyone's wildest imagination. He'd been able to predict three earthquakes in a row with uncanny accuracy."

Ted could feel the coldness within him intensifying. He read on.

"The report is self-explanatory. Even though much of what's in it is couched in scientific terms, you'll still be able to understand the main thrust, which is simply that a monster earthquake is going to hit Los Angeles three and a half weeks from now."

Suddenly, Ted's heart began to pound. At first glance, it looked like Tommy Wilson was out of his mind. What he was reading was . . . impossible.

He read on.

"I know it sounds like the voice of doom and in a way it is. Sad to say, it's true. This earthquake will have a magnitude equal to or greater than anything we've ever experienced on the face of this earth. Ever. The most destructive quake in the history of the world, Ted. And the epicenter will be Los Angeles. Not fifty miles away but right in the middle of the megalopolis! And we *know* it's coming! A first! At least for a great earthquake, it is.

"The problem, and it's hard for me to say this, is that NADAT intends to do nothing with this information. I repeat: Nothing! There'll be no warnings, no evacuations, no emergency preparations . . . nothing. Don't ask me why. All I know is that NADAT, for some reason, carries a lot of weight and that's the route they plan to take. It's completely insane! Why are we trying to discover ways to predict earthquakes if we aren't going to use the knowledge?! I just don't understand it!

"I think Vance found out about this and wanted to do something about it. And because of his feelings, I now fear that Vance's death was caused by something other than a stroke. If that makes me sound paranoid, I just can't help it. Naturally, I can't prove a thing, but I'm planning on telling NADAT this afternoon that I intend to take this issue to a higher authority if they don't do something. They may not want me to do that, so you, in fact, are my ace in the hole.

"If something has happened to me, that should prove my point. I can't think of any other way to make it."

For a moment, Ted put the letter down on the desk and rubbed his eyes. He was still having difficulty believing what he was reading. It didn't make any sense. Then he picked up the report and continued on, the adrenaline coursing through his veins unchecked.

"I turn to you," Tommy had written, "because you are one of the few people in the world I really trust. I'm a scientist, not a detective. I simply don't know

20

where to turn. I figure your past experience as an FBI agent will help you decide what to do. I just don't have any idea. I'm not sure going to the media is the answer. I've heard that studies have been done pointing to a massive panic if such news was released without careful preparation beforehand. Such a panic would create problems almost as terrible as the quake itself. Almost.

"As well, I'm not sure who in government is in league with these people (NADAT) and who isn't. So I can't suggest where you should go there either.

"I'm not asking you to find out what happened to me. That's unimportant."

Unimportant! Ted's hands formed into fists as he read that particular word. Unimportant! It was very important. At the very least, it was a starting point. Aside from that, it wasn't in Ted's nature to blindly accept something that was obviously wrong. He read on.

"I'm asking you to make sure this report gets into the hands of somebody who can do something," the letter continued. "The earthquake can't be stopped, but the lives of millions are at stake here. That's what's really important. It's beyond me why NADAT plans no action. Maybe you can find out. I want you to try. In fact, I beg you to try. In any case, I apologize once again for bringing you into it, but I don't really have much choice."

There was the name and Menlo Park address of the man from NADAT and one final paragraph.

"One more thing. Please see Terry and tell her how sorry I am for messing up both our lives. I realize now, belatedly, how stupid I was. I had a woman who loved me and I let her down badly. I was so wrapped up in my work and what did it get me in the end? Not much."

The letter was signed simply, "Tommy."

Ted put the letter down and opened the report.

Instead of reading it through, he turned to the back pages and looked for the conclusions. It didn't take long to find them. And it didn't take long to read them. They took Ted's breath away.

"As stated earlier," the report concluded, "the dilatancy theory alone is not enough, but when combined with the other three measurements detailed in earlier sections, a definitive estimate can be given as to the location and magnitude of earthquakes within the control sectors.

"Three earthquakes having an intensity of 4 or more have been accurately predicted. Using the methods described, I am confident that an earthquake having a magnitude of at least 5.2 will occur in section 65 of the newly discovered Glendale fault line on May 5 or 6. The epicenter will be within three miles of the intersection of Interstate 5 and the Glendale freeway."

Ted stopped reading the report and grabbed the morning paper. The prediction had been right on. The epicenter of yesterday's quake had been pinpointed and it was right where the report had indicated it would be. Again, Ted looked at the original wrapper that the package had been mailed in. It was postmarked four days ago, just as he'd noticed the first time.

No mistake.

The chills began anew.

These two men had correctly predicted the magnitude and the location of yesterday's quake. There was simply no question about it. And they were predicting . . .

He read on. "The analysis of the data points to an earthquake having a magnitude of at least 4.8 striking section 145 of the San Andreas fault line, located three miles south of Hollister, between May 9 and 10. Another of similar strength will occur in the same region one week later, most likely May 16. While larger than normal, these earthquakes are common in

22

the area and illustrate the steady shifting of the plates as outlined in section 4. These earthquakes, once they occur, will serve to further emphasize the validity of our newly developed prediction techniques."

Then came the real shocker.

"The Oct. 1, 1987 quake that occurred on the Whittier Narrows fault line is now determined to be a precursor to what I believe will be the most devastating earthquake ever experienced on this earth. I expect this new earthquake to have a magnitude in excess of 9.3 and perhaps as strong as 9.5. Its epicenter will be in section 73, located five miles west of the Oct. 1 quake, along the fault line illustrated in figure 53. The earthquake will occur between May 27 and 28. This great earthquake . . ."

The report described in detail the effects of such an unprecedented jolt. Every building that stood over four stories would collapse, no matter how it was constructed. The rupturing of underground gas lines would release invisible clouds of gas into the atmosphere that were sure to be ignited, causing massive fires. Oil and gasoline refineries, smashed into ruins, would provide additional fuel to the fires. Flaming rivers of oil and gas, ignited by fallen power lines, would spill over much of the Los Angeles basin, carried along by waters from heavily damaged reservoirs. What wasn't leveled by the quake would be burned. Fractured mains would reduce water pressure to zero, invalidating any attempts to extinguish the fires.

Roads would be impassable. Medical help would be nonexistent, with hospitals in ruins. There would be no communications, no electricity. Entire communities resting on hilltops would come tumbling down, further blocking already useless highways with tons of clay and debris.

If there was a temperature inversion, common to Los Angeles, and no wind, the smoke and dust would choke the life out of almost every living thing that managed to survive. LAX, Hollywood-Burbank and Long Beach airports would be turned into a useless jumble of broken runways. Fuel reservoirs would be destroyed. The only access to the city itself would be by helicopter.

And that wasn't all. The effects of the quake would be felt in nine states. The range of severe damage would form a semicircle that would include cities such as San Diego, Riverside and Santa Barbara. Outside that imaginary line, damage would be more moderate, but cities as far away as Las Vegas and San Francisco would still suffer substantial damage.

The report also predicted that a *tsunami,* a tidal wave moving at almost the speed of sound, a phenomenon common to great earthquakes, would originate in Los Angeles and move up and down the coast, as well as hurtle across the Pacific Ocean. It was possible that the Hawaiian Islands would be hit by an explosive rush of water that would do terrible damage. The entire western coast of the Northern Hemisphere would feel the effects of such a wave as well. In fact, the incredible effects of this most violent earthquake would be felt throughout the entire world.

But for Los Angeles, the epicenter, it would be a holocaust.

And Tommy Wilson, as Vance Gifford had stated before him, was convinced it was *going to happen.* The report requested that immediate measures be taken to prepare the people of Los Angeles, both physically and psychologically, for what would be the most terrible experience of their lives. A plan for the total uprooting of as many as ten million people would have to be prepared and carried out. Billions of dollars worth of real estate would simply have to be abandoned.

It was an incredible undertaking.

And it had to be done now!

Ted put the report down and stared out the window, numbed by what he had read.

He tried to think.

The prediction of the small temblor had been completely accurate. According to the morning paper, the quake's epicenter had been exactly where predicted. And it had happened yesterday, three days *after* the report had been mailed to Ted.

That made it four accurate predictions in a row.

It was mind-boggling.

God! It was unthinkable!

Ted rubbed his forehead, as if the activity would force his mind to function properly. He was almost dizzy from the shock of learning what was in the report.

He picked up the letter and read it again. It asked that Ted take the report to someone who could force the government to evacuate the city.

Who should that be?

The newspapers? Television stations?

No . . . Not yet.

It was such a terrible responsibility. Once the information was out, there was no bringing it back. What if there was a panic?

This kind of information had to be presented by someone who was respected and immediately believed. Someone who had the power to order the evacuation of the city.

But Tommy had said . . .

Ted looked at the calendar on his desk. May 27 was just over three weeks away. Plenty of time, in his initial judgment, to evacuate Los Angeles, if that's what it came to. But first, Ted felt, he had to read it all. Then he had to understand it. Then he would decide what to do. He couldn't make a decision now. It was too soon. He was still in shock. The decision might be the wrong one. He needed time to think.

He left his office and stopped by Shirley's desk. "I'll

be back in about twenty minutes. I have to make some copies."

She looked almost hurt. "I can do that for you," she said.

He forced a grin to his lips. "I know, but this is personal stuff. I'll be back in a bit."

When he returned with the copies, he put the original in his personal office safe, and put one of the copies in his briefcase. He took the second copy, enclosed a copy of the letter from Tommy, and shoved it all into a large manila envelope. He placed that in his briefcase as well. He wanted to mail it to someone, but for the moment, he didn't know exactly who it should be.

Then he picked up the phone and punched the buttons that would connect him with his boss back in Hartford. In a matter of seconds, Frank Leach was on the phone.

"Frank . . . Ted Kowalczyk."

"Ted, babe . . . how's it goin'? Things still rattlin' out there?"

Frank Leach was one of those people who looked and sounded like a used car salesman. He called everyone babe and slapped shoulders like a ham-handed oaf. Devoid of the social graces, the man was indeed an oaf, but . . . he was one terrific insurance investigator. Had it not been for that, Ted would have been long gone from Connecticut Mutual.

"Frank," Ted began, "I need two things."

"Just name it, babe."

"I need everything you've got on earthquakes . . . and I need a few days off."

"Earthquakes?" The voice was filled with curiosity. "We got nothing to do with earthquakes. You know that."

"I know," Ted said, "but you have the association. You can find out what's going on from your connections there."

He could almost see the little antenna on the back of Frank's head beginning to rise. "What exactly are you after?"

"I don't know yet," Ted said. "All I know is that I want to find out everything I can as soon as I can. The underwriters of earthquake insurance must know a lot of things that might be useful. I'd like to get a handle on some of it."

Frank wasn't buying it. "I don't understand, babe. I read that the earthquake was relatively minor. What's got you so upset?"

Ted had to play it coy. If he told the man nothing, he would get nothing. If he told him too much, the cat would be out of the bag.

"I can't tell you that," he said. "Not just now, anyway. Let's just say that I've picked up on some rumors I want to check out. As soon as I have something solid, I'll let you know. OK?"

For a moment there was silence on the other end of the line. Then, "Has this got anything to do with the hearings next week?"

The words stunned him. He'd completely forgotten about the hearings, even though they'd received considerable attention in the media. Because his company was not involved in the selling of earthquake insurance, they hadn't seemed to matter much, other than to provide a forum for those whose prime interest was in further defacing the image of the insurance industry as a whole. Now . . . they took on a totally different dimension.

"No," he said, "this is something else."

A sigh. Then, "OK, Ted. I'll play along. But be quick, will ya? We're runnin' way behind."

"I'll be quick," Ted said. Then he hung up the phone, grabbed his briefcase and headed out of his office.

Stopping by Shirley's desk again, he said, "Shirley, I have to be out of town for a few days. Something's come up."

She looked mildly surprised. It was the nature of his business to be running all over the state at the drop of a hat.

"Did you call Mr. Jacobs?"

"No," he said, "I didn't. If he calls again, just tell him it's out of my hands. He can talk to the company attorneys. I'm not about to alter my report. His client is a crook and that's that."

"I'll hold down the fort," she said. "You'll call in?"

"Of course," he said. "Like always."

Chapter Two

The man with the outsized, black eyeglass frames looked exhausted. The large pouches under his lifeless eyes, magnified by the thick lenses, were a sickly gray. The thin, white hair on his head was tousled and uncombed, a victim of the wet and windy weather that was raking Washington this day. His fat fingers played with the knot of his tie and for a moment it appeared he might loosen it, but he changed his mind, removed his hand and planted it on top of the blue-covered report he had just placed on the desk. As he spoke, his fingers tapped the cover.

"There are no options," Robert Graves said, his voice raspy from having smoked too many cigarettes. It was a pronouncement, uttered by a man uninviting of dissent, made in a tone of voice chosen to discourage further discussion.

There were two of them in the small Washington office. The visitor was Robert Graves, executive director of NADAT, a 60-year-old veteran bureaucrat, a civilian who'd worked with three different departments of the Pentagon for most of his life. He'd given so many secret briefings and lectures that his manner of speech, once an affectation, was now second nature. When he spoke, he sounded more like a displaced Englishman or failed Shakespearean actor than a man who'd been born and brought up in the Lower East Side of New York City.

The office belonged to Michael Davis, a liaison man between certain Pentagon departments and the Joint Chiefs. He was ten years Graves's junior and new to the position. Both factors made him relatively unsure of himself, a condition that was evident to the canny Graves.

The man from NADAT removed his heavy glasses, closed his eyes and rubbed the sides of his nose. Meetings such as this one were galling to him. Granted, the procedures had been formulated by Graves himself, part of the overall system he'd developed over two decades ago. But now, in his later years, he found it demeaning that he should still be required to use middlemen with limited intelligence to act as go-betweens between himself and those who were the ultimate recipients of his expertise.

Belatedly and to no avail, he'd tried to have the system changed. But those he'd served so well and faithfully over the years had determined that his original concept was perfection and saw no need to make adjustments. As one had put it, "If it ain't broke, don't fix it." Graves had wanted to vomit upon hearing the statement.

With his eyes still closed, he continued with his presentation, his face cloaked in a mask of what Davis perceived to be false concern. "Aside from all military personnel and equipment, which we'll move under cover of announced exercises, there's the problem with essential defense contractors.

"The logistics are staggering. Our resources are almost exclusively devoted to this problem. People, data, equipment . . . much of it will have to be moved in complete secrecy, a forbidding challenge. We simply cannot afford to lose that much production capacity. We might never catch up. As a cover, we'll move some of the less strategic elements overtly, an operation that, I am sure, will raise more than a few eyebrows. It can't be helped.

"But aside from that, there can be no other action."

Graves opened his eyes and repositioned his glasses.

"We have been handed," he went on, "a gift, one might say. Until now, most of our concerns have been focused on the activity associated with the San Andreas fault, these new ones being undiscovered until recently. Fortunately, the inevitability of a major earthquake somewhere in California forced us to carefully examine a score of scenarios. The discussions have benefited from the input of the best available minds. In every case, the majority opinion was the same. Evacuation is simply impossible. Other than those items I have already mentioned, the only answer is to do nothing."

Michael Davis could feel the color rising to his cheeks. Despite the careful tutoring centering on the need for discretion at all times, he wasn't about to let such statements go unchallenged.

"Do nothing?" he exclaimed, a note of pure astonishment in his voice. "That's not an answer. That's nothing! Surely, you don't expect me to deliver that message to the Joint Chiefs! They'll have a fit!"

Graves looked at him as one might look at a man busy picking his nose in an expensive restaurant. "In this case," he said, "I think you'll find the opposite to be true. Doing nothing is the *only* answer. An earthquake is an act of God. Interjecting ourselves into such a cataclysmic natural phenomenon is both foolish and nonproductive. It accomplishes nothing.

31

"I've forwarded transcripts of some of the most relevant discussions for your perusal. I'm sure, after you read them . . ."

"I *have* read them," Davis interrupted. "And I think you are all making a serious mistake. Some of your conclusions are simply unacceptable. You've dismissed all of the other options out-of-hand."

"For good reason," Graves shot back. "The quake itself is largely theoretical. There's no *proof* that it will take place. And that is the very crux of the problem. To take action at this time, when we have only a theory . . . would mean leaving ourselves open to serious political and financial repercussions."

For a moment, the room was silent. "You people," Davis said, finally, the anger now clear in his voice, "are so insulated from the real world, I doubt you have any true comprehension of what goes on in the average person's mind. The only people you talk to are each other. Your reports are filled with wonderful analyses that justify your positions, but what you're supposed to be doing is perfecting the very options you say aren't warranted. I find that unconscionable."

Graves's eyes began to show some life. He wasn't used to being upbraided and he didn't like it. "It's all very well for you to sit there and pretend you are possessed of some infinite wisdom handed down from on high," he said, fairly bristling with indignation, "but whatever talents you possess most certainly lie in other areas. I, on the other hand, have spent a lifetime studying situations that parallel what may lie ahead.

"You might be surprised to know that I am convinced that this earthquake is imminent, despite the strong arguments presented by some detractors who have studied the data and found it wanting. In my view, Mr. Gifford and Mr. Wilson have shown themselves to be dedicated professionals. Their detractors are, I think, more concerned with their own reputations than anything else. Their protestations must be taken in that light.

"No matter. The path I have chosen is presented with considerable insight. In short, Mr. Davis, I know what I am talking about. You don't. If you want to argue the point with your superiors, you do so at your peril. My advice would be to step softly."

He waited for a response, but received only a hard stare.

"Any attempt," Graves said, reiterating his position, "to evacuate Los Angeles will be an unmitigated disaster. Certainly, there have been situations in smaller centers where evacuation has been carried out effectively, during floods or hurricanes, but they were on a relatively small scale. The evacuation of Los Angeles would involve ten million people.

"If, as you say, you *have* read the transcripts, you will have learned that in order to control the situation, you'll need, at the very least, three hundred thousand troops to augment the civil authorities. We simply can't spare them. We'll be using every available man to assist in the movement of vital defense material. Without troops to supervise the evacuation, there is no control whatsoever. You'll have rioting, looting, all manner of problems in what amounts to total anarchy! And if you were to provide the troops, do you seriously suggest that they be exposed to the unnecessary dangers of protecting soon-to-be-useless property from gangs of looters? Not to mention the possibility that they could be killed in the quake itself. It would be stupid.

"As I said earlier, we must take steps to protect the troops, not expose them to unnecessary dangers. As for the methodology employed, leading to our conclusions, certain assumptions are absolute. There will always be a percentage of people who positively refuse to leave. Are they to be hauled away in front of drooling television reporters? How do you think that will look?

"What about the hospitals? Can you imagine trying to move terminally ill people through streets clogged with refugees? The street gangs! Have you thought about them? They would have a veritable feast! And the other hundred thousand misfits? What do you think their reaction would be? You haven't had the opportunity to consider these things but I have!"

He stopped and wiped a handkerchief across his lips. "And for those who do agree to leave . . . do you seriously believe that ten million people are going to walk away from possessions they have spent their life accumulating?

"No!" he said, answering his own question. "They'll want to take everything they own with them. Especially if they think there will be nothing to come back to. As I said earlier, the streets will be full of refugees using cars, trucks, trailers . . . whatever they can get their hands on . . . to haul their worldly goods along with them. A total debacle. Roads and highways would become hopelessly gridlocked, completely ruining our chances of moving those essential elements. An intolerable situation.

"And where will they go? Many of them are mortgage poor now. Their houses will be worth nothing. They will have no borrowing power, no jobs. Nothing. Who will feed them? Where will we find the jobs for them? Don't you see? It's totally impossible!"

Davis's body stiffened. He seemed to be hearing the man for the first time, his face reflecting the horror that roiled within. His jaw slack, his eyes wide, he said, "You . . . you're seriously suggesting that it is better for millions of people to die? You can't possibly be serious! It's inhuman!"

Again, Graves removed his glasses and rubbed his nose. Replacing them, he said, "I'm not suggesting that at all. There are steps . . . but that is not your concern. The purpose of my briefing today is confined to the subject of evacuation. That is your province.

Nothing else. On the other hand, if, and I repeat, *if* . . . there actually is an earthquake of the magnitude predicted by these people, it will be the biggest natural disaster in the history of the world. The entire planet will want to lend assistance. Money, people, medical supplies . . . all of it will be available from all over the world. For a change, the United States will be on the receiving end of a massive relief undertaking. That in itself can be a tremendous unifying force in the world. It may be the very thing that will unlock the doors to understanding that we've been seeking for so many years. I'd call that kind of thinking very humanistic. Very humanistic indeed.

"But nothing will happen before the quake hits. Attempts to convince the citizens of Los Angeles that an earthquake is about to destroy them will fall on deaf ears, I assure you. They will not be swayed by official government statements. They are suspicious of anything the government says as it is. They will see this as some insidious plot. We can't have that."

Again, the room grew silent. Graves seemed exhausted after his tirade. Davis looked almost ill.

"You said there were *some* steps . . . outside my purview. Surely, in view of the circumstances, you could be a little more forthcoming. I am, after all, cleared to the highest levels."

A small smile appeared on Graves's lips. This was the part he relished almost more than anything else. Perhaps it would have been possible to tell this minor official some of the other details, but why should he? He'd asked to be allowed to make his reports directly and had been rebuffed. The classifications were quite inviolate, classifications that had been established by others. They, therefore, would be the ones to live with that decision.

To Davis, he said, "Not the *highest* level, I'm afraid."

Davis's face fell. "It amazes me," he said, the disdain evident in his voice, "how you people can rationalize *anything.* You're prepared to sit back and watch one of our major cities be destroyed without lifting a finger and you think you can actually *justify* such thinking. It disgusts me."

Robert Graves stood up, snapped his briefcase shut and spun the combination on the lock. "It is fortunate," he said, "that the decision is not yours to make. We are both minions, Michael. Each with a job to do. I've done mine. Now you must do yours. Unfortunately, the Joint Chiefs, in their infinite wisdom, have determined that I should work through an intermediary. I realize, of course, why they have chosen to do this. While they see the need for our department, they wish to remain at arm's length from the realities that we are forced to deal with. That makes it much easier for them. Direct contact with me contaminates them, so to speak. Unpleasant decisions can be made and the ramifications thereof are subject to many different interpretations. Misunderstandings might have occurred, and all of that rot.

"However, it has always been this way. I accept that. You must do the same. I won't disturb you any further."

With that, Graves turned on his heel and strode out of the office.

As the door to the office slammed shut, Michael Davis got up from behind the desk and walked over to a small cabinet beneath the French window. He opened one of the doors and removed a bottle of bourbon. For a moment, he considered preparing the drink properly, using a glass and ice, an exercise he once considered a ritual. It had, after all, been a long time between drinks.

Instead, he uncapped the bottle and tilted it to his lips, letting the liquid burn his throat as it made its way to his stomach.

Chapter Three

Ted Kowalczyk tried to get comfortable in the narrow aircraft seat, without success. Whenever possible, he flew first class, an extravagance born of necessity. The seats were broader in first class and allowed him to travel without the prospect of losing all feeling in his posterior. But this commuter plane, on a flight from Los Angeles to San Jose, was a single class flight, with small, narrow seats that wedged big men into position.

To take his mind from his growing discomfort, Ted removed the report Tommy had sent him from his briefcase and began to read specific sections, the first of which was an explanation of the Richter scale. Tommy had taken the time to write the explanation for a reason. To most people, the scale was just a lot of numbers. They were unaware of what the numbers really meant, even though the scale had become synonymous with the measurement of earthquakes.

Ted knew, as did most people, that an earthquake

measuring 6 on the scale was ten times greater in magnitude than one measuring a 5. But it didn't really tell the whole story. As Tommy put it, trying to keep it in laymen's terms, "The Richter scale measures the magnitude of the ground waves created by an earthquake. It also measures how much energy is released. The two measurements are combined to produce a number that allows scientists to compare one earthquake against another.

"If the scale measured magnitude alone and was arithmetic instead of logarithmic, the scale would read like this:

"Let's start with an earthquake having a magnitude of say, 4. Anything under that doesn't matter much anyhow. Using the number 4 as a starting point, an earthquake previously measured as being a 5 would now become a 40, 40 being ten times larger than 4. An earthquake measuring a 6 would become a 400. A major quake of 7 would now read 4,000. And a quake of 8 would measure 40,000 on the new scale."

The section concluded with the information that "an earthquake having a magnitude of 9 would be equal to 400,000 on the new scale. A quake measuring 9.5 would be equal to, roughly, 2,000,000. That would mean a quake having a magnitude of 9.5 would be *500,000 times more powerful* than a quake measuring 4 on the Richter scale."

It was clear that Tommy was desperately trying to illustrate the tremendous power of the earthquake he was predicting. The numbers had the desired effect on Ted. He wondered why, in the light of what Tommy had written, there was no move to take immediate steps to evacuate Los Angeles.

He read on. The report contained other fascinating information. There was a section devoted to geology, which was Vance Gifford's specialty. But it was a bit hard to understand. There was a section on the relatively new science of earthquake prediction that was equally absorbing but even harder to fathom.

But the most fascinating section of all was the one that dealt with theories on how earthquakes could be diffused. Ted had only enough time to skip through it, but until then, he'd had no idea that such things were even considered. As the plane touched down, he closed the report and placed it back in his briefcase, his mind a jumble of confusing thoughts, his gluteus maximus a numbed, flattened mass of flesh.

He signed for the rental car, the largest one available, and took the keys. Quickly, he strode from the counter to the parking lot, where the car was parked, threw his bags into the back seat and got behind the wheel. He was in a hurry.

Three weeks.

This morning, it had seemed like time enough. Now, as the full impact of what he had read bored deeper into his consciousness, it seemed pitifully inadequate.

Terry Wilson lived in a small, one-bedroom apartment in Menlo Park and commuted daily to her job as a librarian at Stanford University. When she parked her car in the shed behind the apartment building, she was surprised to see Ted Kowalczyk standing by the rear door of the brown stucco building. She got out of the car and walked slowly toward him.

"Hello, Ted," she said, "I guess you heard."

"I heard," he said, quietly.

And then, without another word, she was in his arms, her head pressed against his chest, the mascara-filled tears staining his blue shirt. They stood there for a moment while her body heaved with deep sobs. He took the keys from her hand, opened the door, and guided her up to her second-floor apartment.

Once inside, she excused herself and headed for the bathroom. When she returned, she looked little better, her eyes still red and puffy, the streaked mascara not fully removed from her cheeks.

Her skin was deeply tanned. That, and the long, brown hair served to frame a face dominated by deep, dark eyes that heralded her Italian heritage. At twenty, she'd been beautiful. Now, at thirty-five, she was magnificent. Even the pain that pinched her face failed to detract from her true loveliness.

"Can I get you something?" she asked.

"A beer, if you have it."

"I have it."

She went into the kitchen and returned with the drinks. A beer for him, white wine for her. She placed both glasses on the coffee table and said, "I'm sorry I'm such a wreck. It's just . . . I messed up your shirt. I'll wash it for you."

"No need," he said. "I'm sorry about Tommy."

She sat beside him on the couch, let out a deep sigh and sipped the wine. "God . . . I can't believe it. I guess, deep down, I always hoped we'd get back together. That maybe he'd change, realize how much more there was to life. But he never did. And now . . . it's too late. He's gone."

For a moment, he thought she might cry again, but she didn't. She turned to face him and said, "We'd kept in touch. Did you know that?"

"No, I didn't," Ted answered. "It's been two years since I last talked to either one of you."

Once, they'd all been close. Tommy and Terry, Ted and Toni. The Terrible T's, as they'd been called in college. They'd studied together, gone to football games together, eaten together, done everything but make love together.

And when they'd graduated, Tommy and Terry were still in love and Ted and Toni weren't. There'd been no argument, no great issue to drive them apart. It had simply been a passion that had run its course.

Perhaps it was because of the break-up of the

foursome that they'd drifted apart. Tommy and Terry got married and Ted joined the FBI. Toni ended up marrying a stockbroker, he'd heard. Big bucks. And Ted . . . he'd finally married a woman named Erica. With Erica, there'd been passion too. But, as the relationship grew, the passion, while never really dimming, became almost secondary. She aroused in him deep, supplemental feelings he never knew existed. For six wonderful years, they'd . . .

He felt the chill again.

As he looked at Terry now, it seemed so long ago, and yet, like yesterday, if that was possible. A flood of memories, joyous memories, washed over him like a gentle mist. Memories of another time. A simpler time.

"It's nice to see you again, Ted. It really is."

Terry's voice broke his reverie.

"I missed you," she said. He could tell that she was speaking the truth.

"I missed you too," he replied.

She sipped her wine and then put the glass down on the table. "I'm glad you're here . . . but . . . please don't take offense, why did you come?"

It was a logical question. There'd been the obligatory Christmas card, but other than that, no contact between them. And now he was here, sitting in her apartment. She was no fool.

"I was curious," he said, "why I wasn't invited to the funeral."

She looked away. "There *was* no funeral." Again, tears began to form in the corners of her eyes. "Isn't that a bitch? I was surprised when I heard about his will. I knew he'd prepared a new one after the divorce, but I had no idea he wanted to be cremated. And no funeral. I never . . ." She started to weep again, but touched a tissue to her eyes and fought back the tears. "I never even got a chance to say goodbye. They never notified me or anything."

41

Ted leaned forward on the sofa and stared at her intently as he asked, "Who made the arrangements?"

"His mother," she said. "The bitch! Not a word! She never forgave me for leaving him, you know. Once, she came by, about a week after the split-up, and accused me of having a lover. To her, it was the only reason I would even consider leaving Tommy. I tried to explain to her that my reasons for leaving were legitimate. That he was working too hard and I only got to see him once in a blue moon. We had no children and he made it clear, near the end, that he didn't want any. I was devastated. I wanted children, dammit!"

Her face reflected her anger as she remembered. "She wouldn't hear of it. It was all my fault, she said. I was a manipulating, pushy wop. She'd been against the marriage from the start, she said. God! It was awful. I finally threw her out."

Now she was looking at him as seriously as he'd been staring at her, as though seeking some validation for actions she'd felt compelled to take two years ago. It wasn't necessary. He'd told her then that she was right. He still felt that way. But he sensed she needed to hear it.

"You had a right to your own happiness," he said. "You still do, for that matter. Mothers tend to be biased. Some of them are overly protective, even when their children are all grown up. You know that."

For the first time, she smiled. "You always knew the perfect thing to say, didn't you Ted? Even when we were in college you had an insight that was remarkable. That was something Tommy never had. And yet, I was in love with him, and you . . . you were in love with Toni. Does that make any sense at all?"

He could feel his cheeks becoming warm. Her eyes confirmed the directness of her words.

No! He pushed the thoughts from his mind. She was vulnerable. Much too vulnerable.

He shook his head. "Nope," he said, trying to sound matter-of-fact. "Chemistry, I guess." Then he asked, "So his mother took care of the arrangements? She never even told you about the accident?"

"Not a word," she said, bitterly. "I didn't see or hear from her. I don't get the newspaper and I rarely watch television. The people at the library have only known me since I started there. If they heard about it, there was no reason to put two and two together, even though I still use the name Wilson. I only found out he was dead when the man from the insurance company came by the library with a check. That was yesterday.

"He told me what happened. I phoned the police and they confirmed it. By then, Tommy had already been cremated and his ashes dumped at sea. I was horrified."

Trying hard to keep the surprise out of his voice, Ted asked, "Insurance?"

"Yes," she said. "The company Tommy worked for had some group life plan. Tommy still had me listed as the beneficiary. He'd never gotten around to changing it, I guess."

"You didn't know?"

She looked puzzled. "No, I didn't. I thought he'd changed everything after the divorce. He never discussed it with me, and of course I never asked."

"And the insurance man came by with a check? Just like that? You never contacted them?"

She looked confused. "Of course not," she said. "Why are you asking me these things?"

He wanted to tell her everything. But he couldn't. Not yet. "I'm sorry, Terry. I don't mean to invade your privacy. It's just that . . . well, you know I'm in the insurance business myself. We don't usually hand out checks without a claim being made."

She stared at him, her face looking even more confused. "I don't understand," she said.

"I don't either," he said. "I'll ask you one more question about the insurance and then I'll get off the subject altogether. Do you know the name of the company that issued the check?"

"No," she said. "But I have the stub, if you think it's important."

He gave her a small smile. "If it isn't any trouble."

She stood up and walked over to the desk by the window, opened a drawer and removed a piece of paper. When she handed it to him, Ted examined it and asked, "May I hold on to this for a few days? I'll make sure you get it back."

"Ted, why are you so concerned about this? You're not here because I didn't call you, are you? There's something else, isn't there? I can tell by the look on your face. What is it, Ted? What's going on?"

He held the check stub in front of him. "Can I keep this?" he repeated.

She nodded. He put it inside his shirt pocket, then said, "I didn't mean to deceive you, Terry. I *did* come to see you because I was curious why you didn't let me know. But you're right. There *is* something else."

"What?"

He ran a hand through his heavy thatch of sandy hair and said, "I received a letter from Tommy this morning. It was just sort of a newsy thing, bringing me up to date. But I thought it a little strange, for a couple of reasons. He wasn't one to write letters, especially to me, and . . . there was a paragraph that was, well, pretty heartbreaking. He wrote about his feelings for you. How he'd screwed up your life. He wrote to ask that I tell you that."

For a moment she just stared at him. Then she took a sip of her wine and asked, "Are you trying to tell me that he committed suicide?"

"No," he answered quickly. "Not at all. I guess what I'm trying to avoid saying is that he sensed he was in some danger."

Her eyes widened. "Danger? What kind of danger? He was a seismologist. A scientist. What kind of danger could he be in?"

"I don't know," Ted answered. "I wondered if he'd ever mentioned anything to you. You said you'd kept in touch."

"It wasn't like that," she said. "Yes, we kept in touch, but it was a once-a-month thing. How are you? I'm fine, how are you? There was never anything beneath the surface. I think we went to dinner once or twice. He wanted me to find a man. Like it was a project of his. Maybe he felt guilty and thought a man would take care of everything."

Ted watched her closely. "I think he *did* feel guilty."

"He should have." Her tone betrayed the bitterness still within her. And then she caught herself, realizing he was no longer alive, and once more, the anguish was upon her. "Damn! Damn him!"

Neither of them said anything for a moment. Then Ted asked, "How did you find out about the will? Were you in it?"

She shook her head. "No. Everything he had went to his mother. The insurance was a separate thing. The man from the insurance company told me about the will."

"Do you remember his name?"

She thought about it for a moment, then shook her head.

"What about Tommy's mother? Do you have her address?"

"She lives in the same house she always did in San Jose. At least, I think she does. If she ever moved, I never heard about it."

She dabbed the corners of her eyes with the now-soggy tissue and asked, "What are you going to do?"

He stood up. "Nose around a bit," he said. "See what turns up."

She seemed about to cry again. "Would you stay for

dinner? It wouldn't be any trouble."

Ted patted her on the shoulder. "Not tonight. If you ask me again, say for tomorrow, I'll take you up on it."

"It's a date," she said. "I'll look for you around six."

"Sounds great."

She stood up and pressed her face against his chest again. Without looking at him, she asked, "Do you really think he was in danger?"

He wrapped his big arms around her and rested his chin on the top of her head. The smell of her perfume drifted up and with it came more memories. It had been a long time since he'd had a woman in his arms . . . for any reason. Almost reluctantly, he pulled away and said, "I don't know. But I intend to find out."

She looked at him now, his brown eyes intense, the brow furrowed, the jaw set. She knew that he would, somehow.

It made her feel better.

Much better.

She was wise enough to know that he hadn't told her everything.

But it didn't matter.

Chapter Four

Michael Davis licked his lips nervously as he bared his soul to the man from the Interior Department. "Raymond, I've read this over and over and I still can't accept it," he said, holding a report in his hands. "According to Graves, we should simply stand by and let this thing happen. That's what I'm supposed to take to the Joint Chiefs."

He put the report down and ran the back of his hand across his lips. "I can't be a party to this," he continued. "I just can't. I don't care how many studies he and his cohorts have conducted, the idea that we are incapable of evacuating Los Angeles is totally unacceptable. Totally!"

"Did you tell him that?" asked Raymond Ellis.

"I did."

Ellis shrugged and said, "You certainly do like to live dangerously, don't you, Michael?"

Again, Davis licked his lips, his nervousness approaching panic. "It's not a case of living dangerously. It's a case of not being able to live with that kind of decision. Graves! The man is an egotistical Neanderthal. Why the hell anyone listens to him is beyond me."

"You realize he's very good at what he does."

Davis fingered the thick pile of reports on his desk and said, "I'm aware that he's held in high esteem in certain circles. As for me, I always feel the need for a long shower after I've talked to him. And as for the reports, they're so much bureaucratic bullshit, as far as I'm concerned. While I agree that an evacuation of this immensity raises enormous problems, it seems to me that the entire emphasis has been focused on the negative aspects, without any effort to find a solution. It's as though the lives of millions of people are just numbers! Statistics!"

Ellis grunted. "You're losing your objectivity, Michael. I can understand your concern. I share it. But there are times when decisions have to be made that seem heartless on the surface, but are, in the final analysis, best overall. Military commanders face this dilemma many times in their careers. It's never easy."

Davis slapped a hand on the pile of reports. "I'm not asking for something easy. I'm trying to find answers here. That's why I wanted to talk to you before I made my presentation. You've read the report and Graves's recommendations?"

"Yes."

"Well . . . the first thing I want to know is this: are we facing disaster, or aren't we? You people are supposed to be on the cutting edge of earthquake prediction. And yet, we have two people from a privately funded organization developing a system that's been dead right four times in a row. Your people had nothing. Can you explain that to me?"

Ellis tossed a hand in the air and said, "You said the magic words, Michael. Privately funded. That's part of the reason. Dalton Research is funded by an association that is, in turn, funded by a group of insurance companies. Ten years ago, they started hiring away our best people and giving them a blank check, whereas we've been subjected to budget cuts year after year."

Davis pursed his lips. "Why," he asked, "would they cut the budget when there's been almost unanimous agreement that a big earthquake would hit either San Francisco or Los Angeles sometime in the next three decades?"

"Three reasons," Ellis answered, holding up a hand and ticking off the fingers. "One, the deficits have caused them to reprioritize funds, and we happen to be in an area that isn't very glamorous. Nobody really gives a shit, other than a small handful of environmentalists, what the hell we do. Oh sure, there are screams when the redwoods come down and oil leases are given out, or when some animal nobody ever heard of is about to become extinct, but by and large, we don't get a lot of attention. At least, up until now, we haven't.

"And then," he said, as he slapped another finger, "there's Graves and his group. He's got everyone pretty well convinced that earthquakes are something we have to live with. At least, for now. You must take into account the fact that we've had a lot of people crying wolf throughout the years. It might surprise you to know that this isn't the first time we've had successful predictions of earthquakes."

Davis frowned. "Graves mentioned that and it's also in the reports. But this new system seems so sure! They've been right on the money four times in a row. What the hell does it take to convince people?"

Ellis sighed. "For every scientist who believes that you can accurately predict earthquakes, there are a hundred who insist that earthquake prediction is something that belongs in the same category as tea-leaf reading. Oh sure, there's been the odd time when someone seemed to have a handle on it, but until the scientific community has a chance to study the methodology in the open, they'll never accept these findings.

"As Graves told you," Ellis continued, "There have been previous occasional earthquake predictions that were quite accurate. But they were always isolated incidents, almost accidental in nature. When put to the test over a long period of time, the methods came up empty. I'm sure this one will too."

Davis shook his head in disbelief as Ellis continued: "But the third reason is probably the most important. We've always had access to whatever Dalton Research developed, simply by inserting one of our own people within the company. Once we learned what Gifford was working on, we went to Graves, who had a Top Secret label slapped on it. From that day forward, the information came directly to us, and only to us, because of the national security concerns. We benefited from the information without having to put up the funds. The same thing happened with Wilson's data. I'd call that prudent management of available resources."

Davis stared at the man and said nothing for several seconds. The only sound in the room was that of the grandfather clock by the window.

He wanted a drink.

"You mean," he said, a slight quaver to his voice, "that you doubt the veracity of the report?"

"No. But then again, I'm not that concerned about it."

Davis more than wanted a drink. He *needed* a drink. Badly.

"I don't understand," he said, numbly.

Ellis replied, "Whether or not we have an earthquake is beside the point," he said. "We're confronted here with the task of making decisions. In this case, we must address ourselves to one single problem, that being, do we, or do we not, evacuate Los Angeles. Since that specific question has been thoroughly examined and a viable recommendation made, the decision-making process becomes less complicated. You must learn to accept the inevitable, Michael. Evacuation is impossible. Totally out of the question. Even you must agree that Graves has studied the problem well. His thinking on that issue is indisputable. If we can't evacuate, what's left?"

"I'll tell you what's left," Davis snapped. "You can at least *try* to diffuse it. That's better than just sitting on our hands." Again, he ran his hand over the pile of reports on his desk. "There were several suggestions made during some of these discussions, suggestions that were being looked into, according to these reports. Graves alluded to them when I met with him earlier, yet he refused to discuss them with me. What about those?"

"We're still looking into them," Ellis said, his eyes cold and hard.

"That's it?"

"What else can I tell you?"

"You can tell me why I'm excluded from this information, for one."

"You'll have to ask your superiors."

"I intend to," Davis said.

Ellis could see the anger building in this man. Clearly, he wasn't thinking properly. Things that were being explained to him were going in one ear and out the other. It was just as Graves had predicted. Something would have to be done.

Ellis shrugged and said, "I'd like to be able to say we have a more amenable solution to this, but I can't. Even if we did, there's not enough time for its implementation. We'd need years to set it up. Instead, we have days. If there's anything to be salvaged, it's the fact that we'll all learn a great deal from this experi-

51

ence."

Davis jumped to his feet, his face flushed with anger. "What *is* it with you people? Everything is politics! Are you so completely cynical that nothing else matters? Is that it?"

Slowly, Raymond Ellis rose to his feet. "You're new at this, Michael," he said, an edge to his voice. "It's not a case of cynicism at all. It's simply understanding the reality of the way things work. In the first place, there's the money problem, which may seem like a small thing to you, but the fact is, people who perform services have to be paid. Someone has to approve the money and that means telling them why you need it. And *that* means going public. We *can't* go public.

"I know you're not familiar with that problem, having come from a privately held business where you answered to no one, but this is public service, Michael. There's a big difference.

"Secondly," he continued, "we have the reports of two men, two individuals, in which they state their opinions. Opinions aren't facts. Before we make decisions that will impact on the lives of millions of people, at a cost of billions of dollars, we need facts. We have to know that this will not blow up in our faces. Before we start running off in all directions, we need the input of many more people. That's the way things are done around here, like it or not."

Davis's face reflected the frustration building inside him. "What does it take to convince you?" he asked. "Four earthquake predictions proved accurate and you brush them off as being mere opinions? If those aren't facts, I don't know what are."

Ellis sighed. "You miss the point, Michael. Even if these men are right, there's still no way to effect an evacuation. That's what you don't seem to understand. I wish you would listen carefully to what we've been telling you. This isn't something that just fell from the sky. We've been addressing this problem for years. Don't you understand?"

Davis wanted to say more, but realized how futile it would be. Again, he heard the ticking of the big clock. "I guess I'm starting to," he said, his voice thick, his eyes on fire. He stood up. "Thanks for coming."

Ellis wasn't quite ready to be dismissed. He wanted to make one last effort to get through to this man. Extending an arm, he motioned to the chair, saying, "Sit down and listen to me for a moment, Michael. You're letting this thing get to you."

Davis sucked in some air, let it out slowly, then, sat down. "I'm listening," he said, his eyes still fiery.

"Good," Ellis answered, his voice soothing and warm, his manner much like a teacher trying to reach a recalcitrant student. "Let's assume, for the sake of discussion, that the scientists are one hundred percent right in everything they've said. We'll assume that there will be a monstrous earthquake in three weeks. That's number one."

Davis nodded.

"Fine," said Ellis, happy now that he was in control of the conversation. "Now, Graves has outlined the problems with evacuation. Let's, for the sake of this discussion, put that aside for the moment. Let's say that there *is* a way to release the pressure. You know, of course, that the only way to prevent an earthquake is to release the pressure?"

"Yes." It was a weak answer, as though the man was beginning to realize he was defeated.

"Good," Ellis went on. "Now, let us assume that an attempt is made to release the pressure. Let us further suppose that this attempt, however well intentioned, creates the very earthquake it was designed to prevent. What do you suppose would happen then?"

Davis leaned forward and said, "Are you saying . . .?"

Ellis held up his hand. "Please, Michael. Just go along with me for a few moments. What do you suppose would happen then?"

Davis slapped his hand on the desk. "I'm not a child, Raymond! You don't have to draw me a picture! I don't appreciate your condescending attitude."

Ellis gritted his teeth. "Michael," he said, "I'm not being condescending. I'm trying very hard to make you understand something. In fact, I'm sticking my neck out a mile here and you're being obstinate. Will you at least listen for a few minutes?"

Davis took a deep breath and said, "Go on."

"Good. Now, if the earthquake is a result of actions taken by us, who do you think will be responsible financially?"

"That's not the point," Davis protested.

Ellis shook his head. "That's *exactly* the point," he said. "The American people are not yet ready to embrace the concept that life is not without certain risks. They've been coddled and protected to the point where they expect us to solve all of their problems and answer all of their needs without cost or risk to them. Utopia! That's what they want.

"In this case, there are certain measures that can be taken but they are dangerous measures. There's not enough time to either inform or educate the public about the ramifications of such measures. The debate would rage on forever. And should we be bold enough to go forward, take the risks and have it backfire on us, there'd be no end to the damage we'd suffer. Therefore, you must trust in those who have the wisdom and the foresight to see the reality of the problems. You must accept their recommendations for the good of the country as a whole and put your personal concerns aside."

Davis wiped his lips again. He wanted a drink more than anything else in the world. He couldn't stand it any more. He turned to his guest and asked, "Would you care for a drink?"

Ellis looked at him closely and nodded his head.

Davis rushed to the small cabinet. For a moment, he hesitated, remembering that he had vowed to himself that he wouldn't have another drink today.

This morning, he'd had two.

He'd been told that if he took just one, he wouldn't be able to stop. But he'd proved them wrong. He'd had two and managed to keep it at that. And then he'd made a deal with himself that he wouldn't have another for at least a day.

But . . . he needed one drink. Just a small one. These meetings always upset him so much. Tomorrow, he'd have none. But today, he'd have just one more. He opened the door and pulled out the bottle.

Ellis watched as he fumbled with the ice and the water. He also noticed the slight tremor in the hand that handed him the glass. "Michael, I realize how hard it is for you to accept this kind of thinking. It's new to you. I understand that. But sometimes, we have to be pragmatic, no matter how difficult it is."

Davis fought the desire to gulp the drink down. "Raymond, I can understand pragmatism. But I can't accept letting ten million people sit there when we know there's a very good chance they'll be killed. I don't care how you slice it, I can't live with that on my conscience."

"I see," Ellis said quietly.

"I don't think you do."

Ellis stood up, walked to the door and opened it. To Davis's complete surprise, two large men walked quickly into the room.

"You're an alcoholic, Michael," Ellis said, in a voice one might use with a child. "You need help. I'm going to see that you get it."

Michael Davis's eyes widened as a large hand covered his nose and mouth. He felt a sharp pain in his neck and for a few moments, the panic rose in him so fast, he feared he was losing his mind. Then, in a rush, the fear diminished. For a moment, he watched, detached and uncomprehending, as Raymond Ellis gathered up copies of the reports and shoved them into his briefcase.

And then, Davis's world became dark.

Chapter Five

Mrs. Harold Wilson lived in a small, unpretentious house in a quiet section of San Jose. It was a narrow street, lined with tall pines and contrasting eucalyptus trees. The houses stood so close they seemed to touch each other. Houses that reflected the interest people in the neighborhood took in their immediate surroundings. The small lawns were well manicured and dotted with beds of birds-of-paradise, azaleas and other vibrant flowers. Clumps of bougainvillaeas nestled against walls or climbed cedar fences.

Ted Kowalczyk had been on this street before. Several times, in fact. The trees had been smaller then, the houses appearing not so close together, an optical illusion common to new subdivisions built seventeen years ago. Or perhaps it was because he'd been younger then, his powers of observation not so finely tuned. He rang the doorbell of the once familiar house and waited.

Sally Wilson answered the door, dressed in a pink terrycloth robe that only served to emphasize her considerable bulk. Her hair was wound tight in a forest of metallic curlers and her bulbous eyes peered out over half-frame reading glasses. There was a drink in her hand and a cigarette dangling from her lips.

"What is it?" she said, as sharply as she could, her voice scarcely above a harsh whisper. And then, almost as soon as she had spoken the words, her face brightened. She pulled the cigarette from her mouth, a big smile forcing her lips away from the false teeth.

"I know you," she said, excitedly. "You're that Polack pal of Tommy's, ain't ya! Kowalski or sumtin'. Yeah! Jeez, it's been a long time! Come in! Come in!"

"You have a good memory," Ted said, as he moved past her into the house.

"I never forget a face," she said. "Never!"

They moved into the cramped living room where Ted's presence sent the parrot into a frenzy of complaint. Two large black cats got up from the couch and took off for parts unknown, leaving a trail of black hairs in their wake. Ted looked around. There was cat hair everywhere, so he mentally closed his eyes and sat on the sofa while Sally Wilson yelled at her bird, finally putting the cover over the cage.

"Time he went to sleep anyway," she said, her eyes squinting from the smoke that drifted up from the cigarette, once again positioned, somewhat tenuously, in her mouth. "Pain in the ass, that thing. Drives the children crazy."

"The children?"

She puffed on the cigarette and said, "Yeah. Eennie and Meenie. The cats. Had two others, Miney and Moe, but they took off a few weeks back and I ain't seen them since. Want a drink?"

He declined.

"I guess you're here about Tommy. You and him was pretty tight in college wasn't ya?"

"We were good friends," Ted said.

"Yeah. You wuz at that. I remember a few weekends when the four of ya was here. You was quite a group. I still got some pictures somewheres of when you yusta come up here and visit. Tommy didn't visit much after he got married, thanks to that bitch he got tangled up with. I don't think she ever wanted him outta her sight."

Ted removed some cat hair that had attached itself, almost magnetically, to his trousers. It seemed to be alive.

He hated cats.

The inside of the house was in sharp contrast to the outside. It was cluttered and dirty and smelled of stale cat litter. A testament to its owner, a woman who'd lost too much and didn't really care any more. He wondered what motivated her to keep the outside so fresh looking. Maybe she didn't want the neighbors to know, a last-gasp attempt to present an image that was pure fantasy. Or maybe someone else did it for her, or rather, for the neighborhood.

"You must have been very shocked when you heard about the accident," he said.

"Shocked? Jeez, that doesn't begin to cover it. I just couldn't believe it. The cops came to the door at two in the morning . . . ya ever notice it's always in the middle of the night when ya hear about these things? Same with Harold. It was three in the morning when they tol' me about him, the poor bastard."

She refilled her glass, stubbed out the cigarette

59

and promptly lit another. "Yeah," she continued, "Ol' Harold, he jus' plain drank himself to death. Passed out in some bar and by the time they got him to the hospital, he was gone. I 'magine he's laughin' up a storm now watchin' his widow drinkin' like this. Well, screw him!"

She held her glass up high, as though making a toast.

"Tommy, now," she went on, "he was much too young to die. Jus' like Trudy."

"How did it happen?" Ted asked, keeping his voice low and soft. "Tommy, I mean."

"You don't know?" she asked, surprised.

"No, I don't," he said. "All I heard was that he'd been killed in an accident, but I never heard . . . exactly what happened. If you'd rather not talk about it . . ."

"No," she said, holding up a hand. "I don't mind. They say it's better if ya talk about it." She sighed and then said, "They say he musta fell asleep. Car went off the road and down the side of a ravine, right down to the bottom. Caught fire and burned up . . . with him in it. There wasn't all that much . . ."

She placed the drink on the table and the cigarette in the ash tray and then covered her face with gnarly hands. Almost as if they sensed something was wrong, the cats reappeared and took up positions on her ample lap, stretching their bodies so that they could try to lick away the tears. She stopped, hugged them to her body and then took a tissue and wiped her eyes.

"I'm sorry," she said. "Don't mean to carry on like this."

"Don't apologize, Mrs. Wilson. You have every right in the world to be upset. Perhaps I should come back . . ."

She waved him off. "No, no," she said. "I'm all

right."

She blew her nose and then continued. "It was awful," she said. "They made me look . . . at his remains, you know? I couldn't even be sure it was Tommy 'cept for the ring. It was the one I gave 'im on graduation. It was engraved and everythin'."

"I'm very sorry," Ted said.

"He was the last," she said, staring at the plastic curtains that covered the dirty front window. "First Harold and then Trudy. She died of cancer, you know. And now Tommy. Jeez, I don't have nobody no more. I'm too old and too ugly to start again. I guess I'll just live out my years with the cats and that stupid bird. Maybe I'll get me another Miney and Moe. I think the others miss them, you know?"

He nodded. "I'm sure they do."

She looked directly at him with eyes that seemed suddenly hostile again. "What you doin' here anyway? I haven't seen ya in fifteen years."

Ted ran a hand through his hair and said, "I came for two reasons. I wanted to express my sympathy to you, of course. Tommy and I were, as you said, pretty tight when we were in college."

"And the other reason?"

"I was curious about a couple of things."

"Curious? Why? The FBI send ya?"

He shook his head. "I haven't been with them for a number of years."

The hostility went out of her eyes for a moment. "Oh yeah. I forgot about that. Jeez, I'm sorry. Tommy told me about it when it happened. I guess ya had your own share of shit in this life, ain't ya?"

That was one way of putting it, he thought.

"So, what are ya so curious about?"

"I was wondering . . ." He stopped and said, "This really isn't the time. I can see you're upset. I shouldn't have bothered you."

"It's all right," she protested, again. "I don't get

that much company. It's nice to see one of Tommy's old friends, even if it is because of . . . go ahead. What's on your mind?"

"Well," he began, "I was surprised when I found out about Tommy, which was this morning, as a matter of fact. I called the police, asking if they knew who to contact about funeral arrangements because, naturally, I wanted to attend. They told me he'd already been cremated. I was pretty shocked."

"Ain't that a corker?" she said, almost as though she didn't believe it herself. "That really set me back when I found that out. This lawyer showed up the day after the accident and said he was Tommy's executive or whatever they call themselves."

"Executor?" Ted asked.

"Yeah, That's it. He worked for the company, he said. Anyway, he had this will and there it was, plain as day, Tommy sayin' he wanted to be cremated. No funeral, no memorial service. Like he'd never set foot on this earth. The lawyer said he'd take care of everythin', so I let him. I didn't know what else to do. He said that's what Tommy wanted."

"I realize," Ted said, "that this isn't any of my business, but . . . was there anything else about the will that you thought unusual?"

For a moment, she just stared at him. Then, her gaze fell to the two cats she was stroking, one at a time. "Well, I guess ya could say I was surprised about that bitch wife of his. I never liked her, ya know. Even when you wuz all together, the four of ya, I could see she was a real pushy one. I never cared much for Eye-talians anyway. Harold got wounded in the war and it was Eye-talians that did it. Good-for-nothings, far as I'm concerned. Bunch of criminals is all they are.

"But Tommy, he was crazy about her and wanted to marry her and then he did and look what happened. She found herself a boyfriend and took off. Still, he never seemed to get over it and when he never left her anything in the will, it made me wonder. He even changed his insurance over to me."

Ted tried very hard to keep his voice even. "Insurance?" he asked, innocently.

"Yeah," she said. "It wasn't much, but it was all he had. That and some furniture. A few stocks. I don't know what the hell he did with his money. 'Course, he didn't make all that much to begin with. His savings was less'n a thousand dollars. Ain't much after thirty-five years of livin', is it? 'Course, he had to split everything with that bitch when she took off. They oughta change that law, you know? Woman takes off and the man has to split everything right down the middle. Ain't right. They shouldn't get a damn dime. I got his furniture out in the garage. Ain't got no car. Guess I'll give it to Goodwill."

She started to weep. Almost as if on cue, the cats started licking her face again.

The cigarette in the ash tray had almost burned out, the still-smoldering filter casting off an acrid stink. She lit another and gulped down what was left of her drink.

The feeling that something wasn't quite right was growing in Ted Kowalczyk. He wanted to ask some more questions. He wanted to look at the furniture, on the off-chance that there might be a stray paper or two. Almost as quickly as the thought occurred to him, it was discarded. If Tommy had been murdered, the furniture would yield no clues. These people, whoever they were, were professionals.

At the moment, what he really wanted was to get out of this house and away from this woman who had lost everything that ever meant anything to her. He stood up, brushed some of the hair off his trousers and said, "I'm sorry, Mrs. Wilson. Tommy was a good man. I'll miss him. Thanks for your help."

She looked at him strangely. "Help? What help?"

"I just meant," he said, "that I appreciate you telling me what you've told me."

"If it makes you feel better," she said.

She let him find his own way out.

In pleasant contrast to the house, the air outside smelled like expensive perfume. Ted brushed some more cat hair off his suit and climbed into the car. He headed towards the airport, found a Holiday Inn with a vacancy and checked in.

Over a chopped steak dinner and a beer, which he had in his room, he made some notes to himself and then started to read again the report that Tommy had sent him. Maybe this time, it would make some sense.

Four hours later, it was starting to.

The report acknowledged that the large bulk of scientists in the field were convinced that earthquake prediction was a hopeless pursuit. It went on to describe, in considerable detail, why it was vital that research continue until a breakthrough was at hand. In fact, it was clear that Vance Gifford was convinced he had made just such a breakthrough. Gifford had developed a new system that seemed to work. It had, after all, accurately predicted four earthquakes in a row. That had to be more than coincidence.

There were two main types of faults, the report stated. Some faults, called strike-slip faults, consisted of large masses of rock moving in two different horizontal directions, such as in the case of the San Andreas fault, where there was almost constant movement. On one side, the rock was moving north and on the other, south. Movement was usually several inches a year. Every year.

Sometimes, the rock would become locked, as one jagged edge of solid rock hooked onto another moving in the opposite direction. Pressure, hundreds of billions of tons of pressure, would build up until finally the rock would break loose from its lock, and an earthquake would ensue.

Another type of fault was the thrust fault, where two blocks of rock were pushing directly against each other, deep beneath the surface of the earth. Sometimes, one would force itself either above or below the other, causing the ground to shake. Millions of years ago, these faults had created mountains. The very same energy that had produced the mountains was still alive, deep in the earth. There were several theories on earthquake prediction. One was called the dilatancy theory. It held that bedrock, under pressure, developed microscopic cracks that caused the rock to swell. The swollen rock's ability to conduct electricity was affected, and sound waves took longer to pass through. By constantly monitoring a section of a fault line, and measuring these changes, then matching deviation from the norm to quakes that had taken place, scientists could anticipate future quakes. The trick was in picking the right spot to monitor.

The temperature theory explained that the friction of two massive rock formations moving in opposite directions created heat. A drop in temperature at a specified location along a fault line would indicate the formations were gridlocked.

And the theory concerning seismic gaps, spots on the landscape where certain waves emitted by moving rock weren't picked up by sensitive equipment, seemed to have been considerably significant to Tommy Wilson. According to Wilson, there were two types of waves emitted by moving plates of rock: P waves and S waves. Each wave had its own characteristics that could be measured. As well, the difference in the time it took for the different waves to reach sensitive equipment sometimes varied. Analysis of those differences had meant something to Vance Gifford.

Vance Gifford had spent ten years of his life entering almost everything known about earthquakes into computer data banks. Information from hundreds of sources and literally thousands of earthquakes, inside and outside California, had been compiled and cross-referenced. Patterns had been drawn from the most recent ones and these patterns were analyzed and reanalyzed.

Gifford had taken the raw data and used it to develop a complex formula based on as many as fifty different criteria. He'd taken these theories and put them to work in the field, using equipment of his own design. Equipment that probed beneath the earth's surface, sometimes reaching as deep as three miles. Equipment that measured even the smallest movements or slightest pressure in the earth, even the moisture content of seemingly solid rock.

Using his new formula, he'd made a number of predictions. So far, he'd been right on the first four.

Tommy Wilson had studied Gifford's methodology for two months and had not found it wanting. He'd taken the equipment into the field himself and conducted his own experiments. He was as convinced as Gifford that they had made a major breakthrough. The results of all of the experiments were included in the report. As far as Ted could tell, the probes were still in place and others were continuing with the work, which was still classified Top Secret.

Scientifically, it was more than Ted could understand, but there were three facts that stood out.

The two men had been right four times in a row.

They had both died mysterious deaths.

In the case of Tommy Wilson, life insurance benefits had been paid with incredible haste to two women.

His eyes aching, he switched off the light and rested his head on the pillow, not bothering to change out of his clothes. He could hear the traffic as it roared by in a never-ending stream on the nearby freeway, even at this late hour.

Traffic. People.

He thought about Los Angeles and what might happen in three weeks if Tommy and his colleague were right. And they had to be right. And then he thought about the evacuation of Los Angeles.

The largest American evacuation ever undertaken had been in Florida, Labor Day weekend, 1985. Hundreds of thousands of people had been evacuated from low-lying areas in the path of hurricane Elena. The costs had been staggering. The hurricane, after dancing around in the Gulf of Mexico for some thirty-five hours, had failed to come onshore in Florida, choosing instead to move up the gulf, weakening, and finally striking Louisiana. That movement had served to minimize the damage, but the evacuation itself had been looked upon by many, in the clear light of hindsight, as overkill. Many evacuees had complained that their uprooting was unnecessary, refusing to recognize the capriciousness of hurricanes. Had Elena come onshore in central Florida and had the evacuation not taken place, many of the complainers surely would have died. The logistics of the evacuation had been examined and re-examined and pronounced successful in every way. A triumph, in fact.

But . . . as successful as it was, the evacuation had involved hundreds of thousands, not ten million. Was it the sheer numbers that were daunting? Was it possible that the government was unable or unwilling to undertake the evacuation of Los Angeles because it was just too unwieldy? Or was it that they didn't believe the prediction?

In either case, how could he, Ted Kowalczyk, make a difference? If Tommy had been murdered and he could prove it, would that be enough? Was there time?

He struggled to sort out his thoughts.

For a moment, he thought of Mrs. Wilson with her cats and her parrot, her bitterness and hate. He wondered how a woman like her could produce such a brilliant man as Tommy.

And then, as every night, his thoughts turned to a woman named Erica and a little girl named Grace. He could see their faces clearly, floating like ethereal guests at a seance.

He pressed his fingers to his eyelids to make sure they were closed. Sometimes, he wasn't sure they were just visions in his mind. The images would go away soon, he assured himself. They always did.

And then he'd be alone once more.

Alone . . .

Almost desperately alone.

Chapter Six

Michael Davis heard the key being inserted in the lock and immediately felt the adrenaline rush through his veins. The plan he'd been formulating in his mind for the last hour was about to be put into action. An almost hopeless plan. He knew that. But, he had to try, at the very least. To do nothing would, he was sure, drive him mad.

He started shaking his arms and legs and rolled his head back and forth. At the same time, he emitted a series of grunts and moans. The reaction was just as he expected.

The door to his hospital room opened and the nurse, a small tray in her hand, flicked on the light switch, bathing the room in bright light.

"George!" she exclaimed, speaking to the beefy orderly who always accompanied her whenever she made her nocturnal "needle rounds," "help me strap him down. He's having a convulsion."

She placed the tray on a side table and the two approached the bed, taking positions on either side of the writhing Davis. As they reached for the straps affixed to the bed frame, Davis sprang upright and swung his right arm in a wide arc, the edge of his stiffened hand crashing against the neck of the orderly. In another fluid motion, the arm slashed in the opposite direction, smashing into the neck of the astonished nurse, her eyes already wide with shock.

Both of them fell to the ground with a dull thud.

Instantly, Davis was out of bed and on his feet. He removed a set of keys from the nurse's belt and padded to the door of his room. He opened the door slowly and looked down the hall.

No one was about.

Tiptoeing on bare feet, he crept down the hall in the direction of the nurse's station, his heart pounding, beads of sweat popping from his forehead. At the end of the hallway, a locked door with a small, reinforced window blocked entry to the nurse's station, which was positioned much like the hub of a wheel. As he reached the door, he crouched down and peeked out the bottom of the window.

From his position, he couldn't see the entire area, but he could see that there was another nurse, sitting at a long desk, making entries in aluminum-cased medical charts.

There were six keys on the ring. The fourth one unlocked the door.

He peeked through the window again. The nurse was still engrossed.

Carefully, he opened the door just enough to allow him to move through it, then kept his hand against it as it closed silently behind him.

Moving in a crouch and holding his breath, he headed toward the long desk, hoping the nurse wouldn't hear the pounding of his heart. With each step, he anticipated the sound of alarms or the shouts of someone who had seen him. Finally, he was standing behind her, his right arm in position. He covered her mouth with his left hand as his right smashed against the side of her neck. Then, he lowered her unconscious body to the ground.

The object of his search was right in front of him. A telephone. Did it have an outside line? That was the question.

Quickly, he looked at the unmarked line buttons. There were seven of them, all unlit. He pressed the one next to the hold button and brought the receiver to his ear. He almost shouted with joy as he heard the dial tone.

He punched some buttons and waited as the phone rang at the other end.

One . . . two . . .

Come on, Mary!

Three . . .

God! Had she disconnected the phone?

Four . . .

He heard a click and then a muffled, "Yes?"

"Mary, it's me. Michael. Listen carefully. I don't have much time."

"Michael? Michael?"

"Mary!" He tried to keep his voice as low as possible. "Just listen. I'm in a private hospital. A prisoner. It's called Harbor View. Get a lawyer and get me out. And get out of the house. You've got to get away from there."

"They said . . . "

"Just listen! You remember Bill Price?"

"Yes, but . . ."

"Listen! He's in L.A. now. I don't know what paper. I want you to call him. Tell him I said—off the record—that Los Angeles is going to have a terrible earthquake in three weeks. He's got to warn the people. He can't use my name. Got that?"

There was a hesitation and then, "Michael! For

71

God's sake! What's going on?"

"Just do it. Remember! Get out of the house, call a lawyer and then call Bill. He can't use my name. I gotta go! I love you!"

He hung up the phone and moved quickly to the door leading to his hallway. Then he was through it, locking it behind him. Seconds later he was back in his relocked room, the keys were back on the nurse's belt, and he was wiping her face with a wet towel.

As she started to come to, he asked, "Are you all right?"

"What?" Her hand went to her neck. "You . . ."

"I'm sorry I hit you," he said. "I was having a nightmare. I guess I kinda went nuts there. I'm really sorry."

She struggled to her feet and, with unsteady legs, moved to the other side of the bed. George, the orderly, was still out. The nurse took the wet towel Davis had used on her and began wiping George's face with it. Davis, trying to appear helpful, rubbed the man's wrists. Then the door flew open and two burly, white-uniformed orderlies rushed in.

"You all right in here?" one of them asked.

"It's all right," the nurse answered. "We just had a little problem here. It's fine now."

"A little problem? Like what?"

George was coming around. "Mr. Davis was having a nightmare. He thought George and I were attacking him and he . . ."

"Bullshit!" one of the orderlies yelled. "The bastard cold-cocked Patricia. He used the phone!"

Michael Davis chewed on his lower lip as he felt the heat emanating from three sets of very hostile eyes.

It seemed innocuous enough. A release from the Pentagon's public relations department, low-keyed and understated, not unlike as many as a hundred that the newspaper would receive over the course of an average month from the same source.

It was called "Operation Move."

At the top of the single page that had just come over the wire was the legend, "For Immediate Release."

The body of the announcement read, "The Pentagon today announced a special exercise dubbed, 'Operation Move,' which will involve the temporary relocation of certain unspecified defense contractors.

"The operation is designed to test the preparedness of critical defense contractors should the need arise because of possible attack or natural disasters such as hurricanes, floods, brush fires or earthquakes. It will be combined with a similar operation to be carried out by all arms of the nation's defense forces.

"Because of the sensitive nature of the operation, details are classified. The operation is the first of its kind and will be concluded within four weeks."

Bill Price looked at the single yellow sheet and scratched his head with the eraser-end of the blue pencil in his hand.

The release was one of six that had come over the wire at the same time. The other five had dealt with matters that seemed much more important. A new policy with regard to the operation of the Sixth Fleet in the Middle East; A report on the investigation into the latest crash of a B-1 bomber; A major personnel shuffle in the Marine Corps. Of particular interest was a very major story involving the Coast Guard. The biggest cocaine bust in their history had been achieved after a ferocious fire-fight with well-equipped drug runners. Eight men, all of them smugglers, had been killed and three ships sunk. The ever-increasing boldness of the drug runners had been stunted, at least on this run.

And this story, "Operation Move."

Price, editor of the Los Angeles *Globe,* walked over to the wire-service machine and checked the copy. The story was there, but it had been given a bland, national slant. He wanted a local angle. He looked around the office, searching for a reporter, but they were all out of the building for the moment, so he decided to check it out himself. He returned to his desk, entered a key on his computer terminal and brought up an alphabetical list of names and telephone numbers of various defense contractors located in the Los Angeles area.

The first six claimed to know nothing of the exercise. The seventh was more forthcoming. The man's name was Lester Barnes and he was the public relations director for Exton Aviation, a subcontractor that produced small, electronically controlled motors for the "Stealth" fighter.

"What can I do for you, Bill?" he asked.

"Well," replied Price, "I'm a little confused. We just received a hand-out from the Pentagon concerning something called 'Operation Move.' I wondered if you people were involved in this thing."

Barnes chuckled and then said, "Well, you know the Pentagon, Bill. They like to make things a lot more mysterious than they need to be. Fact is, the exercise is something that's been talked about for some time. No big deal. But, the actual details are classified, so I can't really say much."

"Tell me what you *can* say."

"Well, as long as you don't attribute this to me."

"That's a deal."

"OK. Well, what they're doing is seeing just how fast certain contractors can move out of an area. It's not just here, it's all over the country. They want to see if it's possible to move the essential elements, including the people, from one city to another, in the event that something unforeseen might happen."

"Are you telling me that your whole company is being moved to some other location?"

"Not the whole company, Bill. And it's temporary.

It's just the critical stuff. Certain dies, jigs, computer programs, stuff like that. Things you wouldn't want lying around."

Bill Price rubbed his head with the pencil again. "You gotta be kidding me. Where the hell are you moving to?"

"I don't know."

"Do you know when?"

"No. We're supposed to react when we get the word. It's sort of a test. Like I say, no big deal."

"No big deal? Sounds like it to me. You said the people go too?"

"Again, not all, just some."

"You?"

"I can't say."

"Have you any idea of the cost?"

"I can't talk about that."

"Who's picking up the tab?"

"I can't talk about that either, Bill."

Price shook his head. "Lester, this is nuts. You say they've been working on this for some time?"

"It's something that's been discussed for at least two years, far as I know. To tell you the truth, I never thought they'd actually go through with it, 'cause it's such a pain in the ass, but I guess I was wrong. But what can we do? When the customer says do it, we do it."

"What else can you tell me?"

"Nothing much. As far as I know, we pack up when we get the word, load up some trucks and we're outta here. Then, within four weeks, we're back. Later, we get compared to the others and I guess there's some grading system to tell us how we did."

They talked some more, but there wasn't much information that Lester felt free to impart. Finally, Price grunted and said, "OK, Lester. Thanks a lot."

Price hung up the phone and looked at his watch. The morning conference, the first of many conferences that determined the content of tomorrow's newspaper, would begin in half an hour. Time enough to make a couple more calls.

He looked through the names on his computer list again and found one he recognized. Jim Sokol was the P.R. man for a company called Triad Electronics. Price remembered Sokol. They'd been paired in a charity golf tournament a month ago. He picked up the telephone and punched the number. In a moment, Sokol was on the line.

"Jim? Bill Price, Los Angeles *Globe.*"

Sokol's voice was cheery. "Morning, Bill. How's the handicap?"

"Getting worse. No time. Listen, I just got a Pentagon release this morning regarding a thing they call 'Operation Move.' You know anything about this?"

There was a hesitation and then, "Some."

"Is your company one of those involved?"

Again, there was a hesitation. This time, it was a long one. Too long.

"Jim? You there?"

The voice that answered was decidedly less cheerful. "Yeah, I'm here. Look . . . I can't talk about it, Bill. Sorry, but this whole thing is classified. You understand, I'm sure."

"Yeah, yeah. We'll see ya."

"Right. Have a nice day."

Price slammed the phone down and looked at the computer list once more. Then, the phone beeped. He picked up the receiver, and still angry, barked, "Price!"

"Bill Price?"

"Yeah! Who's this?"

It was a woman's voice, and she sounded terrified. "Mr. Price, this is Mary Davis. You and my husband used to work out together when you were both in Detroit. Do you remember?"

The anger vanished. He smiled as he remembered. "Sure," he said. "I remember both of you. Jeez! It

76

seems a hundred years ago. I was going through a divorce and Michael was fed up with the business world. We both took karate lessons just so we could bash some people around. You treated me like a long-lost brother. How the heck are you two?"

"That's why I'm calling," she said. "Michael's in terrible trouble."

"Trouble? What kind of trouble?"

"Well, it's a rather long story, but he works for the government now and he . . ." She was starting to cry.

Price lowered his voice an octave. "Take it easy, Mary. Just take a deep breath and tell me all about it."

Bill Price's mind was racing as he went back to his work station after the morning conference, a conference that had seen him strangely silent throughout. Instead of concentrating on the business at hand, hundreds of previous stories were being replayed in his mind's eye. He was trying to sort out those that might have a bearing on what he had just heard. By the time he sat down at his desk, one set of stories stood out above all others. He brought one of them up on the computer and read it over.

The story was one of several that dealt with an official hearing that was scheduled to begin Monday morning in Sacramento. The hearing had been receiving a lot of interest from both the electronic media and the press because it was looking into the behavior of the insurance industry, always a popular subject.

This time, the attention was focused on a small segment of the insurance market, specifically, earthquake insurance. In recent years this insurance, something that was purchased by less than 5 per cent of the population of California, had increased dramatically in cost while benefits had been reduced. Some large corporations had been refused any coverage, while others had been denied the opportunity to renew existing policies. The uproar had finally caused the California legislature to schedule a hearing to investigate the matter.

It was all coming at a bad time for the insurance industry. One of the insurance associations had already been sued by the State of California and seven other states on antitrust violations. Another association had gone to court, trying to avoid appearing at the hearings, claiming the inquiry was unconstitutional. All in all, the industry as a whole was bound to come out of this with bloody noses. For what? Unless . . .

For the last few days, the *Globe* had run several stories on the pending hearings, focusing attention on the fact that many scientists had contended that a great earthquake, one destined to cause massive damage, was expected to strike California within twenty or thirty years. The *Globe* had speculated that the insurance companies had reacted to that certainty by reducing their risk, further supporting the view that an earthquake was inevitable.

The *Globe* had championed a program that would further educate Californians on the steps to be taken before, during and after an earthquake, as a public service.

There were some other related stories. Price read them all. The more he thought about it, the more it made sense.

He picked up the telephone and punched the number for the communications center.

"Communications."

"Yeah, this is Bill Price. Get me Darlene Yu in Washington, will ya?"

"Yes, sir."

Darlene Yu was the *Globe's* chief Washington correspondent. Equipped with a beeper and mobile phone, she was usually available at a moment's notice. Once, she'd held a telephone conversation with her boss while using the rest room facilities of one of Washington's posher restaurants, to the consternation of some other patrons. She was, by any standard, an overachiever of the best kind. Today was no exception. She was on the line in seconds.

"Where are you?" Bill asked, "You sound like you're in the bottom of a well."

"I'm on the Beltway," she answered, "on my way to Langley for a CIA press conference. What's up?"

"Did you read the latest from the Pentagon?"

"Not in depth, but yes. Any one in particular?"

"Yeah," Bill said. "This 'Operation Move.' What's that all about?"

"I have no idea," she replied. "I read the release but I don't know what it means. You want me to find out?"

"Yeah, I do," he said. "Forget Langley, will you? I don't think it's all that important. Swing by the Pentagon and see if you can get some sort of explanation. This doesn't make any sense to me."

There was a short burst of interference on the line and then he heard her say, "I'm on my way. Anything else?"

"Yeah," Price answered. "I have an old friend in Washington. Works for the Pentagon. He's a civilian. I tried to get ahold of him last night but there was no answer. See if you can track him down for me, will ya?"

"Sure! What's his name?"

"Michael Davis. I'm not sure what department he works in, but they should be able to find him."

"Okay, I'm on it. When I find him, what do you want me to say?"

"Just tell him to give me a call."

"That's it? Why don't you just call him at work?"

"I could do that," he said, "but I thought he'd get a kick out of seeing a beautiful woman like you asking after him."

"Really."

"Really. He and I were pals in Detroit a few years ago, if anybody asks."

"OK."

Price hung up the phone and looked around the room again. He spotted just the man he was looking for. He walked over to Rusty Coleman's desk and said, "Rusty, I need you for a bit. Let's head down to the lounge where I can smoke."

Coleman grinned and followed his boss down the elevator and into the basement lounge. As soon as they were seated, Price lit up, leaned back with a satisfied smile on his face and closed his eyes.

"God! I've waited an hour for this. It's almost as good as . . ."

Coleman laughed and said, "Never! Don't even say it."

Price opened his eyes and leaned forward. "Yeah . . . come to think of it . . ."

They both laughed.

"Rusty," Price said, nonchalantly, "about two years ago, you did a multi-day feature on earthquakes. Ran about thirty thousand words if I remember. You researched the hell out of it. Talk to me about that. Especially the part about preparation."

Coleman grinned and shook his head. It was always like this when Price was on to something. He'd start out with a question from left field and then keep pursuing it, like an enthusiastic middle-aged teenager. His freshness was one of the qualities that kept employee turnover low at the newspaper, despite the crummy wages.

"I've still got prints of that if you want."

"No," Price said. "I don't have the time. Give me the main points."

Rusty Coleman shrugged and started talking. "Well, there are the Red Cross and the Civil Defense teams that . . ."

"No," Price interrupted, "I mean the big picture. Didn't you attend some seminar where they said that a full-scale evacuation of L.A., assuming they knew there was going to be a big earthquake, was impossible?"

Coleman thought about it for a moment and nodded. "Sure. I remember. There were three days of seminars, all told. They were talking about what would happen if everyone knew there was going to be a really *big* one, you know, like Mexico City had, only worse, and the consensus was that evacuation was out of the question."

"Totally?"

"Well, it was all hypothetical, of course. Right now, there's no way to predict an earthquake, so, like most of these seminars, not a hell of a lot was said that was worthwhile."

"But, they *did* say that evacuation was impossible," Price insisted.

"Right. For a lot of reasons."

"Like?"

Coleman walked over to the soft drink machine and deposited some coins. A can clattered down the chute, and he picked it up, popped the top and took a swallow. Turning back to his boss, he said, "I'll get the article and give you the basics. I can't remember all of the points that were made, but there wasn't all that much interest anyway because nobody knows exactly when the big one's gonna hit. So what the hell difference does it make?"

Price took the Pentagon announcement out of his shirt pocket and handed it to his reporter. "What do you make of this?" he asked.

Coleman looked it over and shook his head. "Not much, on the face of it. Looks silly to me. Obviously, you've got an angle."

"I'm not sure," Price said. "But supposing the Pentagon knew there was going to be an earthquake and wanted to protect some of the more critical defense contractors?"

Rusty Coleman grinned. "Boss . . . you've been working too hard. There's no way they could know that."

"Why not?"

"I just told you! Because earthquakes can't be predicted."

"You said otherwise in your piece."

Coleman's eyebrows shot up. "Oh? You remember that part but you don't remember the seminars? What is it with you? Selective memory cells?"

"Never mind," Price said brusquely. "The fact is, you said that they *could* predict earthquakes."

"Not really," Coleman said. "What I wrote was that there was a lot of research being done, especially by the Russians. This is one case where they can honestly say they're ahead. Sure, some techniques have been developed, but the big problem, like everything else, is money."

"Explain, please."

Coleman took a deep breath and said, "In order to accurately predict an earthquake, you'd need to have probes in the ground, covering, say, twenty-five square miles. That's just to cover one small part of a known fault line. One small area, where there is evidence that the plates are locked. With a probe every three hundred feet, running down as deep as three miles, you'd have in the neighborhood of seven or eight thousand probes. The cost of drilling the holes, all by itself, would be around half a million bucks per. Right there, you've got a cost of three or four billion dollars. And that's just to cover one possible problem area. In California alone, we've got hundreds of them. Then, you've got . . ."

"What do these probes do?"

"Well, for one thing, they can be used to measure

ground movement over a long period of time. But a stick in the ground can do the same thing. The probes measure heat, conductivity of the rock to electric current, P waves, S waves, the time variations between the two . . ."

"Hold on," Price barked. "Are you telling me that you *can* predict earthquakes? It's just a question of money?"

Rusty shook his head. "No. Not really. Let me put it another way. There are some scientists who claim they can predict earthquakes if given enough time and money. There are some theories that seem to work, but no one, at least not in this country, has been able to really check them out. There've been some earthquakes predicted, but most of those in the scientific community put that down to chance.

"If, for example, there was a portion of the San Andreas fault line that was known to be locked, and if they spent about ten billion bucks checking it out, they *might* be able to prove that the theories were right. But nobody is about to lay out that kind of money. It would take years before they'd know enough. So the theories are just that. Theories. Nothing more. Except for Hollister, which seems to have a quake every day, there isn't much going on in the way of serious research."

"But," Price protested, "*Somebody* seems to know something. We've been saying for years that there was going to be a biggie within twenty years at the outside, either here or up north."

"True," Coleman said. "But that's based on past history. The San Andreas fault is something you can actually see. It's right there on top of the ground. The movement has been measured and access is relatively inexpensive. That's why there's so much interest in Hollister, which lies right in the middle of the fault line. Also, they've been able to track every earthquake along the whole thing. It's got a record of quakes that allows them to make calculations about the future. But most faults are far below the surface. First you have to find them, then you have to find the location of the pressure points. You're talking *big* bucks.

"The Geological Survey people have been trying to score some funds to really track both ends of the San Andreas for years and they just can't shake them loose. The attitude is that if there is a big quake, the losses will be less than the cost of trying to predict the quake."

Bill Price's eyes lit up. He stubbed out the cigarette and quickly lit another one. "Rusty, I was just going over that piece Helen did about the earthquake insurance flap and the hearings next week."

"So?"

"They raised the deductible limits, right? And stopped renewing policies, right?"

"That's what I understand."

"And now we get this announcement from the Pentagon, saying that they're not only going to move a bunch of military personnel, but they're moving critical defense contractors as well."

Rusty Coleman was beginning to get the drift. "Boss, I see what you're getting at, but you've got a problem."

"Which is?"

"There are no probes! Except for Hollister. Hollister is the earthquake capital of the world, so a lot of research is going on there. But outside of that, there aren't any signs that the kind of research needed is being done. Without the research, how could they have discovered something that would indicate a big earthquake was coming?"

For a moment, neither man spoke. Then, Price, his eyes flashing with excitement, said, "OK. One: money. The insurance companies have lots of money. Two: money could buy the kind of research needed to accurately predict earthquakes. Maybe the research is being done in secret. Three: evacuation is out, but they would want to save what they could. Four: the Pentagon is conducting a really weird exercise that they are playing down. They have to make it public because with all of the movement, there'd be a million questions anyway. What's that all add up to?"

"Coincidence."

Price stubbed out the cigarette and shook his head.

"No way," he said. "No way. There's something to this. I want you on it. Now."

"Boss . . ."

"Don't argue with me. I have a very strong feeling something's up. Talk to some scientists, especially those involved in earthquake prediction. You did that piece two years ago. A lot of things have happened since. Maybe they've found an easier way to predict these things."

Rusty Coleman stared at his boss for a moment and said, "You've got something. I know it! I can see it in your eyes!"

Price grunted. "Maybe. Just maybe. But I have to be sure, Rusty. I want you to find out."

Chapter Seven

For the past few days, the weather had behaved as though Nevada was in the dog days of midsummer. A time when, on rare occasions, superheated air would rise into the sky. The space once occupied by the rising air would be claimed by cooler air dropping down. Then, it too would heat, expand and start its rise. The cycle would continue and intensify until the sand would begin to stir, carried along by the invisible currents, smashing into wood and metal, rubbing it raw. Six hours in this kind of storm would leave an automobile denuded, its steel shell devoid of paint, even primer, looking forlorn in the morning light, gray and dull and sick-looking.

But this was different. It was deep in the night. This particular sandstorm was caused by another kind of weather phenomenon. The jet stream, roaring along at two hundred miles an hour some six miles above the earth, was sucking lower levels of air along with it.

Because of a rapid and unusual change in barometric pressure, it was pulling, like a magnet, vast quantities of air from the ground, causing the winds to howl through the canyons and sweep across the flats, the air filled with tiny bits of sand, making it opaque, blotting out the moon and the stars.

The Nevada Nuclear Test Range.

A place of foreboding. Where engineers and scientists tested the newest instruments of death and destruction in the never-ending quest to be the first with the most.

In one small laboratory inside a long, low building, the heavily tinted windows pitted from previous sandstorms, six men sat around a green metal table, examining blueprints and schematic diagrams.

It was three in the morning and they were all tired.

An hour ago, the discussions had become heated. Now, filled with frustration and close to exhaustion, the men were starting to vent their feelings on a personal level.

Insults were being hurled back and forth. Aspersions were being cast on character, sexual preferences, loyalty, trust, even appearances.

Four of the men were there because it was their job to be there. Two of the men were there because they'd been taken there against their wills.

They were prisoners.

They'd committed no crime. They'd heard no charges leveled against them. They'd had no trials. Still, they were prisoners being forced to engage in something they would have been happy to do, if only they'd been asked.

That was the rub.

They hadn't been asked. They'd been ordered to perform.

One of them still found it unacceptable. Instead of participating in the discussions, he'd remained mute, sitting stiffly in his chair, his arms crossed, his eyes aflame, the rage in evidence all over his long, bearded face.

Throughout the night, the others had asked questions of him which he refused to answer. They had pointed to the diagrams and cajoled, almost begged him to answer. Always, he'd refused. They'd turned away from him and carried on, as though he weren't in the room until, sometime later, they would ask another question.

Finally, he spoke. "You bastards," the dissident said. "You'll never get away with this. Never! If you've gone this far, who the hell knows where it will end!"

The room was silent, save for the sound of the sand as it pummeled the outside walls of the room. After so many refusals, his decision to speak came as somewhat of a surprise. Five sets of eyes stared at him.

Finally, one of the men, the one from Washington, sensing that a breakthrough was at hand, said, "All right. That's enough for the moment. We're not getting anywhere this way. We're all tired. Let's all get some sleep. Things will look different in the morning."

He pressed a button on the table. The door to the office opened, and three uniformed soldiers entered. Jason Shubert, the man from Washington, pointed to the two prisoners and said, "Get them some food and bed them down for the night."

"Yes, sir," one of the soldiers said. He reached down to grasp the arm of the bearded man.

The man jerked his arm free and said, "Keep your fucking hands off me, you sonofabitch!"

Shubert sighed and shook his head. "You're making this much more difficult than it needs to be," he said.

"Really?" the prisoner said, his voice filled with sarcasm. "Difficult? Is that what you call it? Jesus Christ! You people are incredible! You really think you can get away with this. It amazes me. This is America, not some goddam dictatorship! Sooner or later, no matter what the hell happens to us, this will all come to light and you'll spend the rest of your lives in prison. Hell, maybe they'll shoot you."

Shubert smiled and said, "Look . . . I understand how you feel. You're pissed. But it's only because you don't see the problem. Your friend here is cooperating because he knows we're right. Give it time—you'll feel the same way."

The bearded man looked into the eyes of the other prisoner, a short, overweight man in his forties. "Is that really how you feel, Vance?"

Vance Gifford shook his head and answered, "Tommy, I know how you feel. I don't like it any more than you do, believe me. But the fact is, we're running out of time. If this doesn't come off, a lot of people are going to die. If I can help prevent that, I'll do it. You should too. Every small piece of information heightens our chances of success. We need you, Tommy. We really do!"

Tommy Wilson hung his head in frustration. "You were against this," he said, softly.

Vance sighed deeply and rubbed a hand across his eyes. "Yes, I was. No question about it. But the decision has been made, Tommy. That's the thing you have to face. Nothing you say or do will change that. All you have left is to help pull this off. It's something you have to do."

"How am I supposed to live with myself if I do that?"

The man from Washington said, "Tommy . . . Listen to me. During World War Two, my father was a bomber pilot. He took part in the Dresden raid. They fire-bombed that city for two days. Killed almost half a million innocent people. Innocent people! But it was something that had to be done.

"I've talked to him many times about that raid. Certainly, he feels bad about those who were killed, but he understands the reasons for the raid. He sleeps at night. Maybe the analogy isn't such a hot one, but what I'm trying to explain to you is this: sometimes we're forced by circumstances to do things that seem totally wrong at the time. We're not given all of the facts because . . . well, that's just the way things are sometimes.

"Right now, we're faced with the task of saving the lives of millions of people. We've been told we can't evacuate the city because there are just too many problems. Now, I may not agree with that, and I know you don't. But it doesn't matter what you and I think. Somebody else has already made that decision. I know you have trouble with that and I'm sorry. We've been all over that. We've beaten it into the ground. The fact is that the decision *has* been made. So we have to deal with what we *can* do. And what we *can* do is something that might prevent the quake.

"You've seen the test results. You know what we're facing. If you *don't* help us with this thing, you'll never forgive yourself. If you're any kind of a man at all, you'll realize that by refusing to help us, you're risking the chance that we might fail because of it. That one small contribution that you could have made might be the difference. You've been brought here against your will. That lets you off the hook. Why not do what you can to help us with this?"

Vance leaned forward and rested his hand on Tommy's arm. "I'm cooperating," he said, "for one reason and one reason only. It's like the man says. There are millions of lives at stake here. Something has to be done. Right now, these assholes are the only game in town. It's wrong, dead wrong, but it's the way things are. If I don't contribute to this effort, it will lessen the chances of success. That's all I care about right now."

Tommy shook his head. "This is crazy. I don't care what you say. This is just crazy. By cooperating with these idiots, you're giving credence to this whole insane operation. I don't buy it. Not for a second. This isn't the way it should be done and I'll never be a part of it. You might as well take me out there and bury me now. Sure as hell, that's what's going to happen as soon as this is over."

Shubert sighed and said, "Nobody's going to get hurt. You've got my word on that."

Tommy laughed out loud. "Your word! What the hell's that worth. Zip! You people are so crazy, you're liable to do anything. The moment we're let go, the shit hits the fan and you know it. You can't let that happen." He turned to Vance and said, "Don't you see that, Vance? Don't you see what's happening?"

Vance stood up and paced the floor for a moment. Then he turned to Tommy and said, "OK! So we both agree that Los Angeles should be evacuated. For reasons they think are sound, the powers that be have decided they can't do that. All of the screaming and stamping of feet isn't going to change that, dammit! Don't you understand that? All that's left is to try and stop it from happening. What happens to us is of little consequence."

He took a deep breath, shoved his hands in his pockets and added, "You've seen the plan. You *know* there's a slim chance it could work. Can you really sit there and do nothing?"

Tommy looked at his friend and wanted to scream in pure frustration. It was a nightmare. Some horrible, impossible nightmare. Silently, he cursed his mother and father for having committed the act that conceived him. He cursed God for having allowed him to live through the ordeal of birth. He cursed the fates for steering him into his profession. And he cursed Vance Gifford for having discovered a way to predict earthquakes. Not knowing would have been infinitely better than this!

He thought about the package he'd sent to Ted Kowalczyk. Surely, by now Ted would have received it. Why hadn't he done something?

Then again, he remembered cautioning against

going to the press. Perhaps Ted had gone to his old employers, the FBI. Perhaps the FBI was in this up to their ears. Perhaps Ted was already stashed somewhere in a prison of his own.

Almost in tears, he turned to face Vance and very slowly nodded his head. "OK," he said. "In the morning. I'll work with you in the morning."

Chapter Eight

Los Angeles *Globe* Executive Editor Sam Steele pushed his glasses up on his forehead and glared at Bill Price, sitting across the desk, smoking a cigarette. The two men were sitting in the glass-enclosed office of the executive editor, discussing Price's latest wild idea.

It had been Steele who had been the moving force behind bringing Price to Los Angeles after Price had found himself out in the street for the fifth time. They had worked together once before. Worked well together, as a matter of fact. Sam knew that Price liked to shoot from the hip. He was fully aware of the fact that Price had embarrassed publishers of other newspapers by jumping the gun on a story that later had to be retracted. But, he was also cognizant of the fact that Price had also broken several hard-hitting stories that had covered the same publishers in all sorts of glory. It was the nature of the business that you were expected to be right all of the time.

Steele had managed to convince the apathetic owner of the *Globe* that Price would be an asset. He'd promised that he would ride herd on this man, exploit his talents and personally guarantee that no embarrassment would befall the newspaper. It had been quite a gamble. So far, it had paid off. The newspaper's circulation was rising, the staff was relatively happy, and there'd been no increase in the number of legal actions taken against the newspaper.

"When are you gonna wise up and get off those things?" Steele snarled, referring to the cigarette in Price's mouth.

Price ignored the question. "So, what do you think?" he asked.

Steele shrugged, ran a hand across his stomach and said, "I think you're wasting your time. You've got Rusty on this when he could be doing something more important. I think you should forget the whole deal."

Bill Price looked like he'd been stabbed in the heart. "You don't see it?"

"What's to see?" Steele said, his face taking on a pained expression. "You've got some guy you refuse to identify who says that an earthquake is coming. You say he works for the government, but you won't say anything else because, to use your words, you think his life is in danger. Jesus Christ! How would he know an earthquake was coming anyway? Come on, Bill! Give me a break! You put two and two together and come up with nine.

"You've got two scientists who are prepared to state unequivocally that it's possible to predict an earthquake. Great, except that's old news. Those two managed to successfully predict one . . . repeat, one . . . earthquake a year ago. They tried to predict four others and they were dead wrong. They have very little credibility. There are a hundred other scientists who will say it's all crap. So where does that leave you? Nowhere! And then there's 'Operation Move.' You say it's just a scam, but you can't find anyone to support that contention."

"It'll come. There are others in the media who are curious about this thing."

"Yes. But because they think it's a waste of time and money, not because they think it's a scam. Jesus! You've got nothing to go on worth a damn! You know that!"

Price groaned. "That's why I want Darlene to pop the question," he said. "I figure if she throws a curve at Murphy, they'll get nervous. They'll figure somebody leaked something. That might smoke 'em out. It's worked before."

Steele winced. Not from the statement, but from a spike of pain that shot through his midsection.

"What's the matter?" Price asked.

Steele rubbed his stomach again. "I don't know. Ever since I got up this morning, I've had a steady pain in my gut. Every once in awhile, it gives me a real shot. Maybe I'm getting an ulcer. Jesus! Working with you would give anybody an ulcer."

Price grinned. "You only say that because you mean it. Ever had your appendix out?"

Steele shook his head.

"Maybe you better go to the hospital and check it out."

Steele tried to shake it off. "No. It's just something I ate, that's all."

"You sure?"

"Yeah. Now, as I was saying, I think you should . . ." He stopped in midsentence and grabbed his stomach. "Jesus," he groaned, a look of surprise on his face, "this is really starting to hurt."

Price reached over and grabbed the telephone. He punched some buttons and said, "Get some paramedics up here. Something's wrong with Sam!"

Darlene Yu's sleep was interrupted by a telephone call from Bill Price. It was three in the morning.

"Darlene?" he asked, "Did I wake you?"

"Of course not," she answered, some heat in her voice. "I've been sitting up in bed waiting for your call. This makes two, I think."

She heard him mumble something under his breath, and then, "Look, I'm sorry, but I keep getting new information. I want you to be prepared when you finally talk to those clowns at the Pentagon."

"If you keep calling me, I won't be able to stay awake once I finally get there."

"OK. Last time. Murphy said he wouldn't see you alone, right?"

"Right. He's upset about all of the interest in this and he says he'll see a group of us together and answer a few questions and that's it."

There was a pause and then, "You told me about three months ago that you wanted to come back to Los Angeles. That still true?"

She felt her heartbeat quicken. Los Angeles! God! It had been three years. Three years of listening to prepared statements read by boring, harried assistants to the undersecretary of whatever. Or long-winded speeches by politicians, each with that same stupid smile on the face, the glad hand, the phony friendliness.

She'd been lied to, propositioned at least a hundred times, promised exclusives that were anything but, and through it all, she'd felt she was just another media soldier, part of an army chasing the same tired stories.

Oh sure, she'd had her moments. There had been stories written under her byline that had found their way to the front page of the *Globe,* even some that had been reprinted in other newspapers. Had that not been the case, she'd have been yanked out of this prestigious office long ago.

But she hated it. The politicians, the bureaucrats, the lobbyists, and the city itself.

All of it.

Los Angeles was her home. A place that hummed from the pulse of a different heartbeat, with its Hispanic flavor, its craziness, its unpredictability. She loved Los Angeles. Compared to Washington, it was heaven.

"Are you kidding?" she said. "You know I'd love to come back. I told you that. I'll even take less money."

"I just wanted to make sure," Price said, "before I told you about this idea I have. A way for you to get an exclusive meeting with Murphy. But, it might cost you."

"I'm all ears," she said.

So he told her.

And now, four hours later, as she dressed and applied her makeup, she almost shivered with anticipation.

If Price was right, and she was sure that he was, she'd either have a story, or be on her way to L.A. in a matter of hours.

An hour later, she was crammed into the small press room of the Pentagon, along with the maximum limit of fifty-nine other reporters, from print and electronic media. In idle chatter prior to the meeting, it occurred to most of them that the Pentagon was reluctant to talk about "Operation Move." Their observations seemed right on target once the spokesman, a civilian named Jack Murphy, began to speak.

"OK," he said, "I know why you'll all here and frankly, I'm a little nonplussed by all of this attention to what is basically a very simple exercise. I note that the big drug bust by the Coast Guard got some press yesterday and today, there's nothing.

"These things don't happen every day. It would be nice if you spent a little more time giving credit where credit is due instead of inundating us with questions concerning a relatively unimportant exercise."

He paused to allow his diatribe to sink in. If Murphy was nothing else, he was predictable. He seemed to harbor a constant dislike for the press which he took every opportunity to express. Behind the scenes, there had been quiet efforts by some senior members of the press corps to have him removed from his post, but nothing had come of it, which only served to confirm the widely held attitude that it was the Pentagon, not Murphy personally, who disliked the press.

"As for 'Operation Move,'" Murphy continued, "which, for reasons that are a mystery to me, seems to have captured all of your attention, the release speaks for itself. This is a classified exercise to test certain capabilities of the private sector in the event of a possible attack by an unfriendly nation, or certain natural disasters. We've brought it to your attention for one reason, that being the fact that you'll see a lot of trucks on the road during the next few weeks, not to mention increased activity at many military bases throughout the country.

"We didn't want you thinking that there was a major flap in progress, or an attack on some poor, unsuspecting Central American country in the works. This is an exercise designed to give us some information that we feel is needed. Maybe not now, but sometime in the future.

"As you know, it's common practice during hurricanes, for example, for all land-based aircraft to be moved to safer locations. As well, the Navy has, at certain times, repositioned nonessential units to calmer seas. Let's face it, it would be pretty stupid to allow billions of dollars worth of equipment to be sitting ducks in the event of a hurricane.

"The military has been trained to make sudden moves if need be. This is only prudent. But, for some reason, we've never involved essential defense contractors in any of these exercises and that's pretty dumb, to put it bluntly.

"To give you one small example, using an incident that I think most of you are familiar with, we have a very important subcontractor in Florida who suffered severe damage during Hurricane Grace last year. The company had a fire caused by downed electrical wires that

98

practically gutted the building. It set production back two months. During that time, a critical part for the F-18 had to be produced elsewhere. As it turned out, we suffered no ill effects from this shortage, but we could have. We want to establish procedures that will ensure such things never happen again.

"As well," he continued, "we must be prepared for the possibility of attack from our enemies. In the event that we believed an armed conflict was imminent, we wouldn't want our enemies to be able to pinpoint specific targets at will. 'Operation Move' is an exercise that will not only determine how fast we can move certain industries, but will also study the possibility of developing alternate permanent sites for these industries. We will be studying the viability of having key defense contractors positioned in more than one area, with the flexibility to function from one, two, or three different places as the situation dictates.

"Now, I'll answer what questions I can."

A reporter for one of the television networks asked, "If I understand you correctly, you seem to be saying that not all industries are being moved. Is that right?"

Murphy nodded and said, "Of course that's right. It would be impossible to move every one of them. It's by no means certain that we can effectively move *any* of them. That's the purpose of this exercise, to determine the feasibility of moving a civilian contractor under any circumstances. It may turn out that the entire idea is unworkable, but we won't know until we test it out.

"The idea has been kicked around for several years and nothing ever came of it. Now, we've been given the green light to begin some preliminary exploration and that's what this is all about."

Another reporter asked, "Isn't it true that the main contractors, people like the airframe makers, the sub builders, are not being moved?"

"I can't say."

"But isn't it true that they would be impossible to

move? For logistic as well as financial reasons?"

"That hasn't been determined," Murphy answered. "Again, this is more of an experiment than anything else.

Another reporter asked, "But if the people being moved are relatively small subcontractors, what's the point? If there are no ships or planes or tanks to put the parts in, their usefulness is redundant."

Jack Murphy sighed and said, "You haven't been listening. I said that the list of those involved in the exercise is classified. Therefore, I can't comment on that."

Darlene Yu had her hand up. Murphy looked at her and then pointed. She stood up. It was time.

"Jack," she said, smiling sweetly, "isn't it true that this entire exercise is simply a smoke screen? That you have information that a large earthquake is about to strike Los Angeles very soon and you're simply trying to save what industries you can?"

For a moment, the room was silent. Then, everyone was shouting at once. Half of them were shouting at Darlene and half were screaming at Murphy. The spokesman held up his hands and once order was restored, placed them solidly on the lectern.

"That," he said, his face grim, "is almost beneath contempt. But . . . just so you don't run off and print that we have something to hide, I'll answer it.

"No . . . that's not true. In the first place, there is no way we could know an earthquake was about to hit Los Angeles. As any competent scientist will tell you, earthquakes are impossible to predict. In the second place, all defense contractors are housed in buildings that are designed to withstand the largest earthquakes. In California, for example, earthquakes are relatively common and yet we have a number of key defense contractors located in that area. Anyone who thinks that we are so stupid as to fail to consider earthquakes when assigning projects must hold the people who work in this building

100

in very low esteem.

"Frankly, I resent it and I'm sure they do too. Your remarks imply that we're being less than honest with you. It's a charge that's been made before and never substantiated. I resent it very much. It represents an attitude that I find disgusting and unworthy of the newspaper you represent.

"In fact, I think I'll draw this meeting to a close right now. Darlene, I'll see you in my office in ten minutes. If you don't have an apology ready by then, I'm on record as saying I'll ask that your credentials be lifted. Things are tough enough around here without this kind of gutter journalism. As for me, I've had my fill of it."

With that, he turned and stomped out of the room.

Immediately, Darlene was besieged by her colleagues, most of whom were angry with her.

"Where the hell did you get that?" one asked.

"Jesus Christ, Darlene, Murphy's mad at all of us again. What got into you?" said another.

There were other less kind remarks which she took with a hollow smile on her face, responding to none of them.

She trusted Bill Price. If he'd asked her to make a fool of herself in front of these people, it was probably for good reason. If nothing else, it would get her back to Los Angeles.

Ten minutes later, she presented herself to Jack Murphy in his private office. If he'd seemed angry in front of the others, here, in the sanctity of his own office, he was livid.

"Well?" he said. He was standing, his arms folded in front of him, his eyes almost spitting flames.

"Well, what?" she said, defiantly.

The arms dropped to his sides. "OK, smart ass, consider your credentials lifted. You are no longer welcome in this building. I'll see to it that you're blocked from entering any federal buildings, for that matter. A letter to that effect will be sent to your paper.

"You're finished here."

"I can live with that," she said, "but the fact remains that I was right."

"Are you going to print that?"

"Yes."

For the first time, he smiled. "Good. I hope you do. It will give us the chance, finally, to discredit your newspaper. It'll afford us the opportunity to show the American people what you really stand for. You're a cheap rag and it's time people were made aware of it. Print what you like. In the meantime, I'd appreciate it if you'd get the hell out of my office."

"That's it? That's all you've got to say?"

He simply stared at her for a moment. Then, he reached for the phone and punched some buttons. "Security . . . ? This is Murphy. I'd like someone . . ."

She was gone before he could finish the sentence. On her way out of the building, she smiled sweetly at the Marine sitting behind the desk near the entrance to one of the halls. The same one who had informed her the day before that Michael Davis, Price's old pal, had been taken to a hospital, suffering from some unknown illness. After some prodding, he'd found out the name of the hospital and passed it on to her. Price had seemed quite upset when she'd given him the news.

Now, she reasoned, he'd be even more upset. Whatever his reasons for wanting her to confront Murphy, they hadn't worked. Oh well, she thought. At least she was heading back to Los Angeles. That was the good news.

Chapter Nine

It was like watching some horrific science fiction movie. Buildings . . . tall, majestic structures of glass and chrome and reinforced concrete . . . buildings considered earthquake-proof . . . were crumbling and crashing slowly to the earth, their movement akin to a ballet, each twisted remnant floating through the air with the gentleness of a butterfly. A sickening display of destruction played out in vivid slow motion.

And as the buildings broke apart, the bits and pieces were joined by the bodies of men, women and children . . . spilling out of the buildings, being thrown into nothingness, like seeds from some giant plant.

The ground was shaking violently, vibrating with a noise that was almost deafening. Telephone poles snapped, power lines crackled, their wires twinkling in a burst of yellow, like grotesque holiday sparklers.

All around him, Ted could see nothing but death and destruction. Fires raged everywhere. Rivers of flame sloshed down hills, devouring houses, trees, people . . . anything in their path. Other people ran aimlessly up and down streets, screaming, their clothes on fire, their skin charred black. Large crevices opened up in the surface of the earth, swallowing entire blocks of Los Angeles, as though the earth itself had turned into some insatiable monster on a diet of glass and concrete.

And in the middle of it all stood Tommy Wilson, his bearded face wrinkled in agony, his arms outstretched, the finger on one hand pointed directly at Ted. "I warned you," he said, as the flames licked at his feet. "I asked you to help and you did nothing. It's all your fault, Ted! It's all your fault."

Ted wanted to scream at the man. Wanted to tell him that there was still time. That the earthquake wasn't due for another three weeks. That it had been Tommy, not himself, who was at fault. But he couldn't get his mouth to work. His feet were stuck to the asphalt as if nailed there. He was immobile, unable to speak. Unable to do anything except watch as the world disintegrated in front of his eyes.

He fought to make his legs work. He struggled to make his mouth work. And finally, he was able to utter a scream. A tortured wail of agony that reverberated off the walls and assailed his own ears. Even above the sound of the traffic.

Traffic . . .

The incessant growl of nearby traffic combined with the early take-offs of jet aircraft brought Ted Kowalczyk awake at seven, still fully dressed, his body covered with a thin film of cold sweat which had soaked through his shirt in several spots. He'd left a window open during the night and the cacophony of sound blended with the last vestiges of the nightmare that was now receding, leaving him almost limp with relief.

He climbed out of bed, closed the window, stripped, and headed for the shower.

For a while, he let the water run cold, as was his habit,

until his entire body felt the chill, almost to the bone. The shivering signaled it was time to warm things up. He turned the knob, let the warm water wash over him for a few minutes and then soaped and shampooed.

As he stood in front of the mirror, wiping away the condensation, he felt a twinge in his stomach. Almost reflexively, his hand reached down and rubbed the scar that had defied all attempts by plastic surgeons to remove it. The scar was one of two that marred the otherwise flawless skin. There was one just below the navel, the one that twinged many times during an average day. And there was another one on his chest, just to the right and below the left nipple.

The scars were the only physical reminders of a few violent seconds that had changed his life forever. The scars on the inside, the ones to his psyche, were far from healed. They were still red and raw, thinly covered by layer upon layer of logic and rationalization, which hardly served to hide the trauma fully. The layers would, it was hoped, take root and grow, eventually filling the wound and making it whole. But he wasn't there yet. Far from it.

Ted Kowalczyk was a man well used to nightmares. Whereas the earthquake was but an apparition, the nightmare that had become his constant companion was anything but. It was a vision that could never be erased.

It had happened inside a restaurant. A mad moment of impulse that had taken a woman named Erica and a child named Grace away from him . . . and almost ended his own life.

It was a restaurant they favored about every two weeks, with no particular pattern. A small, family place with inexpensive food that was both tasty and abundant. As usual, Ted and Erica had taken a booth, sitting side by side, their backs to the wall, while Grace was seated facing them, so that her mind would be on them and not what was going on in the restaurant.

Ted had looked up as the woman approached the

105

table. He'd noticed the strangeness in the eyes, the set to the face that spelled trouble, but for the briefest of moments, he'd failed to react. He was, after all, simply having dinner with his wife and daughter and the woman was unknown to him. It would look stupid to pull out a pistol at the mere approach of a strange woman.

But he should have.

For a moment, she just stood there. And then, the woman's eyes widened, her nostrils flared and there was a gun in her hand. It had happened faster than was humanly possible, as was often the case when insanity was involved. But there it was, the gun staring him in the face, his hand reaching for his own handgun even as he knew it was much too late.

With a scream of outrage, she aimed and fired.

The first bullet hit Ted in the chest, the force of it knocking him against the wall and back again, his head slamming down on the table. Instinctively, Erica had grabbed at him, pulling him back, perhaps trying to protect him, and another bullet hit him in the stomach. But he didn't feel it. He was already unconscious.

It wasn't until four days later that he learned the crazed woman had continued to fire, emptying the semi of its entire clip, fourteen bullets in all.

Six of the shots had missed everyone, making big holes in the wall and almost killing a woman who worked in the store next to the restaurant. Two shots had hit Ted. Two more had slammed into the skull of Erica, another in her neck, and one in her heart. And two had ended the life of little Grace.

It had been almost an afterthought, the witnesses had said. The woman had let out another scream and blown the child's head off with two shots.

The shrinks had said that in some ways, it was fortunate that Ted was the first one hit. It saved him from seeing what happened to his loved ones. But he knew better. He'd seen it all right. In his mind's eye, he saw it almost every day.

The killer had been the daughter of a man he'd helped put away for life. A drug dealer who was probably unaware, until it all hit the newspapers, that his own daughter was one of his best customers, albeit indirectly.

Three years of snorting coke had fried her brain. She'd taken to carrying a gun with her wherever she went. And when she saw the man with his wife and child sitting at the table in the restaurant, she recognized him as the man from the FBI she'd seen in court. The one who'd testified against her father, sending him away forever. Something had snapped. Maybe it was the thought of losing her father. Perhaps it was anxiety over her future access to the drugs she craved. They were never able to determine her motives.

For whatever reason, she'd walked over and tried to kill them all, with no thought at all to what would happen to her. It simply didn't matter.

Not then, it didn't.

Now she was herself in another kind of prison. A place where they gave different kinds of drugs, legal drugs. Drugs to keep her from screaming twenty-four hours a day. She was alive in one sense. In another, she was already in hell.

And Ted, after six months of intensive rehabilitation, both physical and mental, had quietly left the FBI and taken a job with Connecticut Mutual, supposedly whole again.

He wasn't even close to being whole. But he was trying.

They'd told him there was no way he could have known. No way anyone could have known. The woman had never been investigated, had not been known to be involved with her father. An oversight not uncommon. It was just a freak coincidence, they'd insisted, that the woman and Ted had been in the same restaurant at that particular moment.

But he had trouble with the rationale.

He should have known. At the very least, he should have reacted sooner. He'd been trained to be observant and when it counted most, he'd let it get past him. He was supposed to protect the public from the crazies, and most of all, themselves. Above all, he was supposed to protect his family. And he hadn't done that. He'd failed. His work had cost them their lives. His mistakes had killed them.

And he was still alive.

He was too hard on himself, they said.

They were wrong. It was obvious now that God had chosen this time to punish him. Why else would Tommy have burdened him with this fearsome responsibility? Why else would this terrible knowledge be thrust into his hands? Why else would Ted Kowalczyk be sitting in this motel room trying to figure out his next step? It was punishment, pure and simple.

Or . . . was it his chance for redemption?

He shaved and put on fresh clothes. Then he phoned Frank Leach in Hartford.

"Where the hell are you?" were the first words out of the man's mouth. He sounded upset.

"I'm in San Jose," Ted replied, fully awake and craving a cup of coffee.

"What's in San Jose? Just what the hell is going on?"

"Frank . . . I can't say just yet," Ted said. "I told you that yesterday. What's got your motor running this morning?"

"Listen, babe," Frank barked, "I did like you asked, started asking some questions and I'm tellin' you, there's something fishy goin' on here."

Ted was all ears. "I'm listening," he said.

"First, you gotta tell me what the hell rumor you heard. You can't leave me in the dark like this. You just can't. It's driving me crazy!"

For a moment, Ted mulled the idea around in his

mind. On the one hand, Frank Leach was a man he could trust. That had been proven several times. Maybe he should tell Frank everything and let *him* decide what to do.

"Ted?"

No . . . he couldn't do that. It was a cop-out.

"Frank," he said, "I'll fill you in on everything as soon as I have a handle on it, but right now I just can't. You've got to go along with me on this. I need your help. I don't ask for it that often."

He could hear the sound of his own voice. It seemed to be begging. For a few moments, there was silence and then he heard Frank say, "OK. OK. But you keep stallin' me and I'm comin' out there. Understand?"

"Understand."

"These guys at AAIS," Frank said, speaking of his contacts in one of the monolithic insurance associations, "are really nervous. They don't want to talk about earthquakes or earthquake insurance. All of a sudden, it's like some dirty word with them. But I managed to find out some things."

AAIS was only one of the associations that Connecticut Mutual belonged to. It was an association that lobbied, on behalf of its members, various government bodies on pending legislation. In addition it provided generic advertising for the industry as a whole. It also maintained a data bank on every individual or corporation that had ever applied for insurance of any kind, which it shared with other associations.

Exchanges of information were routine, made in the interests of preventing fraud, such as supposedly stolen automobiles that got pushed into some river in the hope that a killing could be made on the insurance. Frauds perpetrated by surprisingly stupid people who took out four different policies on the same car and thought the companies wouldn't find out. Insurance fraud was one of the most common crimes committed by Americans and one that the industry was constantly trying to stamp out.

AAIS was only one of several organizations that maintained a data bank containing scraps of information gleaned from hundreds of sources. Most Americans didn't realize it, but somewhere information on almost every facet of their lives was stored on thin strips of magnetic tape. Extensive information that would astonish them, if they knew.

The information was available to any member of the organization. Every job they'd ever held was listed. Information on every car, home or major purchase they'd ever made. A list of their credit cards and information on how they paid them. Their various wives, husbands, even lovers. Lists of children, grandchildren, habits, any criminal activities, even the comments of some of their neighbors, old and new. Records of any health problems. Pages of information that helped an army of underwriters determine whether someone was a good risk.

Or not.

"You found out some things? Like what?" Ted asked.

"Like the fact that the deductible on earthquake insurance is due to go up again real soon. Maybe to twenty-five per cent. Even in the face of the hearings. That's almost asking for it.

"They went after the feds to try and get back-up and got turned down flat. There's no pool on this stuff, Ted. Everybody covers their own. Near as I can tell, some of these guys would be wiped out if there was a real bad quake. They don't have near enough the reserves to cover the losses. All of the numbers were crunched with a moderate earthquake in mind. Now, it looks like they're worried about covering their asses.

"If I had to make a guess, I'd say that your rumor concerns the big quake that everybody talks about. Maybe it's coming sooner than we think. Like next week. And maybe it's gonna be a lot worse than anybody figured. These guys are all acting like rats trying to jump ship. It's like they know sumthin' and can't talk about it. And the hearings don't seem to concern them at all, even though it won't be pretty. That fit in with what you're after?"

Ted grunted. "Yeah, that helps a lot," he said. "I need a couple of more things."

"I had a feeling."

"Two people. A guy named Vance Gifford. Another one named Thomas Wilson. Both worked for Dalton Research, an earthquake research company in Menlo Park. I need to know the details of any life payouts. Everything you can get. You should be able to get that from central data."

"Earthquake research? They weren't your clients?"

"No."

"What's your interest?"

"Tommy was an old friend of mine. I'm just curious."

"Yeah, sure. Anything else?"

"Yeah," Ted said. "Check with your pals in Washington and see if they ever heard of a Pentagon outfit called NADAT. It means National Disaster Alert Team. It's supposed to be a secret outfit, but you know Washington. Got it?"

He could hear Frank take a deep breath. "Ted," he said, "You're messing around in heavy water here. Why don't you level with me? I can do you more good if I know what the hell you're really after. Besides, we're carrying life and disability on about sixteen thousand people in California. Even with the pool, if there was a real bad quake, there's a chance we could lose our ass. If you know something, you've got to share it with me. I'm talking about our survival here, babe. You got an obligation, you know?"

Ted could feel the genuine concern in the man's voice. "I know," he said. "I've just started looking into this thing. Give me a chance to get my facts straight before I shoot off my mouth, will you?"

"No way, babe. If you know something, you should tell me now."

For a moment, Ted said nothing, his ear filled with the sound of a dull rush from the microwave equipment that moved the signal across the country. Then, he said, "Frank . . . you're a pretty smart guy. You know what you've heard with your own ears. Let that be your guide."

"Jesus Christ!" Frank exploded. "Stop playing games with me!"

"That's all I've got to say right now," Ted said as he quietly hung up the phone.

He leaned back in a chair, thinking over what had been said during the conversation with Frank and matching that with what he already knew.

Earthquake insurance was something that was available to residents of certain states, particularly California. There were a few restrictions. Like deductible, for instance. The deductible figure had already been increased from 5 percent to 10 percent. That meant that if a house was valued at $300,000, the first $30,000 worth of damage would not be covered. The raise in deductibles had been done without formal announcement, but had still managed to create a furor. A further increase would just add fuel to the fire, but the carriers were going to do it regardless of the consequences. That smacked of desperation.

There was no pool, Frank had said. That meant that each insurance company was responsible for their own loss, instead of the loss being divided among various companies in a pool. It seemed to point to one thing. The insurance companies were acting as though they *knew* a major quake was coming. Soon. They knew about it and so did state and federal government people, or so it appeared.

Tommy had said his work was classified Top Secret.

It seemed to Ted that much of what was in the report was no longer a secret. And yet, aside from what Frank

112

perceived as mild panic within the insurance industry, not much was happening.

Why not?

The old thoughts came back in a rush.

He removed the envelope he'd previously put in his briefcase, the one containing the copy of Tommy's report, and set it on the desk. Then he took another manila envelope and addressed it to his personal attorney, Sam Hughes. He wrote a short note to Sam and put the note and the report inside the envelope he'd just addressed. He sealed it and mailed it on his way out of the hotel.

But not before he checked out.

Originally, he'd planned on staying in one spot a few days, while he investigated the sudden death of Tommy, among other things. But a sudden hunch, a sixth sense, told him to check out.

He'd wanted to send the report to Frank, but it wasn't fair. The man's curiosity was burning him up. Asking him to hold on to the report without looking at it constituted cruel and unusual punishment. Besides, Frank simply wouldn't do it. Not for a minute. There were limits to trust.

A little over three hours later, Ted was seated in the reception area of the Menlo Park police station, waiting to see a sergeant named Drucker.

Inside his briefcase were copies of two death certificates, one for Vance Gifford, the other for Tommy Wilson. Both had been obtained at the county courthouse. They had two things in common. Both men had worked at Dalton Research and both death certificates were signed by the same M.E. Coincidence? Maybe. Maybe not.

Also tucked away in the briefcase was a copy of the official police report on the death of Tommy Wilson. Nothing was available on the death of Vance Gifford, because the man had died of natural causes. It wasn't a police matter. At least, not at the moment.

The uniformed policeman behind the counter barked his name and Ted headed for the counter.

"Sergeant Drucker can see you now. His office is upstairs, third one on the left. Name's on the door."

Ted thanked him and moved over to a set of double doors that led into the office area. A buzzer sounded and he pulled one of the doors open. In these crazy days, even police stations had to take precautions. Ted's briefcase had been searched earlier, his credentials examined and his licensed semi-automatic taken away for safekeeping.

Sergeant Alvin Drucker was a portly man in his mid-forties, his face and demeanor not much different than most cops who'd been on the job more than a few years. His eyes had that world-weary look of resignation, with a touch of wariness for strangers, no matter who they were. Most cops were xenophobic, an occupational disease that affected even Ted. Drucker's jowls made him look older than he was and the carelessness with which he shaved them, along with the frayed collar on his shirt, gave him a slovenly appearance which he tried to overcome by applying large quantities of cheap aftershave. His body seemed to be in a permanent slouch, even when standing. The mouth turned down at the corners, reflecting a pessimistic attitude that was probably a self-fulfilling prophesy.

"What can I do for you, Kowalczyk?"

The way he pronounced the name was another tip-off that the man had been around. So had the cop in the reception area. Veteran cops can speak small sentences in many languages. But most of all, they know how to pronounce names correctly in almost every language. It's a thing with cops.

They were both standing. Ted handed the man his card. Drucker glanced at it and then threw it on the desk. Without suggesting that Ted take a seat, he said,

114

"So?"

"I'm investigating the death of Tommy Wilson. According to the . . ."

Drucker cut him off. "What do you mean, you're investigating the death of Tommy Wilson?" His eyes were suddenly hard and mean.

"You have a problem with that?" Ted shot back.

"You bet your ass I do." Drucker said. "Your company's got nothin' to do with this."

"How do you know that?"

Drucker's eyes widened and his cheeks began to flush. "Look, asshole, I been at this awhile, so don't try to con me. What's your angle?"

"I don't have an angle, Sergeant. I told you that I'm investigating the death of Tommy Wilson and that's what I'm doing. I'm not required to share with you my reasons, since this is a closed case at the moment. But you, being a public servant, are required to cooperate with me. If you choose not to, I'll include that in my report."

"What report?" Drucker yelled.

Ted stood his ground. "What's the problem, Drucker? You act like a man with something to hide."

The heavy jowls quivered slightly as the man fought to control his temper. "*Sergeant* Drucker," he corrected. "I need your action like a hole in the head," he said. "What is it?"

"Tell me about the accident," Ted said.

"You got a copy of the accident report. What else is there?"

"You know as well as I do that no written report covers everything," Ted replied. "You were the investigating officer. I want to hear it from you."

"Hear what?"

"OK. There were no skid marks. The autopsy report says there were no signs of drugs or booze. It's a road the man was familiar with, even though it was ten miles from his home. What was he doing there? How come this time he falls asleep and goes over the side? How come the car burns to a crisp? Doesn't that strike you as just a little convenient?"

Drucker rolled his eyes and sat heavily in his worn leather chair. "Jesus Christ! The insurance company that took the hit didn't find anything wrong. They paid off without a peep. What makes you so suspicious?"

Ted looked at the chair in front of the desk and decided against using it. He wanted to intimidate this man. Remaining standing, looming over him, was what was called for here. "I find it strange," he said, "that the insurance company acted with such haste. I find it strange that Tommy had two different policies payable to two different people. I find it strange that he wanted to be cremated. I find it strange that the dental charts were available within fourteen hours for the purpose of identification.

"In fact," he continued, "I find so many strange things about this death that I'm about to make it my life's work."

Drucker looked confused. "What's your interest in this? Really?"

"He was an old friend of mine," Ted answered.

A look of relief seemed to wash over the man's face. "So. He was a friend of yours."

It was a statement that, for Drucker, explained everything. He was dealing with a person who'd lost his objectivity, as was often the case in the sudden death of friends. They always thought there was something suspicious. It was a personal thing with this guy. That made more sense. He decided to be benevolent.

"Have a seat," he said, struggling hard to work up a smile.

Ted sat down.

"Coffee?"

Ted nodded.

Drucker poured coffee into two foam cups from a pot that sat on a small table beside three green filing cabinets. He handed one of the cups to Ted.

It was fresh and astonishingly good for cop coffee, thought Ted.

"There's really nothin' strange about this deal," Drucker said, putting his elbows on the desk and trying to look avuncular, which for him wasn't easy. "There weren't any witnesses, which is unfortunate, but we've been able to piece it together pretty good. We talked to some people he worked with and they said he was working very hard. He was tired a lot."

"Did they see him that night?"

"No. They said he had a meeting with some government people in the afternoon. Late. Around five."

"Did you talk to them?"

"Who?"

"The government people."

"No. We never found out who they were."

"So . . . who was the last person to see Tommy alive that you've talked to?"

Drucker made a sour face and sipped some of the coffee. "Look," he said. "One of the problems here is that the man was working on very secret stuff. We don't know who he talked to and there's no way we can find out. It's all classified."

"I can tell you who they were."

"What?" The look on his face was a mixture of genuine astonishment and fear. A look that was not lost on Ted.

"He was working for an outfit called the National Disaster Alert Team," Ted said, continuing to observe the reaction. "His meeting was with them that afternoon. Nobody saw him alive after that."

Drucker's eyes narrowed into thin slits. "How do you know?"

Ted almost smiled at him. Almost. "I'm an investigator," he said. "It's my job."

"You said it was personal."

"I didn't say that. I said he was a friend of mine."

A big hand slammed on the desk. "All right!" Drucker bellowed. "Let's cut the shit right now! What the hell's going on here?"

Ted rose to his feet and said, "I don't know about you, but I'm about to talk with the feds. The guys Tommy was meeting. You're welcome to come along if you like."

There was genuine fear in the eyes now. Not fear of Ted Kowalczyk, but fear of another kind. The feds had power. Lots of power. The kind of power that could end a local cop's career. Alvin Drucker may have been a world-wise cop, but he wasn't very good at hiding his emotions.

"As far as I'm concerned," he said, "the case is closed. I got no reason to hassle anyone."

"Supposing," Ted asked, "Tommy was murdered? Would that be of interest to you?"

Drucker scowled. "Murdered! There's no evidence to suggest that. There's no motive either. Nobody had a beef, near as we can tell. You've been watching too much television, Kowalczyk."

Ted started toward the door and stopped. He turned and asked, "Who talked to you, Drucker?"

"What?"

"I asked who it was who talked to you. I told you that I knew who the people were that were the last to see Tommy and yet you have no interest in talking with them. That means you've already talked to someone. Who was it?"

"You're crazy," Drucker said. "We talked to his employers. That was enough."

Ted shook his head. "No, it isn't. It's never enough for you guys. There's a hole there. Seven or eight hours that are unaccounted for. You guys never close a case until you have the holes filled in. Except this one. Somebody talked to you. Who was it?"

"I told you," Drucker protested, his eyes wary again. "The whole thing is classified. The case is closed. That's all I got to say."

118

Ted stood there and stared at him for a moment. Then he turned and walked out, closing the door quietly behind him. Just before heading down the stairs, he stopped, turned around and returned to Drucker's office. The door was still closed and Drucker's secretary was hard at work typing reports, her back to Ted.

He put his ear next to the frosted glass and tried to hear what was being said inside the office.

Drucker was on the phone.

". . . says he's gonna look into it. I thought you oughta know."

For a moment, silence. Then, "Well, I don't like it. I think you better have that letter of authorization here before the day is over or I'm gonna have to take this to the chief, like I said. I don't mind cooperating with you guys but there's a limit, you know?"

Ted didn't want to press his luck. He moved quietly away from the frosted glass and headed downstairs. In seconds, he was out of the police station, more convinced than ever that something was very, very wrong.

Chapter Ten

Robert Graves hung up the phone and cursed under his breath. Would it never end? It was like trying to nail Jello to the wall, keeping the lid on this, potentially the most dangerous situation with which he'd ever been associated.

In all his years of public service, he'd never experienced what one could call fear. He was a problem solver. He and the other members of his think tank, of which he was executive director as well as spokesman, would be asked to assess a situation and provide various options, rating them on a scale. The actual decision would be made by someone else.

Usually, the preferred option was the one that was implemented because the wisdom, both perceived and demonstrated, was almost unassailable. Graves was known to possess an I.Q. of over 175 and was rarely, if ever, wrong. At least, that's how it seemed. There were times when his advice was rejected, usually with near-tragic results.

He was considered a genius at anticipating the human response to any given situation. It had been a lifelong obsession of his, first as a student, then as an academic, and now, as a highly paid consultant with only one client, the Pentagon.

At first, he'd used his intellect to make money, working for an advertising company that had made millions quickly and showed no hesitancy in sharing their riches with him. But money was not the thing that made him tick.

Power made him tick.

It gave his already prodigious ego an additional lift when he would advise the rich and the famous and the powerful and they would bow and scrape and exhibit further evidence that he was imbued with some mystical insights not normally associated with mere humans.

It wasn't just the brilliance that he'd inherited, locked mysteriously in strands of DNA. It was his capacity to work. To study. To absorb great quantities of information relating to the human condition. And now, at the peak of his powers, his name was whispered with reverence.

It had been his idea to set up the National Disaster Alert Team, charged with the responsibility of providing reasonable courses of action in the event of catastrophes, be they natural or unnatural. There were others engaged in the same activity, to be sure. Every branch of government had a department that went through the same machinations as NADAT. But his department, attached to the Pentagon, was the one with the power.

His department was the one that could move generals with a phone call. Make politicians blanch at the mention of his name.

It was all so secret, and yet, they all knew him.

And he loved it.

Except when there were problems like this one.

Usually, they discussed potential disasters in the comfortable environs of total secrecy. NADAT was a division of the Pentagon whose functions were protected by a veil of secrecy that even excluded the most senior people in the government. Very few of their discussions ever saw the light of day, and when they did, it was only to reaffirm the legendary accuracy of their suppositions.

But this situation was different.

Vance Gifford had threatened to make his report public, despite full knowledge of the consequences. Very unprofessional. Then, to Graves's horror, he'd learned that the very man picked to verify Gifford's work had himself threatened similar action. Both of these men had been dealt with in the only way that made any sense.

There was the fear that the insurance industry association funding Dalton Research was itself in possession of some of the data. That was bad enough.

Now there were two additional threats. The Michael Davis situation was being handled with dispatch, but the other . . . A man, an insurance investigator no less, looking into the death of Thomas Wilson. More problems. Before deciding what to do, Graves needed to know more about this man.

He switched on his computer and modem. Within minutes, he was tied in to one of the giant Pentagon computers and running a search on the name one of his staff people had received from Sergeant Drucker. It shouldn't take too long, he thought to himself. There weren't that many people with the name Kowalczyk living in California.

He was right. The screen lit up with the information he was seeking. A few seconds of perusal convinced him that this was his man. He hit the print key and watched as the information was transformed into hard copy. It filled eleven pages.

Kowalczyk, Theodore Joseph.
Born: Los Angeles, June 23, 1950.
Caucasian, Complexion: fair. Hair: brown.
Eyes: brown.
Height: 6′ 4″. Weight. 215.
Scars: Bullet wound on chest. Bullet wound on stomach.
(see reference 32)
Marital Status: Widower (see reference 32)

The file was a storehouse of pertinent information. Ted's high school records, his military service record detailing his two-year stint in Vietnam, his college records, his marriage date, a short profile on Erica, his security clearance at the time of his joining the FBI. A follow-up clearance done three years later. Excerpts from his fitness reports when he was an agent.

There were references to his present employers. A psychological profile, financial records, sexual preferences, even notations regarding his maternal grandfather, a man who'd died in the Warsaw ghetto in 1943, and his paternal grandfather, who'd died in Treblinka's notorious gas chambers.

That little detail, thought Graves, explained why the man had not Americanized his name, like many others with strange, European monikers. For this man, changing his name would be like turning his back on his dead grandfathers. It would be unthinkable and no amount of persuasion or ridicule could move such a man.

Graves looked for confirmation of his judgment. Yes, it was there.

Yes.

Kowalczyk was considered bright, energetic, hard-working, stubborn, imbued with a clear sense of values that were unwavering. Until the death of his wife and child, he'd been considered a comer, in the best sense of the word, by his superiors in the bureau. The tragedy had affected him deeply, but he was now coping well, working without the crutches of drugs or alcohol, seemingly putting his life in order.

It was a pattern. There'd been other times when his life had been severely disrupted, and each time, he'd taken his lumps and come back, seemingly stronger than before.

Both of Kowalczyk's parents had died relatively young, probably as a result of deprivations suffered during the war. They'd spent six years in the Polish underground, coming to America in 1947. The father had died in 1963 of cancer and the mother in 1975, again, of cancer. Ted had been the only child of the union.

Under the heading of college activities, both on and off campus, Graves found the name of Thomas Wilson. Wilson was listed as a close friend of Ted's during their college days. Surprisingly, there was no current information on the status of their friendship.

Graves put down the file and stared into space, thinking.

Here was a man who was trained to be suspicious. The death of Tommy Wilson would stand out like a red flag waving in the wind.

He wasn't a bumbler. He was a skilled professional who would know he was stepping into a hornet's nest even before he started his quest. Kowalczyk was a problem, no question. He'd used the name NADAT when talking to Drucker. That meant his investigation wasn't simple curiosity. It meant Wilson had done some talking before being taken out of the picture.

Damn!

For years, Graves had asked for his own special force of men who would be authorized to carry out certain tasks at his bidding. Time after time, he'd been refused. He'd have to use the FBI, he'd been told.

It was ridiculous. In the first place, the FBI was subject to public scrutiny. NADAT wasn't. It was insane to have a super-secret agency dependent on people whose every move could someday be made public.

In the second place, there were times when there were obvious conflicts. Like this case. Kowalczyk was a former FBI man. That was bad enough. He was a threat to the entire operation. But it would be asking for trouble to expect FBI men to handle him the way he should be handled. Not until Graves knew a lot more about his possible actions. At the same time, they couldn't afford to give him too long a string. He'd have to be watched. If he got too close, Graves would have to resort to other means.

Damn!

He looked at reference 32. It contained data concerning the events surrounding the death of Kowalczyk's wife and child. And the name of another man almost leaped from the page.

George Belcher!

The very man assigned to keep an eye on Kowalczyk was a former FBI associate!

Robert Graves stared at the name in shock. It was too much of a coincidence to be anything but a horrible portent.

Attorney David Rosen leaned forward and looked into the eyes of a distraught Mary Davis.

"I'm very sorry, Mrs. Davis, but I don't know what else I can do. The people at both the Pentagon and the hospital have been most cooperative. They're prepared to give me depositions, they've shown me documentation and . . ."

"Lies!" she exclaimed. "All lies!"

Rosen sighed and shook his head. "I can understand how you feel, Mrs. Davis, but you must accept the fact that your husband was treated for depression once before. In fact, he withheld that information from the Department of Defense when he was hired.

"As I told you, my associate interviewed the people at the hospital and he saw the bruises on those who were attacked. There's no question that an assault took place. The evidence clearly supports their claim that your husband left the hospital of his own free will, after attacking three hospital employees. Other witnesses have spoken to the problem with alcohol. You've confirmed that your husband has studied the martial arts, so you know he's physically capable of doing this. All in all, everyone we've talked to has been most forthcoming."

"What about the phone call?"

Rosen took a deep breath and said, "The doctors who were treating your husband have stated that paranoia is common in these situations. Right now, it appears that your husband is suffering from a serious mental disorder. He needs treatment. I'd suggest that you return to your home and, hopefully, he'll contact you again. Dr. Williams has asked that you come and talk to him. He wants to discuss with you the things that you might say to your husband to encourage him to come home and get the treatment he needs."

Mary Davis took a tissue from her handbag and dabbed at her swollen eyes. "You're sure about this?"

The attorney nodded and said, "I'm absolutely sure, Mrs. Davis. No one is trying to hurt your husband. In fact, they're very concerned about him and want to help him."

Chapter Eleven

By 1:30 in the afternoon, a thoroughly frustrated Ted Kowalczyk was beginning to feel the full weight of the enormous problem that confronted him. Initially, he'd been stunned by the information contained in the report he'd received from Tommy, but now, in spite of the pressure, or perhaps because of it, his mind was functioning properly, carefully analyzing the data and considering the options open to him. They were frightfully few.

He needed to be careful. Tommy's death was, in his opinion, no accident. Ted further believed that Tommy was correct in assuming that Vance Gifford's death was no accident either. Obviously, both men were murdered for a reason. Clearly, it was because they were the possessors of information that was considered too dangerous to be made public. Information that was now in the hands of Ted Kowalczyk. He would certainly meet the same fate if he failed to act with reasoned care.

Everywhere he turned, doors were closing in his face, in what was clearly a concerted effort to keep the lid on tight. Drucker had called someone and warned them that Ted was looking into things. Even before that call was placed, a series of events had taken place that looked extremely suspicious.

For one, Dalton Research was closed. A single sheet of white paper had been taped to the inside of the thick glass on the door, stating that the firm was in Chapter 7. All inquiries were directed to the trustee.

The trustee, a man named Rose, was out of town for a few days. A death in the family, Ted was told.

Tommy had written down the name and address of the man from NADAT. Someone named Jason Shubert, who operated out of a small office in Menlo Park. Under his own name, of course. The building directory listed him as a business consultant.

He wasn't there. The office was locked. This time, there was no indication as to why.

The police report had indicated that the hulk of Tommy's burned-out car had been taken to a compound outside San Jose.

It wasn't there either.

The man who looked after the compound said that the car had been written off by the insurance appraiser and hauled away to a scrap yard.

When Ted arrived at the scrap yard, he found that they, with uncommon haste, had reduced the car to a two-foot-square cube of twisted metal that was, at this very moment, on its way to a metal reclamation factory in Gary, Indiana.

A second visit to Shubert's office had again been fruitless. He was listed in the telephone directory, but the outgoing message on the answering machine was like a hundred others. A disembodied female voice apologizing for the fact that no one could come to the phone right at the moment, but if you'd leave your name. . .

Ted decided to give Frank Leach another call. He stood in the street and punched a series of numbers into the pay phone outside Shubert's office building. When Frank came to the phone, he sounded considerably more upset than he had been earlier in the day.

"Don't you ever do that to me again, you sonofabitch!" he yelled, the noise practically rattling the earpiece. "I don't deserve being hung up on. You want my help, you treat me with some goddam respect!"

"Listen, Frank," Ted replied, some heat in his own voice, "I don't have time for this. If I hung up on you it was because you were pushing too hard. If you want to help, help. If not, we'll say goodbye right now!"

"Ted, babe," Frank replied, his voice uncharacteristically and suddenly warm, "I'm comin' out there tonight. You're into something that's just too damn big. I want to help."

Ted, staring down the street as he stood by the pay telephone, found his attention drawn by a particular car parked about a half-block away. "Not yet, Frank," he said, his eyes fixed on the car. "I need you there."

"Listen to me! I've just been visited by two people from the FBI, for chrissakes! They wanted to know where the hell I heard the name NADAT!"

Ted's attention was now completely on Frank. "What'd you tell them?"

"The truth! What the hell else could I do? I told them that you'd mentioned the name because it had come up in an investigation you were doing and that's all I knew. They seemed upset, babe. I wouldn't be surprised to learn this phone is tapped. I got a guy comin' in to check it out, but in the meantime, you better not say anything. This really pisses me off."

Ted's attention returned to the car. There were two men sitting in it. A real tip-off. He seemed to remember having seen the car before in his travels, as he made his way from office to office, compound to junkyard. At the time, he hadn't given it a thought, but now, as he replayed the morning's activities in his mind's eye, a mind jarred by the paranoia of Frank Leach, he could recall it clearly. The car was never behind him but always in front, one or two cars away. One minute it would be there and then it would be gone. A plain, gray Ford, working a tail the way a well-trained agent would function. Keeping the subject *behind* him. Rear-end tails were too easy to spot. The average person never suspected they'd be followed from in front.

Except Ted wasn't the average person.

Now the car was sitting next to the curb, probably with the mirror arranged to allow them a clear look at him. So be it.

"This happened after you talked to your friends in Washington?" Ted asked.

"Within three hours," Frank said.

"OK . . . Frank . . . stay put. Don't come out here just yet. You've got access to a hell of a lot of information that I may need to tap. Besides, there's nothing you can do to help me here. The less people in on this the better. What did you find out about the payouts?"

There was a grunt at the other end of the line. "Ted, babe," Frank said, almost in agony, "I just finished telling you this line might be bugged."

"That's OK. What'd you find out?"

The respect that Frank Leach demanded was already there. A respect earned through months of working together. A respect that was mutual. Right now, the man might not understand what was going through his employee's mind, but he was going to honor his wishes. "Not much," he said, after a short pause. "Whoever carries the freight on Dalton Research doesn't belong to the pool or the association. I've got some feelers out with some other people, but so far, I ain't got squat. I can't seem to find out anything on Dalton either."

He paused for a moment and then said, "Ted, this is really getting creepy, babe. I don't know what you're into, but it's serious, you know?"

Ted sighed and looked at the gray car again. "I know, Frank. Look in your directory and see if there's a company called. . ." He mentioned the name of the company that had issued the check to Terry.

"Hold on."

After a short pause, Frank returned to the phone and said, "No such animal, babe."

"It figures. OK. Keep plugging. Obviously, we've got some people nervous. See what else you can find out. I'll get back to you tomorrow."

"Ted! I still think I should come out there. Whatever you're into, you could use some help."

"Frank," Ted said, almost pleading, "I appreciate the concern, but there's nothing you can really do here. If you want to help, stay put. Find out what's going on in Washington. Find out why they're so nervous."

There was a another pause and then, "I think you already know the answer to that one. Take care, babe."

"I will."

Ted hung up the phone and walked towards the gray car. When he was beside it, he reached down, opened the rear door and climbed in. Two very startled men turned and glared at him. One of them said, "You outta your mind, Mac? Get the fuck outta the car."

"As soon as you tell me why the FBI is on my case," Ted replied, his voice flat and cold.

The two men looked at each other and then back at Ted. They were both wearing suits and ties, so they weren't the usual undercover types. The one who had spoken, the driver, said, "You're nuts! Get outta the car or we'll call the cops."

They were both young. Probably fresh out of the academy. Too young for the name Kowalczyk to ring any bells.

"Is George Belcher still RAC in San Jose?" Ted asked.

The eyes told him what he wanted to know.

"Who?" the driver asked, too late.

"My name is Ted Kowalczyk," Ted said. "I used to be with the bureau, in L.A. George was an agent then. Why don't we go and talk to him. Maybe we can straighten this out."

Again, they looked at each other, seemingly mystified. Then, the driver, weary of the charade, grabbed the radio mic from under the dash and pressed the "talk" button.

"Central, this is thirty-four."

"Go ahead."

"Patch me through to Belcher."

"Stand by."

In a moment, Ted heard a voice he recognized. "Go ahead, thirty-four."

"Sir, we have the subject in the car. He wants to talk to you. Should we bring him in?"

There was a pause and then a short laugh. "He made you?"

Ted could see the blush on the man's cheeks. "I'm afraid so, sir."

"OK. Talk to you soon, Ted."

George Belcher was all smiles when Ted entered his office. He stuck out his hand and gripped Ted's firmly, then slapped him on the shoulder.

He was older than Ted by two years, but looked younger, almost baby-faced. His eyes were alive with good humor, a rarity in people with jobs like his. He was tall and slim and seemed like a rich man's son cruising through life on a free pass. His blue suit was well tailored and expensive. He looked like anything but a cop.

It was all a carefully crafted illusion. George Belcher was, to the unknowing, a highly intelligent, hard-nosed agent with a diffuse proclivity for the psychological aspects of police work. He had stated, on many occa-

132

sions, his professed belief that good humor and a pleasant demeanor were essential elements in a successful interrogation. That more people would talk to a man who appeared to be a potential ally than one who was an obvious enemy. It was a philosophy that wasn't shared by many of his colleagues, but it seemed to work for him. The persona he'd developed was an affectation that was so well done, it almost seemed natural. Only those who'd had the experience of working with him knew of the darker side that lay beneath the surface of the man.

He was, despite his appearance, a true manic-depressive, fighting every step of the way to control his wild mood swings. The affected affability was born of necessity, not ego.

"So . . . how've you been?"

It was as though they were meeting in the park. A chance encounter between two old associates. Ted wasn't having any of it. It had been a long and disconcerting day.

"George," he said evenly, his eyes narrowing, "What's going on?"

Belcher stood behind his desk and motioned to the two chairs sitting in front of it. "Take a load off, Ted. Can I get you anything?"

"Just some answers."

"I don't really know what to tell you. We got a flash from Washington asking us to keep you in sight and report. You apparently mentioned the name of an outfit that's supposed to be a big secret, which made some people in the Pentagon nervous. They want to know what you're up to. They told us you'd probably try to contact somebody named Shubert. We staked out the guy's office and sure enough, there you were. I don't know a thing, other than that. Maybe you can tell me what's going on."

"That's it?"

"That's it," George said, his face the picture of

innocence. "No shit. When I saw your name I practically freaked. Last I heard, you were in L.A. with an insurance company. What's happening?"

The face had lost the jovial look. The false persona had been stripped away, now that they were alone. The look in the eyes was one of concern. Genuine concern. Self-involved concern.

Ted took a seat. "Well," he began, "it's a long story."

"For you," George said, trying in vain not to make it sound treacly, "I've got all day."

I'll bet you do, thought Ted.

"Well," Ted said, "I don't mind telling you what's happening. Yesterday, I received a letter from an old friend of mine from college days, guy by the name of Tommy Wilson. He said he was doing some research for the National Disaster Alert Team, NADAT for short, and he was getting nervous. A friend of his, involved in similar research, had died under what Tommy took to be mysterious circumstances and he was getting a little paranoid.

"So, I decided to give him a call. Just to chill him out a little, you know. Make him feel better. Unfortunately, he was already dead."

As he said it, he watched the eyes of George Belcher very carefully. They reacted the way he expected they would. It was a bad sign.

"We weren't close," he continued, "but I felt obligated to at least look into it. You'd do the same, if you were in my shoes."

George nodded. "I sure as hell would. Jesus! You find anything?"

"Yeah, I did. You really want to hear about this?"

The interest seemed intense. "Damn right!"

Ted pursed his lips for a moment while he thought about what he would say next. He wanted to choose his words carefully. "I've only been on this half a day, but already, there are lots of things that don't add up."

"Like?"

"Well, for one thing, I talked to the locals and they can't account for the seven or eight hours immediately prior to Tommy's death, which was supposedly an auto accident. But they closed the case anyway, without talking to the last person to see Tommy alive, which, according to them, was this Shubert guy."

As he talked, he discerned that none of this was news to George Belcher. The realization gave him a sinking feeling in the pit of his stomach. Belcher was part of the cover-up. How deep did it go?

"I don't have to tell you how weird that is," Ted continued. "Then I found out that the insurance company paid off on Tommy's life insurance so fast it would make your head spin, but the data bank at the insurance association we belong to has no record of it. And then I talked to my boss in Hartford who started making inquiries in Washington about this secret disaster team and all of a sudden, you guys are on my tail. Mighty strange, don't you think?"

Belcher smiled and said, "We didn't do all that well, did we?"

Ted smiled himself. It was time for some stroking. "Oh, I don't know. If I had to guess, I'd say that you were pretty curious when you got the instructions to keep an eye on me. I'd say that you told your guys to make sure I spotted them, so I'd come here and make your job a lot easier. I'd say that whoever sent the orders didn't take the trouble to check on whether or not we knew each other. If they had, they would have given the assignment to someone else."

George tried to look hurt. "No way, Ted. I was playing it straight all the way. Who's this guy Shubert?"

"He's the local NADAT man. The secret outfit. National Disaster Alert Team."

Belcher thought about it for a moment and then asked, "What exactly did Wilson say he was working on?"

"He didn't," Ted answered. "But I know he was a

seismologist, so I assume it had something to do with earthquakes."

"Earthquakes? And he was working for this NADAT outfit?"

"No. He was working for a company called Dalton Research. He just said that he was requested to make a report to Shubert, who he said was the NADAT man. I have no idea what was in the report."

Belcher chewed on his lower lip a moment and then shook his head. "This really sucks, Ted. Naturally, we can't get involved in investigating your friend's death, at least not at this point. If you dig up some evidence to indicate that things aren't kosher, that might change things. We have to be careful not to upset the locals, as you well know. Right now, you don't have enough. But I can try and find out what has the Pentagon so interested."

"No need," Ted said, "I already know."

Again, the eyes gave him away. "You do?"

"Certainly," Ted said. "NADAT killed him for reasons unknown, and now they're trying to cover it up. They want you guys to keep an eye on me and if I get too close, they'll move in and take me out. It doesn't take a rocket scientist to figure that one out."

Belcher looked like someone had kicked him in the groin. Almost breathlessly, he said, "Those are pretty serious allegations, Ted. You're practically accusing a government agency of murder!"

"I'm not practically accusing them. I *am* accusing them. Just between you and me, of course. I know you'll respect that."

If anything, the shortness of breath was getting worse. "I do, I do," Belcher said, too quickly. "But Jesus! You're putting yourself out on a hell of a limb."

"I realize that. But there's no other answer. Nothing else makes sense." He pulled out the bottom half of the settlement check Terry had given him and handed it to George. "This," he said, "is the payout given to Tom-

136

my's ex-wife. I checked. The insurance company doesn't exist. And yet they gave her fifty thousand dollars. That make any sense to you?"

Belcher just stared at him for a moment. Then he asked, "Mind if I hold on to this?"

"As a matter of fact, I do. Make a copy, if you like."

Belcher did just that. When he returned to the office, Ted was standing. Belcher handed him back the check stub and said, "What now?"

"Well," Ted said, pocketing the check stub, "I still have a few people to talk to. Why don't we do it this way? I'll nose around and call you at least once a day, giving you a full report. That way, you can save some manpower and I'll be able to get more done. The next guys on my tail might not be yours. If I know that, I'll be able to take care of it. I wouldn't want anything to happen to somebody because of a misunderstanding."

The smile returned to Belcher's face and the eyes took on their innocent look again. "I like that. I like that a lot. You'll keep in touch?"

"Yeah. You'll drop the tail?"

"No problem, Ted. No problem at all."

"OK."

"Good to see you again, Ted. I mean it. You're looking really great. Fit as a fiddle. It's nice to see."

"Thanks, George. I'll be in touch. Oh . . ."

"Yes?"

"How about a ride back to my car."

George Belcher grinned and said, "No problem."

Ted watched the FBI car pull away after depositing him outside the offices of Jason Shubert, then went inside. The office was still closed. He went back outside and hit the pay phone again. He called Terry at work and the sound of her voice lifted his spirits. She sounded surprised and happy to hear from him. "I hope you're still planning on coming for dinner," she said, cheerily.

"I'm looking forward to it," he said. "Right now, I need a little information."

"Yes?"

"Who's a real authoritative expert on earthquakes around here? I'm looking for someone who's not connected with anybody official, like the Geological Survey or Dalton. Maybe somebody retired. An ex-professor, somebody like that. Oh . . . and they would need to be able to keep a secret."

"A secret? What kind of secret?"

"I'll tell you over dinner," he said.

"I know just the person," she said, without hesitation. "There's a woman named Glenda Wickshire. Dr. Wickshire, actually. She's retired now, but she comes to the campus often, to give lectures, things like that. Really fascinating woman. What she doesn't know about earthquakes isn't worth knowing. She lives in Palo Alto. Hold on and I'll get you her address."

In a minute she was back with the address. Ted wrote it down.

"What can you tell me about her?" he asked.

"Well. . . she and Tommy used to be friends. Then he stopped seeing her . . . and everyone else for that matter. She's a spinster lady, an academic who was a geology professor for thirty years at least. She's got a good mind and she's still very sharp. As for her personality, she's tough. Independent. She's been a consultant off and on for years with various groups, but never stuck with any of them. I'm afraid she doesn't suffer fools gladly, as they say."

Just the ticket, he thought.

"Thanks, Terry. I appreciate it. I'll see you tonight."

"I'm looking forward to it," she said, her voice betraying her curiosity.

Ted hung up the phone and started walking towards the parking lot where he'd parked his car some hours ago. He got in and drove aimlessly for a few minutes,

138

making a lot of turns, using alleys, side streets and main thoroughfares. It didn't take him long to spot the tail.

He parked the car in another lot and headed inside a hotel, baggage in hand. Minutes later, the baggage checked, he was in the alley behind the hotel, using his credentials to gain access to the rear of a dry-cleaning establishment. Then he was out on another street, hailing a cab and heading for the nearest car rental agency.

He paid the cabby an extra twenty to go and get his bags while he signed for another car.

Then, his bags in the trunk of the new car, he went through the same procedure, his eyes carefully scanning in front and behind.

The tail was gone, but the anger was building. It was deep, this cover-up. Very deep. It was going to make things difficult.

Chapter Twelve

Dr. Glenda Wickshire lived in a small home nestled in the residential hills of Palo Alto. She answered the door with a small poodle in her arms and a twinkle in her eye.

"Yes?" she said, speaking through the mesh of the locked screen door.

"My name is Ted Kowalczyk," Ted said, holding up his card so she could read it through the screen. "I wonder if I might talk to you for a few minutes."

She peered at the card through half-glasses perched on the end of her nose and said, "Insurance? I'm afraid not, young man." The twinkle had gone out of her eye.

"I'm not a salesman, Dr. Wickshire," he said, smiling. "I'm an investigator. I'm looking into the death of a seismologist named Thomas Wilson."

"I don't understand," she said. "I understood that Thomas's death was investigated by the police and . . . What exactly do you want, Mr. Kowalsick?"

"Kowal . . . sis . . . ick," he corrected. "Doctor, I realize you're busy. I won't take long."

She was a tall woman in her mid-seventies. Still handsome, with deep lines etching her face, particularly around the eyes. Her gray hair was piled atop her head and held by a flowered band. Her makeup was fastidiously and artfully applied. Even the hands that held the dog were carefully manicured, the nails polished in a clear lacquer. She was a woman who looked after herself as a natural part of living, like many older women who had always been considered beautiful.

"I'm not all that busy, Mr. Kowal . . . sisick, but that's beside the point. All I know about Thomas's death is what I've read in the papers, like anyone else. I can't be of much help to you and it would be a waste of your time."

Ted looked deeply into her eyes, made a snap decision and played it out. "Actually," he said, "what I wanted to talk to you about was Tommy's work. He was a friend of mine. Before he died, he wrote me a letter in which he stated his belief that a very large earthquake would hit L.A. this year. In fact, his letter indicated that he thought it would be the biggest earthquake the world has ever known. He seemed quite sure of himself."

She almost dropped the dog.

"Come in," she said, holding the screen door open.

She may have been in her seventies, but Dr. Glenda Wickshire was a very contemporary woman. The house was furnished in what might be called California modern, all chrome and hot colors, lots of glass and mirrors and art that ranged from Yamagata serigraphs to Picasso prints. There wasn't a doily in sight.

"Would you like a cup of coffee? Perhaps a glass of wine?"

"Coffee would be fine," Ted said. "Thank you."

She let the dog down and he immediately pranced over to check Ted out.

"He'll leave you alone in a minute," she said. "He's very good."

The dog sat at Ted's feet, his mouth open, panting, his eyes shining, the small powder-puff of a tail carving a temporary pattern in the thick carpet as it wagged back and forth. Then, he ran his nose all over Ted's shoes and socks, his little nostrils almost vibrating with excitement. He was still there when Dr. Wickshire returned with the coffee.

"Pierre!" she exclaimed, her voice filled with condemnation. The dog moved back, hung its head in shame and practically crawled to a corner of the room where it plopped down, resting its small head on its front paws, the eyes never leaving Ted.

The coffee was hot and fresh. Dr. Wickshire, her face white, her hands trembling slightly, apologized. "I'm sorry. He's normally very good."

"It's quite all right," Ted said. "I was wearing these same pants around a bunch of cats not too long ago. I think he smells them on me."

The doctor glared at her pet for a moment and then turned her attention to Ted. "So," she said, "tell me how you know Thomas."

She was being careful, something that Ted appreciated immensely. He liked her instantly. For the next five minutes, he gave her a complete briefing on his relationship with Tommy. When he was done, she seemed to regard him as less of a possible threat.

"So Thomas told you he thought a great earthquake was coming?"

"Yes," Ted said. "He said it would measure between 9 and 9.5 on the Richter scale."

For a moment, she simply stared at him, her

breathing coming in short, shallow gasps. Then she put a hand to her forehead and said, "My God! No wonder!"

"No wonder?"

Again, she said nothing, instead seeming to concentrate on her labored breathing. Then, she said, "For years, Thomas, I, and a few others have had informal discussions about the possibility of such a quake. We certainly weren't alone. It's something that most of us in the field discuss constantly. Notwithstanding the fact that we were all engaged in the business of studying earthquakes, we are all intensely interested for other reasons, not the least of which is the fact that we live here. It's more than just a vocation. As you can appreciate, those of us who live in California are interested in earthquakes as a matter of course."

"Yes," he said. "I live in L.A."

"Well, then . . . You've no doubt heard the prognostications. Unalterable fact, young man. Not geomancy. Without question, there will be a great earthquake in California within the next three decades, either up here or down in your end of the state. We're all convinced of that. But . . . while we talk a lot about it, there's never been anyone who could really put their finger on when and where. Not to mention the magnitude of such a quake.

"Thomas was almost consumed with this pursuit of his. He was very single-minded, actually. Earthquake prediction was his stated purpose in life and he inculcated us with each and every new step that was being taken. He was quite effusive. And then, quite suddenly, he stopped coming to our little gatherings a few years ago. He said his work had been classified by the government and he was no longer able to talk about it. Naturally, we all wondered about that, because we've all been involved with data that was turned over to the government with no thought towards classifying any of it. After all, most of the research is paid for by taxpayers' dollars. It had simply never happened before.

"After some discussion, we concluded that Thomas was not being honest with us. We took the position that he and the people he worked for were simply on to something that they did not wish to share with us, for reasons we took to be personal. Fame, fortune, something along those lines. It's not uncommon for scientists to become greedy when they're close to a major breakthrough, whatever their field of endeavor.

"For Thomas to say what he did to you—no offense—but an outsider—comes as a very large surprise. It sheds an entirely new light on his motives. But, I still cannot believe he was working for the government. It doesn't make any sense."

"He was," Ted said. "There's no mistake about that. And he told me what he did because he thought he was going to be murdered."

His words had the impact of a sharp blow. Involuntarily, her hand flew to her throat. "Murdered!" she cried. "You can't be serious!"

"I'm very serious, Doctor. That's why I'm looking into his death. I believe he *was* murdered."

For a moment, he thought she might faint. He made a move to reach toward her but she held up a hand. The dog came running from his resting place and leaped into her lap.

"It's all right, Pierre, it's all right," she said as she petted him, calming him down. The dog hesitated for a moment, then bounded back to the carpet and jogged back towards his favorite corner, but not before giving Ted what seemed like a dirty look.

People and dogs. It was easy to see why some people treated them better than they would human beings. If they were trained properly, they were loyal, undemanding companions. Never an argument. Always glad to see you. Agreeing with everything you said without question. Not like cats. He hated cats.

Dogs were different.

"I can't believe that Thomas was murdered," she said, recovering her self-control quickly. "I just can't. You seem to be saying that he was murdered because of his convictions. That simply isn't possible."

"Why not?"

"Because there's no proven way to predict earthquakes. Not yet. Certainly, much research is being done and there have been some impressive case histories, but . . . we're a long way from being able to really do what you suggest. And even if we could, the costs would be enormous. In the billions. Even if Thomas *was* working for the government, and even if funds were almost unlimited, that kind of breakthrough is still years away. You simply have no idea."

Ted sipped his coffee for a moment and then asked, "What can you tell me about earthquakes?"

She looked at him as though he were mad. "That's a rather lengthy discussion, Mr. Kowal . . . sisick."

"Please . . . call me Ted. It's easier."

"I'd rather not," she said, pointedly.

Ted leaned forward. Pierre was immediately back on his feet, ready to move. He was just a little thing, but he had the instincts of a tiger, ready to take on anything or anybody.

"Dr. Wickshire," Ted said, keeping his voice as even as possible, "I don't mean to be offensive. I really don't. I'm not here to badger you. If I seem a little hostile it's because I'm a trained investigator who knows when something isn't right. I have good reason to believe that Tommy was murdered, and that makes me angry.

"I also have reason to believe that Tommy was on to something. I think he was right about a big quake in L.A. and I think there are people trying to suppress that information.

"I'm looking for help. A lot of help. I need a friend, someone I can trust. Someone who can work with me

145

and keep her mouth shut. Someone who isn't all that trustful of governments. Someone who has a mind of her own and isn't afraid to use it."

He looked at her, his eyes filled with pleading, and said, "Will you help me?"

For a moment, she stared at him intently, trying to take the measure of this stranger who'd just entered her house and thrown lightning bolts of shock at her. This man, who spoke directly and to the point. Who seemed sincere, if not obsessed. There was a sense of danger about him. A certain tinge of mystery. At this point in her life, she welcomed some excitement.

It had been a lonely life indeed. She'd never married. There'd been men, early on. Men who'd said they had no objections to her working, following her fascination with nature, especially rocks. But she knew differently. She knew that as soon as she married one of them, the pressures would start. Pressures to stop working, have a family, become a housewife like every other woman of that era. It was expected.

Until recently, she'd never regretted her decision. But now, in the twilight of her years, there were times. . . .

"How can I help you?" she asked.

"I'm not sure," he said. "Perhaps, I just need someone to talk to. Someone who knows about earthquakes, the people involved with them . . . the bureaucracy. . . ."

"Yes," she said, without hesitation. "I'll help you."

Very deliberately, Ted opened his briefcase and withdrew the second copy of Tommy's report. "I think you should read this," he said, handing it to her.

"I thought you said this was only going to take a few minutes," she said, as she hefted the report in her hands.

"I lied," Ted said, looking apologetic.

First she read Tommy's letter. Then she quickly leafed through the report. When she had finished, she

146

looked at Ted, her face white and drawn. "My God," she said. "I was aware, of course . . . aware that discussions had been held relative to the possible evacuation of a major city, but. . ." She stopped and touched a hand to her cheek, "It was such conjecture. We all assumed it would be decades before we would be able to effectively predict a great earthquake. The discussions seemed so *redundant!* I never expected to live to see the day when . . ." Her voice trailed off.

Ted leaned forward again and asked, "These discussions . . . why wouldn't they have developed a workable plan? Why isn't something being done right now?"

"It's always been a question of priorities," she said, almost wistfully. "Since earthquake prediction is in its infancy as a science, we were constantly fighting to procure more funds for research. They were very hard to come by and never enough. Then again, you must understand that undertaking the development of a plan for the evacuation of a city the size of Los Angeles is enormously expensive as well. First the plan has to be devised and then it has to be maintained. Things change. New roads are built, new buildings . . . previously available resources become unavailable. It requires constant updating . . . a full-time staff, equipment. . . .

"It's a case of what comes first, the chicken or the egg. If there is no effective way to predict an earthquake, what is the point of spending precious resources on evacuation plans that will never be implemented? You see?"

"I see," he said.

"So . . . we were all more concerned with the aftereffects of such a quake. Getting medical facilities in place, devising emergency measures to cover a wide range of problems. Evacuation beforehand . . . was something that seemed a fantasy. At least for some time. I had no idea that the matter had been

147

seriously addressed . . . and by a secret government agency . . . My God!"

She seemed close to tears.

"Will you help me?" he asked.

"I told you I would," she said. "But . . . could you let me keep this report for awhile? I'd like to look it over thoroughly."

Ted rose to his feet. "That's not a problem. But I would caution you to not discuss this with anyone. And I mean anyone. Until I have a better handle on this situation, I'm not sure who we can trust and who we can't. And, as I said earlier, I'm convinced Tommy was murdered. I wouldn't want . . . anything to happen to you."

She stared at him for a moment and slowly nodded her head. "I'll keep it to myself," she said. Then, "What exactly are you planning on doing with this information?"

"I'm not sure yet," he said. "I only know that somehow . . . I have to find a way to make them change their minds. Los Angeles has to be evacuated. This cannot be allowed to happen."

She continued to stare at him for a while longer. Then her attention returned to Tommy's letter, her face mirroring the emotions that churned within her. After looking it over one more time, she lifted her head and sighed deeply. "There's the possibility," she said, "that this report is inaccurate. Have you considered that?"

"I have," he said. "But somehow, I don't think it is. Do you?"

For a moment she said nothing. Then, in a very quiet voice, she said, "I'll let you know tomorrow. After I've had an opportunity to really study it."

He extended his hand. "OK, Doctor. Thanks for your help. I'll see you tomorrow."

She stood up and gripped his hand firmly. "Yes. Tomorrow." Then she asked, "Are you a religious man, Mr. Kowalczyk?"

"Not really," he said, quickly.

"Then I'll have to do the praying for both of us," she said, a sad little smile on her lips.

Chapter Thirteen

He could smell it in the hallway as he walked purposefully toward the door to her apartment. The door was already ajar when he got there, the delicious smells wafting through the small opening.

"I hope I'm not too late," he said, as he stepped into the apartment and closed the door behind him.

"No, it's fine," she called from the kitchen, "We have time for a drink and then it'll be ready."

She peeked out from around the entryway to the small kitchen and motioned to a tray sitting on a side table in the living room. "Help yourself to a drink. I'll be right there."

By the time he fixed his drink, she was there, her hair carefully combed and framing the high cheekbones and full lips. Her eyes, unlike yesterday, seemed to sparkle with new life.

She was wearing a simple white blouse and a full black skirt. Her legs were bare and her feet were shod in leather thongs. She carried a glass of white wine in her hand as she walked into the living room, her body a study in fluid, sensual motion.

"Did you find out anything?"

"Not yet," he lied. "I talked to some people but it'll be a few days before I really get some answers back."

"Did you talk to Dr. Wickshire?"

"Yes."

"And what did you think of her?"

He grinned. "She's a hell of a woman. Sharp as a tack, independent, like you said. I like her. She's doing some research for me. She said she'd have some answers tomorrow."

She looked at him intently. "You said you came up here because of Tommy," she said. "What would she know about Tommy's death?"

"Nothing really. I'm just trying to understand a little of Tommy's work. I'm trying to figure out why he thought he was in danger."

For a moment she just looked at him, the big eyes trying to take a read. "And have you?"

He wanted to tell her badly. At the same time, he didn't want her involved any further than she already was. Tommy was dead, murdered, and she'd been paid off on a life insurance policy that never existed, by a government agency that worked in the shadows. It wasn't the time.

"Not yet," he said. "As I told you, I talked to some people and I'm still trying to sort it all out. Once I have a feel for what's going on, I'll fill you in. Really."

"Then, you're going to be here a few days?" She said it quickly, her voice betraying her excitement.

"Yes," he said.

"I'm glad."

The glow in her cheeks told him that she meant it.

"I hope you like chicken *cacciatore*," she said.

"I love it," Ted replied, honestly. "I can't cook a lick and you have no idea how wonderful it is to have a genuine homecooked meal for a change."

"And you," she said, "have no idea how nice it is to have a man for dinner who isn't a total sleazeball."

She was right. It hadn't even entered his mind.

He'd rarely thought of her as anything but an appendage, granted a beautiful one, but an appendage nonetheless. Or maybe Tommy was the appendage. Whatever. They were two, not one of each. A pair. A couple. It had always been that way, ever since the first day they'd laid eyes on each other. Tommy and Terry. Together. Holding hands or hugging or kissing or simply talking. But always together.

In college, they'd been four, but he'd always seen them as a unit. It never occurred to him that after the divorce, she'd be sought after by other men. It was only natural, but it just never occurred to him. It was foreign. It didn't fit.

"I guess it's a little tough out there," he said. "The single marketplace."

"Tough? God! I think sometimes that I wanted Tommy back because he was a known quantity. He ignored me, he had a hundred other faults, but at least I knew what to expect, even if it was nothing. Meeting new people, knowing that it might develop into a *relationship*, is brutal. You hear yourself speaking words you've never used before in an effort to impress. Impress who? The guy is usually married and lying about it, or he thinks you've got a case of the hots because you're divorced and getting sick and tired of . . . being alone.

"Men, present company excepted, are such turds, Ted. Really, they are. Oh sure, I met some real up-front guys, men with character, who made no bones about the fact they were married. Some of them were nice but there's no future in that. As for the available ones . . . there were a few nice ones, but they were generally self-absorbed, like Tommy. They'd talk for hours about themselves. I'd try to be interested, but

God! They were so damn boring! After the divorce, I swore to myself that the next man would have to . . ."

She stopped talking and blushed. "God! I sound awful. I'm prattling on like a fishwife. You must think I'm terrible. I'm sorry."

He could see the hunger in her eyes. It wasn't a hunger for sex. It was a hunger for companionship. For someone she could talk to without being constantly on guard. Someone who wasn't posturing, putting their best foot forward in conversation that was a prelude to what amounted to a mating dance. Someone who wasn't making judgments, playing the angles, determining the best way to make the score.

Someone who could be a friend.

She desperately needed a friend.

So, for that matter, did he.

"Don't apologize," he said. "You're right. It's not a pleasant experience at all. I guess when you get married, you think it's going to be forever and when it isn't, it throws you. No matter what the circumstances."

The hunger in her eyes turned to pain. Not her own. She was thinking of Ted.

"It . . . must be awful for you."

He didn't want her to think that. "No," he said, smiling. "It's better now. Much better. I've been dating some myself. Nothing serious, just some casual dates. People I know. Mostly divorcees. They think as you do, for the most part. There are a lot of sleazes out there, no question. It's always easier for the man."

That brought a smile to her lips. "At last. A liberated male. And have you met someone yet?"

"No," he said. "I guess I haven't really made an effort. I know I should. None of us are getting any younger. But, it's just such a bunch of crap, you know? They all ask a lot of questions that I really don't feel like answering. I understand their need to know, but I usually end up lying, just to avoid talking

153

about it. And then I feel like a shit and things go downhill from there.

"Once, I told the truth and it was terrible. I was something to be pitied. It was sickening. I don't want to be pitied. What happened happened. I can't change that. Life goes on."

He stopped and took a deep breath. He didn't want pity from anyone. It was the reason he'd left the FBI, knowing that every man who'd ever worked with him in the past would see him in a new light. They all would look at him with a mixture of pity and fear in their eyes. A double-edged sword aimed at his heart. They'd wonder if the same thing might happen to them some day. Or they'd wonder if he was really all right, able to face whatever came with a clear mind and sharp eyes. Would his reactions be dulled by the tragedy that had been visited upon him? Would his own grief cause him to hesitate a moment too long, putting their own lives in danger?

He couldn't have that. So, he'd left.

Life goes on, he'd said to himself. Too many times.

But it wasn't true. Life didn't go on. Not in that sense. There was no continuity, no blending. Instead, there was an end to something and the beginning of something else. It was a shearing, a severing. And then there were two lives proceeding in tandem. Like two trains going in the same direction on parallel tracks, the memories of the old life being carried along like baggage on one train, while the new experiences were being transported by the train beside it. Side by side. In a way, it was the antithesis of the fault lines Tommy had written about, where two slabs of rock moved in opposing directions.

She looked at him intently, aware of what he'd said, understanding it the way he'd meant it. Trying hard to keep the pity out of her eyes. He didn't want pity. And she didn't want to provide it. Still

"I think dinner's ready," she said.

154

It was delicious. chicken mixed with celery, toma-
toes, carrots, onions, herbs and spices . . . just
enough garlic so you knew it was there. What was
Italian cooking without garlic? The wine was a California Cabernet, slightly chilled.

For dessert, they had strawberries and cream.

They ate slowly, both talking a lot, exchanging
memories, until both of their hearts were filled with
nostalgic mellowness. The initial tension that both
had felt, as if they were doing a mating dance of their
own, had left, and now they leaned back in their
respective chairs, looking at each other, relaxed and
enjoying the moment. For over an hour, they sipped
decaffeinated coffee and rambled on like teenagers
encapsulated in a world of their own brought about by
the first blush of discovery.

"What does *cacciatore* mean?" he asked.

She grinned at him. "It means hunter style. I guess,
In the old days, the hunters would throw whatever
they brought with them into a pot and cook it up. I
imagine there are hundreds of different recipes."

"This one was wonderful."

"I'm glad you enjoyed it."

She started to clear the table. "You sit and relax. I'll
make some more coffee and we'll sit and listen to
music and talk. Lots and lots of talk. I'm *starved* for
talk."

There was a certain timbre to her voice that he
found attractive. In fact, he found everything about
her attractive. The way her eyes searched his face
when he talked, open and frank in their approval of
him as a man. Letting him know that she found him
interesting and attractive. Flattering him without being mawkish. Keeping her own conversation devoid of
guile, simply spilling out her thoughts on a variety of
subjects that were of interest to both of them.

155

He found himself drawn to her, almost against his will. She created stirrings in him that he'd thought were dead forever. And to his surprise, he realized that his mind and body were in concert, silently expressing a desire he'd thought was part of that other life, dead and gone forever.

Memories flooded his mind. Memories of silky skin, warm lips, tender hands. Memories of shared bodies, shared souls, a giving of each other that renewed the spirit. It wasn't sex he craved. It was that union, total absorption with another human being, an act of love that pushed away the darkness and let the sun shine in.

And then, reflexively, he felt guilty. The guilt descended upon him like a blanket, shutting out the light created by his desire, and in his mind's eye he saw the shattered body of Erica before him. The vision sent a chill down his spine.

Almost as though she could read his mind, Terry was beside him, bending over, placing her lips upon his, gently at first and then, as his big arms encircled her neck, harder, her tongue darting inside his mouth, urging him on. For a moment, there was little response and then . . .

Ted was shocked at first. He waited for the horrible image to return. Mercifully, it didn't. He could feel the warmth, smell the perfume, sense the need in both of them.

He started to fumble with her blouse and felt her hand upon his, the touch electric, the fingers directing his hand to her breast.

"Come with me," she said, a new note of huskiness in her voice.

She led him to the bedroom and sat him on the bed. She lit a candle on the dresser and then, slowly, deliberately, started to remove his tie and unbutton his shirt.

Their eyes never left each other.

And then he was shirtless, sitting on the bed, and she was kissing the scar on his chest.

His hands were in her hair, pulling her toward him so his lips could meet hers again. And then, they stopped, as though some secret signal had been given, and both removed the rest of their clothes.

They lay beside each other, moving slowly, exploring with their hands and their lips and their tongues, his cologne and her perfume blending into an aroma that both found intoxicating. Time was suspended. What went on beyond this small bedroom ceased to exist.

In the dimness of the light cast by the candle, her skin was a soft, almost glowing yellow, her large, firm breasts rising and falling with each breath. The nipples, long and taut, seemed to beckon him.

He felt her hands upon his manhood, now engorged with desire, throbbing and aching, begging for fulfillment.

They each moved with an almost studied calmness, as though both wanted this moment to last forever. A man and a woman, each seeing the need in the other, wanting to fill that need above all, and by doing so, receiving in return a joyful satisfaction of their own.

She was astride him now, moving slowly, her long neck arched, her eyes closed, her lips parted, the tongue flicking up and running along the upper lip, her long hair hanging down and tickling his neck as her nipples brushed his chest.

He was deep inside her, moving equally slowly, enjoying every exquisite sensation, experiencing a passion that brought tears to his eyes.

She looked at him with passion-filled eyes as his big hands cupped her breasts, the thumbs and forefingers caressing the nipples, now gently squeezing and then releasing, and she noticed the mistiness that covered his eyes. Her own eyes immediately filled with tears of understanding, the liquid falling in drops upon his chest.

"Oh, Ted!" she moaned, as her pelvis moved in more deliberate fashion, as though her body wanted to consume his own, devour it, bring it all inside her.

His arms went around her back and he hugged her tightly. For a few moments, they just held each other, neither moving. And then, they began again.

Her head was resting on his chest. His arm was around her, one big hand gently brushing against the skin on her back. Her eyes were closed, her breathing slow and relaxed. She seemed totally comfortable, at peace with the world, if only for these few precious moments.

"I have a confession to make," she said, her voice low and purring.

"What's that?"

"I shouldn't tell you."

He laughed and said, "You can't start off like that and leave it hanging. It isn't fair."

"You'll think I'm terrible."

"No, I won't."

"Promise?"

"Promise."

She sighed and said, "I often wondered . . .Oh . . . I can't."

Again, he laughed. He sat up and plopped the pillows behind him. Then he leaned back against the headboard. Instead of joining him, she laid her head back down, this time on his stomach.

"I often wondered what it would be like with you. Isn't that terrible?"

"No."

"Yes, it is."

"No, it isn't. I did the same."

She sat up and looked him in the eye. "You did?"

"Yes," he said. "When we were all together, you and

Tommy and me and Toni. I wondered. Often."

"I thought it was just me."

He shook his head.

"And how was it?" she asked. "Now that it's happened."

"A fantasy come true," he said.

She made a face. "Oh . . . I know that's not true. But you're sweet for saying it."

He put an arm around her and brought her close again. He kissed her, long and deeply. Then he said, "Terry, you are a very sensuous woman. A delight. It was wonderful, just wonderful."

Her eyes started to mist. "You were crying," she said.

"Yes. I haven't felt like that in a very long time. I never thought I could feel like that again. You brought out something in me that I thought was gone forever. I haven't felt such pure passion for . . . It was . . . I can't find the words."

She kissed him again and asked, "Will you stay the night?"

"What about the neighbors?"

"I don't care about that. I care about you. Will you stay?"

"Yes," he said, as he brought her close to him again.

Chapter Fourteen

The ferocious winds of the night before had faded to a gentle breeze as George Belcher drove his rented car down the narrow roads within the confines of the Nevada Nuclear Test Range. The sun was perched just above the horizon, its light, as it bounced off the bleached brown sand, almost blinding.

He parked the car outside a low, mottled green building, hunkered down in the waste, the drifts of sand against its wall vivid testimony to last night's storm. He left the car and headed for the front entrance. After ringing the bell, the door was unlocked and opened and a uniformed soldier checked his credentials, then escorted him to the office of Jason Shubert. Shubert looked like a man who hadn't slept in days. Belcher just looked angry.

"So you lost him?" Shubert said, as Belcher entered the office.

"For a few hours. But we have him again. It was like I figured. He's shacked up with Wilson's ex-wife. At least he was when I left. Don't worry. My men are on top of it. If he takes off again, they'll keep him in sight. We won't lose him again."

Some of the tiredness went out of the eyes, replaced by anger. "What the hell are you waiting for?" Shubert shouted. "If you have him located, go in and drag his ass out here! The woman too. Damn it, man! That's what you were supposed to do!"

George Belcher gritted his teeth and said, "That's why I came out here to see you, Shubert."

Jason Shubert's eyebrows rose as he leaned forward, resting his elbows on the desk. "Don't tell me we're going to have this discussion again. We've been all through that."

Belcher took a seat in front of the desk and rested his own elbows on the desk, his arms outstretched as though in supplication. "Look, Jason, he said. "This guy is an ex-agent. He was a damn good one, who played by the book every day of his life. I've talked to him and I can tell you that he already has most of this put together."

The eyebrows moved up even further. "Then why in God's name didn't you grab him at that point? You were told that if it appeared he was making waves, he was to be brought in." He slammed a hand on the desk in frustration. "You're not handling this well, Belcher. Not well at all. I suggest you get on the phone and have your people go in now. Bring them both in. You're wasting valuable time."

"No."

It was a flat, matter-of-fact statement.

Shubert looked astonished. "No? Do you realize who you're talking to?"

"Listen to me," Belcher barked. "You people have handled this stupidly from the beginning. So far, I've gone along because I was ordered to, but this is it. No more. I'm not going to trash my career because of the poor judgment of others. I know you have some powerful people in your camp, but sooner or later, this thing is going to crash and burn. You'll never be able to maintain secrecy for any length of time and once the word gets out, everybody's ass will be in a sling, including yours. I don't want mine to be one of them."

He dropped his voice a few decibels and continued. "Maybe you're right about evacuation and the rest. Maybe you're right about being able to stop this thing, but the way you're going about it is wrong. You're operating like this is some tin-pot banana republic. You can't get away with shit like this any more. In the old days, maybe . . . but not now."

Shubert sighed and shook his head. "We've done what we had to do. And for very good reason. If this ever hits the press, we'll never be able to get anything done. It'll be a circus. Damn it, man. We've been all over this! Why is it every time I see you, you want to reinvent the wheel?"

Belcher clenched his jaw. "Did you talk to Wilson?"

"Yes. He's decided to cooperate."

"He has?"

"Don't look so surprised. He's an intelligent man. He sees the logic of our position."

"I want to talk to him."

"You don't believe me?"

Belcher blushed. "I believe you. But if he's decided to cooperate, maybe he can tell me how much he told Kowalczyk. That's something I'd like to know before I go any further."

The FBI man stood up and stuffed his hands in his pockets. "I want to talk to him," he said, his voice reflecting his resoluteness. "Then, I want you to contact Graves. He needs to come out here. We all need to have a talk. This thing is almost out of control. It can't go on like this."

For a moment Shubert looked as though he were going to argue. Instead, he pressed the button on the desk and a uniformed soldier entered the room, marched to the desk, and stood at attention.

"Take Mr. Belcher to see Mr. Wilson," Shubert ordered. "After he's finished, he's to come back here."

"Yes, sir."

Belcher and Shubert eyed each other angrily for a moment and then Belcher turned and walked out of the office, accompanied by the soldier. The two men walked down a long, narrow corridor to a room marked B-226. The soldier fished out a small ring of keys, put one in the lock, then opened the door, standing aside so Belcher could enter the room.

The room looked very much like a standard medium-priced hotel room. There were framed prints on the grasscloth-covered walls, a carpet on the floor, and a minimum of furniture. Atop the low dresser stood a small speaker, from which emanated what some would call "elevator music." Night tables stood on either side of the double bed, both adorned with lamps. A coffee table held some out-of-date magazines. One of the walls was fully draped, but it was simply a stage set, there being no windows in the room. A large vent in the ceiling and a smaller one in the wall above the dresser took care of air circulation.

The only things missing, aside from the window, were a television set and a radio. Clearly, they wanted Tommy Wilson to be kept unaware of activities outside the complex.

As for Wilson, he was lying on the bed, his arms behind his head, his eyes focused on the nothingness of the ceiling. He glanced at Belcher for a moment, then returned his attention to the ceiling. "Ah . . . the Gestapo," he said, his voice filled with scorn. "What brings you to this fair place at the break of dawn?"

Belcher spread his arms out and looked around the room. "This isn't so bad," he said, his eyes shining, a large smile on his face. "I hear you've decided to cooperate."

Tommy glared at him for a moment and then sighed. "They didn't leave me a hell of a lot of choice," he said. "Of course, you knew that would happen, didn't you?"

The FBI man pulled a chair from its position in the corner and drew it up close to the bed. Then, he sat down and leaned forward.

"Look, Wilson," he said, his voice warm and friendly. "I know you're pissed. I can't blame you. You've been kidnapped, dragged out here and ordered to assist in a project you don't believe in. That makes you angry. Hell, it makes *me* angry. If it's any consolation, I think it was the wrong thing to do. I'm taking steps to see what I can do to change all of this."

"Really?" Tommy said, his voice filled with sarcasm. "And what steps would they be?"

Belcher rubbed his chin for a moment and said, "For one, I've talked with your old pal, Ted Kowalczyk."

"Who?"

Belcher laughed. "Come on, Wilson. I know you wrote Ted a letter. He told me all about it. He thinks you're dead and I didn't let him know any different. But I intend to, if I get some cooperation from you.

164

The fact is, I want to tell him everything. I don't think it's right that the man spends his time trying to solve a murder that never took place. Do you?"

Again, Wilson's eyes turned back to the ceiling. "You're the man who made it all happen, Belcher. You and your associates. If you didn't think it was the right thing to do, why did you do it in the first place?"

"You don't know this," Belcher went on, not bothering to answer the question, "but Ted and I were real close when we were agents together. As a matter of fact, we worked together on the case that got his family killed."

At that, Tommy bolted upright.

Belcher pressed on. "It's true," he said. "In fact, I was the man in charge of that entire investigation. I was the one who checked out the daughter and concluded she was not involved with her father. If anyone was at fault, it was me, not Ted. I've had that on my conscience for long enough. If you think I'm about to bring any harm to him now, you're crazy. Fact is, this thing has gone too far already."

He sighed and ran a hand through his hair. "I understand what they're trying to do. You must, too. Otherwise, you wouldn't have agreed to help them. We've got one chance to stop this thing and one chance only. The problem is we have to do it in total secrecy. Shubert and Graves may be total assholes, but they're right about that. Having said that, I still don't think it's right that people are kidnapped and held against their will, no matter how important the reasons. I want you to believe that."

Wilson grunted. "If you're looking for some sort of understanding from me, Mr. Belcher, you're wasting your time. I've agreed to help these people because they hold the key to saving a lot of lives. You, on the

165

other hand, hold the key to nothing. You're just another dumb cop. If you really feel the way you do, you should have done something about it before you grabbed Vance and me and made it look like we were dead. That was the time to stand up and be counted. Not now. They'll never let you make a move." He smiled and said, "Hell, you might have a room out here yourself before the day is out."

Belcher stood up and started pacing the floor. "You might be right at that." Then he turned and faced Tommy. "Look . . . you think you're so goddam smart . . . how come you didn't go to the press yourself instead of shooting your mouth off?"

Tommy waved a hand in the air. "I didn't want to create a panic," he said. "Besides . . . I never had a chance to really think it out before you and your goons clapped me in here."

"Weak excuse, pal. Very weak. I'd call it a cop-out. As much as you want to sit there and bitch, you know damn well that this is the only thing they can do. Problem is, more and more people know about this. You gotta help me."

"Help you? Why?"

"I'll tell you why," Belcher said, his voice rising. "I'm trying to save a mutual friend a lot of grief. Ted Kowalczyk is one stubborn cookie. He's liable to get himself in serious trouble if he pushes this thing too far. Already, he's talked to your ex-wife. If I have to bring him in, I'll have to bring her as well. You want that to happen?"

Tommy Wilson's face turned beet red. "She's got nothing to do with any of this. You bastards stay the hell away from her!"

Belcher extended his arms. "It's not me you have to worry about, pal. That's what I'm trying to tell you.

I'm on your side. I need to know what you told Ted."

Tommy shook his head. "I told him nothing! Maybe I mentioned NADAT by mistake, but that's all it was. The reason he's nosing around is because he thinks I'm dead and he wants to make sure it was really an accident, that's all. He knows nothing about anything else."

"Why'd you write him at all?"

"It's personal."

Belcher snorted. "Personal? You think getting killed isn't personal?"

Tommy stood up and pointed a finger at his interrogator. "So . . . now you're going to start killing people, is that it? I was right! As soon as this is over, you'll bury Vance and me out in the desert." He shook his head and lay back on the bed. "You people are crazy! Nuts! A lot of people are going to die because of your incredible stupidity. Jesus! If I wasn't observing this with my own eyes, I'd have said such a thing was impossible!

"And if," he continued, "if you and Ted *did* work together . . . and if you *were* involved in the case that cost him his family . . . If you do anything that brings harm to him, you'll burn in hell, Belcher. No project is worth selling your soul for. And that's what you'd be doing. If I were you, I'd make sure that you did everything in your power to see he was protected from the vultures that inhabit this place. I really would."

An almost involuntary groan escaped from the lips of George Belcher. He'd tried to be honest with the man and it hadn't worked. The man still didn't trust him. Now he had to face Shubert again and . . .

Jesus!

* * *

Moments later, Belcher was back in Shubert's office, his face wearing a phony smile. "After talking to Wilson, I think I can get Kowalczyk to go along with us voluntarily."

Shubert shook his head. "That isn't your decision, Belcher. You're to do as you're told. This operation is in the hands of Robert Graves, not you."

"Look," Belcher said, his exasperation wiping the smile from his face. "You had us grab Gifford and what happened? Wilson got suspicious and contacted Kowalczyk. Now Kowalczyk is all over the place and in less than a day, he's pretty well got things figured out. I guarantee you, he's already made enough contacts that if we simply go out and grab him, this thing will bust wide open.

"Let me talk to him," he pleaded. "Let me bring him out here on his own hook. I know the man. He's sharp. If we handle it right, maybe we can turn things around, but right now, you guys are about to mess it up totally."

Shubert sighed and threw a pencil at the wall. "What does it take to make you understand, Belcher? This operation is set. You're to grab Kowalczyk and bring him out here. That's it. If you don't do as you're told, we'll give the assignment to someone else and your career will be at an end."

"Is that what Graves said?"

"I don't need to talk to him about this."

At that precise moment, George Belcher wanted more than anything else in the world to smash a fist into the arrogant face of Jason Shubert. But he didn't. Instead, he held his hands in the air as though surrendering and said, "Maybe you're right. But at least let me find out what he knows. Let me determine how far he's gone before I bring him in. It would make sense to do that much, don't you think?"

Shubert rolled his eyes. "What difference does it make? Bring him and the woman out here. *Then* we'll find out what he knows."

For a moment they just glared at each other. Then George Belcher sighed deeply and said, "OK, OK. I'll get on it."

"Good," Shubert said, sounding like a harried parent who'd just had an argument with a recalcitrant child. "You do that. And stop trying to outthink Robert Graves. It can't be done, believe me."

Belcher sighed again and said, "I believe you."

As he drove back along the narrow roads, George Belcher fully expected a jeep full of soldiers to stop him and haul him off to some dungeon. But, much to his relief, it never happened. When the plane left the ground at the Las Vegas airport, he finally started to relax, if only for the short duration of the flight.

As for Jason Shubert, he sat behind the desk chewing his nails. Security was his responsibility. If George Belcher went off the deep end and failed to carry out his orders, it would be Shubert who would feel the pain. But he had no other choice. Because of the strict guidelines, he'd been severely limited in the number of people he could use in this operation. He'd brought Belcher into the program after carefully interviewing the man and making a judgment about him. A judgment that now seemed in error.

Belcher wasn't the cool, collected professional Jason had thought he was. The pressure was getting to him and it was starting to show. All because of the fact that he and this Kowalczyk character had known each other in times past. Something that had not been known to Jason Shubert until much too late. The two men shared a bond that went even deeper than simple acquaintanceship. A fluke. A coincidence.

But it was too late to make a change now. Time was of the essence. It was Belcher or no one.

And in his gut, Jason Shubert had the horrible feeling that George Belcher was going to ruin everything. He shuddered at the prospect of explaining his failure to Robert Graves. But it had to be done. If Belcher . . .

With hands that trembled, Shubert picked up the phone and started punching numbers.

Chapter Fifteen

When Ted awakened in the morning, the beautiful woman beside him was still sound asleep, her dark hair strewn across the pillow, her mouth partly open, a look of complete peace on her face.

It was Saturday. Surely, she didn't work on Saturday.

Carefully, he slipped out of bed and padded, still nude, into the kitchen. He looked around and located the coffee and the brewer, put some coffee in the basket, water in the reservoir, and switched it on. It began to gurgle immediately, and the room quickly filled with the welcome aroma of fresh coffee.

He went through the cupboards, looking for cups, when he heard a partially suppressed giggle behind him.

She was standing there, dressed in a soft blue silk robe, one hand covering her mouth, her eyes dancing in glee.

"I thought you were asleep," he said, sheepishly.

"I felt you leave."

"Oh."

She came to him and gently placed her hands on his shoulders. Another giggle. "Do you always traipse around the house naked?"

"Only when I'm visiting members of the opposite sex," he said, grinning, as he wrapped his big arms around her. "Actually, all my stuff is still in the car. I was afraid I'd wake you. Now that you're up, I'll get dressed."

"Please don't," she said, pulling away from him and slipping off the robe.

And then they were in the middle of the kitchen, embracing each other, standing there like kids in the first thralls of fresh awareness.

Again, her hand clasped his and she was pulling him back to the bedroom.

"What about the coffee?" he said.

"Later. First you, then coffee."

Actually, she took him to the shower first. She soaped him down and he did the same to her. Then they stood under the needle spray, its warmth making him almost sleepy again. He reached around her and turned it full to cold, then laughed as she let out a horrific screech, practically flying from the stall.

"You rat!" she screamed, as she rubbed her shivering body with a thick towel.

He stuck his head out over the shower door and grinned at her. "Come on back in," he said. "It's good for you. Really! Gets the adrenaline going."

"My adrenaline is already going," she answered,

her eyes sparkling with feigned anger. "At least, it was."

He turned the water back to warm, shut it off, then stepped out onto the thick carpet. He took her into his arms and said, "I'm sorry."

"Do you always do that?" she asked, the towel wrapped around her, the dark, still-wet hair plastered all over her face.

"Yes. It's a good way to jump-start the heart in the morning. Gets the blood moving."

"Some day your heart will just stop. God!"

"I really am sorry," he said. "I didn't mean to turn you off."

She handed him a towel of his own and then put an arm around his neck, drawing his head down to hers. "I'm not turned off," she said, "I'm just not into cold showers before making love. Is that a Polish custom or are you just a little weird?"

"I think I'm a little weird," he said, as his lips covered hers. "I have a sure-fire way to warm you up."

Then, they were back in the bed, making love in the semidarkness of a not yet risen sun. By the time they were finished, the room was aglow with bright light.

They showered again. This time, he kept his hands off the temperature dial. After helping each other dry off, he started getting dressed while she threw on a robe and headed for the kitchen. By the time he reached it, the coffee was poured and some raisin toast sat on small plates beside it. Blessed coffee. His body ached, making him realize how incredibly long it had been since he'd last made love like this. All of a sudden, he felt old.

He wasn't, really. It was just that so much had happened in a very short period of time. And then, as he looked at her across the table, the feeling left him as quickly as it had arrived. A whole life, a new life, lay ahead of him. It was there if he wanted it.

He wanted it.

"Do you work on Saturday?"

"No," she said.

"Well, I have to see some people."

"I know. Will you stay here while you're in town? I'd really like it if you did."

He grinned and said, "I don't know. You might wear me out."

Her face took on a look of deep concern. "Am I too . . . aggressive?"

He took her hand in his. "No, no. I was only kidding. It was wonderful. It *is* wonderful. I didn't mean to hurt your feelings. There's not a damn thing wrong with you. You're terrific. You know that."

"You make me feel terrific," she said.

For a moment they just stared at each other in that special way that lovers have of looking beyond the eyes, into the very souls of each other. And then the visage of her lovely face was replaced by another . . . Tommy's face; it seemed to loom in front of him, as if reminding him why he'd come.

There was never a good time, he thought, hating that he'd have to bring sadness and pain into her warm, gentle eyes. But it had to be done. It had to done before this thing went too far.

"We have to talk," he said, abruptly.

"OK," she said, suddenly on guard, still worried that she'd been too forward, too quick to let her feelings be known.

He told her everything.

He told her about his suspicions, Tommy's letter, the report, the FBI surveillance of him . . . every-

174

thing. When he was finished, she was stunned. Much like he'd been when first confronted by this excruciatingly complex problem.

For some, it would be a simple thing. They'd pass the information along to someone else and wash their hands of the entire matter. But for Ted Kowalczyk, it was anything but a simple matter.

He'd been brought up in a home darkened by terrible memories that refused to fade. His father had died when Ted was just a child. His mother, embittered, had turned her pain into a crusade. As soon as he was old enough to understand, she'd told him about his heritage and inculcated him with a value system that placed the sanctity of human life above all things.

The death camps were not only a regular topic, they were the focal point of her entire philosophy. It wasn't just that the Germans had murdered millions. It was the others she railed against. The ones who knew and failed to act. To her, they were just as evil.

He'd been taught to respect life. He'd been taught to be responsible. He'd been taught to carefully weigh each decision with respect to its effect on others.

In his darkest moments, he wondered if all of that teaching had slowed his reaction to danger when it had counted most. It was a question that could never be answered.

And now this.

It wasn't simple. It wasn't simple at all.

"So," he continued, pushing the thoughts from his mind, "I'm going to see Dr. Wickshire today and depending on what she has to say, I'll decide what to do. I have to do something. I just can't sit by and let this happen. But you can see that turning this

175

over to the newspapers is not the thing to do."

"I agree with you," she said.

"And," he continued, "I won't rest until I know who killed Tommy."

"I know."

"The problem is . . . there are risks here. Big risks. I don't know how deep this thing goes. It might be better if we didn't see each other until . . . well . . . until it's all out in the open. I don't want to put you in any danger."

"You don't mean that," she said, her face losing that look of shock. "I mean about not seeing me. I understand your concern, but . . ."

"Yes, I do."

She smiled thinly and said, "No . . . you don't. You could have lied. You could have not told me. You wouldn't have told me if you'd really wanted to stay away from me. You just wanted me to know the risks. I understand that. I accept them. I want to help. I want you to be with me. I'll take my chances. I have that right, Ted."

Was she right? Was that the real reason he'd told her? He wasn't sure himself. But her response warmed him. That, he was sure of.

"OK," he said, rubbing her hand, now suddenly cold. "I'll be back as soon as I can. This time, I'll bring up my bags."

"Good."

"You're sure?"

She shook her head. "Ted," she said, "Will you please stop acting like a sixteen year old? I'm a big girl now. OK?"

There was a spark of anger in the eyes which he found strangely reassuring.

"OK," he said.

* * *

He'd driven about ten blocks when he realized he was being tailed again. This time, it was obvious, the car following behind him too closely to be missed. He stomped the gas pedal and forged ahead. After another half-mile of turns and switchbacks, he was sure of it. They weren't even trying to be subtle.

It enraged him. It was confirmation George Belcher was part of this hideous conspiracy. That never would have happened four years ago. Once they'd been allies. Now they were on opposite sides. Of what? What was this madness! It wasn't like George to be involved in something like the cover-up of a murder, no matter what the reasons.

What enraged him even more was his own stupidity. He'd thought he'd shaken the tail yesterday. Now they knew where he'd spent the night. He'd placed Terry in danger unnecessarily.

God!

The thought of it stabbed at his heart. Why had he spent the night? The report from Tommy had scrambled his brain. He should have stayed the hell away from her. His only contact should have been by telephone. He never should have gone near her. He'd sworn to himself never to place a woman in any sort of danger again. And he'd broken that pact. Worse yet, he'd told her everything.

In his frustration, he slammed his fist on the steering wheel. Then, sighting a pay telephone box, he pulled over and screeched to a stop. He had to warn her. She had to run.

He was halfway through dialing the number when the car that had been tailing him stopped behind his and the secondary object of his anger stepped from the car. And then Belcher was striding toward the phone box and Ted was holding the receiver out in front of him, listening to the sound of a busy signal.

Ted slammed the receiver on the hook, stepped out and, without a word, threw a right hook that sent George Belcher sprawling to the ground. Within seconds, men stood on either side of Ted, their guns drawn, their fingers tight on the triggers, the look in their eyes one of surprise and anger. One of them screamed, "Grab the wall, you bastard!"

"No!"

It was Belcher, lying on the ground, one hand on his aching jaw, another held up in the air. "Leave him alone. Get back in the car! I'll deal with this."

Ted just stared at him, his hands still formed into fists, as he struggled to his feet, shaking his head to clear the cobwebs. "Jesus Christ! You pack a wallop! An inch in either direction and I don't think I'd have a jaw left. What the hell did you do that for?"

The two agents were still standing there, guns drawn, not really wanting to get back in the car.

Belcher motioned to them and barked. "I told you! Get in the fucking car! I'll talk to him . . . alone!"

Reluctantly, the two men put their guns away and got into the car.

"You told me," Ted said, his voice cold and harsh, "that you'd drop the tail. We had a deal, you bastard."

Belcher ran a hand through his hair. "I'm sorry. I'm just following orders. This morning, I realized I needed to talk to you. I didn't want to involve the woman, so I waited until you came out. I thought I was being discreet, damn it. If you'd given me a chance to explain . . ."

"Talk? What about?"

"Can we go somewhere?"

Ted scanned the street. There was a pancake

house about a half-block away. "Come, follow me," he said brusquely.

They walked to the restaurant, taking a window booth in the rear of the place, far enough away from the few other patrons so as not to be heard. Once the waitress had left the coffee on the table, Ted nodded and said, "OK, what's on your mind?"

George Belcher looked extremely uncomfortable. His face was pinched, the brows furrowed, all of his usual affectations cast aside. He looked like a man who'd undergone a hemorrhoid operation less than five minutes ago.

"First off," he said, his voice almost a whisper, "Tommy Wilson is alive."

For a moment, it looked as though Ted would hit him again. The man's entire body stiffened and his eyes became dark, smoldering coals. He fought to control his rage while he continued to glare at Belcher.

"And Gifford?" he asked, his voice a harsh whisper.

"The same. He's alive too." Then, his eyes opened wide as he realized what Ted had said. "You know!"

Ted sipped his coffee for a moment and said, "A variation on the witness protection program?"

"Exactly. Both bodies were unclaimed cadavers."

"Where are they?" Ted asked, his voice barely disguising the fury that was still building within him.

"It's a long story," Belcher said, his face a picture of anguish, "but bear with me, OK?"

Ted didn't answer. He simply glared at his former associate. Belcher cleared his throat and started talking.

"Obviously, you know a lot more than you told me yesterday. I had a feeling." He sighed and ran a hand through his hair. "Tommy told you about NADAT. What else did he tell you?"

"You said you wanted to talk, not ask questions," Ted snapped, the voice sharp and hard, the hostility twisting his face into an angry mask.

"OK, OK." Belcher looked around, as though to reassure himself that no one was listening to their conversation.

"NADAT," he said, "is an arm of the Pentagon. They're basically a think-tank run by a guy named Robert Graves. They're supposed to advise the Pentagon on what to do in case some disaster happens. Well, we've got a dandy coming. Are you aware of that, too?"

Ted continued to glare at him. "Just keep talking," he said.

Belcher swallowed hard, looked around once more and leaned forward. "About two years ago, a scientist . . . this Gifford guy . . . after a number of years of research, developed a complicated system that not only predicted earthquakes, but explored various ways to stop them ahead of time. Graves found out about it and had the research classified. At the same time, Graves started testing some of the man's theories on stopping quakes. So far, the results are inconclusive, but they haven't given up yet. They're still testing.

"Anyway, Gifford, still testing out his prediction theories, suddenly announced that he was sure a monster quake was going to hit L.A. and soon. He spelled out the day and everything. According to him, it was going to be the biggest quake in history, leveling L.A. and causing damage all over the West Coast. He demanded that L.A. be evacuated. Said he'd go public if it wasn't.

"Well, You can imagine what a flap that created.

180

Graves and his people had apparently done a lot of research on the problems surrounding the evacuation of large cities and had concluded that such a thing was logistically impossible. At the same time, he had these tests going on whereby they were experimenting on ways to prevent the quake from happening. Naturally, going public would throw everything in the ash can. Christ! The panic would be terrible. Besides, there was always the chance that Gifford was full of shit. So, he had him snatched and we set up a phony death to keep things cool.

"Then," he continued, his face becoming pinched, "Graves gave Wilson, who'd been kept pretty much in the dark, a look at what his friend and colleague had developed and asked him to check it out. All hush-hush, of course. Wilson did just that and came to the same conclusions that Gifford had. Including the one that the whole thing should be made public. So, they had him snatched as well."

"I ask you again," Ted said, his patience wearing thin, "Where are they?"

Belcher sighed and ran a hand across his forehead. "They're both out in the desert. The nuclear test site."

"Why there?"

"Because," the FBI man said, "that's where they're testing the gimmick."

"The gimmick?"

"Yeah. If you can believe it, they're going to try to stop the earthquake by exploding a series of small nuclear devices. The idea being that the heat created will melt the rock and let it slip a bit at a time. According to Gifford, there are other ways to stop an earthquake, but with one this big, this is the only thing that has a chance. Real tricky stuff."

Ted couldn't help himself. "They have to be out of

their minds!" he said.

Belcher looked around the coffee shop again and said, "Keep it down, will ya?"

Ted continued to stare at him in shock. The report Tommy had sent him had made reference to several proposed methods for preventing earthquakes, but the references, while interesting, were minor, almost insignificant. A nuclear solution had been given a single sentence. Clearly, Tommy Wilson was not keen on that idea.

Belcher took another gulp of coffee and continued. "You see," he said, "I don't know diddly about earthquakes, but the way I understand it, they're saying that the rock is locked together along a line that's about a mile long and two miles deep. They think that they can explode a small device which will create enough heat to melt some of the rock and let it slip just a little. Then they do it again, and again, maybe five or six times, until all of the pressure is released. That way, there'll be a series of small quakes, but no big one. I haven't a clue if it'll work, but I don't know what else they can do.

"Naturally, if this got out, every goddam pressure group in the world would raise hell. The whole operation would be stopped in its tracks. You know as well as I do that there's no way on God's green earth they'd be legally allowed to explode a series of nuclear bombs practically in the middle of Los Angeles.

"Even though Gifford and Wilson have been proven right four times in a row, as far as predicting earthquakes is concerned, ninety-five percent of the scientific community would never buy this. The only way they'll be convinced is when the big one hits. By then, it'll be too late.

"So what it boils down to is this," he said, winding

up. "As crazy as it is, this is our only shot, Ted. I kid you not. If this works, we'll avert a catastrophe. If it doesn't, we may in fact trigger the very quake we're trying to prevent. It's a real crap shoot. With the lives of millions at stake.

"I'm no scientist. I don't have the answers. Jesus! I just don't know if it's right or not. But I do know this: if you take this information to the press, it's all over."

Some of the shock was wearing off. "Can it work?" Ted asked.

"Like I said, I don't know," George replied, honestly. "But what the hell else is there? If this becomes public, all hell will break loose. I've looked at some of Graves's data. His views on evacuation, while appearing very cruel on the surface, are pretty solid, as far as I'm concerned. You know what people are like, Ted. Talk about being between a rock and a hard place. God!"

"Maybe," Ted said, "but that shouldn't be his decision. Who the hell is this guy? He's never been elected to anything. Neither have those guys at the Pentagon. This kind of decision has to be made by . . . well . . . I'd say the president. Nobody less. We're talking about people's lives here!"

Belcher said nothing.

"So Gifford and Tommy are prisoners?"

"Sort of. It started out that way but now both of them are working with the group doing the testing. They've both come around to Graves's way of thinking, but they won't be let loose until it's all over, and even then, they'll have to be somebody else for the rest of their lives. Even if this deal is successful, they won't be able to make it public for obvious reasons."

Belcher drank some of his coffee and said, "Right now, my problem is you. I thought if I talked to you, I could get you to come out there voluntarily. They're real worried about you. If you don't come out on your own, I'm gonna have to take you there. The woman, too."

Ted couldn't help it. A smile found its way to his lips. "You haven't lost your balls, George. I'll say that for you."

Belcher smiled himself. "I know. Neither have you. It's a good thing to see."

There was a certain look in the eyes. A set to the jaw. A total look about the man that was compelling. Ted was convinced that the man was telling him the absolute truth. At least, as far as he saw it. The raw, unvarnished, impossible truth. It was too crazy to be otherwise.

"This Graves character," Ted asked. "This is all his doing?"

George nodded. "Yeah. He's in charge of the entire operation. I think they've kept this from the politicians because . . . well, in the first place, they don't trust them . . . and in the second place, if it all goes bad, the pols can say they didn't know a thing. And mean it."

Ted should have been surprised, but he wasn't. The pattern had been set years ago.

"Very thoughtful of Mr. Graves," he said. "How'd he hook you into this?"

George took a mouthful of air and said, "I was approached by Shubert. At first, he just told me that this thing involved the national security and that he'd been authorized by the director to talk to me. But gradually, he opened up a little more. I don't think the director even knows about it."

"You didn't check?"

Belcher shook his head. "In the beginning, I was sure he was involved. Besides, I was sold on what they were trying to do. By the time I realized this whole thing was Graves's doing . . . the full extent of Graves's influence, it was too late. I was in it up to my ears.

"Keep in mind," George continued, "that this guy Graves has seen six or seven administrations come and go. He stays on. He knows how they think. No matter what the situation, politicians have this built-in penchant for shooting off their mouths. Sometimes, they don't have a clue as to the damage they do. Look! You know as well as I do that this problem is an impossible one. You had the chance to go to the newspapers and you didn't. You were smart enough to realize what would happen."

For a few moments, they sat there and stared at each other, neither speaking, both lost in thought. Then George asked, "What are you going to do?"

Ted shook his head. "I don't know. First, I want to talk to Tommy on the phone. Then . . . we'll see."

Belcher's face blanched. "That's impossible!"

"Why?"

Belcher squirmed in his seat for a moment and then hung his head. "I've told you these things in confidence. If I ask them to put Wilson on the phone, they'll know I've talked to you. I wasn't supposed to do that."

"That's too bad," Ted said, the anger surging within him again. "Look, you're up to your ears in something that's flat-out wrong. According to you, this whole thing is the brain child of some chrome-dome who works for the Pentagon. Maybe . . . maybe not. But you know damn well that this is not the way things should be done. I don't care what the problems are with evacuation, the fact remains that if there's a chance that a terrible earthquake is going to hit L.A., the people have to be warned. Jesus!

185

You can't just sit back and let it happen. That's criminal!"

Belcher squirmed in his seat. "If you feel that way, why didn't you go to the press when you had the chance?"

"Because," Ted said, "I'm not sure going to the press is the answer. There has to be something else. You've answered some of the questions in my mind, if what you've told me is the truth."

"It is."

"Well . . . if that's so, the person we have to talk to is the president himself."

Belcher laughed out loud. "You can't be serious."

"I'm dead serious, George."

"You think you can just phone up the president of the United States and talk to him?"

"Of course not. I have to work through channels. And I have to make sure the channels I pick are ones I can trust. If, as you say, this Graves guy is operating on his own, I have a chance. If the president is in on it, I'm well and truly screwed. The only alternative then will be to let the press have the story and to hell with the panic."

A sick grin came over Belcher's face. "Nobody will believe it, you know."

"They will if you work with me. They will if we pull Tommy out of there. That's what has to be done."

Belcher threw his hands in the air. "You're crazy! You'll never get in there! It's impossible!"

Ted shook his head. "Nothing is impossible, George. You know that. It's just a question of making the right moves at the right time. Between us, we can make it work."

"Us?"

"Yes . . . us."

186

Again, they sat there, looking at each other, saying nothing. Then Ted said, "Look, George, I know you're a little fucked up. So am I. It all stems from something that happened years ago. The time when Erica and Grace got killed because you and I botched things up. We're both carrying around a lot of guilt about that, George. You know it and I know it. Frankly, I'm sick of it. I don't intend to spend the rest of my life in pain because of it. And if I blow this thing, I know that's what I'll be doing. Same goes for you.

"I'm no scientist, but I know enough about the workings of the Pentagon to realize that they aren't exactly geniuses either. Whatever their plans are, there's too big a margin of error. Much too big. The city of Los Angeles has got to be evacuated and that's all there is to it. Maybe there will be loss of life because of the panic. Maybe it'll be a real disaster. But it won't be anything like the disaster a big earthquake will cause."

George pressed his fingers to his temples. "How can you be so sure those guys are right?" he asked. "What if there isn't any earthquake?"

Ted clenched his jaw tight and hissed the words. "I had to make a decision about that and I have. I could spend the rest of my life debating this with myself and do nothing. There's no time for that. I've made my decision, George. Now it's time for you to make yours. What's it going to be?"

George looked like he wanted to cry. For a moment, he just stared out the window. Then, he lowered his head and said, "OK. I'm with you. What do you want me to do?"

Ted slapped him on the shoulder. "First, I want to talk to Tommy. Phone those assholes and tell them that I found out somehow. Tell them I'm willing to cooperate . . . come out there . . . but before I do, I want to be sure Tommy is alive. Tell them that."

Without a word, George left the booth and headed for the pay phone near the front entrance. After what seemed like a heated discussion, he finally motioned to Ted, who walked up and took the receiver from the man's hand.

"Who am I talking to?" he asked.

"Ted?"

He recognized the slightly nasal voice of Tommy Wilson. At least, it sounded like Tommy.

"Yeah. Tommy?"

"Jesus, Ted! How the hell did you manage this?"

"You OK?"

"In a manner of speaking."

"I want to ask you a question."

"What?"

"Remember the time you and me and Terry and Toni went up to Arrowhead? Friend of Toni's had a cottage up there."

"Yeah, I remember, but what . . ."

"Just hold on. I want to make sure I'm talking to the real Tommy Wilson."

"OK."

"That night, one of us got locked out in the cold. Do you remember which one it was?"

"Of course," he answered without hesitation. "It was me. Damn near froze my ass off."

It was Tommy all right. George hadn't lied about that.

Almost instantly, another voice was on the line. "Tell Belcher to get back on the line."

"I'm not through yet."

"Yes, you are, buster. Get Belcher on the line or we hang up. Now!"

Reluctantly, Ted handed the phone back to Belcher. George took it, listened for a minute, and then, a frown on his face, slammed it home. "Prick!" he yelled.

Belcher turned to Ted and said, "Well, that should get the pot boiling. What now?"

"There are a still a few things I need to know," Ted said. "Who was the guy on the phone? Graves?"

"No. It was Shubert. He works for Graves. Graves is in Washington."

They walked slowly back to the booth. After having their cups refilled, Ted asked, "Did he buy it?"

George shrugged. "I told them you'd come voluntarily once you talked to Tommy. I don't know whether he bought it or not. In either case, I'm supposed to bring you and the woman out there. If I don't have you there within a few hours, I'm unemployed and they'll expect you to go to the press. I think they're ready for that. Graves is a man who thinks of everything."

Ted felt a small shudder go through his body. "How did you know where I'd be last night?"

"I didn't," Belcher responded. "I simply had teams stake out the homes of everyone in the area you might possibly contact. One of the stake-out teams saw you visit Mrs. Wilson."

"Terrific!"

"Take it easy. The people under my direction don't know about this. As far as they're concerned, you're a suspect in an insurance scam, that's all."

"An insurance scam? All of this attention?"

"I had to tell them something."

For a moment, both men were lost in thought. Then George said, "I'm really scared, Ted. All my life I've been able to make decisions without too much trouble. Some of them seemed important. At least to me. But this! I just don't know what's right! There are so damn many variables. These guys are experts! They've been studying problems like this for years. Are you sure we aren't messing with something we shouldn't be?"

Ted shook his head. "The only thing I am sure about is this: experts have been wrong before."

"What do you want me to do?" Belcher asked.

"First," Ted said, "I want you to talk to your boys and tell them we're taking a ride together. Tell them you'll be back in an hour or so. Make it sound convincing. Then, we'll see."

Without argument, George Belcher pulled the small walkie-talkie from his inner pocket and barked orders into it.

They both watched through the dirt-streaked window as the car containing the other FBI men drove off.

"Now," Ted said, smiling in earnest for the first time since he'd left Terry, "let's you and me take a ride."

Chapter Sixteen

It was one of the smallest nuclear devices ever designed: a two-foot-long tube less than three inches in diameter. Earlier, it had been carefully lowered down a two-mile deep shaft drilled in the desert to a fixed position deep in the bedrock.

It was a relatively clean bomb, as clean as they could design it, but there would still be long-term radioactivity in the ground for years after the test. It was, however, the kind of radioactivity that would remain in the rock, not finding its way to the surface as long as the proper precautions were taken once the thing was triggered.

Designated TT-366, it was the thirtieth device in a series that had begun production some two years ago. A bomb designed not to kill, but to create intense heat for just a few seconds; heat that would be high enough to turn solid rock into a molten mass of magma.

The previous tests had been successful to a degree. The designers of the device knew they could melt the rock. The problem was the explosion itself. Always, it had been too strong. Time after time, the device was redesigned, the yield revised downward, until now, they had something that they hoped would be enough to do the job without creating the very shock the device was designed to prevent.

Two years.

They'd been working on this project for two years. Now, it was down to a matter of days. If this one was too strong, they would have to admit failure, because there was not enough time to produce the eight devices needed to do the job.

As they gathered around the forest of instruments in the low building in the desert, the faces of those involved in this critical project were grim and drawn. It wasn't just the test that concerned them. It was the mounting attention they were receiving.

The project was supposed to have been carried out in total secrecy. But already, there were rumors flying around the site about FBI agents not performing their assigned tasks, insurance investigators asking a lot of questions, newspaper reporters popping off at press conferences. It seemed as though the entire country was on the verge of becoming aware of exactly what they were doing. And if that happened, it would be all over. The bright lights of publicity would doom the project forever. Two years of work would have gone for naught.

"Three minutes and counting!"

The project director had checked his monitors. The area was clear, the instruments in place and functioning properly. Everything was set.

They all waited tensely.

"Two minutes and counting."

The countdown continued unimpeded. Everything was in order.

Finally, a button was pressed and all eyes were on the monitors. The instruments suddenly came alive, needles gyrating wildly, digital readouts flashing numbers on scores of tiny television screens. Seismograph needles wiggled violently, drawing ever-increasing squiggly lines on a roll of paper, then, almost suddenly, relaxing, the needle now looking like a thin, shaking, steel finger.

"Six thousand, three!"

The project director was reading the heat created. More than enough.

"Initial readings are 3.2 and 2.5!"

The blast had created a shock equivalent to a 3.2 on the Richter scale, measured at the surface. Less than a half-mile away, the reading was down to 2.5. Well within limits.

The men all looked at each other, a new feeling of hope in their eyes. So far, so good.

It would take at least twenty-four hours before they would know for sure. The rock would have to be cooled, measurements taken and analyzed. Even a small television camera would be lowered into the hole, allowing the scientists to see the actual extent of the blast. Then, the hole would be filled, sealed and capped. And if they had finally arrived at the proper mix, orders would be sent out to a bomb factory in the state of Washington. Orders for at least eight small bombs to be produced within days. Normally impossible, but in this case, the pump had already been well primed.

Twenty-four hours.

They wouldn't really know until then.

Bill Price hung up the telephone and shook his head. He'd just talked to the hospital again and this time, they were sure. Sam Steele was suffering from appendicitis. An operation was to be performed within hours. That meant that Sam would be away from the office for at least a week. Decisions would now have to made by the publisher, Brian Cantrell.

But Brian Cantrell was not in the office. In fact, he was hardly ever in the office.

Price picked up the phone and punched some numbers. In a moment, he heard the voice of Cantrell's maid.

"Cantrell residence."

"Is Brian there, please?"

"Who's calling?"

"Bill Price."

"Uuhhh. Sorry, Mr. Price. Mr. Cantrell is sailing today."

"I see. Well, leave a message for him, will you?"

"Of course."

"Tell him that Sam is in the hospital having his appendix out. We need Brian to come in and run things for awhile."

There was a small pause and then, "I'll tell him as soon as I hear from him, but it might be a day or two. I think they were planning on staying over in Avalon."

Price grunted and said, "Well, try and track him down if you can. OK?"

"Yes, Mr. Price."

Price hung up the phone and leaned back in his chair. In a way, it was a bit of a thrill. For at least another day, he would be completely in charge of the newspaper. There was a certain satisfaction in that.

On the other hand, there were risks. Already, he'd done something Sam had asked him not to do. He'd used Darlene to try and smoke out a story that he was sure was being covered up. It hadn't worked. Sam was sure to be upset, once he returned. Unless he was able to make it work.

He scratched his head as he thought about it. He had two reporters digging hard. If . . .

The phone rang. He picked it up. It was Mary Davis and she was almost beside herself. He could hardly understand what she was saying.

"Mary . . . take it easy. Take a deep breath, slow down and tell me all about it. There's no hurry."

She did as she was told and, between sobs, started to speak more coherently. "They say that Michael went crazy. They say he attacked the nurses and left the hospital. Even our own lawyer says it's true!"

Price's knuckles were white from the pressure being exerted on the receiver.

"Mary," he said, calmly, "back up a little and start at the beginning. I want to help, but I need to know it all."

Chapter Seventeen

George sat silently in the car as Ted drove a circuitous route to Terry Wilson's apartment. George's baby face looked troubled, the soft skin wrinkled, the eyes seemingly unfocused, as though the man was deep in thought. As he drove, Ted stole frequent glances at a man who'd once been his friend and wondered if he'd made a mistake in trusting him. How far did loyalty extend? And where did the allegiance really lie? Was George responding to pressure by bending with the wind or was he really made of sterner stuff?

Pressure.

Once, George Belcher had responded to pressure in predictable fashion. Now, the inner workings of his mind were more deeply masked and much less calculable.

Or was it more a case of Ted succumbing to the

ravages of paranoia? And why not? Who *could* he trust? George had confessed to being part of a massive cover-up perpetrated by those in the Pentagon, the FBI, local law enforcement officials and God knew who else. He'd said that NADAT was working on its own, but who really knew? How many times had that game been played?

Instinctively, Ted perused the rear-view mirror and the road ahead, watching every movement, cataloguing every vehicle, his senses attuned to the slightest indication that they were being followed from in back or in front. If someone was following them, they were doing it in such a professional manner that Ted couldn't spot it. He hoped that was not the case.

When they finally reached their destination, Ted parked the car in the rear of the apartment complex and waited a few moments. Then he turned to George and said, "I'm going to go in and get Terry. Soon enough, if my guess is right, a few of Graves's other friends will be looking for all of us."

Belcher looked at him with empty eyes and nodded. "You can count on that . . . for sure." The voice was flat, lifeless, tired.

"Second thoughts?" asked Ted.

"No," the FBI man said, quickly. "I'm fine. Really. I just hope you know what you're doing."

"Me too. You want to come in or wait in the car?"

"I'll wait here, if it's all the same to you."

Ted looked at him carefully. "George," he said, softly. "I need you. I have to be able to count on you. Can I do that?"

Belcher reached out and clasped a hand on Ted's arm. A smile worked its way to his lips, but not the

197

eyes. "I'm fine, Ted. I won't let you down. It just takes a little getting used to, you know? I've never been in a situation like this before."

The understatement of the year.

Ted patted the hand on his arm and said, "OK. I won't be long."

He made his way to Terry's apartment. She greeted him at the door with a long, warm kiss. When they finally pulled apart, she looked into his eyes and said, "You look agitated. Have you found something?"

Ted took her by the hand and sat her on the couch. Sitting beside her, he said, "Terry . . . I'm afraid I've gotten you mixed up in all of this. I've just spent some time with a man I used to work with. George Belcher. He's with the FBI."

He stopped and searched for the right words. There weren't any. "They have orders to bring me in," he said. "And you as well."

"The FBI? What for?"

He ran a hand through his sandy hair and said, "It's a very long story. The bottom line is that you need to come with me. Pack a few things. Enough for a week, at least."

Some of the color seemed to drain from her face. "You mean the FBI is part of this whole thing? Tommy's murder too? My God!"

He gripped her hand tightly.

"Tommy's alive," he said, flatly.

"Alive?" Her eyes searched his face, looking for answers to questions she was unable to utter.

"He was kidnapped by the FBI," Ted said. "They've got him stashed in the desert. Gifford too. They're both being forced to work on a project that . . . look . . . we need to get a move on. There

198

isn't much time. I'll explain everything to you on the way."

"Where are we going?" she asked, her face a portrait of confusion.

"You aren't going anywhere."

They both turned and stared at George Belcher, standing in the doorway, a gun in his hand.

"Sorry, Ted," George said, the voice almost pleading, "I can't take the chance. These people have too much power. They can *destroy* me! As much as I want to help you, and I do, honest to God. I . . . just can't. God! I'm really sorry."

It was the second time this day that Ted had looked down the end of a gun barrel. It made him very uncomfortable. And once again, angry at himself.

He'd known George Belcher a long time. He'd known how unstable the man was. How subject he was to sudden shifts of mood and attitude. And he'd foolishly trusted the man.

Stupidly!

He felt a cold chill sweep his body and then . . . suddenly, an icy calm seemed to overcome him. As he looked straight into the eyes of George Belcher, he felt his senses being fully activated, his mind clicking like a well-engineered machine. Various bits and pieces of information were being sorted by the living computer inside his head, the pertinent data fed to his nerve-endings, now poised and ready.

He was tired of making mistakes. Tired of being taken for the fool that he was. Tired of trusting those who could not be trusted. But more than anything, he was angry. Furious! At himself more than anyone else. Long ago, he'd been taught to use that anger in a positive way. Make it work for him.

Turn it from a liability to an asset. And that was what he had to do now.

This very minute.

Very slowly, he stood up.

"George, he said, his voice deceptively calm. "You're a lot of things, but you aren't a cold-blooded killer."

"I'm not going to hurt anyone," Belcher said, his voice almost a childish whine. "I just want you and the woman to come with me. We'll go to the site and Shubert will decide what to do."

Ted stared at him, the brown eyes turning dark and cold. "No, George. We're not going anywhere. I'm going to walk over there and take the gun away from you. You aren't going to shoot me because you aren't that kind of man. Besides, you're my friend. You've been my friend a very long time. Friends don't shoot each other, George."

Ted's eyes focused on the gun hand. There was just enough of a tremor to give him hope.

"This has nothing to do with friendship!" Belcher cried. "This is business! You understand that."

Ted shook his head. "No, George. It isn't business. You said I could count on you." He started moving slowly toward the man. "You said I shouldn't worry. You said you wouldn't let me down. And now you're going to kill me? I don't believe it."

Another step.

"Stay where you are!"

"I can't, George," Ted said. "I have to take the gun away. I know you won't shoot me, because I know what kind of man you are. You're not the kind of man who would shoot a friend."

He was five feet away. Belcher's face was twisted

in agony.

"Ted!" he screamed, "I'll shoot! Goddamit! You hit the floor. This is my career here! I'll shoot. I will!"

"No, you won't, George. I'd stake my life on that. In fact, I *am* staking my life on that."

Ted took another step as Belcher, almost involuntarily, retreated until his back was pressed against the door frame.

"Ted! Don't!"

It was the critical moment. Ted could see George's eyes begin to narrow, a signal that he was about to shut them tight and pull the trigger, commit an act that he couldn't bear to watch. An act of desperation.

Ted moved with the quickness of a panther, his left hand lashing out at the gun hand just as Belcher pressed the trigger. The room was filled with the sound of an exploding shell, the slug burying itself harmlessly in the ceiling. Then the gun clattered to the floor and again, as it had once before this day, Ted's right hand, formed in a fist, came sweeping across and met the side of Belcher's face.

This time, the blow was right on target. There was the sickening sound of bones cracking and a tortured, bloody scream came boiling out of the broken mouth of George Belcher. He bounced off the door frame and fell in a heap to the floor, unconscious.

Ted picked up the gun and stuck it in his belt. Then he turned to a thoroughly frightened Terry and said, "There's no time to pack. Just gather up what you need."

She seemed stuck fast to the couch, her hands

201

pressed so tightly to her cheeks they seemed bloodless. Her eyes were fixed upon the immobile creature on the floor, the blood forming a small pool on the parquet.

"Shouldn't I call an ambulance or something?" she gasped.

"No," Ted said, sharply. "Somebody will have heard that shot. This place will be swarming with cops in no time. We have to move! Now!" It was a shout.

She jerked back against the couch and stared at him. Then, galvanized, she sprang to her feet and grabbed her handbag.

They were in the car and moving in less than a minute. Even then, with the apartment building visible in the rear-view mirror, they could hear the sirens howling in the distance.

On the way to Dr. Wickshire's, Ted told Terry everything he'd learned. Throughout the short trip, she held one of his hands in both of hers, clutching it tightly, listening intently, shaking her head in disbelief from time to time.

"I can't believe it!" she said, when he finally finished.

He didn't know if he believed it himself. It seemed more a living nightmare than anything else.

When they arrived at the home of the scientist, something new had been added. A long motor home was parked in front of the small house. It was an older model, boxy and unattractive, bristling with antennae, the rear panel covered with colorful decals heralding various national parks and other well-known natural wonders.

For a moment, Ted thought the woman had received unexpected visitors until he saw the legend painted on the spare tire cover. It read, "Rock Doc."

He parked the car and together, he and Terry went to the front door. Before Ted could ring the bell, the door flew open and Dr. Wickshire stood there, the poodle in her arms, a look of excitement in her eyes.

"Where have you been?" she asked.

"Well . . . I . . ."

She cut him off. "No matter." Then she recognized Terry. "Theresa! How nice to see you. Come in, come in!" she said, unlocking the screen door and holding it open. Once they were inside, she put the dog down and Pierre went through his regular routine, checking both visitors out before heading back to his favorite corner. Then Ted and Terry sat down in the living room while Glenda Wickshire made a fresh pot of coffee.

As she came out of the kitchen, the coffee and the cups on a silver tray, she was all smiles. "I read a lot of detective novels," she said, directing her attention to Ted. "From what I understand, you people drink a lot of coffee."

Ted smiled back at her. "I'm afraid that's true, Doctor," he said. "I sometimes wonder if we'd be able to function without it." Then he asked, "Are you planning a trip?"

"Indeed I am."

"Where?"

"Hollister. I'm leaving almost immediately. According to Thomas's report, he expects an earthquake tomorrow in Hollister. I want to be there when it happens. *If* it happens."

"You doubt it?" he asked.

203

She rubbed her chin for a moment and said, "To be perfectly honest with you . . . I don't know what to think. There is so much that is confusing."

"Like?"

"Well, to begin with, there's the peculiarity of Hollister itself. As many people, even those outside the scientific community know, Hollister is a town that lies right along a very active part of the San Andreas fault line. Because of its unique location, it suffers earthquakes more than almost any other place in the world.

"You see," she continued, "the San Andreas fault is a wonderful example of a strike-slip fault line. And Hollister, being where it is, is besieged by scientists and tourists alike. We—by that I mean the scientific community—have blanketed the area with every conceivable monitoring device. Seismometers, magnetometers, strain gauges, geodolites, tilt-meters . . . all in an effort to learn as much about earthquakes as possible. Have you ever been there?"

"No."

"Well, it's quite something to see. The town is literally being torn apart by the constant stresses created by the fault. Streets and buildings are gradually being ripped asunder because they straddle the fault lines, either the San Andreas itself or one of the many small tributaries. The movement of the plates, which averages about a centimeter every year, is inexorable. On one side, the plate is being pushed northward. On the other, southward. It's really quite fascinating. That's why there's so much interest in the place.

"But—and this is but one problem I have with Thomas's report—it isn't just we, by that I mean Americans, who have research facilities in the region. There are expeditionary groups from many countries, primarily those experiencing regular earthquake activity. Japan, Mexico, Chile . . . actually, a score of countries. And almost all of the information gathered is shared quite freely. It's been that way all along."

She paused and sipped her coffee for a moment, then continued. "Thomas contends that the research carried out by himself and Mr. Gifford was classified by this . . . government agency. He further contends that the new techniques developed by Mr. Gifford have been proved effective. I really find that most difficult to believe."

"Why?"

She pursed her lips for a moment and then said, "If Hollister was a closed area, inaccessible to all but a chosen few, I could understand it. But such is not the case. It's open to anyone. If there'd been a breakthrough of this magnitude, I think I would have known about it. All of us would have, in fact. Much of the data available to Thomas and Mr. Gifford was available to others. I don't understand why some of the others haven't made a similar prediction."

"But," Ted said, "didn't he write that they were using new techniques . . . new equipment? New interpretations of existing data?"

"Yes, he did," she said. "It's the interpretations that are different here. The methodology." She threw her hands up in the air. "Oh, listen to me! I'm the archetypical scientific doubting Thomas!"

As soon as she said it, she realized the strangeness of the remark. Her hand flew to her mouth and she said, "Oh my!"

They all laughed.

"I guess," she went on, "I'm no different than the rest. We scientists hate to accept new ideas at first. We're always looking for solid evidence. And the older we are, the harder we are to convince." She took a deep breath and placed her hands in her lap. "However, if there is an earthquake in Hollister tomorrow, I'll be completely convinced of the veracity of the report."

"What about the other four earthquakes?" Ted asked. "Why would they mean nothing to you and this one . . . ?"

"You must understand," she said, "that data can sometimes be created to fit the desired results. In the case of the other four earthquakes that were predicted, I have no *real* evidence that the quakes occurred *after* the predictions."

"But . . . ?"

She waved a hand at him. "Yes, yes. I know what you're about to say." She fixed her unwavering gaze upon him. "I'm a scientist, Mr. Kowalczyk. I deal in facts. I have in my hands a report that predicts an earthquake in Hollister tomorrow. If such an earthquake occurs, I will have *my* evidence. That will suffice. Nothing less.

"As for Los Angeles . . ." She stopped talking and stared at the floor for a moment. Then, her eyes began to cloud over and she put her hands to her face. Terry moved to her side and put an arm around her.

"I'll be all right," she said. "It's just such a shock. All of those people!" She patted Terry's arm and said, "I'm so sorry about Thomas."

Terry looked at Ted, her eyes bespeaking the question.

"Yes," Ted said. "You had better tell her. Tell her

everything."

The old lady with the young spirit looked up and asked, "Tell me what? What is going on?"

Ted grinned. "Quite a bit. Terry will fill you in. But before she does, I need to use a telephone and I also need to hide my car."

"Hide your car?"

"Yes. I'm afraid . . . Would it be possible for us to travel with you in the motor home?"

Dr. Wickshire looked confused. "I don't understand," she said. "If you want to use a phone, there's one in the kitchen. But why would you need to hide a car? Hide it from whom?"

Ted stood up. "I thought that, in the interests of time, Terry could tell you everything while I went out and made my phone call. May I use your car?"

"Yes . . . of course. It's an old one. In the garage."

She fished out the keys from her handbag and handed them to him.

"Do you drink, Doctor?" Ted asked.

She looked at him sharply. "On occasion. Why do you ask?"

Ted looked at Terry and smiled. "I think you better give her a stiff belt before you tell her everything."

While Terry was left to brief Dr. Wickshire, Ted switched cars. The doctor's car was, of all things, an old, beat-up '56 Chevy. At long last, he was able to sit up straight again. He felt right at home.

He found a phone booth about ten blocks away from the house. It being Saturday, he expected to find Frank Leach at home. He wasn't. He was at his office.

"Anything new?" Ted asked.

Leach was almost beside himself. "Listen, babe. I talked to some people. I got some information. But I'm not giving you anything over the phone. Damn it, Ted! I'm coming out there!"

It was useless to argue any further. From the sound of the man's voice, it was a total waste of time.

"OK, Frank. Come on out."

"Where are you?"

"I can't tell you that."

"How the hell are we going to get together?"

"I don't know that we can, Frank. There are some people looking for me. They may tail you all the way out here. You might lead them right to me."

He could almost hear the man's mind clicking as he considered the problem. Then he heard, "I had the place swept. They didn't find any bugs."

"Frank," Ted said, almost casually, "the ones they have now you'd never find. Trust me."

"Jesus."

"That's why I don't think we can get together."

The line was silent for a moment. Then Frank said, "OK, babe. I got the picture. I know what to do. You remember a case we worked on last year? Good-lookin' broad with the bad back?"

Ted remembered. She'd claimed disability for a bad back. The medical workup had been inconclusive, but that wasn't unusual in cases of back pain. X-rays were almost useless and even MRI's were of no help unless there was damage to a disk. They'd watched her for a while and finally found her in a motel in Santa Barbara, enjoying herself in a way that no bad back would tolerate.

"I remember," Ted said.

"That's where I'll be. I'll register under her last name. You remember?"

"Yes."

"OK. You contact me there. I'll shake any tails. Don't you worry yourself about that. OK, babe?"

Ted smiled to himself. It was OK. For a lot of reasons. Frank Leach was a man he could trust completely. He was also a man with a powerful mind. Right now, Ted Kowalczyk needed all of the help he could find.

"Tomorrow," he said. "I'll call you tomorrow."

"See ya, babe."

By the time Ted got back to Glenda Wickshire's place, the woman had been fully briefed. It was clear, from the expression on her face, that Terry had spared no details. The scientist seemed dazed and upset.

"It's incredible!" Dr. Wickshire said. "I'm no child. I've always known that there were things going on in this country that were being kept from us. But this! This is monstrous!"

She would get no argument from Ted on that. "What do you plan to do?" she asked.

"I don't know," he said.

And he didn't. Not really. A idea was formulating in his mind. But it wasn't set yet. There were bits and pieces floating around, like parts of a jigsaw puzzle.

For a few moments, the three of them sat lost in their own thoughts, saying nothing. Then Ted said, "I guess it's like you said earlier. If there's an

209

earthquake in Hollister tomorrow or the next day, then it would make Tommy's report even more viable. If there isn't . . ."

Dr. Wickshire held up a hand. "Clearly, it doesn't make any sense for this . . . NADAT . . . to be doing what they're doing unless they're certain the report is accurate. The risk they're prepared to take . . . it could actually trigger . . . my God! It's beyond me!

"In any case, you mentioned coming with me. You're quite welcome to do so. I assume you want to use the motor home as a hide-out. Is that the right word?"

Ted smiled. "It's perfect, don't you think?"

"Yes, I do. You can both help load up the vehicle. We'll stop on the way and get some groceries. I wasn't expecting company, but I welcome it. We'll be quite comfortable. The motor home is old but efficient. It sleeps six."

"If you'd . . ."

She smiled. "No . . . it's fine. I welcome you. I welcome anyone who can get to the bottom of this mess. I don't think I've ever been so upset in all my life."

Ted smiled at her. He admired her spunk, her guts. But, at the same time, it concerned him. "I want you to realize," he said, "that by helping us, you may be involving yourself in something that could land you in jail . . . or worse. It's possible you could even lose your life, Doctor. Are you aware of that?"

She looked at him with eyes that were filled with sadness. "The fact that what you say is true causes me much pain, Mr. Kowalczyk. Not because of the danger, but because somehow, somewhere, the wrong people have been allowed too much power.

"I couldn't live with myself if I didn't help you. I imagine it's much the same with you."

He nodded.

"No . . . Don't worry about me. Besides, I haven't had this much excitement since . . . I don't know when. I'd suggest we get started immediately."

"When we stop for groceries, I need to pick up some other . . . things," Terry said. "I didn't exactly have time to pack."

Dr. Wickshire smiled. "There's a shopping plaza on the way to the highway. I'm sure you'll find everything you need there."

They loaded the motor home with blankets and towels and other essentials.

And then they were on their way.

Chapter Eighteen

Robert Graves hung up the telephone, removed his glasses and rubbed both sides of his nose. The glasses he wore were heavy and formed deep indentations in the skin that caused his nose to ache almost constantly. He'd heard that there were newer, lighter glasses available, but that would require a visit to the doctor. Graves, for all his brilliance, had a phobia about doctors. He'd gone though the last ten years of his life with a number of medical problems that could have easily been attended to. But he'd delayed and avoided and finally conceded that he'd never willingly see a doctor unless his life depended on one.

He pushed the thoughts from his mind. Shubert had contacted him with a far more important problem. A problem that had not been entirely unforeseen. Graves had anticipated that there would be those involved in the project who might yield to pressures brought about by conscience or some other ill-defined value system. It was a sign of the times. The country suffered from a paucity of true patriots willing to put the needs of the country ahead of personal considerations. There were too many who questioned too much. A vast proletariat with neither the breeding nor the training to allow them to make proper decisions was represented by shallow men with little wisdom.

Weak men representing spoiled, even weaker men. It was killing the country, just as it had brought an end to other great cultures.

He rubbed his nose once more.

He had undertaken this mission, the gravest he had ever encountered, with the knowledge that it could well be his last. He had determined to proceed with due caution. Those in critical positions had been carefully interviewed and given a series of psychological tests before being assigned their tasks, but even then, there was always the chance they'd crack. No test was foolproof. Not all human reactions were predictable. Just most of them.

For that reason, among others, there were only a few of the project workers who knew the details of the entire undertaking. Most were carefully monitored. Not all of them would suffer pangs of guilt, thank God. But the weak ones were like grains of sand thrown in the oil of a magnificently engineered engine. If not properly eliminated, the tiny grains of sand could bring the most powerful engine to a shuddering stop. There were weak minds everywhere.

There was the FBI man, Belcher, supposedly a professional, who'd been told to deal with the Polack and hadn't. Instead, he'd probably blabbed everything he knew. It was something not unanticipated, in light of the information contained in Kowalczyk's file. Belcher had allowed the Polack to gain the upper hand and now lay in the hospital, his broken jaw wired shut, refusing to communicate by other means the circumstances surrounding his injuries. But he'd been found in the home of the ex-wife of Thomas Wilson. Graves could almost visualize what had happened.

Belcher's incompetence had resulted in interest from other, deliberately uninformed, factions of the FBI. Questions, quiet and discreet, were being asked of certain people in the Pentagon. They, in turn, were asking questions of their own. It was building ominously. As long as Belcher continued to refuse to communicate, there would be few problems, but Graves was by no means sure of anything the man might do. Belcher would have to be enlightened as to the consequences of further indiscretions.

He had been Shubert's choice. And a bad one. Shubert . . . another fool. But a necessary one. And irreplaceable at this late date.

And then there was the curiosity of a reporter in Washington, a Chinese, who'd stood up in a Pentagon press office and announced that "Operation Move" was simply a way to get some critical defense contractors out of Los Angeles before a big earthquake struck. Why had she taken such an unwarranted risk? Certainly, not without the full knowledge and consent of her employers. And where had they obtained their information? What did they really know? The newspaper wasn't saying. Neither were they publishing the story. It appeared to be a trial balloon, but what had triggered the interest?

Michael Davis had made one phone call while on the loose at the hospital. But that call had been to his wife. And she had run to a lawyer. The lawyer, in turn, had come to the hospital, but that entire situation had been well handled. Davis was now ensconced in a more secure hospital. His wife had been interviewed but had made no mention of any contact to the newspaper. So where had the interest come from?

He shook his head. Graves knew that some of the defense contractors had been contacted by the newspaper, but nothing had been revealed that wasn't part of the plan. Even now, trucks were moving men and equipment along the freeways, the very beginning of an operation that would take three weeks to complete.

The insurance companies had acted in a way that had been fully anticipated. After all, it was their money that had financed the very research that had resulted in their knowing about the quake. Certainly, the research had been classified immediately and steps taken to prevent the information being circulated to those who'd paid for it. But Graves had assumed all along that the companies would somehow find a way to gain access to the data and indeed, they had. The insurance companies had quickly taken steps to cut their losses and for that, no one could blame them. Their actions were further proof that Robert Graves was indeed a genius. He'd anticipated their every move. And prepared for it.

The entire project had been meticulously planned down to the last detail . . . but . . . there were tiny cracks now appearing in the very foundation of the plan. Too many things were going wrong too quickly. While he'd expected some of them, he hadn't foreseen all of them. And he was supposed to. That's what he was paid to do. There was more at stake here than the lives of millions of people.

There was the reputation of Robert Graves.

He put the glasses back on and looked over the papers on his desk. Something had to be done. He could almost visualize the domino effect taking hold.

It was time to implement a contingency plan. Now.

It was time to use his ace in the hole.

He'd wanted to reserve that for later, when the real crunch came. But things were moving too fast. Much too fast. And they still didn't know if the test had been successful. If it wasn't, that would change everything. Still another plan would have to be implemented.

But for now . . .

He picked up the phone.

First he called Shubert in Nevada. Then he called a Washington number. To the person who answered, he said, "This is Robert Graves. I wish to speak to Jack Murphy."

Chapter Nineteen

A very tired Rusty Coleman plopped himself down in an old wooden chair and rested his head in his hands. As usual, his boss, Bill Price, was on the telephone.

Saturday was normally a day off for both of them, but today was the exception. An army of reporters had been covering the strange movements of several truck convoys ever since the first ones had been spotted at four in the morning, tooling quickly along the relatively traffic-free highways, headed east. They had made it out of the city before the morning crush began. Even on Saturday, it was formidable.

So far, the group of reporters covering the operation had tracked seven convoys, each made up of a number of Army green eighteen-wheelers escorted front and back by trucks carrying armed troops.

Army helicopters hovered over the convoys as they made their way through the heavily populated areas, then into the high desert and, finally, out of California, into Arizona and Utah. They were still moving toward their assigned destinations when those following the convoys had been stopped. A series of roadblocks had been set up and all reporters had been told that, in the interests of national security, they were to stop following the convoys.

It was completely unconstitutional and everyone knew it. By the time the legalities were attended to and the roadblocks torn down, the convoys were nowhere to be found. It was as though they had disappeared into thin air. The *Globe* had leased a light airplane in an effort to pick up the trail, but had drawn a blank. The beginnings of what seemed like an exodus had gone off with uncommon precision, which only served to heighten the suspicions of Bill Price.

And now, he slammed the telephone down and cursed. Then, he reached into his shirt pocket and pulled out his pack of cigarettes, putting one in his mouth.

"Uh-uh," Rusty said. "Better not light that."

"Screw it," Price said as he placed a lighted match to the end of the cigarette and inhaled deeply. "Damn it! I can't function like this! If this newspaper wants me to work here, they're gonna have to give me my own office. Then, I can smoke when the hell I want to. I can't keep running downstairs all the damn time."

"Why don't you quit smoking?"

The look in his boss's eyes told Rusty Coleman to drop the subject. Fast.

"Well? What have you found out?"

Coleman groaned and said, "Boss, I've been on the road all day. You've had me running all over town trying to find a couple of thousand drill sites that don't exist. I told you it's too expensive!"

"And I told you they've got to be there," Price replied. "You just aren't looking hard enough! What the hell kind of reporter do you call yourself, anyway?"

For a moment, Coleman opened his mouth, as though to respond in kind. But he held his tongue. Bill Price had been on a tear for over a day. The man was in a foul humor, unusual for him. And everyone knew why. It wasn't the first time the man had had an idea that hadn't panned out. It wouldn't be the last. But in between the failures, there'd been some spectacular successes. Ideas originally hatched from vague hunches had developed into big stories as a result of hard work and knowing where to look.

The man had hundreds of contacts. Normally, they'd provide little bits of information that were like pieces in some jigsaw puzzle. Price and his crew of reporters would keep finding a piece here, a piece there . . . until the picture was complete.

Another exclusive for the *Globe*.

But this time was different.

Aside from what had been revealed by the Pentagon, there was practically nothing.

Through the wire services, they'd learned that several defense contractors located in other parts of the country had begun to act out their roles in this crazy relocation, bearing out what Jack Murphy had said.

Murphy. He was a puzzle. He'd reacted as expected in one sense, lifting the credentials of Darlene, but in another sense, he'd surprised Price by telling her to go ahead and print the story. He was acting in a manner that was unfamiliar to Price, who'd known the man for years. Usually, Murphy was defensive, especially off the record, where he would pour out his guts, knowing that none of what he said would ever see the light of day. But with Darlene, he'd been anything but defensive. He'd been laconic and arrogant. Sure of himself. Refusing to utter another word, either on or off the record.

It was unaccustomed behavior for Murphy and somewhat baffling to Price. Even more baffling was the lack of interest being shown by other media in the movement of billions of dollars worth of equipment all over the country in an exercise that could only be termed as suspect.

Retired high-ranking military personnel had been interviewed at some length. Those that would talk had said they didn't understand "Operation Move," but some of them thought it wasn't that bad an idea.

And then there was the subject of earthquakes.

Aside from the two discredited scientists who insisted earthquake prediction was a reality, his reporters had talked to nine other experts in the field of earthquakes. All of them were respected. And all of them were adamant. They were convinced that there was no way on earth anyone could know a great earthquake was imminent. According to them, small successes notwithstanding, the field of earthquake prediction was not nearly far enough advanced for anyone to make such a claim. Even the retired military people had backed them up.

They bore out Murphy's claim that defense contractors used buildings that were considered earthquake-proof. So what would be the point?

Already, the rival newspaper had printed the story of Darlene's outburst and subsequent black-listing. They'd interviewed some of the same experts and concluded that Price and the *Globe* were simply trying to manufacture a story to sell newspapers. They were gloating. The fact that the story had yet to run in the *Globe* made them gloat even more. In fact, an editorial in the morning edition had been so condescending it had made Bill lose his appetite.

"We don't often talk about our competition," it had read, "but today we feel compelled to tip our hat to the fine people at the *Globe* for allowing reason to temper their normal penchant for sensationalism.

"Yesterday, one of their reporters made an intemperate outburst at a Pentagon press conference called to discuss an exercise now under way, an exercise called 'Operation Move.' The exercise is reported elsewhere in this paper, so we won't delve into it here. But the reporter for the *Globe*, in what can only be called a fishing expedition, practically accused the Pentagon of carrying out this exercise for one reason and one reason only. According to the reporter, who will, mercifully, be unnamed here, a major earthquake was about to hit Los Angeles, hence the need to remove the defense contractors.

"We've talked to several eminent seismologists and geologists, all of whom are united in the view that earthquakes are unpredictable. That's one thing. But the damning thing here is that a reporter would think that the only concern of the government would be defense contractors and military personnel. The question posed by the reporter indicated that the *Globe* thinks no efforts would be made to evacuate the citizens of this city, should such a fanciful idea be actually true.

"Perhaps the reporter's judgment was clouded by a report that was circulated some years back in which it was stated that evacuation of a major city was not feasible. That report was studied and subsequently discounted by civil defense authorities. As everyone knows, there are many agencies hard at work on perfecting evacuation plans, should they ever be necessary for whatever reason.

"It's bad enough when people in public service do keep important facts from us. But it's totally unfair to accuse them of such actions when there is no proof whatsoever.

"We tip our hat to the *Globe* because, in spite of the intemperance of one of their reporters, they have not printed a story that holds no water. They've refrained from backing a reporter who was obviously out of line and for that we applaud them."

Price leaned back in his chair and sucked on the cigarette. Already, several of the staff were casting stiff looks in his direction. For sure, another memo would be written and Bill would be called in and told that the rule was for everyone. No smoking in the open office area.

It was so stupid. He was an experienced editor with a string of awards. His people, most of them, anyway, liked and admired him. But this was a new age. An age when smoking was out. An age when a cub reporter could actually have an editor dismissed because he insisted on breaking the rules. And the newspaper, ever-devoted to the bottom line, would rather lose a good editor than provide him with a closed-in place where he could indulge his addiction.

Crazy!

He could almost see it coming.

He stubbed out the cigarette in the ash tray secreted in his desk drawer and slammed the drawer shut.

"Rusty," he said, his voice almost a snarl, "we have to break something loose on this. I'm being laughed at and I really don't like that a whole lot. I know I've been wrong once or twice in the past, but this time . . . damn it! I'm right! I know it! I can feel it in my gut."

"Boss . . ."

"Don't 'boss' me. I know! You think I'm off my rocker. Well, I'm not. I'm . . ."

He was interrupted by a copy boy who dropped three pages torn from the wire service teletype on his desk. He glared at the back of the "boy," a man of sixty, and pointed a finger at Rusty. He was about to say something when his eyes were drawn to the wire service report. Actually, it was one word in the report. The word "earthquake" in the lead.

He started to read.

The further he progressed, the more excited he became. When he'd finished, he let out a yell and handed it to Rusty. "Read this!" he chortled.

Rusty looked at the report. It read: "JUSTICE DEPARTMENT TO INVESTIGATE INSURANCE ASSOCIATION RE EARTHQUAKE FLAP.

"Washington: May 8. The Justice Department today announced a full-scale investigation into activities of the American Association of Insurance Specialties (AAIS) after complaints were received from a group of California legislators scheduled to begin hearings next week. The hearings were originally called to look into the earthquake insurance situation as it exists in California today, but according to Senator Jake Simpson, chairman of the committee, information has been received that 'requires a complete and extensive investigation by the Justice Department.'

"Senator Simpson went on to say that, 'We have reason to believe that the AAIS has financed a ten-year study of earthquakes. A study that concluded the chances of a major earthquake in California in the next twenty years are remote, an estimate that is not supported by the established scientific community, and that they sought to suppress the report, even to the point of possible homicide.'

"Although the senator would not give further details of the possible homicide, informed sources indicated that the Justice Department will be asked to look into the circumstances surrounding the death of Thomas A. Wilson, a seismologist, who died in a one-car auto accident last week. Wilson is believed to be the author of the report mentioned.

"The senator went on to say that full details would be revealed when the committee opens its hearings on Monday. In the meantime, a spokesman for AAIS said that they were completely unaware of either the report or the pending investigation, and would have no comment until they could study the matter further.

"In recent years, the cost of earthquake insurance has risen dramatically, with the deductible percentage rising as well. In actual fact, very few new policies have been issued in the last two months while policies already in force have been either cancelled or renewals denied in many cases. It is believed that the Justice Department will be asked to investigate whether or not AAIS sought to start a rumor indicating that a major earthquake in the Los Angeles area was imminent, when they were in possession of a report that indicated otherwise. Speculation centers on the theory that the association sought to create an atmosphere that would justify the actions of several of their members. Informed sources say that AAIS even went so far as to alert the Pentagon, this action precipitating 'Operation Move' now under way.

"Informed sources say that the drastic actions taken by the insurance companies were the opening gambit in a plan that would eventually see earthquake insurance policies being issued, but at much higher rates and with even higher deductible percentages, some rumored to be as high as 25%. It is believed that the plan was conceived to produce enormous revenues that are to be used as a buffer against losses from an earthquake that the report indicates is expected to strike California sometime between the years 2010 and 2020. Other sources have speculated that the plan was designed to exert pressure on federal authorities who have balked at classifying earthquake insurance in the same manner as flood insurance, which would allow for federal assistance."

There was more, much more, but it was enough for Rusty Coleman.

He put the report back on the desk and said, "Well, you were right. There was something fishy about 'Operation Move.' It just wasn't what you thought."

"Is that how you see it?" Price asked.

"Don't you?"

Price slammed his hand on the desk. "Think! Think!"

Rusty looked hurt. Price didn't wait. He pressed on with his thoughts.

"What is it that insurance companies do?" he asked.

"Boss . . . I'm not a kid, for Christ's sake."

"Then stop acting like one!"

"Boss!"

"Listen," Price went on, "Insurance companies are in business to make money. They've got thousands of guys who figure the odds, just like the bookmakers in Vegas. They've got this down to a science. They know how long the average guy will live; how many accidents there'll be in an average day; what percentage of people will develop cancer in the next two years . . . all of it.

"They issue policies based on the odds. That includes earthquake insurance. In the first place, you were the one who told me that you can't predict earthquakes. So how come they have the results of a ten-year study that says the chances of one within the next twenty years are remote? How can they stick their necks out like that? Does that sound kosher?"

"No," Rusty said.

"OK. Now supposing the report, by some strange deal, *did* say just that. Wouldn't the insurance companies want to write all of the earthquake insurance they could? It would be a sure bet! But they aren't doing that. Just the opposite."

"But . . ."

"But, but, but. This thing really stinks. Remem-

226

ber what I said the other day about that seminar? This is all part of the smoke screen, Rusty. By God! Darlene did shake them up! People are asking too many questions about this crazy exercise, so they've concocted this song-and-dance about some conspiracy on the part of the insurance companies. It's just a bunch of crap. When the earthquake hits, who'll remember?"

"Boss," Rusty said, "I think you're really off the wall on this one."

"Yeah? Does that mean you aren't going to bust your ass to find those probes?"

"No, of course not. It's just that . . ."

"Don't you worry about me, pal. You just find those probes. We may have the biggest story we've ever had here. Don't let me down."

For a moment, Rusty's tired eyes seemed to glaze over. He said nothing. Instead, he just sat and stared at Price, wondering, for perhaps the hundredth time, just what it was that drove this man. Then, finally, he rose slowly from the chair and said, "I won't, boss."

Chapter Twenty

Dr. Glenda Wickshire drove the fifty miles from Palo Alto to Hollister with a practiced precision born of experience. Her firm hands guided the motor home through the heavy traffic on the highway, as well as the more confining narrow road that led into Hollister, with an ease that belied her years. With the "Rock Doc" at the wheel, the thirty-three-foot vehicle seemed almost as agile as a small sports car.

There were two captain's chairs up front, one occupied by the driver, the other occupied by Pierre, the poodle. It was obvious that he, like most dogs, loved to travel. His tiny body was stretched to its fullest, his hind legs on the seat, his front paws on the dashboard, his nose pushed against the windshield as though he were the official lookout.

Behind the dog and his mistress, Ted and Terry

sat in a dining area about midway down the coach and talked in hushed tones. After some time, Terry asked, somewhat anxiously, "What are we going to do?"

Ted rubbed the top of his head. The motor home had a rather low ceiling and every time he stood up, he had to bend his head to avoid striking it. Despite his caution, he'd already banged his head twice on one of the two air conditioners that had been installed in the ceiling. The second encounter had created a small swelling that still ached.

"I've been thinking about little else," he said. "I have a few ideas, but I haven't yet come to a firm decision."

Terry seemed puzzled. "Shouldn't we go to the newspapers, or the television people?" she asked. "At the very least, the police? This should be made public, don't you think? And if Tommy's a prisoner, for God's sake . . ."

Ted brought his hand down from his head. The swelling continued to throb unabated. "It's not quite that simple," he said. "Belcher was involved, and he's FBI. I talked to a local cop who's also involved. I still don't know how deep this cover-up goes. Until I have a better idea—"

"But—"

He held up his hand. "Going to the press isn't the answer either. Not yet. That's a last resort. We could create a terrible panic, the likes of which we've never seen."

She looked out the window. "We have to do something."

He took her hand in his and made her look at him. "I know that, Terry. Believe me, I know that. It's just that making the wrong move right now could be disastrous. Give me a little time. I'll come up with something."

Her gaze dropped to the table. "I'm sorry," she said. "I know you're doing your best. It's just . . ."

"Tommy? I realize how important it is to get him out of there, I can assure you. He's already been declared dead. In view of the circumstances, he may become a liability they can no longer afford to keep alive."

As soon as he uttered the words, he wished he could take them back. Instantly, he could see the impact his words had on her.

"But how could you get him out?" she asked. "The place must be protected like a fortress. What can you possibly do?"

"Again," he said, "I have some ideas. I'm working on it."

She looked out the window. Neither of them spoke. Then she turned back and looked into his eyes. "There's something I want to tell you," she said.

He waited.

"What happened last night . . . and this morning . . . I wanted that to happen, Ted."

He could feel the adrenaline begin to surge through his veins. "So did I," he said.

She placed a hand over his lips. "No . . . don't talk. Just listen for a moment."

Again, he waited. He could feel his heart beginning to pound. For the last two days, he'd been exhibiting all of the signs of a man falling in love. The pounding heart, the clammy hands, the quickness of breath . . . and it terrified him. He felt as though his love was a curse, bringing no good to those who were its recipients. Part of him hoped she was about to tell him that she was still in love with her ex-husband and that she wanted another chance to make it work.

If they ever saw him again.

And yet, another part of him wanted to hear something else.

"Tommy . . ." she said, her eyes cast downward again, as if she was unsure of his reaction and unable to watch for it, "wasn't much of a husband. Not ever. I still love him, and I suppose I'll always love him. But it isn't the kind of love you can build a relationship on. It's the love you might feel for any human being who was once a part of your life. Someone who doesn't realize how selfish he is.

"Tommy had one interest and one interest only. His work. That's not necessarily wrong. It's just the way he is. Maybe a person needs to be like that if they're ever going to accomplish great things. I don't really know. But even though—when he was worried—he thought about me, and expressed some very sweet sentiments, I know he can never change. Sure, he might for a while. A few weeks, maybe a few months. But it will all be superficial. The man is what he is. He can't help it."

She was still staring at the table, both of her hands touching one of his, holding it tight, as though it could provide some strength . . . or maybe a signal.

"So I love him," she continued, "but . . . he's out of my life, if you can understand what I mean. I'll always care for him in a little corner of my heart, but that's the extent of it.

"My needs are greater than he could ever provide. Perhaps that's my own selfishness. If it is, I can only say it's a part of me I recognize and have

231

to accept. I don't need money. I need companionship, affection, caring . . . sharing. I need that.

"No matter what happens, Tommy and I will never be together again. And he'll never be a threat to our relationship . . . that is, if you want us to have a relationship."

Almost reluctantly, she raised her head and those dark eyes were upon him, searching, beseeching. Dark, frightened eyes that made his heart pound even harder.

He was astonished. He felt more for her than he'd dreamed possible. He simply sat and stared at her.

"You can speak now," she said.

His lips twisted into a strange, silly grin. Still he said nothing. He was truly speechless.

"In fact," she said, looking worried now, "I'd really like it if you did speak."

Very gently, he took her face in his big hands and drew her closer. Then he kissed her on the lips. When they parted, he said, "Yes . . . I'd like that."

For a moment, they just stared into each other's eyes and then they heard the doctor cry out. "Hollister! Straight ahead!"

For the next two hours, Dr. Wickshire, secure in her own element, gave her two guests a guided tour of Hollister, California, earthquake capital of the world.

She showed them buildings literally being ripped apart by the conflict of two opposing forces in the earth beneath them; streets in constant need of repair because of the cracks and tears caused by the same forces; trees that had been made crooked by the shifting of the earth; and sections of the ground that showed clear evidence of past quakes.

Aside from that, the town looked like a typical California small town, just off the beaten path, where the pace of life was a few ticks behind.

Except for the equipment.

She pointed out the hundreds of instruments and probes that dotted the landscape; they were positioned to measure each and every twitch in the surface of the earth.

"By taking sightings between these various stations," she said, "we can accurately measure the earth's movement over a specified period of time. We constantly compare one period with another, which gives us a lot of data."

They continued to explore the town. "Most people," she said, as they walked together, looking for all the world like tourists, "assume that California and earthquakes are synonymous. They are totally unaware that one of the most devastating earthquakes this country has ever suffered occurred in a place called New Madrid, Missouri."

Only Terry had ever heard of the place.

"Yes," Dr. Wickshire continued, "there were several large quakes, back in December of 1811 and again in January of the next year. They were so strong they were felt in several states and the course of the Mississippi River was forever altered. Of course, in those days, they didn't have the equipment we have now, but most scientists put the magnitude at somewhere between 7 and 7.5 on the Richter scale.

"Then, in 1964, we had a tremendous quake in Alaska. At one time it was classified as an 8.5, but it has since been upgraded to a 9.2 making it the largest quake ever to hit North America. Even bigger than those in Mexico City."

They walked up to a green box, which looked much like an electrical transformer sitting on the ground, only this one was covered with heavy wire mesh.

"This is one of the probe sites," she said. "You'll see scores of them all over town. The information gathered by these probes is fed by underground cable to a transmission site on the other side of town, and from there it goes directly to Menlo Park, where the Geological Survey people have their monitoring equipment. The green ones are ours. Other countries have them as well, as you can see."

Across the street was a similar box, this one blue. The legend stenciled on the box identified it as belonging to some outfit from Chile.

She took a deep breath and said, "There are so many different theories. You've heard of the Palmdale bulge?"

They had.

"Well, that's an example of the dilatancy effect. A theory contending that the pressure being exerted causes the rock to actually swell, which can cause a bulge in the earth's crust. The same theory holds that rock under pressure develops tiny cracks and fissures which affect its ability to conduct electricity. It seems to have considerable merit.

"Then there's the wave theory . . ." She stopped talking and smiled at them. "Well, you've both read Thomas's report, so I'm sure you know all of this." Then she sighed. "To be able to actually predict an earthquake with that kind of accuracy . . . It still seems impossible."

234

She grimaced and added, "I sound like quite the naysayer, don't I?"

"You have good reason to feel that way, Doctor," said Ted.

The woman patted him on the shoulder and said, "I've worked up an appetite. I'm a terrific cook. Allow me to show off for you."

They made their way back to the motor home.

She was right. She was a terrific cook.

She was also a born leader. There was no discussion about sleeping arrangements. Each person was assigned a specific space and issued a blanket and a pillow.

Dr. Wickshire served coffee and then looked at her watch. "The news will be on now. I never miss the news."

With that, she flicked on the television set that was built in to a spot just aft of the driver's chair.

There were the usual commercials and then the evening news broadcast began.

The lead item concerned an upcoming hearing in Sacramento. A blonde woman who looked to be in her mid-twenties peered into the camera, a plastic smile affixed to her face, and intoned, "What started out to be an inquiry into insurance company practices has now become something much more significant with the announcement today of a full-scale investigation by the Justice Department. Lloyd Hooks has the story . . ."

The picture changed to one of a man standing in front of a darkened building. "Yes, Judy," he said, "Here in Sacramento, the word is that Monday's inquiry will be . . ."

The three of them listened as the story was told. It was a truncated version of the story that had gone over the wire service lines earlier in the day.

When it was over, Dr. Wickshire stood up and turned off the television set. She looked almost ill. "If you don't mind," she said, quietly, "I think I'll take a walk."

She hooked up the dog's chain and together, she and Pierre left the motor home. Ted and Terry just sat there, numbed by what they had heard.

It was a lie. A total lie.

All of it.

Ted knew it and so did Terry.

It only proved that Robert Graves had even more power than they had possibly imagined. The question was: What could they do about it?

Five hours later, Ted was still awake, staring at the dimness of a ceiling just inches away from his nose. His sleeping quarters consisted of a bunk that hung above the captain's chairs in the front of the vehicle. It was the only bed that could accommodate his lengthy frame. And only if he stretched from corner to corner.

He could hear the crickets as they rubbed their legs together in the darkness beyond the walls of the ancient motor home. He could also hear the sound of Terry's breathing, as she slept in the dining area cum sleeping quarters midway down the coach.

It was coming together, the plan. After hours of uninterrupted concentration, it was finally coming together.

The risks were great, the odds against him.

But it was a plan that had a chance.

Satisfied, he closed his eyes and surrendered to the weariness that cloaked him as tightly as the darkness.

Chapter Twenty-one

It was morning. A beautiful, quiet, peaceful morning in a small town in north-central California, where the air smelled sweet and the sky emerged blue instead of yellow. Once again, Dr. Wickshire was showing off and they were all eating a delicious breakfast of bacon, eggs, and freshly baked rolls. The geologist was a woman who liked to rough it first class.

And then it hit.

Precisely at 8:35 A.M. Pacific time, the ground beneath the old motor home began to shake. At first, it was a sharp rattle that lasted less than three seconds, then the ground seemed to turn into an ocean, the vehicle rocking like a ship drifting atop soft swells, gently . . . deceptively so.

The motor home creaked and groaned. The

sound of it mixed with the low rumble coming from outside, as if some unseen freight train was passing just inches from them. Outside, the trees swayed to and fro, the tops sometimes touching. And the sky was filled with birds on the wing, their roosts suddenly unfamiliar.

Another series of sharp rattles sent dishes flying and the dog to chasing his own tail.

And then . . . it stopped.

It had lasted a total of sixteen seconds.

All three of them dashed out of the vehicle and into the vacant lot they had used as a temporary camping ground, a location just on the edge of town. It was a scant few blocks from the main corner of the town where two state highways intersected. Dr. Wickshire carried the frightened dog in her arms as they walked around the town and surveyed the damage. There wasn't much. A few things had been knocked over, a window or two had shattered, and the faint smell of sulfur hung in the air. It had been just a minor earthquake, although it was much stronger than the citizens of this town were used to. From the looks on most of the faces, one could see that their fabled equanimity was being sorely tested.

They returned to the motor home and Dr. Wickshire fired up the generator located in the rear of the vehicle. Within minutes, she was using a ham radio to talk to several contacts back in Menlo Park. Then she switched to a mobile phone and talked to a few more. Through it all, she spoke a language that seemed totally foreign to Ted and Terry, but when she was finished she took pains to explain everything carefully.

Her eyes were sparkling with excitement.

"Here's what we have so far," she said. "The

239

epicenter appears to be right here in Hollister. Initial indications are that the quake registered a 4.7 on the Richter scale, but that could be modified once more data comes in.

"It was felt in San Francisco, probably even further north than that. And they have a report from San Luis Obispo, with more coming in. Not much damage at all."

She sighed deeply and sat down on the sofa, obviously awed, staring at the ceiling. "It's just as they predicted," she said. "I never would have believed it. But, there's no longer any doubt in my mind."

She brought her head down and faced them. "I have my evidence," she said. "No one could guess five in a row. Not this accurately. It's impossible . . . and yet . . . they've done it." Then, her face took on a new expression. Gone was the awe. In its place was something akin to terror. "We have to do something about this," she said, her hands cutting through the air to make the point. "There's no longer any doubt in my mind. Los Angeles is about to be destroyed. Totally! There's simply no question of it!"

She stared at Ted.

They both stared at Ted, their eyes communicating the same thought at the same time. The same question.

What was he going to do about it?

For a moment, nothing was said. Then Ted, his eyes displaying his weariness, said, "All right. I'm going out to make a phone call. I'll be back in a few minutes."

"You can use my mobile phone," Dr. Wickshire said.

"No. Those things can be monitored. I'd rather

240

not take the chance."

He left the motor home and walked the short distance to a pay phone that stood outside the drug store. He punched the "O" button and when the operator came on the line, gave her his credit card number and said, "I'd like to speak, person to person, to a Mr. Webster at the Rest Awhile Inn in Santa Barbara," he said.

"One moment, sir."

In moments, Frank Leach was on the line. He sounded very depressed. "Mornin', babe," he said, almost sadly. "You watch the news last night?"

"Yeah, I did, Frank."

"You see what those sonsabitches are doing to us?"

"It's clear as a bell, Frank. Did anyone from the association talk to you?"

There was a grunt. "Are you shittin' me? I'm sittin' here with the executive director himself. He was supposed to testify, which he had no intention of doin', at that hearing in Sacramento tomorrow, but they've changed the whole schedule. Now it looks like he won't be on 'til Thursday at the earliest. Jesus! He was refusing to testify because this whole thing is unconstitutional, but now . . . They're gonna crucify us, the bastards! How can he stay silent in the face of this?

"When the association heard what was comin' down, they were all over me! They knew, since I'd been nosing around, that I was on to something! They wanted to know what it was."

"And what did you tell them?"

"I told them I knew all about it and had a man already placed on the inside. Now don't get upset. These people can be trusted."

Ted laughed out loud. It was typical Frank

Leach. The man was a legend.

"So," Ted said, still laughing, "You told them that, did you?"

"Listen, babe, you gotta help us here. We're about to get our asses fried. What the hell *is* going on, anyway?"

Ted took a deep breath and said, "It's a really long story, Frank. How's the association figure in all of this?"

"That's a long story too, babe. Better leave that until we get together."

Ted hesitated for a moment. Then he asked, "How much money does the association have in the slush fund for special projects?"

"What've you got in mind?"

"Something that's going to take a lot of people and a lot of money."

"Listen, babe. That's what I'm tryin' to tell you. Hank and I have been talkin' this thing over and we've got the green light. We'll spend whatever it takes. And if you bust this thing open you'll have your own set of keys to the vault. I kid you not. The sky's the limit."

"Good," Ted said.

"Where are you?"

Ted ran a hand through his hair. "First things first," he said. "Are you sure you weren't followed?"

There was a snort and then, "Listen to me! You think you're talkin' to some kid? Where the hell are you?"

Ted laughed out loud again. Frank Leach was an ex-cop who prided himself on his abundant skills. "I'm in Hollister, Frank. That's a town up north. South of San Jose. Now, before we get together, I need some things."

"Lay it on me, babe."

Ted took a deep breath and said, "Jack Scott is one of our sales agents. He and I served together in Vietnam. He wrote up policies on about seventy guys we both served with in Vietnam who now live in the L.A. area. I want you to contact Jack and every one of those people he wrote up. Tell them I have a very serious problem that needs their expertise. Tell them they'll be paid well. Tell them it will be dangerous. Tell them it's local. No Central American stuff. Aside from that, tell them nothing else. And tell them to keep their mouths shut. I figure you can get about half of them."

Frank whistled, then said, "I like the sound of that! What have you got in mind?"

"Later, Frank."

"OK. I can do that. Where do I tell them to go?"

"In a minute," Ted said. "I also want you to get your hands on every insurance investigator you think will come in on some real action. That should net you about another hundred or so guys."

There was silence at the other end for a moment, and then Frank asked, "What else?"

"Tell all of these people to meet in Vegas. Book a block of rooms at one of the hotels so all of them can stay in the same place. Tell them to make it look like they're on a toot. Book a meeting room for tomorrow night at the same hotel. Figure on 150 or so. Say eight o'clock. I'll meet you there to make the pitch."

"OK, I guess. What pitch?"

"Later."

"OK. Anything else?"

Ted said. "We'll need some weapons. Real ones and fake ones. Talk to Gerry Givens at National Studios in L.A. I handled a claim for him about four weeks ago. They have enough stuff to outfit a

243

small army. Tell him you're filming a documentary for the industry and you want to rent or buy what you need, but it has to be a secret. He may balk. If he does, throw money at him. That'll take care of any problems.

"We need fatigues, weapons, and a lot of fake bombs. You know, pyrotechnic stuff that makes a lot of noise but doesn't do a lot of damage. Lots of fake mortars. We want it to look like a full-scale terrorist attack. We'll also need stun guns, about a dozen jeeps, a bunch of trucks, communications . . . the works. You're an Army vet, just like me, so you know what we need. Think of this as a real exercise, Frank. Except we don't want anybody to get hurt unless it's absolutely necessary. You can figure out the rest of the things we'll have to have."

"Yes . . . I can do that. But . . . ?"

"It's an assault on a fixed position with two diversionary actions. One military and one civilian."

"Civilian?"

"Yes. We'll need about two thousand college kids to make a protest at the Nevada Nuclear Test Site. You know, flag burning, chanting . . . all the usual stuff. Have someone go to one of the campuses and organize a protest against nuclear testing. Keep it a separate operation. Don't tell anyone the real reason. Hell, there are several groups that do this on a regular basis anyway. If we give each kid a couple of hundred bucks, it should be a cinch.

"Arrange buses to take them out to the desert. Figure on both operations taking place at 0200 on the thirteenth. That should give us time enough. Have the kids gather in the desert about thirty miles west of Vegas for a briefing at say 2300 on the twelfth. Got that?"

"I got it."

"OK . . . Now, the most important thing."

"Yes?"

"You have to find someone, possibly retired . . . someone you can trust . . . maybe through some of your political contacts . . . who can give us an accurate map of the inside layout at the Nevada Nuclear Test Site."

He could hear the sharp intake of breath. Then, in a voice that seemed choked, Frank asked, "You're going to attack the site?"

"You got it, Frank."

"Jesus Christ! What in God's name for? What's it got to do with anything?"

"Never mind. Just get the stuff. I'll call you in about six hours and see how you've done. Maybe you can get some of those investigators to help you. Now that the Justice Department is coming out of the closet, I don't think they'll be that concerned with your activities, but just to safe, be very careful."

"I will, babe. You won't tell me why this war is being declared?"

"I'll be happy to, Frank. Tommy Wilson, the man the Justice Department is accusing the association of having killed, is alive and well. He's stashed at the site. If I can get him out, I can save the association's ass, for one thing. But that's really the least of our problems at this point. If we screw this up, we may be responsible for the lives of a few million other people."

There was a pause and then, "Ted . . . for God's sake. What are you talking about?"

Ted grunted and said, "I don't have time to tell you everything, but I will tell you this: The biggest snow job in the country's history is taking place right now. I'm not sure how deep it goes, but it

245

involves one hell of a lot of people.

"You were right about the earthquake, Frank. It's a monster. And it's going to hit L.A. in a little less than three weeks. We just had one here in Hollister this morning. It was a quake that we knew was coming. And so did NADAT. So, for that matter, did AAIS. It's a real quagmire, Frank."

Frank was starting to get the full picture. "Jesus, babe. Are you saying . . . the big one is coming . . . and you know when and where? Is that what this is all about?"

"You've got it, Frank. It's the big one. The monster. And it's coming sure as hell. Don't ask me how I know. I just do. Take my word for it. We've got exactly eighteen days to get everybody out of Los Angeles."

"Sweet Jesus! Are you sure?"

"Positive!"

He heard a string of curses. Then, he heard Frank speaking to the man sharing his room. In a few moments, Frank was back on the line asking a series of questions without waiting for the answers.

"Frank!"

It took a few moments before the man quieted down.

"OK," Ted said. "That's better. Now . . . there's a chance we can stop this quake from happening and before you start asking a lot of questions about *that*, take my word for it again. I know it sounds crazy, but there *is* a chance. We have to do this just right. Who've you got who can get next to one of those guys on the inquiry committee?"

"Well . . . there's me, for one. And Hank too," Frank said. "Senator Ballard is on the committee. He's an old friend with an open mind. Not like the rest of those creeps. He'd listen to either one of us.

He's the one who told us the schedule had been changed. He's as confused as we are about this whole thing."

"Great! Don't contact him yet. Just make sure you know where you can reach him at any given moment. OK?"

"OK."

"Is he state or federal?"

"State."

"Who do you know who has access to the president?"

"Of the United States?"

"Yes."

Again, Ted could hear Frank talking to the other man in the room. When he returned to the phone, he said, "Hank has a friend who can make the connection. But . . ."

"Not now," Ted said. "Just make sure we have access when the time comes. Timing is the key, Frank."

There was a pause. Then, "Listen, babe . . . If Wilson is alive, we should let Ballard know. It would really make a difference."

"No!" Ted shouted. "You tip anyone off and Wilson could end up dead! You've got to keep quiet until we have him in our hands. If we fail, we'll go to plan B, whatever that is."

"OK, babe. Anything else?"

"Not at the moment."

"When are we going to get together?"

"We may not until we all gather in Vegas. As I said before, I'll call you in about six hours and you can let me know where this meeting is going to be."

"OK, babe. I'll get to work. You take care, hear?"

"I will, Frank. I will."

They said their goodbyes and then Ted headed back to the motor home. When he entered and took his seat, both women looked at him with questions in their eyes. Dr. Wickshire spoke first. "Whatever it is that you're planning, young man, I want you to know that I intend to be a part of it."

Terry said, "Me too."

He smiled at them both and said, "Before you make the final decision, you better hear what I have in mind."

Then he told them.

When he was finished, they still wanted in.

They were as crazy as he was.

Chapter Twenty-two

Robert Graves looked at the computer printout and grimaced. The results of this, the final test, were still inconclusive. There had been significant liquefaction of the rockbed, but the explosion had been so small that the affected area was smaller than anticipated. To increase the size of the explosion in order to increase the heat would entail the risk of precipitating the very earthquake they were so desperately trying to prevent. They had hoped that this would be the right combination. Now, it seemed inadequate. And there was no time to prepare another test. If they were to proceed, they would have to use a device that had not had the opportunity to be fully tested.

He let the printout slip from his fingers onto the desk and leaned back in the tall, leather-covered chair. He removed his glasses and rubbed his nose, his eyes closed, the beginnings of a serious headache tingling his skull just behind the eyes.

He squeezed his eyes still tighter. Failure was staring him in the face and he didn't want to see it. Failure due to incompetence on the part of those around him. Men and women who simply didn't take their work seriously enough.

The engineers, the scientists . . . the men they had brought to the desert against their wills, Gifford and Wilson. All of them had been given the chance to effectuate a successful mission and they had failed.

The FBI had failed as well. With Belcher in the hospital, still not talking, another man had been hastily pressed into service. A man named Merkle. Merkle had been ordered to find Kowalczyk and the woman.

He hadn't.

Merkle had reluctantly reported that he'd lost Kowalczyk and the woman completely. The best efforts of the FBI had turned up nothing. Where Kowalczyk would eventually turn up was anyone's guess.

No matter.

Fortunately, Graves had had the foresight to prepare for such occurrences, but the evidence of such incompetence was most frustrating.

The earthquake in Hollister had only served to further exemplify and exacerbate the immediate concern. There could no longer be any question that Gifford and Wilson had been correct in predicting the terrible earthquake that would soon hit Los Angeles. "Operation Move," while progressing on schedule, had triggered some curiosity in the press, but it was doubtful that they would be able to penetrate the walls of disinformation in time to make any difference.

The real problem was the decision that had to be made within the next hour. Whether or not to pronounce the test a limited success and produce the bombs.

To declare the test a failure would mean that Los Angeles would be left to suffer the full effects of the quake. Certainly, he would be criticized for being unable to develop the device that might have prevented the quake. But that could be fended off to those who were in charge of actually designing the device. Graves was no nuclear scientist and therefore could not be held responsible for the failures of those who were.

He could not be criticized for the failure to evacuate the city for the simple reason that the decision to refrain from doing so had been made by others. Granted, they had done so on his recommendation, but his recommendation could be well supported by existing evidence. Totally justified. No . . . that would not be a problem.

If, on the other hand, he recommended that the experiment be carried out and it failed, as now seemed more than likely, *he* would be the one most severely criticized. It would have been *his* decision. Therefore, despite the fact that the engineers had failed, their failure would be his.

It was an intolerable situation.

It was unacceptable.

He rubbed his temples. It was a decision he was not going to make. He wasn't going to be the scapegoat for anyone, especially those who occupied temporary positions in government. A new election brought new people, while he, Robert Graves, remained. It had always been that way and would continue to be so. It would be foolhardy for him to make a decision that could cost him dearly when the decision was better entrusted to one who could be expected to move on to other things should the circumstances dictate. For Graves to suffer undue condemnation would mean the country would then be denied the benefits of his experience and talent. A waste. For no good reason.

No . . . someone else would have to make the decision.

He opened his eyes and placed the glasses back on his nose. Just having made the decision seemed to help his mood. He'd done his best. He'd taken it as far as he could. The rest would be up to someone else. He'd give them the unvarnished truth. Complete details unfettered by bias. They would have to decide.

He picked up the phone and punched some buttons.

Chapter Twenty-three

At exactly 9:34 on an unusually warm Sacramento Monday morning, State Senator Jake Simpson banged his gavel and brought the special inquiry to order. An inquiry originally convened to look into the earthquake insurance business in California, but now much wider in scope, thanks to the pending U.S. Justice Department's announced investigation of far more serious matters.

The inquiry was being held in one of the infrequently used chambers designed for just such things. A chamber with high ceilings, walnut-paneled walls and limited seating for spectators.

"This inquiry is now in session," the senator boomed, his voice reverberating through the chamber, helped by a newly adjusted sound system.

Few of these inquiries were held "in camera" and this one was no exception. A trio of pool television cameras had been installed, their electronic images available to a variety of networks and local stations. Permission had been given to allow for the seating of thirty reporters from both the print and electronic media. Aside from the press, the rest of the seats were taken up by interested spectators, some of whom had waited all night to gain entry. It was, as they say, the hottest ticket in town.

Senator Simpson was fully cognizant of the fact that his chairmanship of this committee could give him national exposure, something he'd craved since his entry into political life some thirty years ago. Now almost sixty-five, he was an impressive figure, with pure white hair topping a ruddy, handsome face. A thespian's voice gave him an aura of statesmanship. If there was a stumbling block to the fulfillment of his wish to move to Washington, aside from his age, it was the view held by his contemporaries that he was, to put it kindly, a political lightweight. He was not unaware of the tag and hoped that the inquiry would change that perception.

When he'd originally convened this inquiry, he'd done so reluctantly. He knew full well that any inquiry having a direct effect on the pocketbooks of Californians was a political plus. The only problem was that less than 5 percent of the population of the state carried earthquake insurance. Since the inquiry, when conceived, was intended to address itself to that single issue, it seemed to the senator that less than 5 percent of the people would be interested. Hardly enough.

Now, however, the thrust of the inquiry was taking a decidedly different turn. There was to be talk of earthquakes, skulduggery, possibly murder. Much meatier stuff. The stuff that made the front pages of newspapers and the lead items in television news broadcasts. His visage would be seen by millions, not only in California, but throughout the country.

Much better. Much better, indeed.

"Originally," the senator intoned, his voice modulating in the lower octaves, "I had intended to begin this session with an opening statement. However, in view of recent developments that have already been widely reported in the media, I will dispense with my statement and instead have it entered into the record as having been read, if there is no objection."

There was none.

"Very well. As you know, we had planned to present witnesses in the order they appeared on the original agenda; however, some late changes have been made and a new agenda has now been prepared. As these are being distributed, I will call the first witness. Will Mr. Peterson come forward and be sworn."

As two men moved from the rear of the chamber and took positions at the table facing a semicircular dais behind which sat nine other representatives and senators, Simpson leaned back and practically licked his lips in anticipation.

The witness had been sworn. The room almost crackled with electricity.

"Mr. Peterson," Simpson began, "I note that you are represented here by counsel and that, sir, is perfectly all right. Do you have an opening statement?"

"Yes, Senator, I do."

"Before you begin, would you be kind enough to introduce yourself, giving us your position, and explain your interest in this inquiry and how it relates to everything we're about to discuss. If you would, sir."

"I'll be happy to, sir."

"Please proceed."

Senator Simpson leaned back and fought back a grin. The man at the witness's table, Felix Peterson,

255

was a thin, wiry man in his thirties. His flat, black hair was combed straight back, emphasizing a bony face that seemed oddly out of kilter. The eyes were very close to each other and the lips thin and tight. He wore a blue suit that seemed two sizes too large for him.

"My name," he said, in a frail voice that matched the body, "is Felix Peterson. At the present time, I am unemployed. Previously, I was executive director of Dalton Research, Incorporated, of Menlo Park, California. I was employed there for ten years."

He stopped speaking, took a drink of water, then continued. Clearly, he was nervous.

"During my tenure, I had the opportunity to work on a project that was one of the most important ever undertaken by any research-oriented facility. A project that researched the practicability of successfully predicting earthquakes, using some newly discovered techniques that had shown promise elsewhere in the world, particularly in the Soviet Union.

"I should note that Dalton Research is a company that is . . . was . . . funded by the American Association of Insurance Specialties, which is based in Hartford, Connecticut. Dalton Research was formed purely for the purpose of exploring all aspects of earthquake research, especially the field of earthquake prediction.

"The insurance industry was financing the company because they were concerned that a very large earthquake would strike somewhere in California within the next twenty or thirty years, and they wanted to know if it was possible to more accurately predict its magnitude, epicenter, and general time frame.

"In any case, we were given almost a blank check to pursue our research and initially, there were indications that the research might prove fruitful, if enough

256

effort—by that I mean money—was expended. The numbers were truly impressive."

He stopped and took another drink, then continued.

"In fact, we spent some sixty million dollars over the ten-year period."

He waited to allow that figure to sink in.

"The end result of all of this research was . . . total failure. While it is true that we were able to successfully predict one small quake in the Hollister region, we were unsuccessful in predicting others, despite our best efforts.

"Two years ago, just after the announcement of our first and only success in predicting an earthquake, our president, Mr. Daniel Dalton, was approached by an agency of the federal government and told that the work we were doing would have to be classified. It was the position of the government that if we were able to successfully predict earthquakes, they should be the first to know, in the interest of national security. They wanted to set up contingency procedures.

"Naturally, Mr. Dalton was outraged. The company was using private funds for research and was being told that the people paying for the research couldn't have access to the results. After some discussion, an agreement was made whereby the company *would* have access to the material, but would be required to keep it private until such time as its release was deemed appropriate by the federal government. That meant that the information would remain classified and no members of AAIS would have access to the information until such time as the government had blocked out the procedures to be taken. It wasn't the best of arrangements, as far as the company was concerned, but the only alternative was to close up shop, so we carried on. Later, it became apparent to

257

me why we did so.

"Three months ago, Mr. Vance Gifford, with whom I worked closely, was preparing a final report that disclosed our failure in the area of earthquake prediction. He was approached by the president of the company, Daniel Dalton, and told that the company wanted to produce a report that would indicate success in the area of predicting earthquakes. In other words, a complete fabrication. He was told that such a report was considered necessary for several reasons. One, if the report he intended to produce was allowed to stand, the one suggesting that earthquake prediction was impossible, Dalton Research would cease to exist due to lack of funding.

"Two, the client, AAIS, wanted a report that would eventually allow them to justify both present and anticipated increases in earthquake insurance premium costs. And three, I was given to understand that pressures were being exerted on the federal government with a view to getting them to cover a percentage of loss in the event of a major earthquake. I was given to understand that another report was to be issued later that would state, most emphatically, that a major earthquake was imminent. It was felt that these reports would force the government to capitulate.

"Mr. Gifford discussed the matter with me and I recommended that he refuse to produce a false report. Not only was it dishonest, but it was also illegal. For reasons of his own, he rejected my recommendation and decided to go along with the request. He changed much of the data to make it appear that we were well on the road to making the prediction of earthquakes a reality.

"At that time, I found myself in complete disagreement with what was going on. I reported these activities to the Federal Bureau of Investigation. They requested that I remain in my position and gather evidence for a possible legal action. They said they needed an insider, since what was being done was completely illegal, and charges would be forthcoming at some time in the future. They said I had a duty to stay on and I took it as such. So I did.

"Two months ago, Mr. Gifford appeared to have second thoughts about what he was doing. He went to Mr. Dalton and threatened to expose this travesty. That very day, he suffered an apparent heart attack and died. Another colleague, Mr. Thomas Wilson, was then asked to complete the report, unaware of the fact that it was a fabrication. After examining the data, he realized the true nature of the report. Without discussing his discovery with anyone, he produced a report of his own, which stated that it was impossible to predict earthquakes. On the day that he presented his report to Mr. Dalton, he too threatened to go to the authorities if his report was not accepted as the official document. That very evening, he was involved in a one-car automobile accident and died."

He cleared his throat and took another drink of water.

"I think both Mr. Gifford and Mr. Wilson were murdered."

The room erupted.

Senator Simpson banged his gavel repeatedly until order was restored. Then he asked, "So, if I understand you correctly, Mr. Peterson, you are saying that ten years of research proved that earthquakes cannot be predicted, is that not so?"

"Essentially, that's correct, sir."

"And there was pressure on Mr. Gifford and Mr. Wilson, in fact . . . everyone at the company, to produce a report that indicated otherwise?"

"That's true, sir."

"And that when they did not do so, Mr. Gifford suffered a heart attack and Mr. Wilson died in an accident?"

"Yes, sir."

"And the reports they were working on are classified?"

"Not any more, sir. They have been declassified by the government. In fact, I have brought copies with me for your perusal. The rest of the members as well." As he said it, a man rose from his seat in the back of the room, came forward and started handing out copies of the report to the members of the committee.

"As you can see," Peterson droned on, "the report bears the signature of Thomas Wilson and is dated the day of his death. The report clearly states that there is no way to predict earthquakes."

Again, there was pandemonium. Simpson banged his gavel some more. Then, for a few moments, all of the men on the committee leafed through the thick report. Finally, Simpson looked up and asked, "Now, Mr. Peterson, aside from your suspicions, do you have any direct evidence that Mr. Wilson was murdered?"

"No, sir. But I know that the FBI is conducting a full investigation. I have given them the same statement I've given you today."

Again, the place was in an uproar.

After a few more minutes of gavel-banging, Simpson said, "Very well, sir. We'll get to that in a moment or so. Now . . . just so I have this right, your testimony is that this association . . . this AAIS, was funding this project. They wanted a report produced that would initially suggest that earthquake prediction was a viable scientific enterprise and then later, they intended to make some sort of prediction concerning a major earthquake. At the same time, they were

260

raising their rates on earthquake insurance and refusing to write new policies. In other words, they were trying very hard to make it look like they were getting out of the earthquake insurance business altogether, is that right?"

"Yes, sir."

"And if this report had said that a big quake was coming, they would appear somewhat justified, since the earthquake insurance policies are a year-to-year thing. They never actually cancelled a policy that was in force, as far as we can determine, but we'll hear more about that later. In any case, if the fake report was allowed to stand, they wouldn't have appeared to have done anything illegal. That's what I'm getting at. Is that not the case? After all, this is America. Nobody expects a big company to lose its shirt if it can possibly be avoided."

"True."

"But the report said otherwise, which would make them look a little stupid, wouldn't it?"

"Yes, sir."

"How is it, sir, that you weren't subject to the same problems that Mr. Gifford and Mr. Wilson were?"

"As I said, Senator, I appeared to be working with them. In actual fact, after the death of Mr. Wilson, I was given a copy of the report and asked to change the data myself. That's how I got my hands on it. I contacted the FBI as soon as the report was given to me and turned the report over to them. Then, thank God, I was allowed to leave."

"And what have you been doing since that time?"

"I've been hiding, sir. In fear of my life. I've been protected by the FBI, thank God, but I must tell you, I have been very concerned."

"And this copy of the report that you are submitting . . . this is a true copy of the actual research done over that ten-year period?"

"Yes, it is."

"Thank you very much, Mr. Peterson. I'm sure some other members of the committee will want to ask you some questions. We'll try to do it as quickly as possible. I think Senator Ballard is first. Senator?"

Senator Harold Ballard switched on his microphone and leaned forward. He was twenty years younger than Simpson and not nearly as good-looking. He had just a hint of hair left on his skull, and a narrow face, the features of which were less than outstanding. He seemed a plain man and, in fact, he was. But he was respected for his mind, which was sharp, and his attitude, which was of the no-nonsense type.

At the moment, his face was red with anger which he seemed to be struggling to contain.

"Mr. Peterson," he began. "You have testified that you were the executive director of Dalton Research."

"Yes, sir."

"And you have stated that Daniel Dalton was the president."

"Yes, he was."

"Are both of you scientists?"

"Yes. I am a geophysicist and Mr. Dalton is a geologist."

"I see. And besides the people you've mentioned, who else worked at Dalton Research?"

Peterson looked up at the ceiling for a moment and then said, "There were two secretaries, three technicians and . . . I guess that's all."

"So there was Mr. Dalton, yourself, Mr. Gifford, Mr. Wilson, two secretaries, and three technicians, is that right?"

"Yes."

Ballard scratched his forehead for a moment and then asked, "Where are they?"

Peterson tugged at his already loose shirt collar and said, "I don't know, sir."

Ballard looked at his notes and said, "Well, I see here that the company was placed in Chapter 7 bankruptcy last week. This committee issued subpoenas to every person that worked there and you, sir, are the only one we can find. Doesn't that seem rather odd to you, Mr. Peterson?"

"Not really, sir. I imagine they are all aware they are in some sort of trouble."

"They all knew of this sham and went along with it?"

"Yes, sir."

"And of the entire group, you were the only one who saw fit to bring this matter to the attention of the authorities? That's quite commendable, Mr. Peterson, but I find it a little difficult to believe."

"I can't speak for the others, Senator."

"Of course. But you did say that you suspect everyone who was in disagreement with the idea of producing a false report was murdered. Is it possible that the others were also murdered?"

"I can't say."

Again, the room echoed with the buzz of conversation as those in the audience expressed their shock.

"But you are convinced that Mr. Gifford and Mr. Wilson were murdered."

"Yes, I am."

"And you seem to be suggesting that the AAIS is somehow responsible for the murders. Is that right?"

Peterson took another drink of water and wiped his lips with the back of his hand. "I don't know that to be a fact. All I know is that they were the ones with the motive."

"I see. You said you went to the FBI. Who did you talk to there?"

"Resident Agent in Charge George Belcher."

"I see." Ballard turned to Senator Simpson and asked, "Has the committee issued a subpoena for Mr. Belcher?"

Simpson made a note and said, "It will be looked after, Senator."

"Thank you." Then, turning back to the witness, Ballard said, "You have testified that the report we now have in our hands represents ten years of research. Is that right?"

"Yes, sir."

"And up until now, the report was classified. By whom?"

"The government, sir."

Ballard smiled. "I am the government, sir. As are the other members of this committee. You testified that Dalton Research was approached by an agency of the federal government and told that the work was classified. I am asking you what specific agency."

"That part is still classified, Senator."

"I see. And this report, according to your testimony, indicates that there is no possible way to predict earthquakes. Is that right?"

"Yes, sir."

"And it is your testimony that the AAIS was aware of this report."

"Yes, sir."

"Well then, if the member companies, which is to say the insurance companies . . . were aware that there was no way to predict earthquakes, and were in fact unaware of any impending disaster, why were they so anxious to get out of the business?"

"They weren't," Peterson said. "At least, not long-term. They were interested in making it appear as though they were getting out, which would bring pressure from various government officials. Then they planned to reenter the business, but with much higher rates. That would allow them to build up reserves for damages they felt would be incurred at some time in the future. At the same time, they felt that their actions would serve to exert more pressure on the federal government to accept at least some of the risk for earthquake damage. Right now, the government refuses to accept any of it."

"I see," Ballard said. "Your testimony is based on your own personal knowledge?"

"Well . . . yes. I was told these things by various people."

"Mr. Dalton, Mr. Gifford, Mr. Wilson, a secret government agency, and assorted others who are unable, for a variety of reasons, to appear before this committee. In other words, Mr. Peterson, what you are testifying to is actually hearsay evidence. Every word of it."

"No!"

Jake Simpson banged his gavel. "You're out of order, Senator Ballard. You're well aware that this is not a court of law. The rules are quite different here."

Ballard glared at his colleague and continued.

"Mr. Peterson, you testified that Dalton Research spent some sixty million dollars over a ten-year period. How was that money spent?"

"It was spent on research."

"I understand that. I mean specifically, aside from salaries, of course."

"Well, the research was centered on the town of Hollister, California. Hollister is very active in terms of seismic activity. It sits right on the San Andreas fault line. Various pieces of equipment were installed, including a number of probes that were installed in holes drilled into the ground."

"How many holes were drilled?"

"About a hundred."

"The San Andreas fault lies close to the surface of the earth, does it not?"

"In a way, but it's not quite that simple. The effect of the plate movement can be seen from the surface, but the actual plate movement takes place beneath the surface. Quite far down, in fact. In order to take proper measurements, you need to explore the substructure with probes. Some of them go as deep as three miles. It's very expensive."

"So . . . a hundred holes were drilled and equipment installed. That works out to about six hundred thousand dollars a hole. Less administrative expenses, of course. That is very expensive, just as you said."

"Yes, it is."

"Now . . . this measuring system . . . is this the normal way things are done?"

"Sir?"

"Well . . . by that I mean, all of these holes were drilled in Hollister, a rather small town. And sixty million dollars was spent on one small section of the San Andreas fault. Wouldn't it be prohibitively expensive to examine the entire length of the fault?"

"Yes, it would."

"Well . . . if that's the case, what was the point? Isn't it true that earthquakes occur all along the fault line?"

"Yes, they do, sir. But the purpose of research is to study various techniques. Hollister was picked because of its seismic activity, which is more prevalent than on other sections of the fault."

"I understand that, Mr. Peterson. I'm still trying to get a handle on this. Please bear with me. My point is that sixty million dollars is a lot of money. Even if you were incredibly successful in Hollister, the cost of carrying on the research would preclude taking the research elsewhere. Isn't it a fact that even if earthquake prediction was precise and proven science, the cost of implementation is so high as to make it totally impractical? Isn't that a fact?"

Peterson gulped and said, "I'm not an accountant, Senator, I'm a scientist. All I know is that sixty million dollars was spent in Hollister. I can't speak to anything else."

"I understand. But, aside from that, just as an ordinary person, wouldn't it appear to you that this research was heading for a dead-end? That the cost of employing the knowledge acquired in Hollister would be so prohibitive as to make the entire research effort redundant?"

"No research is ever redundant, Senator."

Ballard leaned back in his chair and smiled. "Of course you're right, Mr. Peterson. Knowledge is a wonderful thing." He stroked his chin and asked, "Was all of the money spent in Hollister?"

"Well . . . not exactly. There were facilities in Menlo Park and others in Los Angeles."

"Field work was done there?"

"No. The field work was confined to Hollister and Palmdale."

"There was no field work done in Los Angeles?"

"Not to my knowledge."

"You should know, shouldn't you?"

Peterson hesitated for a moment and then answered, "Yes."

"So, if you didn't know of any field work being done in Los Angeles, we can assume there was none. Would that be an accurate statement?"

"I guess so."

"I see. Now . . . you've testified that it was the insurance industry's desire to get out of the earthquake insurance business altogether, for a while, at least. Is that not so?"

"That's right."

"How do you know that to be a fact?"

"I was told that by my boss."

"Your boss? That was Daniel Dalton?"

"Yes. Daniel Dalton. He was the president of Dalton Research."

"I see. And Mr. Dalton told you directly that the intention of the industry, insofar as the members of AAIS were concerned, was to get out of the business of protecting individuals and corporations against earthquake damage, is that your testimony?"

"Yes, sir."

"And since Mr. Dalton was being funded by AAIS, you took it for granted that he spoke for them, is that right?"

"Yes."

"And . . . to the best of your knowledge, Mr. Dalton has flown the coop. Is that right?"

"Yes."

"And you have testified that the insurance companies were aware of the fact that it was impossible to accurately predict earthquakes."

"Yes."

"And you have testified that while the insurance companies are making it appear as though they want out of the earthquake insurance business, the opposite is true. Is that not so?"

"Yes"

"You've testified that they are setting the stage, so to speak, for higher premium costs, at the same time as they are trying to pressure the federal government into sharing some of the risk."

"That's right."

"But isn't it also true that the actions of the insurance companies would make a lot more sense if they actually knew that a big earthquake *was* coming?"

268

"I told you," Peterson replied, "that they wanted to give that impression."

"Yes . . . but impressions aside, their actions would make more sense if they were acting on some information not available to us at this time. Information that appeared to indicate they would suffer an inordinate number of claims in the very near future. Isn't that right?"

"I can't answer that."

"You are a geophysicist, are you not?"

"Yes, I am."

"Is it not true that most people in your profession are convinced that a major earthquake is expected to strike either San Francisco or Los Angeles within the next twenty years?"

"Yes, that's true."

"And what is that assumption based on?"

Peterson took another drink of water. "The assumption is based on the fact that a major earthquake takes place along the San Andreas fault every 100 years or so. That's not an exact figure, but more of an approximation. The last major quake occurred in San Francisco in 1906, which would indicate that any time in the next twenty or so years we can expect another. It takes a number of years for the pressures to build up along the fault line and then it snaps, causing an earthquake."

"Do you believe that such will be the case?"

Peterson hesitated for a moment and then said, "Yes, I do."

"Although most experts say it could happen within the next twenty or so years, it could actually happen tomorrow, couldn't it?"

"It's possible . . . yes."

"And that belief is based on sound scientific data? No horoscopes, no soothsayers, but solid, reasoned analysis, is that not so?"

"Yes."

"All right, then. If you were running your own insurance business, where you were insuring individuals and corporations against possible damage from an earthquake, you would want to ensure that you were taking every possible step to protect yourself, wouldn't you?"

"I'm not sure I understand what you mean."

"Oh . . . I think you do, Mr. Peterson. The fact is that we have thousands of buildings in California that are not constructed in a way that protects them from possible earthquake damage. Isn't that so?"

"I don't know. I'm a geophysicist, not an architect."

"Of course. Let me put it another way. If you were selling life insurance, would you sell a policy to a man diagnosed as having cancer . . . cancer that would kill him within six months?"

"I'm not a doctor either, Senator."

"Of course not. You don't need to be a doctor in order to answer the question. It's simply a matter of common sense."

"Out of order!"

It was Simpson, banging his gavel again.

"Senator," the chairman intoned, "it would be helpful if you would confine your questions to the matter at hand. There are a number of others who wish to ask questions."

Senator Ballard turned to face the chairman and said, "I don't see the need for haste here, Senator. The man said he was unemployed. Just where is it he needs to be?"

Senator Simpson shot him a hard look and said, "Senator, we are dealing with very weighty matters here. I think your levity is inappropriate at this time. If you have no further questions of this witness, I suggest we move on."

"I have only one or two more questions, Senator."

"Please proceed."

"Mr. Peterson, is it your contention that someone connected with AAIS was responsible for murdering Thomas Wilson?"

Without hesitation, Peterson replied, "I've already answered that, sir. They were the only ones with a motive, as far as I can see."

"But the FBI is investigating, you said."

"Yes. And so is the Menlo Park Police Department. I understand that they wish to testify at this hearing."

Ballard jerked back in surprise. "Really? They consult with you on these matters?"

Peterson shook his head. "Not at all. I gave them a deposition at the same time as I gave one to the FBI. They told me that they wanted to appear in passing. My understanding is that testimony is being presented at this very moment to the Grand Jury."

The redness had left the face of Senator Ballard. The anger had been replaced with something closer to disbelief.

"I see. We'll look forward to hearing that testimony. One final question, Mr. Peterson."

The man waited impatiently.

"You have testified that the report being circulated here today is a true copy of a report originally prepared by one Thomas Wilson, is that right?"

"Yes."

"And the report being submitted has not been altered in any way, shape, or form?"

"No. It is exactly as he wrote it."

Senator Ballard smiled, nodded, and said, "Thank you, Mr. Peterson."

Chapter Twenty-four

It was a small bar in downtown Albuquerque, New Mexico. The two men sitting at the bar seemed oddly out of place, their expensive suits standing out in a room that was filled with people in blue jeans, plaid shirts, and boots.

The two strangers were engaged in a heated conversation. It wasn't an argument. It was simply a situation where two very agitated men were agreeing with each other, both nodding their heads as each man made his point.

Beside them, another man dressed in western attire leaned over, extended his hand and introduced himself. He offered to buy them a drink and they accepted. Within minutes, he was nodding his head along with the men in the suits, as he commiserated with their problem.

* * *

Rusty Coleman had been at it for almost five hours, working with the "morgue" computer, sifting through the list of articles and features on earthquakes that had previously appeared in the *Globe*, some of them going back as far as fifteen years.

Before "earthquakes," he'd looked under "drilling," hoping there'd be some item relative to strange people drilling deep holes in the ground in the middle of the night. No such luck. He'd then turned his attention to earthquakes.

The articles were all stored in the morgue computer, where everything ever written in the paper was retained on hard discs, all cross-referenced and indexed according to the subject matter. That made it somewhat easier than in the old days, when thousands of index cards had to be sorted through by hand. But because earthquakes were a topic often in the minds of Californians, the *Globe* had run literally thousands of articles related to their happenings.

Rusty was looking for something special. Something other than just a report of another earthquake. It was one of those times when he didn't really know what he was looking for, but knew that when he saw it, he'd recognize it.

He read most of the items' headlines and then moved on to the next one. It was tedious work, like most real reporting, or any other investigative work, for that matter.

Already his eyes were becoming sore and itchy. Item after item flashed by as he scanned the headlines, looking for . . . . what?

And then . . . he saw a headline that seemed to be exactly what he was looking for. He felt his heart skip a beat as he read the entire piece. It was a short article, less than eight hundred words, concerning two very small earthquakes that had occurred just days apart from each other, in the same section of the city. A section of the city that contained the Whittier Narrows fault line.

A fault line that was unknown at the time the article was written.

According to the piece, written ten years earlier by a reporter long since dead, a scientist named Walter Scollard had claimed that the two quakes had been caused by the activities of an oil company. The oil company engineers had been pumping water, under extreme pressure, into two small oil wells that had been yielding less than five barrels of oil a day.

At a time when the price of oil was at an all-time high, the oil companies had taken to trying to reactivate some of the thousands of small wells dotting the Los Angeles landscape; wells that had ceased to be profitable when oil was selling at five dollars a barrel. But at the time the article was written, oil was bringing thirty-five dollars a barrel.

The oil company had determined that, at that price, even five barrels of oil a day was worthwhile, when the well had already been drilled and the oil could be brought up by using a technique that had proved effective in improving the yield of other almost-forgotten wells. By pumping water into the wells under pressure, they had forced the oil to rise to the surface of the cavity where it could be brought up without additional costly drilling. It was cost-effective and quick.

But the scientist, Scollard, had claimed that the pressure was forcing water into small cracks in the rock surrounding the cavity, causing the rock itself to swell. He further claimed that the rock had exhibited evidence that it was actually a fault line. The swelling, in his opinion, had caused a temporary stoppage in the normal movement of the plates.

The plates were alternately locking and releasing, creating small earthquakes. Because the location of the wells was miles away from the San Andreas fault, the scientist claimed that the small earthquakes were proof that there were scores of other, yet-to-be discovered fault lines all over the Los Angeles basin, and that the activity around the well sites was the key to finding them.

According to him, the earthquakes were a direct result of the new techniques being employed by the oil companies, techniques that could be used by geophysicists to seek and find other potential fault lines. On that issue, he stood almost entirely alone.

But it was an idea that struck Rusty like a hammerblow.

He searched through the files for follow-ups to the story. There were several.

In one, the scientist had been roundly criticized, his theories disclaimed by other scientists. In another, the oil companies had recapped several of the wells as being nonproductive, even with the new system.

And a third article had mentioned that the leases on some of the wells had been returned to the federal government; the leases surrendered in exchange for options on other, more potentially profitable leases that might or might not be granted at some future date. Rusty made notes furiously and then headed for the district courthouse to take a look at some old records.

As he headed out the door of the building, he saw Darlene Yu coming in.

"Well," he said, brightening, "How's it feel to be back in L.A.?"

She threw him a big smile and said, "Wonderful!

It's great to be able to taste the air again. That metallic flavor is something my taste buds have craved for years! Bill in?"

Rusty jerked a thumb over his shoulder. "Yeah, he's in. I'd watch my step, though. He's been a grizzly bear for the last three days."

She grinned and said, "Don't I know it. Does he still think there's going to be a big earthquake?"

"More than ever. Especially after that one yesterday in Hollister. He's convinced the feds are trying to cover something up."

She shook her head. "Where does he get these crazy ideas?"

"May not be so crazy."

She looked stunned. "You found something?"

Rusty quickly bit his tongue. "Naw," he said. "This is a wild goose chase if there ever was one. All I meant was . . . well, you know Bill. He's done this before. He gets us going on something we all think is impossible and then . . . well, you know."

"Yes, I do," she said, her eyes sparkling. "Where are you off to?"

"Oh, I'm just doing some follow-up on yesterday's quake in Hollister. See ya later. Welcome back!"

"Thanks," she said.

The courthouse search proved fruitful. A careful search of the records showed that more than a few wells in the same area had been surrendered to the government over a period of six months. In all, over three thousand dormant and semidormant wells had suffered the same fate. All of them within the same ten-square-mile area.

Rusty went to the custodian and asked for surveyors' maps of the area. Then he took some blank paper and drew a rough sketch of the location of many of the wells. Finally, he drew a line around the well field indicating the outside borders of the affected wells. When he was finished, he rushed back to his office, went through the computer files again and printed an old sketch of the Whittier Narrows fault line. He headed to the photocopier and had the sketch sized to match the sketch he had made of the oil well sites. Finally, he made new, larger prints of both items on transparent film.

He took the transparency of his sketch and laid it on top of the rendering of the fault line. What he saw made his heart pound almost unmercifully.

Price! The sonofabitch had been right!

They matched.

All of the oil wells were located either directly on, or adjacent to, the fault line.

Rusty Coleman felt the adrenaline begin pumping madly, coursing through his veins unchecked, the rush making his hands tremble.

It had to be, he thought.

He'd found his probe locations.

Bill Price stared at a small television set propped on his desk and watched the hearings as they progressed in Sacramento. It was high drama, the testimony unfolding as though it had been carefully choreographed for maximum effect.

He glanced at his watch. By now, Darlene should be there, replacing the man he'd earlier assigned to the job.

When she'd reported in, he'd asked her if she wanted to take some time to get settled and she'd said no. Even though she hadn't yet found a suitable apartment and was bunking in with an old friend, she expressed the desire to get right to work, so he'd suggested she cover the story in Sacramento. She'd accepted the assignment with relish.

Price stared at the television set. All morning, he'd had the deep-seated conviction, as he watched the hearings, that they were some sort of a sham. Just another part of what now looked like a massive campaign of disinformation being disgorged by elements of the government. In his own mind, several fingers pointed to the assumption that Los Angeles, in fact, was in grave peril and the decision had already been made to do nothing about it.

Nothing!

Rusty had said he'd attended a series of seminars where the evacuation of Los Angeles had been discussed. The consensus of opinion was that it couldn't be done! If so, it could only mean one thing. They were simply going to let it happen, because they didn't believe it was possible to evacuate L.A. Nothing else made sense!

It was incredible!

How, he wondered, could he break through the defenses? He needed a hook! Something that would sound the alert! Something that would be accepted as proof they were all being lied to!

Now, as he watched the afternoon session begin, he could feel a sense of anxiety building in him. This was the biggest story of all time! Bigger than Nixon! Bigger than anything! Los Angeles was about to be destroyed and the government was going to stand by and watch it happen!

Jesus!

He felt a chill go down his spine.

He was in L.A. Sitting in an old building that would crumble like so much cardboard. His very life was in danger! This minute!

Price lit a prohibited cigarette and stared at the small television set, his anxiety growing by the second.

He watched as a tired-looking man, overweight and slovenly in appearance, raised his hand and took the oath. Then the man sat down, exhaling noisily, as though even this small effort was too taxing.

"Please state your name."

"Sergeant Alvin Drucker, Menlo Park Police Department."

Price snorted. The high rent district of California couldn't afford cops who looked better than this? He visualized this blimp trying to chase a suspect. He wouldn't get more than ten feet. He made a mental note to look into it further. The *Globe* rarely missed an opportunity to stick it to anyone and everyone located north of Santa Barbara. It was almost tradition.

Senator Jake Simpson leaned forward and said, "Sergeant Drucker, the committee thanks you for taking the time to appear here today. Would you please tell us about your investigation into the death of one Thomas Wilson."

"Yes, sir."

Drucker took a deep breath, opened up a file folder and began to read from his notes.

"The initial investigation into the death of Thomas Wilson was carried out according to regular procedures," he said, his voice a flat monotone. "The body was examined by the coroner's office and positive identification was made with the aid of dental records, then released to next-of-kin. Investigation of the crash site . . . Wilson was killed in a one-car auto accident . . . and a full-scale examination of the vehicle . . . failed to indicate foul play. So the case was closed.

"Subsequently, I was contacted by the FBI and told that they wished to cooperate with us in a reexamination of the case. They have since presented evidence to me and to the Grand Jury. An hour ago, an indictment was handed down and warrants have been issued for the arrest of one Theodore Kowalczyk and one Theresa Wilson. Wilson is the ex-wife of the victim, Thomas Wilson."

Simpson leaned forward and asked, "They are accused of murdering Thomas Wilson?"

"Not as yet, sir. They are prime suspects, yes. The evidence is still being gathered and the warrants are for the purpose of further investigation."

"And what would be the motive?"

Drucker sighed and said, "Kowalczyk is an employee of an insurance company that is a member of AAIS. He is an old friend of Mrs. Wilson's. We think that he was hired by AAIS to knock off Wilson and used Mrs. Wilson to set up the hit."

The gallery went wild. Reporters were pushing past people to get to telephones while still cameras clicked, their electronic flashes playing havoc with the television signal.

Bill Price sat at his desk and shook his head. It was so crazy . . . it could even be true. But he knew it wasn't. In his heart, he knew it was just another ploy.

He hoped Darlene was getting it all down.

He felt a finger tapping on his shoulder. He turned around and looked up into the eyes of Rusty Coleman, eyes that were ablaze with excitement.

"You find something?"

"Boss," Rusty said, breathlessly, "I think I found the key. We need a geophysicist, fast."

"The key? What key? What are you talking about?"

"The probes! Remember the probes? I told you there had to be a whole bunch of probe sites? I told you there was no way?"

"Yeah . . . So?"

"I was wrong! You were right! I've found them. I'm sure of it!"

Price switched off the television set, stood up and planted a big kiss on Rusty Coleman's cheek.

In Sacramento, Darlene Yu looked up from her shorthand pad and almost shouted out her anger.

It was all such trash!

She knew this man Kowalczyk. She'd covered the story of the death of his family before she'd been shipped off to Washington. She'd done a big feature on the man's career. His two years in Vietnam, his career with the FBI, his anguish at the death of his wife and child, and his subsequent resignation.

For three months, she'd dogged him, talking to him personally on several occasions. She'd been compassionate, probing gently, assuring him that her questions were not designed to exploit, but rather to help prevent such a tragedy from happening again, if such a thing was possible. And he'd cooperated to a degree. For that reason and that reason only.

She'd looked into the soul of this man. She'd seen the intense pride, the high standards, the genuine concern for others that lay within his being.

He was no actor. No fake. He was a throwback to another time. And there was no way on earth that he would be mixed up in some tawdry scheme designed to enrich a bunch of insurance companies. It simply wasn't possible!

And there was the testimony of this fat cop from Menlo Park. Why was all of this coming out now, at a hearing in Sacramento, when it would normally be something the FBI would speak to directly? Drucker was a local cop involved in a major murder case with national security implications. That was clearly the province of the FBI. Why weren't *they* here instead of this sorry excuse for a cop? Why wasn't the FBI screaming its lungs out? They would never let something like this pass. If they had an APB out on these people, they had to know that it would all hit the fan soon enough. Normally, they were prepared with complete statements regarding high-profile cases. And this one was becoming as high-profile as they got. Besides, Kowalczyk was an ex-FBI agent. An ex-FBI man involved in a conspiracy to kill a geologist? And they were letting this local cop do all of the talking? Crazy!

There had to be another reason for all of this. And she had to find out what it was.

Then she remembered Rusty's reaction earlier in the day when she'd asked him if he'd found something. The veteran reporter had claimed there was nothing, yet she'd seen the fire in his eyes, the excitement in his walk.

He *had* found something!

She slapped her notebook shut and forged her way out of the hearing room, hoping that she'd be able to make it outside before the anger building inside her made her scream.

Chapter Twenty-five

President Byron Walsh stood up from behind the big oak desk near the window of the Oval Office and walked around in front of it. He leaned against the desk, thrust his hands in his pockets and stared down at the man sitting in the chair. "You *cannot* be serious," he said, the veins in his neck standing out, almost pulsing as he fought to control his anger.

"I realize how terrible this appears, Mr. President," said his visitor, "but I assure you, I had no idea how . . . entrenched . . . this agency had become. Not until I discussed it with Graves this very afternoon. I am as shocked and upset as you are. It's conceivably one of the worst scandals in the Pentagon's history. I hope you'll give careful consideration to all aspects of the situation before you . . ."

The look in the president's eyes caused General Simon Howard to let the sentence trail off into silence. Clearly, the man, already renowned for having a prodigious temper, was near the end of his rope.

Byron Walsh's temper had almost prevented him from becoming president of the United States. Throughout the long and arduous primary season and then the campaign itself, he had striven diligently to present the image of a man who took things in stride, who embodied those qualities most admired and respected by the electorate. His opponents, all of them, were well acquainted with his ambition, his passion and his almost blind intolerance of those he considered thick-headed. They baited him constantly during the campaign, hoping that their jibes would break down the carefully prepared facade and reveal the fire within. Three times they had succeeded.

"Stupidity will destroy this country," Walsh had blurted out on one occasion. "Not drugs, not the budget, not wars, but pure and simple stupidity! Education must be our number one priority. But it's not that we need more engineers or doctors or scientists. It's that we need people who can use the brains God gave them. We need an educational system that demands our children be taught to think! The time has come to deemphasize sports and other extracurricular activities. The time has come to concentrate our efforts on developing a nation of men and women, regardless of their means, who are capable of competing, on every level, with the best minds in the world. That will be the salvation of America!"

He'd dropped five full points in the polls after that explosion and it had taken six weeks of almost cynical backpedaling to get those precious points back.

He was a man of fifty-two, with a lean, trim body arranged on a medium-sized frame. His closely cropped hair was flecked with gray and the face, while pleasant, was not one that sent female hearts to racing. When the temper was properly controlled, he displayed a demeanor that seemed relaxed and controlled, as if he was a man who was very capable of making the most important decisions with rational, logical thought. In fact, he was all of that. When the temper flared, it was usually because Walsh was confronted by something he found revolting. Another example of an attitude that he felt exemplified certain aspects of American life that had become tolerated, if not encouraged, by decades of platitudes.

"I'm afraid," General Howard continued, choosing his words carefully, "that we've allowed this situation to get a little out of hand."

President Walsh reared back in mock surprise. "A *little* out of hand? Is that what you call it? I call it something else entirely. You said a man named Graves is behind this?"

"Yes. I should tell you that Robert Graves is considered one of the brightest men we've ever . . ."

A wave of the hand cut the man off. "Save the testimonials for later. Right now, I want the stupid sonofabitch in this office within the hour."

The man in the chair almost leaped to his feet. "Sir, I think before you talk to him, you should . . ."

Again, there was an imperial wave of the hand. "Frankly, General, I don't give a damn what you think. I am anything but a hands-off president. Maybe someday, you people will get that through your heads. I want Graves in this office within the hour and that's an order. This conversation is at an end."

The general stood stiffly at attention, saluted and left the room.

Thirty-five minutes later, Robert Graves was ushered into the Oval Office and took the seat recently vacated by the general. In addition to Graves, the president's chief of staff, Willard Coones, took his position in the other chair that faced the desk.

There were no formalities, no handshakes, no pleasantries. Instead, the president concentrated on the report on his desk and let Graves stew for a few moments. After what seemed like an eternity, he raised his head and removed his glasses, almost flinging them onto the desk.

"As I understand it," he said, his voice an angry rasp, "you're the mastermind behind this debacle, is that right?"

Graves cleared his throat, played with his tie for a moment and then said, "You can spare me the bleats of outrage, Mr. President. I am a man who is paid to do a certain job. I happen to do mine well, as is the case here. If there is a problem, it lies with the failure of politicians to come to grips with the realities of life, choosing instead to spend their days in an endless series of 'photo opportunities.' There are serious problems that must be addressed on a daily basis. I happen to be one of those chosen to be involved with those problems. If you don't like it, that's too bad."

For a moment, Byron Walsh simply stared at this arrogant man, then dropped his gaze to the report in front of him. "Your lack of respect for our system of government is duly noted, Mr. Graves. Perhaps it explains how you managed to operate with impunity all of these years. We'll deal with that later. Right now, my concern is focused on this report. Is it true?"

Unhesitatingly, Graves answered, "Yes, it is."

The president gritted his teeth. "You're telling me that we *know* a terrible, terrible earthquake will strike Los Angeles and we've kept it a *secret!* Is that what you're saying?"

Graves remained impassive; supremely confident in his ability to handle this political animal, as he had others in the past. "Yes," he said, his lips barely moving. "For very good reasons, as are stated in the report."

President Walsh tapped his fingers on the report and said, "I haven't had the opportunity to read it all, but I've just spent the last two hours with General Howard and he's given me the main points. Up until now, you've been making all of the decisions and now . . . now that the fat is in the fire, you've kicked it all the way up to the White House."

A tight smile played over the president's lips. "It doesn't take a rocket scientist to figure that one out, Graves. This one is too hot to handle. You don't want to mess up. Right?"

The words touched a nerve. Graves ran a hand over his lips and said, "It has nothing whatsoever to do with me, Mr. President. The fact is that the decision is one that would most properly be made by you, not some lower functionary like myself."

"Bullshit!"

The president's voice was so loud it made Graves jerk back in the chair.

President Walsh's eyes were thin slits. His cheeks were flushed with anger. "You've made all of the decisions so far," he said, his voice now barely controlled. "Decisions that may have destroyed the credibility of this entire administration. According to you, that's the way it was set up. What a president didn't know couldn't hurt him. God! Who was the first man you conned into going along with that line of reasoning?"

Graves swallowed hard and said, "I don't appreciate your terminology, Mr. President. The fact is . . ."

Walsh cut him off with another sweeping wave of the hand. Tapping the report with his index finger, he said, "According to you, there's no way Los Angeles can be evacuated without tremendous problems. Right?"

Graves's face now took on a bored expression. "The evidence to support that opinion is irrefutable."

"I'll bet. And the bombs? They won't work?"

"The report makes no such claim. It states that there is a very strong likelihood that they will be ineffective. In a worst-case scenario, they could be construed as having been responsible for the actual quake, which would put the government in an untenable situation. It was a worthy effort, but I would recommend not using them."

"Have they been ordered?"

"That decision is yours, Mr. President."

President Walsh sneered at his guest and said, "Yes, of course." He stood up and walked to the front of his desk, as he had with General Howard. Again, he leaned back, resting his small posterior on the edge of the desk, then bent his upper torso forward so that his face was less than three feet away from that of Graves.

"Very well," he said, crossing his arms in front of his chest, "Here's what you'll do. You will order the bombs to be produced. That's number one. Secondly, you will convene your group and you will present a plan for the evacuation of Los Angeles to me within twenty-four hours."

Graves looked stunned. "Mr. President, that would be impossible! I've already . . ."

The president shoved his face directly in front of the man in the chair. "Mr. Graves," he said, "I'm giving you a direct order. You are to carry out that order posthaste. There are to be no more arguments, no long discussions. Just do it!"

Graves stuck out his chin and said, "Mr. President, I cannot . . . will not . . . be treated in this manner. I *demand* that I be treated with the proper respect. I

288

have . . ."

The fuse had been lit earlier. Now, the full force of the explosion was evident on the face of Byron Walsh. "Listen to me, you pompous piece of crap! You'll do as you're told. You'll do it! Because if you don't, I'll have you arrested. For years, you've managed to subjugate those people charged with the responsibility of making decisions. You've made the decisions for them. You've been running a little empire all by yourself. I'm sure, if we look deep enough, we'll find that you've broken enough laws to keep you behind bars for the rest of your natural life. There will be no resignations, mister. You'll be fired, plain and simple. You'll go to trial, like a common criminal. And when you're found guilty, which I guarantee will be the case, you'll be hauled off to some rotting, stinking hell-hole and shoved in a cell with the rest of the scum. If you want to test my will, feel free. But I warn you, you'll live to regret it."

The color drained from Graves's face. "Mr. President, this is a disgrace. You can't talk to me like that! I'm a civil servant. I have rights. I have . . ."

President Walsh's eyes seemed to explode from their sockets.

"No more arguments!" he screamed. "Do you understand! I want that report in twenty-four hours. And you order the bombs to be produced. Understand?"

Robert Graves's eyes were as wide as saucers. He gasped and said, "You're mad! You're utterly mad!"

Walsh stuck his face inches away from that of Graves again and said, in a voice that was now low and soft. "No, Mr. Graves, I'm not mad. Angry, yes. Upset, maybe. But not mad. And you, my dear fellow, don't ever want to see me mad. Now . . . I want you out of this office."

The president stood up and turned his back on the astonished Graves, his arms crossed, his foot tapping impatiently on the thick carpet. "Tomorrow," he said. "Same place, same time. Got it?"

A very shaken Robert Graves struggled to his feet, his eyes almost spinning in his head, his jaw slack, the expression on his face one of total bewilderment.

Again, the president repeated, "Do you understand?"

Numbly, Robert Graves nodded and shuffled out of the room.

Walsh turned to Coones and said, "Better get someone to keep an eye on that idiot. Get in touch with FBI Director Fisher. I want him here within the hour. Also, I want a reprise of the day's hearings in Sacramento. And tell Marie to cancel everything else on my schedule for the next two days at least."

"Yes, sir."

"Better schedule a meeting of the cabinet for the morning. Say eight. We'll do it over breakfast. If Graves doesn't come through, we better have a plan of our own."

"Yes, sir."

The president fixed his stare on his long-time friend and said, "I sense a note of disapproval."

Coones grimaced and said, "You want it straight?"

"You know better than to ask that kind of question," Walsh snapped. "Shoot!"

"Well," Coones said, nervously scratching his nose, "It may be that Mr. Graves is one hundred percent right. He's had a lot of experience in this area. He's had access to the experts. When you consider what's at stake here, I think you might take it a step slower."

"Slower! We've only got about three weeks!"

Coones hung his head. "That isn't what I mean," he said.

"Then what!"

"You aren't in the mood to hear this."

Byron Walsh moved to his chair and sat in it heavily. "You're not suggesting that we follow these recommendations."

"If you don't," Willard Coones said, "you may be placing yourself . . . this office . . . in terrible jeopardy."

"You think he's *right!* Is that it!"

Coones sighed, looked at his friend and said, "I think you have to consider that possibility."

Walsh slapped his hand on the desk and cursed. "Never!" he said. "It's unacceptable. Totally unacceptable!"

Coones walked over to the desk and placed a hand on the shoulder of his friend. "Then get ready," he said. "The worst may be yet to come. Before you speak with the cabinet, I suggest you acquaint yourself with all of the facts contained in Graves's report. I think it's very important. There are some conclusions in there that . . . unfortunately . . . make a lot of sense. You need to have an open mind on this, no matter what your personal feelings may be. Sometimes . . ." He let the rest of his thought go unspoken.

For a moment, President Walsh simply stared at his long-time friend. Then, very slowly, he picked up the report on his desk and began to read.

Chapter Twenty-six

Las Vegas, Nevada. Garish, glitzy, wild. Mile after mile of dazzling casinos filled with people looking for action or simply enthralled by the atmosphere itself. A city where fantasy rules supreme. A city of assembly-line marriages and quickie divorces. Where the vagaries of climate can bring the air to a boil, even on an evening in May.

Like this particular Monday. Hot, dry, without a whisper of wind. The temperature at six in the evening hovered at just under one hundred degrees.

No matter. The city was teeming with tourists and conventioneers. The huge recreational vehicle parking area located adjacent to the Circus Circus Hotel-Motel complex was jam-packed with vehicles from all over the North American continent.

The old motor home belonging to Dr. Glenda Wickshire was parked at the far end of the lot, about a quarter-mile from the entrance to the RV area.

Inside the vehicle, Ted, Terry, and Dr. Wickshire waited patiently, pondering a gamble of a far different kind. They were waiting for two visitors to show up; visitors who had been contacted by mobile phone earlier. Frank Leach and an associate had checked into the Hilton earlier under assumed names. Frank had taken a count of the others who were gathering in the same hotel, awaiting further instructions. The meeting room had been arranged and the conference had been set for eight o'clock. There was only one problem.

Photographs of Ted Kowalczyk and Theresa Wilson had been displayed prominently on television newscasts from coast-to-coast. They were listed as fugitives. Not just ordinary run-of-the-mill fugitives either. In the statement issued by the FBI, they were identified as being possibly armed and dangerous fugitives. That made them special.

All afternoon, as the trio inside the motor home watched the hearings progress, they had been witness to a carefully and exquisitely conceived plan being put into action. Now Sacramento was as much a fantasy-land as Las Vegas, or Disneyland, or any of a hundred other places. But this fantasy was being presented as fact. That almost all of what was being said was a pack of lies mattered little. The effect was what counted. And the effect was telling.

Somehow, the people at NADAT had made it appear as though two old friends had gotten together to commit murder. Several motives were discussed at the hearings in Sacramento, all of them patently ludicrous. But again, it was the effect that counted. In the minds of the most of the public, Ted and Terry had already been tried and convicted. A blanket of disinformation had been unleashed by the clever minds at NADAT. A false scenario that would serve to blunt

293

whatever the twosome had to say about anything, should they ever see fit to surface. And if they did surface, there was a very good chance that they would be shot dead where they stood. They were, after all, considered armed and dangerous *fugitives!*

Even before they'd been heard, their credibility had been destroyed. They were murderers; therefore, they were not to be believed. People in trouble would say anything to save their skins. Lie, cheat, steal, murder . . . It was Machiavellian and ingenious.

And very effective.

It made the prospects of rescuing Tommy Wilson dimmer. It made them consider the possibility that he'd already been killed, his body buried in the vastness of the desert. If that was so, it would make what was to come totally redundant. Another exercise in futility.

The atmosphere inside the motor home was one of deep depression. Even the dog seemed to sense the mood, his bulging eyes turning from person to person as though trying to understand their pain. Three people . . . spending their time watching television with growing unease, waiting and looking at each other with nothing to say.

In the midst of this gloom, there was a knock at the door. Ted lifted one of the slats in the Venetian blind and peeked through the small opening. He saw two men standing by the door. For a moment, the bleakness of spirit receded and he almost burst out laughing. Frank Leach and a companion were both wearing false mustaches, dark glasses, and hairpieces. They were dressed in outlandishly bold short-sleeved shirts and white shorts. The disguise, if one could call it that, made them look like partners in some old-time vaudeville act. Or two middle-aged men on the tail-end of a wild weekend in Las Vegas. What made it even sillier was the fact that both men were carrying attaché cases.

Ted motioned to Dr. Wickshire and she opened the door, allowing them entry.

Frank came in, all smiles, and grabbed Ted in a bear-hug. "Jesus Christ, babe! It's good to see you!"

Introductions were made all around. The other man was Henry Fraser, the executive director of AAIS. Ted, a weak smile on his lips, said, "You certainly know how to develop a disguise, Frank. You two guys are simply beautiful."

Frank shrugged it off. "You laugh all you want, babe, but it was the best I could do. And it's working. Nobody's stopped me yet. I brought something for you, too. You'll never make it inside the Hilton the way you look right now."

The smile left Ted's lips. "Nobody's looking for the two of you."

"Oh yeah? Don't be so sure. The way this thing is going, anything's possible."

"OK," Ted said. "Bring me up to date. Where are we?"

Frank looked at Dr. Wickshire and asked, "You got anything to drink, babe?"

If Dr. Wickshire was offended by being called "babe," she didn't show it. She pulled out a bottle of scotch from the cabinet above the small sink and placed it on the table. In a moment, there were glasses and ice and some water.

"OK," Frank said, after downing half of his drink. The long walk in the dry heat had given him a strong thirst. "We've got over 130 guys parked at the Hilton and the room is all set up. We've got some of our own investigators sweepin' the place now and security'll be no problem once you get in there. *If* you get in there. As for the other stuff you wanted, I've got truckloads.

Enough to make it look like World War Three. The trucks, the uniforms, weapons . . . you name it. Everything is sitting in L.A. and all we have to do is send our people to pick it up. Your boy went for the story you suggested and I promised him a big bonus if he kept his trap shut. I think he will."

"Did you mention my name?"

"Yes. Had to. But it's OK. He's been watching the hearings and reading the papers and he knows somebody's trying to fry your ass. He can't figure out why but he figures this whole deal has something to do with it, so he's eager to help. You've managed to make some friends, babe."

"I hope so," Ted said. "I'll need them all."

Frank grunted something and said, "I've got three people working with the college kids. Right now, things are being set up. We got a break there, babe. There was a group at UCLA already planning on just such a protest. We managed to wire in to their deal so it's perfect. They've been planning this for months so it looks real natural. So . . . so far, we're on track, but this stuff going on in Sacramento is so weird, I don't know if it's gonna do any good."

"I don't know either," Ted said. "But we don't have a choice. Tommy Wilson is the key to this thing. If we can produce him, we may have a chance." He took a deep breath and asked, "The most important item of all. Did you get me a map of the site?"

Fraser beamed, reached inside his attaché case and extracted a folded piece of paper which he opened and laid flat on the table. "One of our board members is a retired Atomic Energy Commission executive named Terrence Garfield. He's quite familiar with the layout of the entire site. As it turns out, Garfield quit two years ago over some policy differences, so he's got a bit of an axe to grind. After watching what was

296

happening to us in Sacramento, he decided to give me this. He was quite interested in helping us. He even suggested the building they might be using. The others, he says, are so busy all of the time, it's unlikely they would use them."

Fraser pointed to an outline on the map. The building was about six miles from one of the several entrances to the site. Then he looked up at Ted and said, "A stroke of luck, I'd say."

Ted grunted. "It's about time something went our way." Then he turned to Frank and asked, "The guys you lined up . . . are they still with us?"

Frank grinned. "You bet, babe. I told the vets that one of their own was in serious trouble and needed their help. That was enough. I didn't mention any names. Didn't need to. As for the insurance guys, they're all freelance and pissed as hell. They know the hearings are a crock. They can see what's going on and they want to set it right. Besides, we're layin' out big bucks. These guys respond to big bucks, babe."

Fraser frowned. "Can you be a little more specific about this operation? As you can appreciate, AAIS is in serious difficulty. *Serious* difficulty. We've been attacked before, but never at this level of intensity. Our involvement in something like this could finish us."

"Really?" Ted said, failing to keep the sarcasm from his voice. "Then why are you here?"

Fraser held up a hand. "Don't get me wrong. I'm behind you one hundred percent. It's just that . . . you seem to be preparing for a full-scale attack on a federal facility. That's something that could land all of us in jail . . . for a very long time. Have you considered alternatives?"

"Yes, I have," Ted said. "And there aren't any. You guys are being made the scapegoats for NADAT's dirty little plan. They figured on keeping everything secret, but they never counted on people like Tommy having a conscience. If we don't make our move, Los Angeles is likely to be destroyed. AAIS will be destroyed along with it. Which leads me to ask a question."

"Yes?"

"You people knew what was going on. Why the hell didn't you do something?"

"We couldn't."

"Why not?"

"Because we weren't supposed to know about it."

"Bullshit! You *did* know about it."

Fraser looked extremely uncomfortable. "We knew, yes. But we didn't believe it. At first, we didn't believe what we were hearing. We thought there had to be a mistake. And then, after we became convinced that Gifford's data was accurate, we were sure that the government would do something. We never, at any time . . ."

Ted held up a hand and glared at him. "Back up a bit. Start at the beginning."

Fraser took a deep breath and exhaled slowly. Then he said, "It all started in 1971. That year, the Russians hosted an international symposium on earthquakes, at which time they presented some astonishing data on earthquake prediction techniques. That was the same year we had the San Fernando Valley earthquake. Some of our members paid off some very large claims that year, so the interest in anything that could predict earthquakes was quite high.

"In any case, we decided to form a research company to explore the issue. We put the company in the hands of a man named Daniel Dalton, a geologist who'd attended the Moscow conference. At first, things moved quite slowly. Then, in 1978, a scientist named Scollard announced that he'd discovered a new fault line, quite by accident. He claimed that two small earthquakes near Glendale were actually caused by water being pumped into oil wells. At the same time, Vance Gifford had been conducting some experiments in Hollister. He'd managed to produce what he thought was a small earthquake himself, using exactly the same technique.

"Naturally, when he heard about Scollard's claim, he went to see him. The two compared notes and Gifford was certain that the man was really on to something. He came up with the idea of using thousands of existing oil wells as probe sites. But how to get our hands on them was another problem. So . . . we went to the Interior Department.

"After some discussion, a deal was made. The Interior Department would take back leases on about three thousand low-volume oil wells in the Los Angeles basin and turn them over to Dalton Research for research purposes. Dalton would insert probes into the wells and monitor every twitch. A considerable amount of money was involved, but we were told that if we came up with something solid, we would share the information with the feds and they would find a way to reimburse us for at least half of the cost. It was a very secret deal, and for us, a real gamble.

"Anyway, as the work progressed, it started to look like we were going to be successful. We'd managed to predict a few small quakes in the areas that we were concentrating on and everyone was getting excited.

"Then . . . we got pole-axed. NADAT came swooping down and slapped a classified label on everything. We were told that the national security was at stake here and that all of the information had to be kept secret. We were also told that if we didn't cooperate, we'd never get reimbursed. Since none of this was on paper, we were in a box.

"So . . . we just went about our business until . . . until Gifford told us he was sure about a big one in Los Angeles. At first, we thought he was crazy, but as time progressed, it looked more and more like he was right. Then he died. Next, Thomas Wilson redid Gifford's research and the next thing we knew, he also was dead. At least, we thought he was until you told Frank that he was alive.

"We were a little confused, to say the least. We had no idea that the feds were doing experiments in the desert on this nuclear thing. No idea at all. We got into this thing because we wanted to find out whether or not earthquakes could be predicted. Now we know they can. But it's still too expensive."

Ted glared at the man. "But why didn't you start screaming when you realized a big one was going to strike L.A.?"

For a moment, the cramped interior of the motor home grew quiet, save for the growl of the twin air conditioners on the ceiling.

Fraser squirmed in his seat. "Because we were suckered!" he said. "We were told by NADAT three months ago that the likelihood of an earthquake in L.A. was remote. Shubert met with me and told me flat out that there were many things wrong with the data. Then, when I started to push it a little, I was told that an evacuation plan was in the works. It's only in the last few days that we've been able to put everything together, thanks to you."

Ted gave the man a hard look. "You certainly made sure that your members did everything they could to cut their losses, though."

"I admit that," Fraser said, his gaze wavering. "But that started two years ago. At that time, we notified our members verbally that we were concerned about a

300

big quake hitting Los Angeles and suggested they take whatever steps they could, surreptitiously of course, to protect themselves. You see . . . insurance companies are required to maintain certain reserves for most of their underwritings. But earthquake insurance is a different matter. The reserves are not adequate to cover something this big. It would wipe a lot of companies out.

"At the same time, we went to the federal government and asked them to help us financially in the event that a major quake *did* strike, but they just dragged their feet. The fact is, insurance company bashing is the in thing just now, so politically, it's not very viable to consider backing us up. But in my view, they should have put politics aside on this issue. After all, we were the ones who made the prediction of the quake possible. Totally unfair.

"Now, the members are in a terrible bind. It's not just the damage claims that will bankrupt them. It's the other claims as well. Death, injury . . . loss of income . . . No reserves are large enough to handle something like this. Without the assistance of the feds, many of our members are out of business. Pure and simple."

"And business is business, right?"

Fraser grunted and said, "You make it sound dirty. It isn't. The fact remains that we are spending whatever it takes to support you on this little exercise of yours. We believe in what you're doing and we're willing to put our money where our mouths are. If that isn't enough for you, I'm sorry. It's the best I can do."

Again, Fraser hung his head. For a moment, no one spoke. Then Frank Leach said, "Ted . . . you're being a little hard on the man. He's here now. He's supporting you all the way. His ass is out a mile here.

301

Maybe the association had a hard time believing this was actually happening. Maybe they thought the government would evacuate at some point. You have to understand . . ."

Ted waved his hand. "Yeah, yeah." Ted could feel his stomach beginning to turn. As much as the man's attitude disgusted him, he could see the problem. Allied against the association were the considerable forces of an agency of the government, with almost infinite power at their disposal. Already, the hearings in Sacramento had been turned into an orgy of wild charges, none of them founded, but all of them damaging. There was an implied threat that lay exposed for anyone on the inside to see. Cooperate and somehow things will work out. Fail to cooperate, and you'll be out of business.

NADAT had played the AAIS for suckers from the beginning. And now, they were dealing their cards face up, using a stacked deck, and there was nothing the association could do about it.

"Well," Ted said, "there's only one way out of this mess. Frank said you have a connection that can get us through to the president."

"Yes, I do."

"OK. Do you know where you can reach him right after the operation?"

"Yes. I have his home number."

"Good." He turned back to Frank. "You said you had something for me in the way of a disguise?"

Frank opened his briefcase and extracted a hair-piece, a pair of horn-rimmed glasses, a false mustache and a stick-on beard. He handed them to Ted.

After putting them on, Ted looked in the small mirror affixed to the wall and shook his head. "If a cop sees me in this getup, he'll assume I'm some freaked-out child molester. This'll never work. It's too

302

obvious."

Dr. Wickshire tapped him on the shoulder and said, "I have an idea, Ted."

"Yes?"

"Why don't you let me speak to them?"

"But you don't know the plan!" Ted protested.

"I realize that," she said. "But I don't need to. All I need to do is divide them into smaller groups. Each of the smaller groups could pick a leader and the leaders of each group could be brought here, to the motor home. You could brief them personally, with a minimum amount of risk.

"Look . . . you're a very tall man. The FBI is looking for you. No matter what sort of disguise you wear, you'll still manage to draw attention to yourself. No one is looking for an old lady and I can move around without having to look over my shoulder. I think it's the ideal solution."

For a few moments, Ted stared at her in awe. Then he said, "You're quite a lady, Doctor. Quite a lady."

She was grinning from ear to ear.

"OK," he said. "You've got yourself a deal. You go over there and talk to them, but don't tell them anything. Not just yet. Just stall them until I have a chance to talk to the team leaders."

She smiled and said, "Very good."

Ted turned to Frank and asked, "Who's your man?"

Frank look puzzled. "A guy named Radley," he said. "Ron Radley. But she doesn't need to worry about that. I'll take her there."

"No," Ted said. "I want you two out of sight. We can't afford to take any unnecessary chances. What's this guy look like?"

Frank looked like he wanted to argue, but decided against it. "He's a tall guy, like you." Then he turned to Dr. Wickshire and said, "Radley will be at the door

303

to the conference room, checking names. He's the guy to see."

Ted stared at Dr. Wickshire and said, "OK . . . you got that?"

She nodded.

Out of the corner of his eye, Ted saw Terry slouched on the sofa, looking tired and drawn. He moved to her side and sat down.

"Are you OK?" he asked.

She threw him a wan smile, then patted his hand. "I'm just a little tired," she said. "I guess it's the not knowing that wears you out. I mean, here you are getting ready to involve yourself in this dangerous effort to rescue Tommy . . . and you don't even know if he's alive. It's . . . very nerve-wracking."

Before he could respond, Dr. Wickshire hugged the dog to her body and then placed him in Terry's lap. "Look after Pierre while I'm gone."

"I will," Terry said.

The doctor left the motor home and started her long walk to the Hilton. With the dog squirming anxiously in her arms, Terry opened the blind just enough so the dog could watch her. The dog's gaze followed the woman's movements until she was completely out of sight. Then he settled down.

Ted had been watching her as well. Watching and marveling. She was seventy-five years old and full of life.

An inspiration.

Chapter Twenty-seven

On the other side of the country, Robert Graves sat at a small desk in his fifteenth-floor Washington apartment and scratched out a note on a white piece of paper embossed with his initials.

A tear rolled down his cheek and dropped onto the paper, blurring what had just been written.

Graves crumpled up the paper and threw it in the wastebasket. He then reached into the desk drawer and took out another sheet.

It was so unfair, he thought. So terribly unfair.

He'd dedicated his life to his country. He'd saved countless people from the specter of facing up to their own mistakes, including two presidents. For his trouble, he'd been treated, over the years, like any other bureaucrat, none of whom had the foresight and the wisdom he possessed. And now, he'd been totally humiliated by a man devoid of even the slightest intelligence and foresight. A political hack, a man who, by some capricious whim of the gods, held incredible power in his hands.

Power that would be ill-used. Power wasted. Power that could send Robert Graves to *prison!*

Prison!

He'd been a patriot. He'd sacrificed his *life* for his country. And the man was threatening him with *prison!*

He shuddered.

Once, he'd considered writing a memoir about his experiences in government service, thinking it might serve as a useful guide for those who would follow in his footsteps. But he quickly discarded the thought. There was no one to follow in his footsteps; therefore, to discuss such secrets would serve no useful purpose. His memoirs would be treated in the same fashion as those dreary kiss-and-tell books written by a string of weak-minded individuals. The readers of his book would surely fail to see the import of the work and would, no doubt, categorize the effort as an exercise in self-aggrandizement. He was above such people and refused to subject himself to their uninformed and subjective criticisms. History would speak for Robert Graves, as it had for other unappreciated patriots in the past. He had faith in his ultimate vindication. Unfortunately, the period of time between the present and the day of his vindication would be long and unbearable. He could see no avenue, other than a lowering of his own standards, that would allow him to escape this undeserved anguish.

It was so unfair.

A score of people within the government deserved

being exposed for the dolts they were. But doing so would only serve to hurt the country. That was something he could not abide. He could not, in all good conscience, convene his committee and instruct them to devise a plan that he knew was wrong to begin with. It would be a lie. A deceit for no good purpose. They had worked long and hard to produce a report that proffered the only acceptable course of action. To make an about-face now — reject their own work — would be dishonorable and perfidious.

No matter what, he would be looked upon as a man who had lost his power base. Soon, everyone would know that he was a man who'd been treated with scant respect by the president himself.

There was no way out. No way to save face.

He'd put the wheels in motion that would save the face of others, but he hadn't anticipated having to deal with a man who left him no room of his own.

It was so unfair.

The note he was writing should expose the man for what he really was.

But . . . he couldn't do that either. It would be misunderstood and only lead to more degrading, wrongful appraisals of his life and service.

There was nothing left. No way out.

All he could do was to write that he was experiencing failing health and wished to end his agony.

And that is what he wrote. Nothing more, nothing less.

There were no messages to friends, because he had none. There were no messages to loved ones, because there were none.

He was alone.

His work had been his life. And now it was gone.

Having finished the note, he signed it and walked

slowly to the window. He turned the latch, opened the window and stared at the street below for a few moments, smelling the air, his other senses absorbing the almost ethereal pulse of power that throbbed throughout the city of Washington.

And then he threw himself into the void.

Chapter Twenty-eight

The conference room was small by necessity. Most of the conference rooms at the Hilton had been booked for some time, but there was this small space left over, and with movable walls placed in position, it was adequate.

Above the group, a large crystal chandelier, almost a symbol of Las Vegas, glowed brightly as the men took their seats and speculated among themselves as to the reason for this hastily prepared gathering. Dr. Glenda Wickshire stood in front of a room filled with 132 men, most of them wearing puzzled expressions on their faces. Beside her stood Ron Radley, an insurance investigator who'd been quickly briefed on why she was there instead of Frank Leach. She rapped her hand on the lectern and smiled sweetly.

"I imagine many of you are wondering what in the world an old lady is doing standing here in front of all of you. Allow me to introduce myself. My name is Dr. Glenda Wickshire. I'm not a medical doctor, but rather a . . . scientist."

The confusion deepened.

"First, let me say Frank Leach is unable to be at this specific meeting for reasons which will become obvious very soon. I know you've all talked to Mr. Leach and you're very curious as to what this is all about. I am most anxious that you know. All I can tell you at the moment is that there is a vitally important . . . mission . . . that needs to be undertaken. A mission so important . . . it may well be the most significant undertaking you have ever been involved with. I say that with the knowledge that your lives, I am sure, have been filled with many notable accomplishments.

"I wish I could tell you more at this point, but I can't. Circumstances beyond my control have precluded that. But the fact that you are here is proof that you are the kind of men we were counting on."

She looked around the room, as though trying to make eye contact with each and every one of them.

"There are two groups of you here. One group is comprised of Vietnam War veterans and the other is made up of insurance investigators. Right now, I would ask that you separate yourselves into the two groups and that each group appoint one man to be the representative from that group. Once that has been done, I will take both representatives out to meet with Mr. Leach and then they will return here and give you a complete briefing. Would you please separate now?"

They all stood up and shuffled into position.

"Very good," Dr. Wickshire said, once they had realigned themselves. "Now, if each group will appoint a representative, we'll continue."

There was a hubbub of conversation. After about five minutes, two men approached the front of the room. Dr. Wickshire shook their hands and then addressed the group once more.

"Right now, I am going to take the men you have selected to another meeting. Then, they will return and give you a complete briefing. In the meantime, why don't you enjoy yourselves for a bit and we'll reconvene here at . . . let's say . . . eleven. I realize how silly this all must seem to you, but once you are fully briefed, you'll understand the need for such caution. Again, many thanks."

As the men shuffled out of the room, still confused, Dr. Wickshire, her eyes alive with excitement, told the two men to follow her out of the hotel.

"We'll all get in a cab," she said. "We don't want to be followed, so we'll have him drive around a bit first. You people with the experience can make sure we aren't being followed. When you give me the sign, I'll take you to *my* leader."

Her face was practically glowing. As they started to walk out of the room, one of the men turned to the man beside him and whispered, "Is this for real?"

The other man shrugged and said, "Beats me. But I'll run with it for a while. It keeps me away from the goddam tables and besides . . . she kinda reminds me of my grandmother."

At much the same time, in Los Angeles, Bill Price was sitting at the conference table along with Darlene Yu, Rusty Coleman, and two other reporters, Helen Horsey and Phil Chambers. There was one more person attending the meeting, the publisher of the *Globe*, Brian Cantrell.

For almost an hour, they'd been reviewing the information that had been gathered over the past few days.

Darlene had expressed her views regarding the

311

allegations made in Sacramento. Rusty had explained the business about the oil wells. The other reporters had chimed in with information regarding the latest on "Operation Move."

Several of the convoys originating in Los Angeles had been traced to their final destination.

One was in Salt Lake City. Another was in Boise, Idaho. Still a third was in Albuquerque, New Mexico.

All three convoys had ended up in large, empty buildings surrounded by recently installed chain-link fencing. The buildings were guarded by armed military personnel. Windows had been blacked out and security was tight.

In Albuquerque, two of the workers had been followed to a local bar where, after a few drinks, they had expressed disgust with the entire operation. Unfortunately, they'd discussed it with Phil Chambers, a veteran *Globe* reporter.

They were supposed to be setting up temporary shop, they'd said, but such was not the case. Crates were sitting in the middle of the buildings and no effort was being made to unpack. All they'd been told was to say nothing.

Each morning, they were to report to work and amuse themselves by playing cards or watching television. At the end of the day, they were to return to their temporary quarters, motels not too far from the selected buildings.

They were, for all intents and purposes, simply waiting for something. What, they didn't know. But they did know that they were away from their wives and families and their normal surroundings. In addition, important work, work that entailed the meeting of specific deadlines, was not being completed. Penalties for nonperformance loomed in their futures. Penalties that would wipe out already-spent bonus money.

They didn't like it. Not one bit.

And then there was the report that had been released in Sacramento by a man named Peterson. The very fact that it had been prepared by two men who were now dead made it completely suspect. Price, after reading it, declared it a complete fabrication, although he had no direct evidence to support his claim. He had, as he put it, a very solid hunch.

Brian Cantrell looked at his watch. It was a rare occasion when this golden-haired son of the newspaper's late founder deigned to appear at anything having to do with the operation of the newspaper. He usually left such matters to executive editor Sam Steele, preferring to spend his time attending to a variety of high-profile charitable organizations in and around Los Angeles.

But on this day, Sam Steele was in Cedars-Sinai Hospital, recovering from an operation performed to remove both his appendix and his gall bladder. Bill Price, a man with a penchant for shooting from the hip, wasn't about to commit to *this* story without permission from *somebody,* so he'd practically begged Cantrell to come to the newspaper office. Now, he regretted the decision. He wished he'd simply printed the story and the hell with the career. Cantrell was proving to be as troublesome as Steele.

"Bill," Cantrell said, impatiently, "I don't think you've got enough yet to run with this."

Price slammed his hand on the table. "How the hell can you say that?"

Cantrell looked at him in astonishment. He'd heard about Price's temper but this was the first time he'd encountered it firsthand. "Don't get me wrong," he said. "I'm not saying you shouldn't print what you've got. All I'm saying is that it isn't enough to allow us to come out and state flatly that the federal government is

313

expecting a big earthquake."

"We don't have enough? You just heard Rusty say that he'd checked with three different manufacturers of diagnostic equipment. They all confirmed that they'd sold enough stuff to Dalton Research to cover all of the well sites."

"Off the record."

"So what! We don't have to mention their names. The fact is that the equipment was sold."

Cantrell shook his head. "You're breaking all of the rules, Bill. You're taking a bunch of facts and making a case like some lawyer in front of a jury, with no regard to the consequences. You can't shake people up like that without knowing for sure!"

"The point is," Price protested, "that for whatever reason, the government doesn't want us to know for sure. And I'm not saying that there's going to be an earthquake. All I'm doing is quoting a reliable source who says that, on the face of everything we've got, it looks that way."

Cantrell grinned. "Come on, Bill! It amounts to the same thing and you damn well know it."

"But look at the facts," Price protested. " 'Operation Move' is nothing but a fraud. That's obvious. They've moved a bunch of defense contractors to safer locations is all. The stuff Phil got is *on* the record. Those two guys didn't know they were talking to a reporter. You've got the insurance companies screwing around with earthquake insurance policies. That's what started the move to have the hearings in the first place. Now you've got the hearings all turned around, becoming a platform for something that has little to do with what was originally intended. And you've got testimony given at the hearing that ties an outfit doing research on earthquake prediction to both the insurance industry and the feds.

314

"You've got a former Pentagon employee supposedly breaking out of a rehab hospital, after phoning his wife and telling her to warn me about a coming quake. Sure, I know . . . his lawyer says it's all craziness, but how come nobody's seen the guy since the escape? He left the hospital with nothing, according to them. No money, no clothes, zip. Just a hospital gown. Are you going to try and tell me that a guy can wander around Washington for days without being picked up? His wife sure as hell doesn't buy it. Come on! They've got him stashed somewhere!

"And then you've got the oil wells. Not to mention this angle of Darlene's."

Cantrell snorted. "I'd discount that. We've been fooled before by people. Maybe this guy *is* a killer. I'm not prepared to say he isn't at this point."

Darlene took up the challenge. "Mr. Cantrell," she said, failing to keep the edge off her voice, "I spent months following up the story on Ted Kowalczyk. I practically crawled inside the man's head. It's just not his character."

Cantrell shrugged. "Look . . . you aren't a shrink. Maybe all of the pressure got to him. Maybe he flipped out. It happens all the time. Besides," he continued, "that's not the real issue. What we have here is a situation that looks very strange, I'll grant you. But it's all circumstantial. The Geological Survey Office says there's no earthquake coming. In fact, most of the geophysicists you've talked to say that earthquakes can't really be predicted. And before you jump down my throat, I'll agree that there have been documented cases of such things happening. But . . . for you to commit this newspaper to a flat-out prediction that everything going on is pointing to a big quake in L.A. is something that . . . once we put it in writing, we'll never be able to back away from.

"Christ! I can see it now. Those that *do* believe us will go bananas! You'll have a panic out there. It's like yelling fire in a movie theatre. There's a limit to freedom of the press and you know that as well as I do. Even if we're absolutely right, we have no protection. None! We could be closed down.

"And if we're wrong . . . we look like fools. Either way, we can't win. I won't place this newspaper in that sort of box. Not now! Not ever!"

Price was seething in frustration. "So what you're saying is that the people of this city can just sit there and let it happen. That doesn't sound very responsible to me!"

Cantrell's face began to redden. "I don't need a lecture from you on responsibility. You've been skating on thin ice ever since you took over that desk!"

"Really?"

Rusty Coleman interrupted what was fast becoming a personal and bitter argument. "Hold it!" he yelled. "Let's not get carried away here. If I understand Brian, he's saying that we can print what we know to be the facts."

Cantrell leaned back in his chair and said, "I didn't say that."

Rusty turned to Cantrell and said, "Sure you did. You said we had to avoid speculation. You said you didn't want us quoting sources that might make it appear we were slanting the story, but you said it was all right to print solid facts."

Cantrell looked confused. "Well . . . ah . . ."

Rusty turned to Price and said, "Boss, that"s good enough for now. We' re running out of time. Let's print everything we know, but group it together. Two or three main stories and then a few sidebars. All related to the same story. Just the actual facts. That will be enough."

Cantrell held up a hand. "If you do that, make sure you print both sides of the issue. You'll need to reiterate the story that Phil did on the lawsuit filed against that insurance association."

"Why?" Price asked.

"Because! That could be your key here! The insurance association is in trouble. They're being sued by eight states for price-fixing, among other things. They've had it their own way for years! Finally, some people are getting a little fed up with it and starting to look under some rocks. I wouldn't be surprised if this whole story was manufactured by the industry just to get the heat off."

"That's crazy!" Price countered.

"No, it isn't," Cantrell said, some anger of his own beginning to surface. "The insurance companies have been screwing everybody for years. Who the hell are you going to believe? The government of the United States or the insurance industry?"

For a moment, nobody spoke and then Darlene said, "You really want an answer to that question?"

Cantrell smiled and said, "OK. So, we can't take the word of either. But this story has to be balanced."

"You mean killed."

"No! I just don't want you drawing any conclusions. Or making it too easy for the readers to draw their own conclusions. It amounts to the same thing."

"Come on!" cried Price. "You just finished saying that we can print the facts. If the reader draws certain conclusions, that's all to the good. You can't possibly object to printing the goddam news. Jesus! If that's no longer allowed, I might as well pack it in right now."

For a moment, no one said anything. Then Darlene said, "Look . . . I think we're looking at this from the wrong perspective."

All eyes turned to her.

"The facts are irrefutable," she said. "The report that was released at the hearing has the official imprimatur of the feds. It was prepared by two men who are now dead. That seems awfully damn convenient to me. I've shown the report to a geophysicist who claims that it seems strangely truncated. There are pages and pages of redundant data which mean nothing. The whole report has no focus. Now . . . it seems to him that a project of this sort, a very expensive project, would have been halted after a few years if that data was accurate. Let's face it, not even the insurance companies are going to piss money away if they keep coming up with the same useless information, year after year.

"And yet . . . this project continued. And . . . here's the kicker . . . two years ago, the information was classified. Why the hell would it be classified if nothing was found? The methodology wasn't changed. There were no startling discoveries. The data *after* classification was the very same as the data *before* classification. That makes no sense."

Cantrell pursed his lips and said, "According to this . . . whatever his name was . . . they thought they were on to something and that's why it was classified."

"You believe that? Then why isn't there some reference to it in the report?"

Cantrell's facial expression changed dramatically, like a man remembering something long forgotten. In fact, he was recalling something his father had told him not long before his death some twelve years ago. It hadn't been forgotten, just stored away. Brian Cantrell had promised his dying father that he would follow in the family tradition. But he'd broken that promise. Instead of running the newspaper as his father had wished, he'd hired a succession of men to do the job for him, which allowed him to follow his numerous outside interests.

318

The newspaper business, in his view, was dying. Television was where the action was. Owning a television station was almost like having a license to print money. Owing a newspaper was more of a curse than anything else.

He hadn't told his father that. Instead he'd told his father that he'd run it just like *he* had. Boldly.

He hadn't. And now, because Sam Steele was ill, he, Cantrell, was being forced to make a decision. A decision that could have a lasting effect on the future of the paper.

He tried to imagine what his father would have done. And then he started putting together some other facts in his mind. Facts that suddenly seemed much more important than they had previously.

"Come to think of it," he said, "there are about five guys at the club who have decided to take long vacations in the last few days. They all have ties to the government. I never even gave it a thought until just this minute."

He stared at Bill Price and asked, his voice a few decibels lower than before, "Tell me . . . do you really think this is happening? Sometimes, we get so caught up in a story that we lose our objectivity. Is that what's happening here? Or are you people really convinced that Los Angeles is about to experience a monster quake?"

They all said yes.

Brian Cantrell tapped his fingers on the table for a moment and then said, "You know, there's a lot at stake here. More than you can possibly realize."

"What do you mean?" Rusty asked.

"This building," Cantrell said, "is not one of your modern earthquake-proof buildings. It's an old brick structure, the very worst kind in terms of earthquake protection. If there is a big quake, we're finished. And

319

I mean finished."

"What about our own earthquake insurance?"

Cantrell shook his head. "It wasn't renewed when it came up six months ago. We tried every company in the business and came up empty. In fact, we were one of the companies working behind the scenes to bring this inquiry to reality in the first place. For obvious reasons, we didn't want it made public. For one thing, we're in violation of the building codes. For another, we're in violation of the agreement with the union."

Coming from Brian Cantrell, it was an astonishing admission.

"The fact is," he went on, "we've been wanting to build a new building for years, but with the bottom line being what it is, we simply can't afford it. Neither can we afford to fix this one up. So . . . we're totally vulnerable. Sooner or later, we're going to have to face some very hard facts."

The room was quiet. Bill Price lit a cigarette. No one complained.

Cantrell said, "If this building falls down around our ears, we don't get Dime One."

They all stared at him. Again, he tapped his fingers on the table for a moment. Then he took a deep breath and said, "Screw it!" He looked around the room, his eyes meeting those of the others, one by one. Then he said, "OK . . . you can print it the way you want. If you want to quote people who claim this all seems to point to a big earthquake, go ahead. Make sure you print the comments of those who disagree. That's all I ask. And while you're at it, I'd suggest you start looking for work elsewhere."

They continued to stare at him, stunned expressions on their faces.

"You don't get it, do you?" he said.

Bill Price shook his head. Cantrell gave him a sick

320

little smile and said, "You people get so wrapped up in a story you can't see the forest for the trees. If you're wrong, and we do create a panic, the feds will come down on us like a ton of bricks, even though we're just reporting the facts. Make no mistake about that. We have a heavy liability here.

"On the other hand, if you're right, the ton of bricks will come down on us all by themselves. Either way, there'll be no newspaper to come back to."

Price grabbed him by the arm. "You sure about this? You sure you want to stick your neck out?"

There was little hesitation. "Yeah, I'm sure."

"What changed your mind?"

Cantrell sighed deeply and said, "I didn't want to believe it, but . . . I think you're right. I think we're in for one hell of a jolt."

He stood up and put on his sunglasses. "As a matter of fact," he said, "for the next few weeks, you can reach me at my summer place. I don't intend to set foot in this building for a while. Sam will able to talk to people tomorrow. You can clear things with him as soon as he's able to take phone calls. I really hate this business, you know?"

Then he turned on his heel and departed, leaving the rest of them staring at each other.

After a few moments, Price recovered and addressed his troops. "All right," he said. "I'll call downstairs and tell them we're gonna be a little late. You people get to work. Forget the balance. Let's just tell it like it is. If this paper is going down the tubes, we might as well go out with a bang."

His face was covered with a broad grin, which he knew made no sense at all. After all, earthquake or no earthquake, he was about to become unemployed.

Again.

* * *

Ted Kowalczyk shook the hands of the two men as they entered the motor home, then offered them a seat in the cramped confines. The dog went wild welcoming his mistress back and then checked both men out carefully before returning to his favorite spot, the co-pilot's seat.

One of the men received more than a handshake. He received a bear-hug that was returned in kind. They'd done it once before, the bear-hug. Many years ago. In a stinking jungle, surrounded by death, both men crying on the shoulder of the other.

Ted stood at the front of the coach and looked into the waiting eyes of his friend from the past, Joe Green, then the others: Frank Leach, Henry Fraser, Terry Wilson, Glenda Wickshire, and a man he didn't know, the representative from the insurance investigators gathered at the hotel. They were quite a group.

Quite a group indeed.

"I guess you're wondering why I called this meeting," he said, a crooked grin on his big, square face.

Chapter Twenty-nine

President Byron Walsh dipped a piece of toast into some egg yolk and chewed on it for a while. Then he tapped a knife on the side of the crystal water glass and said, "I realize we're still in the middle of breakfast here, but I think we need to get started."

His face was dark with an anger that had failed to recede from the day before. He'd spent an almost sleepless night and it showed.

"As you know," he said, "I've invited Mr. Jason Shubert to be with us this morning. Mr. Shubert is here to brief you on the formation and function of NADAT, an agency that has existed for some time without my direct knowledge." As he said it, he shot a hard look at General Howard. "In addition," the president continued, "Mr. Shubert will update us on the situation at the Nevada test site.

"I have also," the president went on, "invited Mr.

Donald Morgan to join us this morning. Mr. Morgan has worked with Robert Graves for a number of years and will give us some insight with reference to the latest recommendations that were made."

He turned to Shubert and said, "Mr. Shubert, the floor is yours. Please carry on."

Shubert looked at his half-eaten breakfast and felt his body tense even further.

Ever since he'd received the phone call the night before, he'd had this terrible sense of foreboding. It had been the president himself on the line, telling him, in a very cold manner, that Robert Graves had killed himself and that he, Jason Shubert, was to present himself at Nellis Air Force base within the hour. He would be flown to Washington by military jet. Once in Washington, he was to present himself at the White House for a meeting with the president at seven in the morning.

He'd arrived in the city at three in the morning. At seven, having had no sleep at all, he was cloistered with this strange little man with the dark eyes and the quick tongue at which time he was asked a series of rapid-fire questions.

He answered them all unreservedly. This was no time for games.

What had astonished him was the total lack of feeling the president seemed to have over the death of Robert Graves, a man who had served his country well for decades. As far as this president was concerned, he was dead and that was that.

And now Shubert was being asked to tell the cabinet everything. Information that had been deliberately withheld from others, for very good reason, was now to be given out freely, with no concern for leaks or other concerns. It was unconscionable and stupid. NADAT had been formed to function in isolation, for good reason. If the president was removing that barrier, it could only mean one thing. NADAT was through. And he'd been told only that he was to do as he was told or suffer terrible consequences.

The shock of Graves's death, combined with the lack of sleep and now food, made him feel weak, both physically and mentally. A life that had seemed orderly and fulfilling was now in complete disarray. His emotions were in turmoil. Nevertheless, he forged ahead, determined to make the best of it.

"The idea for the creation of NADAT came from . . . the late Robert Graves," he began. "In 1961, shortly after the Bay of Pigs fiasco. As you know, the proposed invasion of Cuba was conceived under the Eisenhower administration and it fell to the Kennedy administration to carry it out. At the time, the administration was in a period of transition, and this one was a particularly difficult transition. People who were intimately involved in the Cuban operation were no longer available and new people were not aware of some of the finer points. Granted, the CIA was primarily responsible for the actual invasion, but Mr. Graves's view was that they were still hampered by the changes that had been made to the original plan by members of the Kennedy administration.

"It was the view of Robert Graves that the Bay of Pigs invasion failed because of its timing. Had it taken place either one year earlier, or one year later, in other words, at a time when everything from conception to actual execution was under the direct control of a single group, it would have succeeded and we would not be faced with the threat that now exists some ninety miles from our border.

"As a result, Mr. Graves proposed that a secret agency be set up that would provide continuity in certain cases involving national security. It would be staffed by civilians and managed by the Pentagon. It would carry out certain sensitive missions unilaterally, and in the event that there was a debacle such as the Bay of Pigs invasion, the administration could, with total honesty, claim no knowledge.

"The idea was rejected. At the time, it was felt that such matters should remain within the province of the administration. However, it was determined that Mr. Graves should form what is now known as NADAT.

"The National Disaster Alert Team was originally conceived as an advisory body. But over the years, it evolved into an agency that was assigned control over specified activities where there was a modicum of vagueness as to which department of the administration had jurisdiction. There were certain cases that involved several agencies and when those agencies were not in agreement as to the course of action that should be taken, it would usually result in costly delays. Sometimes, because of intramural conflicts, no action whatsoever would be taken, when such action was clearly indicated.

"So . . . over a period of time, NADAT was allowed to broaden its scope and began to carry out tasks that were considered politically sensitive. It received the grudging support of all agencies of the government.

"Eventually, again, because of political considerations, NADAT stopped reporting on its activities except in rare cases. The less people who knew about our activities, the less chance there was of damaging leaks.

"If Mr. Graves acted in an imperious way, it was because he was encouraged to do so. In fact, his performance was similar to that of General Douglas MacArthur during the Japanese occupation. A dictator, yes . . . but a benign dictator. Able to get things done when they needed to be done."

President Walsh looked at him with undisguised hostility. Shubert swallowed hard and continued with his briefing. When it was over, some thirty minutes later, the president asked, "Tell me, Mr. Shubert. Have the nuclear devices been ordered?"

"Not to my knowledge."

"Do you think the earthquake in California can be prevented by the use of these devices?"

"I don't know."

The president glowered at him. "Make a guess."

"I don't like to guess, sir. You have the data on the last test. You'll have to make your own decision."

"Yes, of course."

For a moment the room was silent and then the president said, "I want you to order the devices now. You can use the telephone in the anteroom. As soon as you've done that, you may rejoin the meeting."

Shubert turned and walked out of the room. The president turned to the other invited guest, Donald Morgan, and said, "Your turn, Mr. Morgan."

Donald Morgan held his arms outstretched and asked, "What is it you want of me?"

"I want you to tell the cabinet everything that has taken place since NADAT first became involved with this earthquake situation."

Donald Morgan was in his mid-sixties, white-haired, overweight, and still grieving over the untimely death of one of his closest friends. A former professor of political science, he'd been with Graves for the last ten years. It was the first time in his life that he'd ever worked with someone with whom he almost always agreed. It was a joy . . . a reaffirmation of his own opinions and attitudes. And now . . . it was over.

He leaned forward, placed his hands flat in front of him, and in a deep monotone, began to brief the members of the cabinet. About five minutes into his presentation, Jason Shubert entered the room, handed a note to the president, and took his seat. When Morgan was finally finished, some thirty minutes later, he leaned back in his seat and actually closed his eyes.

The people in the room sat silently, looking at each other and shaking their heads in disbelief.

It was incredible. An agency of the federal government had been allowed to operate, make terribly important decisions involving millions of lives and billions of dollars, and none of them, except for General Howard, had the slightest idea it had been going on. In terms of potential damage to the administration, it was a catastrophe.

President Walsh said, "As I understand it, you have three men who are prisoners. Vance Gifford and Thomas Wilson are in Nevada. And Mr. Davis is in a V.A. Hospital. Is that right?"

"Yes, sir," Morgan said, his eyes remaining closed.

"And everyone at Dalton Research has been sent off to Guam on some special project?"

"Yes, sir."

"They have television satellite dishes in Guam, Mr. Morgan. What makes you think these people won't become aware of what is going on here and start asking questions?"

Morgan swallowed hard and said, "We offered them tremendous financial incentives to take on the project. They were told they would be completely isolated for at least a month. They accepted the terms and won't be a problem."

"I see. And what were your plans for them . . . actually all of these people, after the exercise?"

"I don't know. Mr. Graves didn't discuss that with me."

President Walsh snorted and said, "I'll bet he didn't." Then he said, "You've managed to have several witnesses appear at a hearing in California giving per-jured testimony."

Morgan kept his eyes closed, avoiding the hard looks being given him by those around the table.

"Yes, sir," he said.

"Just what did you plan to do with *them* once this was over?"

Morgan took a deep breath and finally opened his eyes. "In the event the project was successful, we felt we would be able to convince all of those affected that what we did was necessary. Mr. Graves was sure they would agree to live out the rest of their lives much like those in the witness protection program."

"And if the project was unsuccessful?"

"Mr. Graves never considered that possibility. At least, if he did, he never discussed it with me."

"I see. And you managed to prevail upon local police officials and members of the FBI to assist you in this cover-up. How did you manage that?"

"We . . . Mr. Shubert can best answer that."

The president turned to Shubert. "Well?"

"It wasn't a case of covering anything up, sir. We were under the impression that the national security was at stake here and presented our position from that standpoint."

The president shook his head slowly. For a moment, he said nothing. Then he said, "Your note says that the devices have been ordered."

"Yes, sir."

"Will they be available in time?"

"That is my understanding."

"Very well. I want you and Mr. Morgan to step outside and remain within this building while the cabinet discusses this matter. General Howard . . . I want you to join them."

Byron Walsh stood up and shoved his hands in his

pockets. "Gentlemen. I want this clearly understood. All three of you are to remain inside the building. If you are entertaining any thoughts of leaving the building, reconsider. I have already given the Marine guard instructions that you are not to do so. Please don't embarrass us further."

"Are we under some sort of arrest?"

It was Morgan, looking like a man whose world had come to an end.

"I haven't decided yet," the president said. "I want to consult with my cabinet first."

The three men stood up and left the room.

President Walsh sat down, spoke to someone on the telephone for a moment, and then brought his attention back to those in the room.

"Well," he said, his eyes dark with barely concealed rage. "As you can see, we are in one hell of a spot. Once Congress gets hold of this, there'll be hell to pay. And they'll find out, sooner or later."

He took a deep breath and said, "I'd suggest that we not spend too much time wringing our hands over what has happened. Rather, I think we should address ourselves to the immediate problems. One: Can we be sure there is going to be a big earthquake in Los Angeles on May twenty-seventh? Two: If we are, and I think we'll be able to dispense with much argument on that, do we evacuate? The other questions that need to be addressed are these: Do we use the nuclear devices in an attempt to prevent the quake? Do we make public the attempt?

"We have a plateful, gentlemen. Who'd like to get the ball rolling?"

Before anyone could speak, there was a rap on the door and the president's personal secretary entered the room and handed him several sheets of yellow paper. He looked at them for a few moments and then carefully placed the sheets on the table. His face became ashen and all of the air seemed to go out of his lungs. He slumped in his chair, his body almost lifeless, the spark in his eyes gone, replaced by a glazed look of shock. He looked like he'd aged five years in five minutes.

For a moment, no one spoke. Clearly, whatever was written on those pieces of paper was terrible news.

Finally, Walsh pulled himself together. "This," he said, tapping the pages on the table, "may influence your thinking. It's a story coming over the wire service right now. The Los Angeles *Globe,* in this morning's edition, is claiming that Los Angeles is about to be struck by a great earthquake. They've devoted several pages to articles supporting their contention. One of the articles concerns 'Operation Move.' Their analysis of that little adventure is presented as proof that the government knows about the coming quake. Another makes reference to the oil wells that they're using as probe sites. They've not only found them, they've found the people who supplied the equipment. A third article discounts everything that has gone on at the Sacramento hearings, claiming that it's a put-up job. Their analysis of that fiasco is quite sound."

He ran a hand over his eyes and said, "They're advising everyone in the city of Los Angeles to leave immediately."

He leaned forward and stared at the sheets of paper. "The city is in a flat panic even as we speak. And it's only six in the morning out there. The *Globe* is being quoted by every radio and television station in the city. Once everybody's awake, God only knows what the hell will happen. The governor has called out the National Guard to keep order. He's trying to get through to me to find out if there's any veracity to the story. So is the mayor of Los Angeles. They are both demanding an immediate statement from me."

The president's eyes moved erratically as he sought to make contact with each and every person in the room. "Naturally," he said, "the press is also screaming for a statement."

The room was thrust into an atmosphere of deep gloom.

"Does anybody in this room," the president asked, his voice almost a whisper, "have the vaguest idea what I should tell them?"

Chapter Thirty

It was upon him again, the nightmare. Visions of death and destruction rocketing through his brain unchecked, blending with another, more ancient phantasmagoria that had plagued him for years, like some exotic disease that refused all manner of treatment.

Los Angeles was being destroyed again. And in the middle of the rubble stood a man, his hands holding a small, green metal box festooned with a big, red button. He looked at Ted, his face wreathed in smiles, and said, quite calmly, "Don't worry. As soon as I push this button, it will all be over."

Ted wanted to scream at the man. More than that, he wanted to kill the stupid bastard. But before he killed him, he wanted to tell him that it was already happening. That the earthquake had struck. That they were too late. That it was insane to be standing there in the middle of all that destruction and pretend that it could now be stopped with the push of a button.

But again, he was transfixed. Unable to speak or move.

"Ted!"

He heard his name being called. It wasn't the man. It was someone else. Someone who was pushing him. Shaking him. Or was it the earthquake?

"Ted!"

He opened his eyes and looked into the bloodshot eyes of Frank Leach. The very concerned eyes of Frank Leach. The man was still wearing the stupid wig and the crazy shirt. Behind him stood Glenda Wickshire, clutching a cotton housecoat to her throat. Above her, in the ceiling, in a position almost at eye-level with Ted, the air conditioners roared loudly.

For a moment, he didn't realize where he was.

And then, in a rush, it all came back to him.

He looked at his watch. It was 6:30 in the morning. He'd had exactly two hours of sleep.

"What's happened?" he asked.

Frank held up a hand. "We've got some problems."

Ted leaned toward the edge of the suspended bed and rubbed his eyes. "What problems?" he asked.

Frank looked to his side at Glenda Wickshire and then back at Ted. "I couldn't sleep when I got back to the hotel," he said. "I was watching the news and they announced that some civilian attached to the Pentagon killed himself. They gave his name as Robert Graves. I phoned some people in D.C. and it's the same guy."

"Jesus!" Ted exclaimed. "What the hell does that mean?"

Leach shook his head. "You ain't heard nothin' yet. About an hour ago, they came out with the news that one of the L.A. newspapers has broken this thing wide open."

Ted was instantly awake. "What?"

Frank nodded. "Yeah. L.A. is coming unglued.

334

That's why I rushed over here. President Walsh is going on the tube in a few minutes."

Glenda Wickshire said, "I'll make some coffee." She switched on the television set and started preparing the coffee.

Terry, wrapped in a blanket, approached the bunk and asked, "What is it? What's going on?"

Frank Leach threw his hands in the air and said, "Somebody talked. I don't know who. But somehow, the L.A. *Globe* put it all together. They know about the quake, the probes . . . even the fact that the hearing was a set-up. They printed a warning to everyone in Los Angeles to get out of town. Fast. The place is going nuts. Already, the freeways are jammed solid. People are shootin' each other just tryin' to get outta town. Walsh is going on the tube in a minute or so to make a statement. I can't wait to hear what he has to say."

Ted struggled into a pair of trousers and climbed down from the bed. Bending over to avoid striking his head on the ceiling, he clamped both big hands on the shoulders of Frank Leach and stared into the man's eyes.

"Did you . . . ?"

Frank Leach looked into those eyes and what he saw made him tremble. Never had he seen such anger in the eyes of Ted Kowalczyk.

"So help me *God!*" Frank screamed. "Not a word! I *swear!*"

"What about Fraser?" Ted asked, the voice cold, hard . . . almost vicious.

"*No!* I was with him every minute. It wasn't possible, Ted. They did this without us! You've got to trust me, babe! Jesus Christ! This thing is tearing you apart!"

For a moment, Ted continued to stare at him, the lids stiff, unblinking, the mind almost audible as it churned. Then, he released his grip and slumped into a chair.

Already, the television picture was focused on the lectern at the front of the White House press room, the presidential seal almost glowing in the bright light. An announcer was bringing everyone up to date. Interspersed with the picture of the unmanned lectern were scenes of the panic taking place in Los Angeles, the pictures being beamed from the top of one of the tall downtown buildings.

The streets were filled with cars and trucks, some of them loaded down with chairs and mattresses and cardboard boxes that had been hastily strapped to their roofs. Nothing was moving, except for the people on foot, hordes of them, running blindly in all directions, all of them carrying suitcases or paper bags filled to overflowing. Or both.

A cacophony of sound was being picked up by the sensitive microphones at the transmission site. Car horns blared, blending with the shouts of people in full flight. Then the scene switched to some unidentified news room where the announcer, normally the evening news anchor, looked into the camera and said, "That was a live shot of Los Angeles, where, clearly, a panic of major proportions has the city in complete turmoil. If you've just joined us, we've been reporting for about the last thirty minutes or so that the Los Angeles *Globe,* a newspaper not renowned for its pursuit of the truth, has printed a story . . . oh . . . I see that the president is ready . . ."

An anonymous voice intoned, "Ladies and gentlemen, the president of the United States!"

Byron Walsh strode to the lectern and placed his hands firmly on either side of it. He looked directly into the camera and said, "I have a few opening remarks to make and then I'll take your questions."

He was dressed in a dark blue suit, a blue shirt, and a red tie. His hair was carefully groomed and his face looked calm and relaxed. Only his eyes gave him away. They seemed to burn with an inner fire that was almost out of control.

"First," he said, "let me say that I have been in touch with the appropriate government agencies within the last few minutes and can assure all of you that the story that appeared in this morning's edition of the Los Angeles *Globe* is totally false and without any foundation whatsoever."

He stopped for a moment and shook his head in exasperation. "In all my years, I have never witnessed a more irresponsible act than this one. For a newspaper to declare, without regard to the facts or the welfare of the citizens of the area which it supposedly serves, that a disaster such as an earthquake is about to take place . . . It's just beyond me.

"For years, we've all suffered the tabloids, with their ludicrous stories about alien babies and slanderous keyhole-peeking. But I don't think even they would stoop to the outrageous, disgusting depths to which we have been subjected this morning.

"I have asked the Justice Department to fully investigate the circumstances surrounding the publication of this story. While I fully understand the constitutional guarantees which protect newspapers, there are limits. I want those responsible for the printing of this mendacious and malicious story to be held fully accountable for their actions.

"I have also directed that the National Guard already moving into position be augmented by regular Army personnel so that the city of Los Angeles can get back to normal as soon as possible."

He hesitated for a moment and then said, "As I speak to you this morning, I am painfully aware of the fact that to this point, seven people have died as a direct result of the panic that now exists in Los Angeles. I hold the people at the Los Angeles *Globe* completely responsible for the deaths of those people. And by God! They'll pay for it!"

He took a moment to regain control of his emotions. Then he said, "To all of you in that great city, I wish to say this: as your president, I can assure you . . . there is *no* threat of an earthquake. The story that appeared in this morning's edition of the *Globe* is completely and utterly false."

He stopped and gritted his teeth. "In the first place," he continued, "the science, if you can call it that, of earthquake prediction is in its infancy. In a moment, I will ask Dr. Carl Obersen, one of the country's leading experts on earthquakes, to give you a primer on this fearsome phenomenon. He'll explain to you the reasons why predicting earthquakes is all but impossible.

"But before I do, I would like to point out that the other newspapers in Los Angeles, as well as radio and television stations, have forthrightly denied the story that appeared in the *Globe*. Of all the media in the city, this . . . I hate to use the word . . . newspaper . . . was the only one to publish this totally insupportable story.

"Reference was made to 'Operation Move,' and it was suggested that this operation was simply a device to protect certain of our defense contractors from possible danger. Nothing could be further from the truth, and to emphasize the point, I have ordered its immediate cancellation. All of those involved in the exercise will return to Los Angeles."

He stopped and gripped the lectern more tightly. "Since the immediate question here is the one concerning a possible earthquake, I have asked Dr. Obersen to explain to you what has been going on in the area of

338

earthquake research and why it is impossible to accurately make such predictions. After he has made his presentation, I will be available for your questions."

He turned to a man standing quietly in the corner and beckoned him to the lectern.

The scientist, tall, white-haired, and bearded, moved to the lectern and nodded toward the camera.

"My name," he said, "is Doctor Carl Obersen. I have been a geophysicist for some twenty-nine years. For the last ten of those years, I have been engaged in a research project located in Los Angeles.

"I would like to say that part of the story that appeared in the newspaper this morning is true. Approximately three thousand dormant oil wells *were* used in a research project designed to determine the feasibility of predicting earthquakes This project, a joint venture of the federal government and private industry, has been ongoing for over ten years. But, to this date, no progress has been made. In fact, a complete report was presented to us just a few days ago that suggested the project be abandoned. That report was made public yesterday and was completely ignored by the people responsible for the newspaper article.

"In the report . . ."

Ted Kowalczyk waved a hand at Glenda Wickshire and said, "Turn it off. I don't think I want to hear any more."

She reached up and turned off the television set, then handed him a cup of coffee.

Everyone in the motor home looked ill.

For Ted, it was a terrible blow.

The president of the United States was lying through his teeth. He was placing himself in a position that precluded any possibility of evacuating Los Angeles. Now that he'd publicly stated his position, how would it be possible to get him to change his mind? To do so after this announcement would be political suicide, and Byron Walsh was, above everything, a politician.

Somewhere in the back of Ted's mind, he'd held on to the notion that Byron Walsh would listen to him if and when they got their hands on Tommy Wilson. He'd been sure that once the president learned of the insidious workings of NADAT, he'd want to make things right.

Now . . .

It was not to be. The man was now committed to the idea that no earthquake was forthcoming. He had attached himself to a fraud. All along, Ted had assumed that NADAT was operating on its own. Making decisions that were not in the national interest because of the inflated ego of its executive director. Now, Graves was dead and the president was standing in his stead, taking the same road. A road that would place the lives of millions at risk.

It was devastating.

Ted had placed himself in extreme danger because he believed what he was doing was right. He was about to lead others in an attack on a federal facility. Men who had willingly agreed to follow his lead. But if the president of the United States . . .

He lay down on the sofa and faced the wall. He didn't want the others to see his bitter disappointment.

It was all such a waste. Futile.

He felt drained, emotionally and physically.

"What are you going to do?"

It was Terry, her face inches from his own, her dark eyes peering into his intently, as though by doing so, she'd be able to see inside his head.

He looked at her, his own face pinched in pain.

"I don't know," he said.

And then he extended his big arms and pulled her to

him, holding her close, hoping the warmth and feel of her body would hold him back. Stop him from falling into the abyss of total despair.

"I know what you're thinking," she said, softly, whispering into his ear.

He remained mute.

"You think it's hopeless."

Still, he said nothing.

"You mustn't give up."

He held her even more tightly.

She repeated it. "You mustn't give up," she said.

Finally, he released his grip, held her away from him and looked into her eyes. "There's nothing to give up," he said, flatly. "I'm just an ordinary man. If the president has decided to take this route, maybe it's the only way. Maybe Graves was right. He was supposed to be a very bright man. Who the hell am I to argue with people who spend their lives worrying about things like that? Who the hell am I to think I know better than the government?"

He let his arms drop to his side as he stared at the ceiling. "Terry," he said, "it's not a case of giving up. It's a case of dealing with the facts. There's nothing we can do now. Tommy's probably dead. Even if he isn't, they'd find a way to stop us. They're committed to letting it happen.

"Maybe they'll try the bombs and maybe they won't. Hell, maybe Tommy and Gifford were wrong! Maybe there won't *be* a quake. But we're out of it now. No one will believe us. Look at what's happening to the newspaper. The poor bastards are being crucified!"

Terry continued to stare at him and then quickly, she moved away from him, grabbed Dr. Wickshire by the arm and dragged her to stand in front of Ted.

"Tell him!" she shouted. "You've read the report! The real one! Is there going to be a quake?"

Glenda Wickshire's jaw was firmly set. She looked at Ted with a mixture of compassion and resoluteness. "There's no question about it. Yes! There will be a great earthquake in Los Angeles, just like the report predicted."

Terry turned to face Ted again. "Maybe," she said, almost pleading, "Walsh said what he did because he didn't know what else to do. What *could* he say under the circumstances? Yes . . . there is a quake coming? Everyone should head for the hills? That would tear the city apart! Graves, as far as we know, was working on his own. Maybe the president didn't even know about any of this until now. Maybe he hasn't had time to think it out. All he could think of is that there was a panic in L.A. and it had to be stopped. Maybe he'll change his mind once he knows all of the facts."

Ted stared at her as he tried to make sense of her words.

"And Graves killed himself," she continued. "Why? Maybe he realized how wrong he'd been. We don't know!

"But we do know that if there's the slightest chance that Tommy is alive, he can prove that the report is a fake. You've got a copy of his original report and he'll show how they altered it. The very fact that he's alive will show everyone that he certainly wasn't murdered. If they lied about that, they could be lying about the quake. People will understand that. And those men! You explained everything to them until all hours of the morning. They agree with you. They briefed the others and *they're* with you. They're all as committed as you are! You mustn't let this throw you. You can't!"

Ted shook his head. "You saw what was going on in Los Angeles. There are people dead already. Supposing we do manage to convince everyone that a big quake is coming? More will be killed!"

Her chin was thrust out a mile. "Maybe," she said. "Maybe there'll be thousands killed. But if the quake takes place during business hours, the death toll could be in the millions! Besides, the panic is a result of shock. They aren't prepared! If the evacuation is handled properly, it doesn't have to be like that. Don't you see?"

He looked at her in unabashed admiration. She was a fighter. A tower of strength.

"Do you really think the president will change his mind?" he asked. "How can he after this?"

Dr. Wickshire spoke to that. "It wouldn't be the first time a president flip-flopped in a matter of days. Happens all the time. People are getting used to it, sad to say. But I think it's like Terry says. You don't know what the president knows or doesn't know. He's probably reacting to the panic at the moment. We don't even know if he's seen the real report. I can't accept that he means to sit by and watch the city of Los Angeles destroyed. I just can't. But if you don't go through with your plan, by the time we find out, it will be too late."

He sat up straight and stared at them. He could feel their strength flowing through him. A woman he was quickly falling in love with and another . . . an old woman with a young spirit. Their vitality seemed to energize him anew.

To his great relief, he felt himself being pulled back from the edge of the cliff.

"OK," he said, "We go."

Chapter Thirty-one

The press conference finally over, President Walsh returned to the more comfortable surroundings of the Oval Office and called for General Howard, Jason Shubert, and Donald Morgan. They arrived promptly and were joined by the president's chief of staff, Willard Coones. All of them sat on the two sofas in front of the large desk, except for President Walsh, who placed himself in the large leather chair behind it.

"Well," the president began, "that should quell some of the hysteria in Los Angeles."

Quickly, he turned to Morgan and said, "I've studied the reports submitted by Graves and I must admit, they have been thoroughly backed up with convincing data. It appears to me, however, that very little time was spend determining if any means could be developed to effectuate an evacuation. All I see here are the negative aspects. I don't see much input relative to overcoming those negatives. Can you elucidate?"

Morgan seemed stunned. "I don't think I understand . . . sir. You just finished telling millions of people that there would be no earthquake. Surely, you don't . . ."

Walsh leaned forward, his arm outstretched, cutting off the man's remarks.

"Mr. Morgan," he said, "I know what I said. I don't have time for idle talk. I asked Mr. Graves to present a workable plan for the evacuation of Los Angeles. Rather than do it, he chose to throw himself out a window. I suspect that there was more than his precious ego behind that act of stupidity. I suspect that he, being the leader of your little group of geniuses, had cowed you all into following his lead. He was convinced that an evacuation was impossible, ergo, it *is* impossible.

"What I want to know is how much time you people spent trying to develop a workable evacuation plan."

Morgan loosened his tie, undid the top button on his shirt and pulled out a handkerchief to wipe some perspiration from his brow. "A considerable amount of time was lavished on a multitude of divergent proposals," he said. "Each one was thoroughly examined and subsequently discarded. The reason the report appears to emphasize the negative aspects is obvious. I would have thought this morning's pandemonium in Los Angeles would be chilling testimony to the accuracy of the findings."

"I don't happen to agree," Walsh said sharply. "I want you and Mr. Shubert and General Howard to bring your people together and come up with a plan that will work. And I want it before the day is over."

Morgan looked dumbstruck. "Mr. President," he said, "while I can sympathize with your position, it is ludicrous to suggest that we, after years of careful study, can suddenly pull a fanciful plan out of a

345

magician's hat. It simply isn't possible. As much as we would like, we cannot create something that does not exist. I'm afraid you fail to fully appreciate the accuracy of the report.

"As for the present situation . . . are we under arrest or not?"

Byron Walsh gave him a hard look. "I never said you were under arrest. I said I wanted to discuss your future with the cabinet. I haven't had the opportunity to do that yet. They still await my return. At the moment, I'm trying to solve a terrible problem. To be perfectly candid, your performance in the next few days will have a great bearing on what happens to you in the future.

"I'm in this up to my ears, thanks to all of you. I'm not happy about that, but there isn't much I can do about it. The only thing I can do now is try and prevent a disaster from happening. I need your help. And I'm not getting it."

He turned to Shubert. "I asked you if you thought the bombs would work and you didn't give me an answer. I asked Mr. Morgan to develop a plan for the evacuation of Los Angeles and he tells me it's not even worth considering.

"You people are really something. You can sit around and create these terrible scenarios, but when I ask you for some positive input, you all shake your heads and have nothing to say. It's almost as if you *want* the worst to happen.

"Let me tell you something," he said, the anger growing even more intense, "I'm *demanding* that you put your heads together and develop a workable plan for the evacuation of Los Angeles. I'm demanding that you advise me as to the feasibility of using the nuclear devices. I'm demanding that you do everything possible to prevent a lot of needless deaths. And I'm goddam well demanding that you do it this very day!

"I don't want to hear any more of this negative shit! If you fail to produce, I'll see to it that you suffer for it." So help me God! Now . . . get the hell out of my office.

General Howard almost leaped to his feet. Stammering slightly, he said, "We understand, Mr. President. We'll have the plan on your desk before midnight."

Walsh stared at him for a moment and then nodded. "Good."

The three left the room and Walsh was left with Willard Coones, who calmly poured some scotch into a glass and handed it to the president. "I think," he said, "you had better calm down. You're likely to make some serious errors while you're in this frame of mind."

Walsh cursed and said, "Calm down? Serious errors? I don't have to worry about serious errors, Willard. This whole thing is so screwed up I'm dead no matter what the hell I do. While it's true that NADAT existed without my knowledge, it doesn't matter any more. I'm in it now! Besides, the American people wouldn't believe for a second that I had no knowledge of this. They'll think the whole thing is just another 'Irangate.'

"If I evacuate and there's a panic, it'll make this morning look like a picnic. If I don't and there's an earthquake, I'll be branded a wanton killer. If we use the bombs and they fail . . . worse, if they trigger the goddam quake . . . shit! I'm in serious trouble here and you're telling me to calm down? Forget it! Besides, my problems are not worth worrying about. It's the people of Los Angeles I'm concerned about. The whole West Coast, for that matter."

For a moment there was silence. Then the president hung his head and said, "Willard . . . what the hell are

347

we going to do?"

Willard Coones looked at the president with an expression of compassion. It wasn't fair, he thought. The man had inherited a long-entrenched system that was feeding on itself. But it would be Byron Walsh who took the fall.

"I think," Coones said, "that the cabinet should help you considerably. They're good people, Byron."

Walsh raised his head, swung the swivel chair around so that he faced the window and stared at the scene outside. For most of his adult life, he'd wanted to be president of the United States. Through a combination of hard work, good genes, and luck, he'd made it.

Up until yesterday, he'd loved almost every minute of it. And now . . .

"Byron . . ."

"Yes?"

"Reserve judgment on everything for awhile. At least until you see what the cabinet and those three wise men come up with."

Walsh swung the chair around and faced Willard Coones. "Do I have a choice?"

Chapter Thirty-two

It was the most rancorous and divisive cabinet meeting ever held during the Walsh administration. It lasted the entire day, pitting friend against friend, friend against enemy, and by the late afternoon, the president stood almost alone.

Earlier, confronted with the specter of a full-scale panic in the city of Los Angeles, the cabinet had agreed on a course of action with uncommon swiftness and President Walsh had acted accordingly. But now, perhaps because of that earlier decision, there was a divergence of opinion almost equal to the number of men and women in the cabinet.

There were those who refused to believe that it was possible to predict an earthquake. Even with the original, unaltered "Wilson" report in their hands, they clung to a logic born of another era, choosing to deny the reality of such predictions, sloughing off the string of successful predictions as unexplainable nonsense. Like a cancer patient denying the existence of the disease, they denied the existence of such technology.

There were those who believed that the "Wilson" report was correct, up to a point. Perhaps, they contended, earthquakes *could* be predicted, but surely, the magnitude of *this* earthquake had been grossly exaggerated. It had to be. There had never been a quake of this size in modern recorded history. Why now? And why Los Angeles? Besides, they went on, the scientists had always held that it was the San Andreas that was due for a big quake at some time in the future, not the Whittier Narrows fault line. The Whittier Narrows fault line was unknown a few years ago. How, therefore, could anyone make such a prediction based on so little historical data?

As for the idea of using nuclear devices as a tool to either diffuse or lessen the magnitude of the quake, the opinions again ran the gamut. There were those who believed that the use of an unproven nuclear device in some desperate attempt to obviate evacuation was the height of irresponsibility.

Still others held the view that the use of the devices was too risky even in the event that a decision was made to evacuate the city. They were of the opinion that those responsible for the tests already conducted should be severely punished, in view of the fact that the tests had been disguised as weapons tests, thereby reducing the actual number of remaining weapons tests allowable under recently signed treaties.

And aside from the president himself, not a single member was in favor of going public with the entire matter, feeling that it was political suicide. Going public, they reasoned, would mean that the administration would be held fully accountable for everything that might go wrong, and they were convinced that there were many things that *would* go wrong.

Most agreed on one issue. The short-lived, but almost devastating panic in Los Angeles had convinced them that evacuation was truly impractical.

As the meeting continued past late afternoon, and the hastily prepared report was presented by the "three wise men" as Coones had called them, the arguments began afresh.

Jason Shubert, Donald Morgan and General Howard had been ordered to meet with Robert Graves's group of geniuses and produce a plan for the evacuation of Los Angeles. And so they had. As if to emphasize their negative attitude, the plan had been presented six hours prior to the deadline imposed by the president.

It called for three hundred thousand troops to be moved into the city of Los Angeles before Saturday, the fifteenth. Another one hundred thousand troops would be positioned in other areas close to the major southern California cities. An announcement would be made, understating the troop strength at fifty thousand and claiming that they were being brought in to quell a rumored civil rights disturbance in Watts.

In the meantime, a large section of the Mojave Desert near the town of Victorville would be turned into a refugee camp. For how long, was anyone's guess. It was estimated that the length of time could extend into the following year.

The area picked for the camp would consume some two hundred square miles for the camp itself and an additional fifty square miles just to accommodate the three million plus vehicles expected. Vehicles that would be allowed to make a one-way trip simply due to the lack of other transportation available.

Tents, portable cooking equipment, food, potable water and sanitary supplies, blankets, pillows . . . millions upon millions of tons of equipment and supplies would be commandeered from all over the world on an emergency basis and placed in the camp area. Edwards and George Air Force Bases would be used as marshaling areas for airborne supplies, while the massive freight yards at Barstow would be used for ground vehicles, which would be piggy-backed on flatbed freight cars. All nonemergency freight activities in southern California would come to a halt for as long as sixty days, an action that would all but destroy the cash crops of thousands of farmers.

Another two hundred thousand troops, comprising Army, Air Force, and Marine Corps personnel, would be brought in to maintain order and provide services in the camp itself.

Then, on Saturday, May 15, martial law would be declared for almost all of southern California.

"Operation Move" would be reinstated.

Southern California would be divided into ten areas, according to population strength. Each of the ten areas would be fully evacuated, one area each day, the people directed to the camp in the desert, a minimum of four to a vehicle. Those without vehicles would be bused to rail lines and loaded onto freight cars. Everyone would be allowed to bring some clothes and personal hygiene items and nothing else.

Nothing.

All citizens would be advised as to the nature of the emergency and told that failure to obey orders from those assigned to assist them would mean immediate arrest. Looters would be shot on sight.

Hospitals would be evacuated by Navy and Army hospital aircraft and the patients flown as far inland as Kansas City.

352

As each section was evacuated, it would be sealed off by troops. Barriers would be erected. By the end of the operation, the day before the anticipated quake, the city would be ringed with troops, out in the open, who would remain there throughout. No one would be allowed in until after the quake had struck.

The exact same procedures would be followed, on a smaller scale, in the evacuation of other smaller cities, such as San Diego, Riverside, Santa Barbara, and everything within that perimeter.

The rest of the state, while advised of the quake and its anticipated magnitude, would be on its own and officials advised to take normal precautionary measures. There would be no announcement of the attempt to diffuse the quake by the use of nuclear devices.

There were 163 other items covered, most dealing with the aftermath of the quake, should it occur in the strength anticipated. But the basics were frightening enough. They had fifteen days to move over twelve million people.

Anticipated initial cost: 28 billion dollars.

Total number of troops required: 730,000.

Expected deaths and injuries due to noncompliance: 14,000.

The report was unsigned. As President Walsh finished reviewing the proposal, he turned to one of its authors, Donald Morgan, and asked, "Do you think this is viable?"

Morgan sat stiffly in his chair and said, "No, Mr. President, I do not. The report bears no signatures. You demanded that we produce this report and we have done so. It is the best that we can do. But, speaking for the group, I tell you that this report is prepared under protest. Not a single one of us believes it can work. We stand by our earlier recommendations

353

and resent your attempts to have us change our minds."

At that point, Edward Small, the secretary of defense, rose to his feet and said, "Mr. President . . . This operation, should it move forward, would totally disrupt the normal defense posture of this country. As much as I sympathize with the people of Los Angeles, I must tell you that the adoption of this plan would require my immediate resignation. I cannot, in all good conscience, be a party to this."

Byron Walsh sighed and said, "I take note of that, Secretary Small."

It was the first of many threats the president would hear before they broke for the day, the issue still unresolved, to be carried over the next day. As the meeting was about to break up, Byron Walsh, drained and depressed, stood at the side of the table and made a calculated gamble of his own.

They were getting nowhere. Time was running out. He felt compelled to do something that would drive these people to some sort of consensus. So he said, "I appointed you to this cabinet because I value your judgment. I have no wish to be a dictator. I have no desire to implement any program that does not meet with the approval of a majority of the members of this body. And I will support such a majority opinion, be it in favor of the proposal, or against the proposal . . . or a variation.

"But I say this to you: there are time constraints here. The proposal suggests that the outside limit for implementation of this exercise is tomorrow evening. Therefore, if there is no agreement by 9 P.M. tomorrow, I will be forced to make the decision on my own.

"You owe it to your fellow Americans and yourselves to make every effort to arrive at a consensus. I know you won't let me down."

* * *

The Washington press corps was in a turmoil. It was no secret that important meetings were being held at the White House. But no one was talking.

Coming, as it did, on the heels of the president's rebuttal of the story that had appeared in the Los Angeles *Globe,* speculation was rampant.

Was it possible, some were asking, that there was more to the president's denial than met the eye?

A careful analysis of the *Globe* story had shown that there were a number of items that were other than pure speculation. Court records had been examined. The oil wells *had* been used for earthquake prediction research. The wire services and others had reported that "Operation Move" did indeed seem strange, with almost no effort being made to establish alternate facilities for the companies involved.

A San Diego newspaper, digging into the case, had profiled both Ted Kowalczyk and Theresa Wilson. Her divorce records were made public. His history was reexamined. Witnesses were found who swore that they hadn't been seen together for over two years. Sergeant Drucker of the Menlo Park Police Department was now unavailable. None of the people who had worked for Dalton Research were available.

And there was the insurance industry itself. It was true that they had been working with the government in the pursuit of finding a dependable method for predicting earthquakes. And now, they were taking every possible step to assure that their losses would be minimal should a major quake strike. The analyses that had been made in Sacramento seemed silly. Everything was pointing to the opposite.

It was starting to stink. Veteran reporters were finding that their sixth senses were being fully activated.

As for the Los Angeles *Globe,* they issued a statement welcoming a full and exhaustive inquiry into their story. A story they continued to stand behind 100 percent. Even the executive editor of the paper, speaking from his hospital bed, had words of praise for Bill Price, not condemnation.

The owner of the newspaper, Brian Cantrell, was unavailable, but the speculation was that he'd flown to Europe for a lengthy vacation.

And in Los Angeles, Darlene Yu received a strange telephone call. The caller wouldn't give his name, but insisted that she would not be disappointed if she came to a secret meeting in Las Vegas Wednesday night.

"Las Vegas?" she asked. "Look, you'll have to tell me what this is about. I'm not about to . . ."

"Listen, babe," the caller insisted, "this is the biggest story you'll ever cover. Ever! Trust me!"

"Trust you? I don't even know who the hell you are!"

For a moment, the man said nothing. Then, "I understand that you know Ted Kowalczyk."

She felt her heartbeat quicken immediately. "So?"

"I need your promise that you'll keep this confidential."

It was against her principles. Her first inclination was to hang up. The fact that she knew Ted had been part of the story that had appeared in the *Globe.* But there was something about the voice.

"I'm sorry," she said. "I'm a journalist. I report the news. I can't make a promise like that to someone I don't know."

The man tried again. "You interviewed him when his wife and child were murdered."

"Yes."

"He told you things then that were never published."

Her interest was increasing. "Give me an example."

"He told you about his father. About the time they talked about the Holocaust. He told you how his father felt about that. How ashamed he was. How ashamed he was of *being* ashamed. It was a family secret."

She remembered. Vividly. Ted Kowalczyk had cried like a child when he'd told her that. Only someone very close to Ted would know he'd told her that.

"All right," she said. "You have my word."

She heard the caller let out a deep sigh. "OK, babe. Ted wants to meet you tomorrow night. After midnight."

"Where?"

"Vegas. The Riviera, on the strip. Stay near the check-in counter. I'll meet you and take you to him. Deal?"

"Deal," she said.

"Bring your camera and your tape recorder."

"OK."

"See ya, babe."

She hung up the phone and stared at the wall. Something in the back of her mind told her that she was on the threshold of a major, major story. It made her entire body tingle with excitement.

On Wednesday, a majority of the members of the cabinet, after another grueling session, and fully cognizant of the mounting interest in the press, finally agreed on a course of action. Unfortunately, in the view of Byron Walsh, the majority decision was to follow the recommendations originally proposed by the late Robert Graves.

They would not evacuate southern California.

They *would* employ the nuclear devices.

"Operation Move" would begin — again — on the twenty-fourth.

Nothing would be made public.

The president had pledged that he would support the majority decision and he did so now.

But, it was the saddest day of Byron Walsh's life.

Chapter Thirty-three

While the Nevada Nuclear Test Site sprawled over an area of desert and mountains encompassing some four thousand square miles, the administration buildings were confined to a heavily secured compound that consumed less than two square miles of the tract. Except for one, the buildings were laid out in clusters, six clusters of eight buildings each, the clusters standing quite close to each other. Almost a half-mile away stood another building. A solitary green building that housed, it was hoped, Tommy Wilson and Vance Gifford. The main entrance to the compound was situated in the town of Mercury, some seventy miles northwest of Las Vegas, just off Highway 95.

A fence and two guarded gates would have to be penetrated before the group could get to the target building. Two gates and six miles of open road within the federal facility. A facility that boasted a full complement of soldiers.

Twenty-four miles to the west of Mercury lay the small town of Amaragosa Valley, which Ted Kowalczyk had picked as the staging area for his makeshift army of Vietnam veterans and insurance investigators. Still further west, sixty-five miles away, near the town of Scotty's Junction, the diversionary group of students were assembled and given their final briefing.

All of them, students and Ted's counterfeit army, had made their way from Los Angeles to the site within the last twenty-four hours. The students had boarded rented buses and been driven along Interstate 15 until they reached the town of Baker, California. From there, they had turned north, travelling along mountainous Highway 127 to the Nevada border, where the highway became 373, dead-ending at Amaragosa Valley. The buses had turned left and gone on to Scotty's Junction.

Throughout the day, half of Ted's people had trekked back to Los Angeles to pick up the trucks, jeeps, and equipment that had been arranged for by Frank Leach and ferry them back to the staging area. They had taken the same path as the students, stopping just outside the town of Amaragosa Valley. From there, trucks shuttled back and forth from Las Vegas to round up the rest of the people and bring them out.

While it might have seemed odd that the two groups, students and "Ted's Army" were so far apart, it was intentional. Ted wanted to keep the two units as far apart as possible until the time of the actual attack.

The trucks and jeeps all looked authentic. Ted's people wore Army uniforms, a calculated gamble. The highways had been cluttered with genuine Army vehicles as they escorted the convoys that formed part of

"Operation Move" *back* to Los Angeles, a result of the president's announcement that the operation had been cancelled. Other Army units were moving *out* of Los Angeles after quelling the panic that had occurred some thirty-eight hours earlier. So Ted's group failed to draw attention to itself, due to circumstances that seemed almost providential.

For the last two days, Ted Kowalczyk had planned for this operation, using the motor home as a command center, having the chosen representatives come and go as unobtrusively as possible as they reported on the progress of each and every step.

The planning had gone well. Better than expected, actually. Frank Leach had chosen well in those he'd sought out.

Now, as he sat rigidly in one of the jeeps, dressed in the uniform of an Army major, he hoped he hadn't forgotten anything. If he had, it would all be for naught. A wild, desperate gamble would result in nothing but more trouble for Ted and those who'd chosen to join him.

For almost an hour, he sat there, staring into the night, running everything through his mind over and over again. He could feel his heart pounding with excitement.

Suddenly, he saw lights in the distance, many lights, boring holes through the darkness. For a moment, his heart skipped a beat and then he looked at his watch. The lights were coming from the west. It had to be the school buses, right on time, as they came charging down the highway on their way to the Mercury entrance.

It was indeed the buses, their yellow bodies shaking and rattling as they hurtled past his position, the engines whining at full song.

361

Even though they were right on time, it still startled him. It was a signal that the operation was under way. No more planning. No turning back. They were now fully committed.

It was time.

The UCLA students had been briefed, briefed again and supplied with costumes that made them look like overgrown Halloween revelers. They all wore white robes and white luminescent death masks as they poured from the scores of buses and took up their positions at the main Mercury entrance. They formed into thirty groups, each with a large banner that proclaimed, "No More Tests!" As they moved toward the entrance, they broke out in chants that bespoke a similar sentiment. Their sheer numbers seemed daunting.

Almost sixteen hundred of them.

"No more tests! No more tests!" they screamed, as they moved quickly toward the entrance to the site. Facing them, the small group of security personnel tensed, fearing the worst.

The protest was not unexpected. Several anonymous tips had been received during the past twenty-four hours. But its size was an astonishment. All of the tips had mentioned a group of some one hundred protesters, not sixteen hundred. Enough troops had been assigned to handle one or two hundred, but no more. There were, after all, hundreds of miles of perimeter to protect.

In the main security headquarters some six miles away, alarms sounded and the call went out for additional soldiers to move into position. The troops at the gate were simply not enough to handle another in a series of demonstrations that had plagued the site over the years.

This demonstration was, by far, the largest protest seen in years. And the protesters, instead of pressing their obvious advantage, seemed to be waiting for something, satisfied to mill about the entrance and chant their slogans.

Within a few minutes, the additional troops were in position, their uniforms laden down with riot gear, tear gas canisters at the ready. Still, the confrontation was relatively peaceful, the students continuing to stay by the gate and string themselves out along the fence, chanting and singing and waving their signs. No attempt was made to breach the fence or the entrance.

To the captain in charge of the troops, the scene seemed very strange.

First, it was almost two in the morning. Pitch dark. Usually, these protests were held in midafternoon, to enable the television people who always accompanied such demonstrations an opportunity to get their pictures in plenty of time for the evening news broadcasts. But this . . . in the middle of the night . . . As a result of the timing, there were very few television crews covering the event.

Second, despite the chanting and the singing, the students seemed almost subdued. The protest seemed passionless, undramatic.

And third . . . the sheer numbers of them. So many students at this particular moment. Why now? With the newly signed agreement that severely restricted underground nuclear testing, the site was less of a contentious issue than it had ever been.

The captain raised a bullhorn to his lips and yelled, "All of you are to disperse immediately! This is federal government property! Disperse immediately or you will be arrested!"

The students stayed in position and continued to sing. But several miles from Mercury, five other groups moved into position. These groups were not composed of students. Two of the groups were made up of Vietnam vets. The other three consisted of independent insurance investigators. All five groups had been armed with real and fake weapons. They all wore Army fatigues and full battle gear.

One of the groups was led by Ted Kowalczyk. He was seated in the lead jeep, one of eight that sat on the side of the road in the moonlight on a clear, warm night in the desert. He was wearing the uniform of an American Army major, preparing to go into battle once again.

It brought back a flood of memories, few of them pleasant.

He looked at his watch as he waited impatiently.

And then, after what seemed like an eternity, part two of the assault was under way.

The students started first.

En masse, they started pushing at the fence, trying to bring it down. Hundreds of them stormed the entrance, to be beaten back with clubs and rifle butts. The air was quickly filled with the stink of tear gas.

It continued like that for almost a minute. And then, three miles west of the Mercury entrance, the sky was filled with the sight of exploding balls of orange flame. Seconds later, the sound of thunderous explosions reached the ears of those at the entrance. The staccato sound of smaller exploding shells mixed with the deep, booming sound of what appeared to be extremely large high-explosives. It looked and sounded like an invasion.

The students were as astonished as the soldiers

protecting the entrance. They stood where they were, staring into the emblazoned sky and asked each other questions as to what it all meant. The captain in charge of the troops got busy on a radio asking for further instructions. He was told to stay with the students. At the same time, another alarm was sounded and more troops were rushed to yet another location as the bombs continued to detonate unabated.

Thirty seconds later, almost four miles away from the student protest, and in the opposite direction, still another series of explosions could be seen . . . and heard.

The security forces began to suspect that they were now under a full-scale attack. More alarms were sent out and panicky requests were made for additional assistance from civilian police and military bases within a fifty-mile radius of the site, including Las Vegas. The request was for every available man to assist in what seemed like a massive terrorist invasion of the testing site. That was exactly the word that was used.

Terrorist!

Radio signals were sent to Washington as well as the Strategic Air Command Headquarters at Omaha, Nebraska. The security people at the nuclear site were not taking any chances.

Thirty seconds later, at still another location, the sky lit up with more explosions and the sound of small-arms fire.

And . . . Ted Kowalczyk, his face blackened with charcoal dust, frantically led his group of twenty-five men as they used wire-cutters to breach a section of fence some two miles west of Mercury. That done, they drove their jeeps through the hole and across the sands until they reached the main road leading to the compound. They were now inside the site, one mile behind the main entrance.

Gate number two was manned by less than ten soldiers. Frightened, confused soldiers—but alert and aware.

Ted's driver brought the jeep to a screeching halt at the barrier and Ted leaped from the jeep. The soldiers saluted. One of them, a corporal, barked, "Sir!"

"You got a problem here, soldier?"

The corporal pointed to the sky and said, "Can't you see it, sir? We're under attack!"

"I see that, son. That's why we're here. Who do we report to?"

"Captain Lewis is in charge of security. He's at the main Gate. You should have talked to him."

"We did, soldier. He told us to come in here. Didn't he advise you?"

"No, sir. I better talk to him . . ."

"No need. We'll stay here. They may attack this entrance soon enough."

Even as he spoke, the men in his group were moving toward the entrance, automatic weapons in their hands. The corporal, now quite confused, said, "I'll contact the captain and . . ."

Before he could use his portable radio, the hapless corporal and the rest of his men were looking down the barrels of twenty-five automatic weapons.

"OK," Ted shouted to his men, "tie them up and stash them in the guard-house. Ten of you take their places. The rest of you follow me."

Five remaining jeeps roared down the narrow road leading to the last gate and the building that housed, it was hoped, Tommy Wilson and Vance Gifford. Ted held on to the windshield as the vehicle bounced down the road, overrunning its headlights. In the air above

366

them, to the left and right, booming explosions continued to split the air while orange, red and yellow displays lit up the sky. Ted allowed himself a little smile. Over a hundred men were hard at work, making it look, for all the world, like the site was being attacked by thousands.

Aside from his group, the others were constantly on the move, leaving behind them bombs and skyrockets timed to explode at precise times, while still more devices had been thrown over the fence, their timers set for even longer periods of time, assuring massive confusion.

It seemed to be working.

The jeeps raced through the night.

Ted's group reached the main compound gate in three minutes, the convoy of jeeps coming to a stop in a cloud of dust. Several soldiers and civilians were standing by the gate while other civilians milled about the buildings, watching the pyrotechnics in the sky and wondering what was going on. Ted leaped out of his vehicle and gesturing with his arms, said, "It's a full-scale terrorist attack. We've got to get the civilians out of here!"

One of the soldiers leveled his rifle and said, "Identify yourself!"

Before another word was spoken, the prong from one of the stun-guns imbedded itself in the soldier's arm and he was immobilized by a low-amp jolt of some twenty-five thousand volts. The other soldiers met the same fate. Quickly, the civilians outside the buildings were subdued and bound.

At last, Ted's men were inside the compound. They circled the buildings while still in the vehicles. Through a bullhorn, Ted yelled, "Everyone, run for your lives! The site is under attack. Terrorists! Run for your lives! Head for the rear gate. There are troops there to take you away!"

Like lemmings, the few engineers, accountants, and other civilians still in the buildings, poured out of the structures and began running toward a little-used rear gate to the compound, located a half-mile to the north. Not one of them thought to stand fast and ask some questions.

Ted and his men then headed their jeeps toward the main target, some one thousand yards to the east.

When they reached it, there were just a few soldiers standing outside, surprised looks on their faces. Ted yelled, "The place is under attack! We've got to get the civilians out of here!"

As the soldiers began shouting questions, the stun-guns did their work and within seconds, all resistance was at an end. With his heart pounding unmercifully, Ted raced inside the building, his men in tow, and started searching the rooms. To his relief, there were no more troops inside. The building seemed deserted. With the aid of some of his people, he raced through the open rooms, then headed down the long hallway, opening doors to accessible rooms and pounding on doors to those that were locked.

Nothing.

The locks were shot away and the rooms inspected. Still nothing.

And so far . . . no sign of Tommy or Vance Gifford.

He continued down the long hallway, his spirits sagging, until he came to the very end.

There were two doors left, on opposite sides of the hall, both locked. His heart seemed to stand still as his anxiety level increased. If these rooms were unoccupied, this entire effort would have been in vain. He'd picked this building because it had been recommended as the most likely one. Had they been misled? Or had Tommy and Gifford been moved? If this wasn't the building, there was no way they would get another chance.

He kicked one of the doors. "Anyone in there?"

There was no answer.

He yelled, "This is Ted Kowalczyk! Tommy or Vance! If you're in there, say something!"

For a moment there was nothing. Then he heard a voice that made him want to shout out in pure joy. The voice was coming from just inside the door, and it was Tommy's.

"Ted?"

"*Yes!* It's me! Stand back! I'm going to shoot the lock."

When he finally kicked the door open, a thoroughly frightened Tommy Wilson was huddled on the bed, his eyes round as saucers, his mouth open, his hands extended as though to ward off a bullet.

"It's OK, Tommy," Ted said. "I've come to take you home."

Tommy bolted upright, as though he'd been given an electric charge. His eyes searched the blackened face. Even though the tall frame of Ted Kowalczyk was very recognizable, the face was blackened and the uniform made no sense at all.

"Ted?" he asked, still unsure.

Ted's face broke into a big grin. "None other," he said. "Come on. We've got to move. Where's Gifford?"

"Across . . . across the hall. What the hell's going on? Is all of this your doing?"

" 'Fraid so, pal. Move!"

They moved across the hall and rescued a stunned Vance Gifford. Then everyone rushed out of the building and into the waiting jeeps.

The sky was still filled with the sights and sounds of explosions as the jeeps hurtled down the road. Then, thankfully, they were out of the compound, through the hole in the fence, and back on the highway, their jeep alone now, as the other seven vehicles cut away to make good their own escape from this madness.

Three miles down the road, the motor home lay waiting. They made it without incident. A hiding area had been prepared beneath the queen-sized bed that occupied most of the rear of the vehicle. That was where they would stay until safely back at the RV park.

As they entered the motor home, Tommy saw Terry and his jaw dropped open in surprise. "What are *you* doing here?"

"Later," she said, as she directed them to the hiding place under the bed. "Everyone has to be quiet now."

A breathless Vance Gifford looked at Ted and asked, "Who the hell are you?"

Ted grinned at him. "I don't have time to explain. Just crawl under the bed and keep your mouth shut until we get where we're going. I'll explain it all to you then."

Ted, Tommy, Vance, and Terry crawled beneath the bed.

Dr. Wickshire put the motor home in gear.

On the drive back to Las Vegas, they encountered only one roadblock. Two State troopers entered the motor home, gave it a quick, cursory inspection and waved them on.

Throughout the trip, Ted suppressed the desire to scream out in pure joy. The adrenaline was still surging through his veins. He was so filled with

370

exhilaration he trembled.

They'd done it!

Tommy Wilson was alive, breathing, wide-eyed, and lying beside him at this very moment!

He felt heartened for another reason. When Tommy had first entered the motor home, Ted had carefully watched the expression in Terry's eyes when she looked at her ex-husband. There was relief, yes. But there wasn't the special warmth in her eyes that he saw when she looked at Ted. His joy was twofold, so intense he was afraid he'd burst.

The highways were a madhouse. Police cars, fire trucks, Air Force and Army vehicles, ambulances . . . all with sirens and horns blaring as they headed in the opposite direction toward the test site. It was chaos.

At the site itself, the explosions had stopped. The students stood meekly as police and Army personnel took names and addresses.

As for the whereabouts of the others, it was a mystery.

Trucks and jeeps had been found abandoned all around the southern perimeter of the site. Deep holes in the ground gave evidence of tremendous explosions, but the explosions had taken place in the sand and no real damage had been done. The hole in the perimeter fence had been the only other evidence of the actual attack. That, and some door locks that had been shot away.

Scores of civilian and Army personnel had been found bound and gagged, but no one was seriously injured.

Except for the students, who seemed as genuinely mystified as everyone else, not a single attacker had been captured. The students, when questioned, were of little help. All they knew, according to their spokespersons, two men and a woman, was that some outfit had wanted to pay them a lot of money to sponsor their next protest. Why not? they'd decided.

Who were they and what did they want? That was the question that was being asked by everyone. No one seemed to know.

Except for those members of NADAT. They knew, but refused to divulge anything to anyone.

An hour later, the motor home was back at the RV park, where an anxious Frank Leach was waiting. As soon as Dr. Wickshire shut off the engine, she gave them the okay and the four crawled from beneath the bed.

Leach opened the door to the motor home, stormed inside the coach and gave Ted a bear-hug. He was almost beside himself with excitement.

"These the guys?" he said, as he looked at Tommy and Vance.

Ted nodded.

"Jesus Christ! I never would have believed it. God! The whole town is going crazy. They think it's a war out there. They've never *seen* this much action! Jesus!"

Ted slapped him on the shoulder. "Did you find Darlene?"

"Yeah, babe! I brought her over here and told her to wait in the lobby. She's been on the phone ever since this started, trying to find out what's going on."

"Get her. Now! We'll meet at the dog walk."

"Right!"

"Ted!"

It was Tommy, still shaken. "What in the hell is going on?" he asked.

Ted turned to Terry and said, "Terry, you tell them. I have to get moving."

Five minutes later, he was at the dog walk, towering

over a diminutive Darlene Yu, looking down into a pair of sloe-eyes that were full of questions. He'd changed into civilian clothes, but there were still streaks of black on his face.

"It *is* you!" Darlene said. "And from the looks of it, you're got something to do with all of this mayhem. What's it all about?"

He didn't answer. "Did you bring a tape recorder and camera?"

She opened her large handbag and showed the items to him. He nodded and then looked away.

"What is it?" she asked.

He turned and looked down into her eyes again. "That story you printed."

"Yes?"

"It created a panic. It took all day for them to get people settled down."

She sighed. "I know. But what are we supposed to do? You know as well as I do that the hearings are a farce. And as far as I'm concerned, our story is right on the money. You should be complaining to those idiots, not me. Did you kill Tommy Wilson?"

"No."

"I didn't think so."

"I know. I read your article. I appreciate the comments."

"Are you going to tell me what this is about or not?"

He pursed his lips for a moment and then said, "What if everything you printed was true . . . and you could prove it? How would you handle it?"

She felt her heart begin to pound. Clearly, the man knew something. She paced the ground for a few moments as she thought about it. Then her face brightened and she said, "I wouldn't print it right away. First, I'd go to the governor with it. I'd tell him what was happening and give him a chance to set up some sort of evacuation plan. Then . . . the moment he went public, I'd print the story. That way, there'd be less of a panic."

"What could the governor do?"

"He could force the feds to come clean," she said. "He's an old-time pol. He knows how to play that game."

"And if he was successful, and the feds did come clean. What then?"

She shook her head and said, "They'd *have* to evacuate. There'd be no other choice!"

"You're sure?"

"Yes. Now . . . what have you got?"

He grinned at her. "How would you like to meet two dead men?"

Chapter Thirty-four

Sacramento, California, the capital of California, lies some five hundred driving miles from the fantasyland of Las Vegas. In Sacramento, Governor George Tasker was having a fantasy of his own. He was dreaming that he was on a cruise ship in the middle of the Caribbean, dancing in the Grand Ballroom. His dancing partner was none other than Jaclyn Smith. She was looking up into his eyes adoringly, telling him how much she admired him. . . How much she desired him . . . How much she wanted to leave this room so that they could be alone . . .

He tried to think of the right words. And as he did so, he was struck with the incongruity of the sound of a ringing telephone. Why on earth, he thought, was a phone ringing in the middle of this dance floor? He could hear the music of the big band clearly. But it was being drowned out by the incessant ringing of the infernal . . .

His eyes snapped open and he was instantly awake. The band had stopped playing. Jaclyn Smith had vanished. He was in his bed. The phone was still ringing.

He looked at the bedside clock and cursed out loud. As usual, Martha slept on, undisturbed. The woman could sleep through anything.

It was 3:37 in the goddam morning! Nobody called him at this hour! Unless . . .

"Yes!" he barked into the phone.

"Governor, it's Jack." Jack Browne was his press secretary.

"What is it, Jack?"

"Sir, I've got a reporter from the L.A. *Globe* on the other line. They patched me through. I thought . . ."

Governor Tasker exploded. "Are you nuts? The *Globe!* Jesus Christ, Jack!"

"Sir . . . Hear me out. She's got solid proof, sir. Solid! The story they wrote is true, for God's sake! She's got the evidence!"

"Evidence! What evidence?"

"It's about the earthquake, sir. There really is going to be an earthquake. In L.A. In a matter of days! She's got the proof!"

"Proof? How the hell can she have proof?"

"Well, for one thing," the press secretary said, his voice almost a wail, "she let me talk to Thomas Wilson. He was supposed to be dead. He isn't. Jesus . . . you aren't going to believe this . . ."

George Tasker could feel the hair on his arms starting to stand on end. The name of Thomas Wilson had impacted on his consciousness. "All right! Take it easy, Jack. Is she still on the line?"

"Yes . . . I thought . . ."

"It's all right. You did the right thing. I'll talk to her."

He opened the drawer to the bedside table and pulled out another telephone. He punched the lit button and picked up the receiver.

"This is Governor Tasker. Who am I speaking to?"

"This is Darlene Yu, Governor."

The name was seared into his brain. Just like the name of every other reporter who had participated in the story that had almost torn Los Angeles apart. Names that were forever on his personal shit-list. "What the hell's this all about?"

"Governor . . . We can't come to you, so we thought you might want to come here."

"Come where? What the hell are you talking about?"

She told him everything. Then she had him talk to Ted Kowalczyk and Thomas Wilson. Throughout, the governor asked some pertinent questions until he was fully satisfied it was no hoax.

Within forty-five minutes, his plane was in the air on its way to Las Vegas.

Governor Tasker and Jack Browne were met at the airport by Darlene Yu, who drove them in a rented car to the RV park. They parked beside the ancient motor home and went inside. After the introductions were made, Tasker, a big man with curly black hair, looked at Ted and said, "You broke into the test site to get these guys out?"

"I had some help," Ted said.

"You've got balls, fella. I'll say that. On the way over, we listened to the radio news reports. Nobody mentioned anything about these two."

Tommy Wilson stroked his beard and said, "The reasons should be obvious, Governor." As he said it, he handed Ted's copy of the report he had written for NADAT to the governor. "This is the *real* report," he said. "The one that was presented at the hearing was faked. They're trying to cover up the fact that we've managed to predict a great earthquake."

"In God's name. Why?"

"Because, Gifford answered, "they're afraid that evacuation is impossible. For some reason, they're convinced it can't be done. So they've pinned their hopes on trying to stop the quake from happening."

"Stop it from happening? Using those bombs? How the hell can they do anything?"

First Wilson, then Gifford, then Dr. Wickshire explained it all to him. When they were finished, the man was almost purple with rage. He turned to Dr. Wickshire and asked, "You seem to be the one with the experience here, Doctor. Is this all poppycock or what?"

Dr. Wickshire looked into his eyes and said, "Not a word of it, Governor. Unless you evacuate Los Angeles, the death toll will be staggering."

The governor turned to Darlene Yu. "I suppose," he said, "you'll have this in the goddam paper before I can even make a move."

She shook her head. "Not at all, Governor. I want to work *with* you on this one. I don't want to see anyone hurt any more than you do. I'll do whatever has to be done. But . . ."

"But what?"

"If you take the same tack as the president did, then I'll just have to do it without you."

Governor Tasker ran a hand over his eyes. "I can't understand it. I know Byron Walsh as well as anyone. I can't imagine what has caused him to react this way."

"There's one way to find out," Ted said.

"You can use my mobile phone," Dr. Wickshire chimed in. Governor Tasker stood up and banged his head on the ceiling. He rubbed it for a moment and then said, "If it's all the same to you, I think I'll use a pay phone."

Chapter Thirty-five

President Byron Walsh sat in the wing-back chair near the window and stared idly at the horizon as the sun, hidden by clouds, burned its way through the day. He was still dressed in the blue pajamas he'd worn to bed, even if precious sleep had failed to come.

It was after eight in the morning. By this time, he should have showered, shaved, dressed, eaten, and been at his desk for at least an hour. That was the way it had been ever since he'd assumed the office, except for those rare days off. But on this bleak morning, he seemed to have no energy at all. Nor enough desire to even make an effort to get ready for the day. He felt like a errant schoolchild, wanting to play hooky from class, perhaps to attend a baseball game, or play with his friends. Except his playing days were over. He was all grown up now, ensconced in a job he'd craved and until now, enjoyed.

This kind of depression was new to him. Most

unwelcome, yet somehow recognizable. It was just that he wasn't quite sure how to fight it.

He turned away from the window as he heard his wife of thirty-two years come into the room.

"Byron?"

"Yes, dear?"

She was dressed in casual clothes, which was her custom. Her face was almost devoid of makeup, with eyes that expressed warmth and caring. "What is it? The California thing?"

She always seemed to know what he was thinking. It had been that way almost from the moment they'd first met. Now they rarely saw each other except on official functions. It was unusual for her to come to his bedroom. What surprised him even more was that she could still read his mind.

"Yes," he said, quietly.

"Did you sleep at all?"

"Oh, I managed some," he lied. "I'm fine."

She walked over to him and placed her hands on his shoulders, then reached up and gently drew his head to her breast.

"You look very tired," she said.

He patted her arm and said, "Don't worry, I'll be fine."

She lifted his head and looked into his eyes. "Byron," she said, softly, "You are the president of the United States. If you really feel that your people are wrong, then you must do what *you* think is best. Just because you made an agreement doesn't make it right. Presidents, like women, are allowed to change their minds."

"You heard?"

"There are few secrets in these halls, my love."

He smiled weakly. "It's not quite that simple, my dear. I would lose at least five cabinet members instantly. Probably more later. There would be a terrible scandal. Just terrible!"

He fought to maintain a smile on his face. "Wasn't it Harry Truman who said there were too damn many secrets in government? Can you imagine Harry in this situation? What do you think he'd have done?"

The telephone beeped quietly, saving her the task of answering her husband. Extricating himself from her grasp, Byron Walsh stood up and walked over to the telephone.

"Yes?"

It was Willard Coones. "Mr. President . . . I'm afraid we have some real problems."

He felt a chill go down his spine. What now! The Middle East? Central America? The Tokyo stock market? What horrors would befall him this day?

"I'll be there in a minute," he said.

It took six.

He was dressed, shaved and his hair was combed. They were waiting for him in the Oval Office, Coones and Jason Shubert.

He took a seat behind the desk and looked at Coones. The man's face was a ghastly shade of white. Pointing at Shubert, Walsh asked, "What's he doing here?"

Coones rubbed a hand across his lips and said, "There was an attack on the nuclear test site in Nevada a couple of hours ago. A heavily armed group of men broke in and took Vance Gifford and Thomas Wilson with them."

President Walsh looked at though he'd been struck in the face. He stood up and said, "What! How in God"s name . . ."

"That's not all," Coones continued. "We know who set up the raid. It was a man named Ted Kowalczyk."

"Who?"

"The man who was accused of murdering Wilson."

382

"But how . . . ?"

Coones stared at the ground and waved a hand at Shubert. "I think our resident expert can explain that."

President Walsh stared at Shubert and asked, "So?"

Shubert looked like a man who'd been through hell. If anything, he looked even worse than Coones.

"We . . . thought . . . at one time . . ." His voice wavered as he tried to find the words, "That George Belcher, being a friend and . . ."

Walsh slammed his hand on the desk and said, "What in the hell are you talking about? Speak up!"

Shubert was in pure agony. He'd made a mistake and now it had come back to destroy his life. He could see that now as he looked into the almost violent eyes of President Walsh.

"Belcher was our FBI point man. He talked to Kowalczyk in an effort to get him to stop his investigation. You see . . ."

"Get to the point!" the president screamed.

Shubert took a deep breath and tried again. "Belcher let Kowalczyk talk to Thomas Wilson," he said. "He knew Wilson was alive. We never expected . . ."

The president's eyes were almost bulging out of his head. "You mean you let this man know about the whole operation?"

"No! Not all of it. Just the fact that Wilson was alive."

"And you didn't tell anyone?"

Shubert extended his arms outward. "I didn't think it would come to this. Belcher was convinced that if we let this guy talk to Wilson, we could get him to cooperate. Instead, Kowalczyk assaulted Belcher, gave him a broken jaw, in fact. The man is in the hospital and hasn't uttered a word since."

The president took a deep breath and asked, "But why? Why in God's name would you let this man talk to Wilson in the first place? What ever possessed you to make such a stupid mistake?"

Shubert's eyes rolled toward the ceiling. "It was . . . the man was investigating the death of his friend. He was starting to make some progress. I thought that if he was given a chance to see what we were trying to do, he'd come around like the rest of them."

President Walsh's jaw dropped as the full impact of what was being said hit him. Pointing his finger at Shubert, he said, "And when he didn't, you had the FBI make him out to be a murderer. You had them pursue him in the hope that he'd be killed. Am I right?"

"No! That was Graves's doing, not mine."

"But you *knew!* You let it happen! God! Is there nothing you people stand for?"

For a moment the room grew silent. Then Walsh turned to Coones. "So . . . what happened at the site? You said it was attacked by a heavily armed group. What group? Where there any casualties?"

Coones shook his head. "No casualties. They used a lot of fake bombs. All we know is that there were about five hundred of them. Maybe more. They were all dressed as Army personnel. There were also a couple thousand students protesting at the same time. We think they were part of it. The FBI is investigating. So is the Army."

"No one was caught?"

"Just the students, and they don't really seem to know that much. There were some people involved in organizing the student protest but they took off before it was even halfway over. The names they gave don't show up on any files."

"And . . . his people. None of them were caught?"

"No. We have no idea where they are."

The president slammed a hand on the desk again.

"My God! The press! Has anything come across the wires?"

"No, Mr. President. Just the story of the raid itself."

"How long ago was this?"

"About three hours ago."

"Three hours! Jesus!" President Walsh sank into his chair and covered his face with his hands. Then, acting deliberately, he tore them away and asked, "What are we doing?"

Coones straightened up and said, "Other than contact the FBI, I haven't done anything yet. I wanted to talk to you."

Byron Walsh sagged even deeper into the thick leather chair. Coones cleared his throat and asked, "What do you want me to do?"

President Walsh simply shook his head. Then he said, "Better get Director Fisher in here."

"Shouldn't I prepare some sort of statement for the press?"

The president looked at him with cold, dead eyes. "No," he said. "Not yet. Not until I see what happens next. I've already made a total fool of myself. I'd rather not compound that just yet."

"But . . ."

President Walsh held up a hand. "Would you two please leave me alone now? I'd really like to be alone, if you don't mind."

Coones looked at his friend, grabbed Shubert by the arm, and very quietly, the two men left the Oval Office.

An obviously angry FBI director John Fisher was ushered into the Oval Office. The country's top cop stood rigidly in front of the desk and glowered at Byron Walsh as the president made notes on a yellow legal pad.

"You wanted to see me, Mr. President?" he said, his voice cold and hard.

Walsh slowly laid down the pen he was using and looked up. He leaned back in his chair and asked, "Have you found out anything yet?"

Fisher nodded. "Some."

"And?"

"I don't think you really want to know."

President Walsh seemed confused. "I don't understand," he said.

"I think you do," the director said, harshly. "I've just received a message from the RAC in San Francisco. He's been trying to break one of our people's silence for days. He finally succeeded. I've been given to understand that some of my people have been working for the Pentagon. I was unaware of this until this moment. I'd like an explanation."

President Walsh took a deep breath and then told the man everything. When he was finished, Fisher, still standing, removed a single sheet of paper from the inside pocket of his jacket and laid it on the desk. President Walsh didn't have to look at it to know what it was.

"John," he said. "I realize how you feel. Truly. But I ask you to please . . . hold off for just a few days. You weren't a part of this. There's no reason why your career should suffer because of it."

"Mr. President," Fisher said, his eyes glistening, "to remain would indicate my tolerance for what has transpired. I cannot do that."

"I understand. I assure you, if you remain, at least until after the twenty-seventh, I will make a statement absolving you of any complicity in this affair."

Fisher grunted. "And who would believe it?"

President Walsh fought to hold off the tears beginning to form in his eyes. He could see his carefully crafted career being destroyed with each passing second. "I'm not asking for myself," he said. "It's just that we have a terrible crisis on our hands. You must realize what's at stake here. There are millions of lives . . . You can't walk away from that. You can't!"

For a moment Fisher said nothing. Then, shoving his hands in his pockets, he said, "We have an attack on a federal facility to contend with at this moment. We have some strong leads. I expect we could make some arrests before the day is out. But I also expect that by doing so, we will bring even more ridicule down on our heads. This is the most incredible disaster I've ever witnessed."

President Walsh shook his head. "Not even close," he said. "The real disaster lies ahead if we aren't able to stop this earthquake."

He leaned forward and said, "I want you to forget about the raid. We both know why it was done. My only hope is that the man who perpetrated it realizes the damage he can do if he doesn't think this out."

"You want me to cancel the warrants?"

"Yes. We'll need to concentrate all of our efforts on the evacuation plans. There's no other choice now. If you would, I'd like you to work with the Pentagon and a man named Jason Shubert. They'll brief you on the evacuation plan and the status of the weapons. We need you, John. Badly."

Some of the stiffness went out of the FBI director's body. "In that case," he said, "I'll stand by. For the moment."

President Walsh stood up and shook Fisher's hand. "Thank you, John."

Less than two hours later, Willard Coones reentered

the Oval Office. Alone.

His face was even more drawn, with eyes that seemed to have sunken inside the sockets. He looked like he'd aged five years.

He took a seat beside the desk and looked at his long-time friend as though he were a condemned man. Byron Walsh looked, if anything, even worse than Coones. His face was puffy, the skin covered with light red blotches. The body sagged in the chair, as though the very life had left the man.

Walsh looked up and asked, "What is it?" in a voice that was barely audible.

Coones hardly knew where to begin. The news he was bringing was the worst. He worried whether or not Walsh could even take it. But there was no choice. None. He was still the president.

"I've got Governor Tasker on the telephone," he said, trying to keep the urgency out of his voice. "He's in Las Vegas. He just finished talking to Wilson and Gifford. He's about to go public. But before he does, he wants to talk to you."

"Governor Tasker? They went to him?"

"It would appear so."

President Walsh rubbed his eyes for a moment and said, "We're finished, Willard. Do you realize that? We're finished!"

Willard Coones knew it. He'd known it the moment he'd talked to Tasker.

The room seemed to smell of death.

President Walsh could feel the air leave his lungs. For a moment, the room seemed to be spinning and he feared he would faint. But he fought the panic that threatened to consume him and picked up the telephone receiver with trembling hands. Then he pressed a button on the desk speaker and placed the receiver back in its cradle. That allowed Coones to hear both ends of the conversation.

"This is President Walsh."

"Mr. President . . . this is Governor George Tasker."

"Yes, Governor. I know why you're calling. I was just about to call you, in fact. I wanted to advise you that we are about to put into action an evacuation plan that includes much of southern California. The details are being forwarded . . ."

"You bastard!" the governor said, his voice quivering with emotion. "Why don't you cut your fucking heart out before I do it myself!"

Even as the words stuck him like hammer blows, the president felt compelled to continue the facade. "Governor Tasker, I don't think . . ."

The voice was raging now. Almost screaming into the telephone. "Listen to me, you son of a bitch! I'll see to it that you're impeached! Goddammit! I'll have you fucking well hung!"

"Governor, for God's sake . . ."

"The evacuation plan. How long have you had it?"

"Well . . . it was just . . . I'm afraid it's not perfect, but there is . . . yes . . ."

"I want it forwarded to me immediately. I intend to put California under martial law and I'll expect your full cooperation. If I get it, I'll cover your ass for a while, which should give you the chance to leave office with a little dignity, but if I don't, you won't be fit for dog food before this day is out. You hear me?"

"Governor . . . I . . ."

"You bastard! You were going to let us all sit there and take it!"

"No! We have a plan! We have some nuclear devices that we think will . . ."

"Yeah. I heard about that too. Right now, I need to move twelve million people. Do I have your full support?"

"Yes, of course. I wouldn't think . . ."

"Just tell me something, Byron. Why? That's what I want to know? Why?"

Byron Walsh swallowed hard and said, "You see . . . we had these experts. They convinced everyone that an evacuation was impossible. They'd conducted a number of studies that indicated any attempt at evacuation would be hopeless. They said it was impossible! But I knew they were wrong. That's why I insisted that . . ."

The governor cut him off. "Sure, you did. That evacuation plan. I want it faxed to my office right now. Will you do that?"

"Yes, of course."

"And the nuclear devices. I'm going public with this. I want your guarantee that you'll still make the attempt."

"George . . . I don't think going public is wise. There are . . ."

"I don't really give a shit what you think! You've already shown us where your brains are. I want your guarantee!" the governor screamed.

President Walsh hesitated for a moment and then said, "Yes, of course."

"I'll have one of my people in constant touch for the duration. We'll arrange for a line to be kept open at all times. Is that agreed?"

"Agreed. But, George . . . I really think . . ." He stopped talking and looked up at Willard Coones. Then both of them stared at the speaker on the desk, the wail of the dial tone evidence of the fact that the governor of California had just hung up on the president of the United States.

Chapter Thirty-six

At three o'clock in the afternoon, Pacific time, on Thursday, May 13, an unusual joint press conference was held in Sacramento and Washington. In the White House press room, a large television screen had been installed, enabling those in attendance to see George Tasker in Sacramento. Similarly, in the governor's press room, another screen had been installed, from which stared the stern visage of President Byron Walsh.

The press conference was the result of intense negotiations between staff members for both men that had been ongoing throughout the day. It couldn't have come at a better time. Speculation by both the electronic media and the press had reached new heights during the previous twenty-four hours.

Whereas the Los Angeles *Globe* had been, just hours ago, branded as an irresponsible, almost malicious purveyor of wild, unsupported lies, second thoughts and solid investigative reporting by a phalanx of journalists had succeeded in directing the attention away from the *Globe* and towards Washington. The raid on the Nevada test site was still an unexplained mystery. Earlier in the morning, the hearings on the earthquake insurance question had been suspended without explanation, which further served to fuel speculation.

The reporters in attendance at both press conferences were, therefore, almost manic as they waited impatiently for what was clearly an important announcement. Both rooms seemed to crackle with tension.

The president spoke first. His face had been carefully made up, but it was impossible to completely disguise the anguish that roiled within the man. His voice was strong and clear, but the lips seemed to tremble as he delivered his remarks.

"Two days ago," he began, "I held a press conference in this very room, a press conference that was necessitated by a story that appeared in the Los Angeles *Globe* contending that a large earthquake was about to strike California.

"At that time, I was unaware that there existed, within the Pentagon, an agency that has for some time, been immersed in the scientific exploration of earthquake prediction. This agency, created and directed by a man named Robert Graves, functioned in secret . . . even to the extent of excluding the president of the United States.

"Robert Graves committed suicide earlier this week. Since that time, members of his organization have come forward and enlightened me . . . and the members of the cabinet, as to their activities and the results of their research.

"It now appears, on the basis of the evidence presented, that a strong possibility indeed exists . . . that southern California may be struck by an earthquake of some magnitude in the very near future."

Both rooms erupted with the babble of scores of voices. President Walsh held up his hand and asked for quiet. It was some time in coming.

"I will deal with the specifics of that possibility a little later. Right now, I want to impress upon you the fact that there is some good news. In fact, I would call it very good news."

He stopped, took a drink of water, and continued. "This research was not confined to the study of earthquakes and the prediction thereof. It included a comprehensive examination of the causes of earthquakes, even to the point of looking into methods whereby their incredible destructive power might be measurably reduced. The research points to a possible answer that has yet to be employed, but shows considerable promise. Without getting into the technical aspects, I can tell you that it involves the use of small nuclear devices that are detonated deep in the fault line."

Again, there was a buzz of conversation on both rooms. Some questions were hurled toward the president. They were ignored.

"Like any new scientific discovery," he continued, "there are perils. But the perils are inconsequential when compared to the destructive power of a great earthquake.

"Since learning of this threat to the people of southern California, I have been in constant communication with Governor George Tasker, who has agreed to accept a leadership position in our efforts to minimize what could be the worst natural disaster in this nation's history. At this point, I would ask that Governor

Tasker advise you as to the measures that have been and will be taken from this point forward."

The scene switched to California where Governor Tasker cleared his throat and, staring glumly into the television camera, said, "Thank you, Mr. President.

"As of this moment, the state of California is under martial law."

There was a stunned silence. The governor pointed to a map of the state on the wall behind him and, with a pointer, indicated an area that had been outlined in black.

"The area within these lines has been designated as an emergency evacuation area. Everyone within . . ."

Even as the press conference was just getting under way, C-5 transports were landing at Long Beach International Airport, their fuselages filled to bursting with troops and equipment. Other planes were landing at the El Toro Marine Base, south of Los Angeles, while still others arrived at Edwards and George Air Force Bases in the desert. From Air Force, Army, Navy and Marine bases in and around southern California, hundreds of thousands of additional troops were pouring into Los Angeles.

Surveyors were already marking off areas of the desert just outside Victorville, preparatory to the erection of chain-link fences. Three-page cables were going out over fax and Telex machines to every law enforcement agency in a twelve-state area.

At the headquarters of the Los Angeles *Globe*, the presses were already running with the biggest story in the newspaper's history, a story that had already been approved by Governor Tasker.

Throughout the entire world, via cables sent to U.S. embassies, the call was going out for everything from tents to blankets to doctors, and feverish preparations for transport of people and supplies to California begun.

The press conference continued. The complete evacuation plan was outlined. The plan for using the nuclear devices was revealed in detail. References were made concerning the creation and function of NADAT, and some mention was made of the attack on the Nevada test site. The names of Ted Kowalczyk, Theresa Wilson, Thomas Wilson, and Vance Gifford were mentioned. It was revealed that the latter two were now back at the test site, working voluntarily on the effort to diffuse the earthquake. As for Ted and Terry, they were told, albeit obliquely, that warrants for their arrest had been rescinded.

Almost everything was made public. Selected information was held back because, it was felt, the knowledge would serve only to further frighten an already terrified public. Even an apology was given to the Los Angeles *Globe*, much to the surprise and delight of one Sam Steele, as he hobbled around in pure frustration in his hospital room. His stomach still hurt like hell and he felt very weak. But the thought of being cooped up in the hospital while the biggest story in the *Globe's* history was being written was enough to make him even sicker.

Both the president and Governor Tasker had chosen their words carefully, wishing to appear positive in their approach to this immense problem. They each stressed the need for cooperation, the importance of remaining calm, and the fact that much of the world was about to assist everyone involved in the next two weeks. But before the press conference was halfway through, the streets of Los Angeles were once again grid-locked with cars, trucks, and other vehicles as hundreds of thousands of men and women tried desperately to escape what they perceived as certain death.

Again, as it had been just two days earlier, the city of Los Angeles was in total chaos.

Chapter Thirty-seven

Ted Kowalczyk rolled over on his back and stretched his aching body. He hurt all over. The tension of the past few days had been unrelenting, the stress manifesting itself in his muscles, stretching them taut almost to the point of inflexibility. Now, as they began to relax and uncoil, they broadcast their belated protest by throbbing in unison.

He opened his eyes and tried to determine exactly where he was. The white acoustic ceiling of the room was bathed in what dim, yellow light that managed to filter through the heavy drapes. As he began to scrutinize the furniture in the room, his nostrils picked up the scent of a woman's perfume on the pillow beside him.

The two senses acted in concert and he realized that he was in Terry's apartment.

It all started to come back in bits and pieces.

They had done what they had set out to do. That much he remembered clearly. The rest was somewhat of a blur.

He remembered a conversation with the governor of California. And there were conversations with Tommy and Gifford and Frank Leach and a few others.

Then he had met with some of the men who had helped him, as they reassembled to celebrate in a suite at the Las Vegas Hilton. He'd thrown his big arms around each and every man who'd come by and thanked them for sticking with him in what had been a risky undertaking. He remembered thinking how precious those bonds were and resolving to keep them more active in the future.

He remembered Tommy and Vance saying they wanted to get back to the nuclear test site and continue working on the project. There were tears in Tommy's eyes when he'd expressed his deep-felt thanks for Ted's involvement.

Then there was Dr. Wickshire saying she wanted to get back to Hollister and study the effects of the small quake that was expected to strike there on Sunday. And as the motor home negotiated the narrow desert road, there were the radio reports of the press conferences. Then they'd stopped short of Reno, so everyone could catch a few hours of sleep. Even then, as exhausted as he was, the sleep was fitful. He'd been fully awake as the ancient motor home wound its way through the spectacular scenery surrounding the Lake Tahoe area, and then he'd fallen asleep again.

When he awoke, there were radio broadcasts that told of the panic that raged in Los Angeles and the steps that were being taken to bring it to an end. He remembered feeling partly responsible for the suffering that was being felt by those caught in the panic, and the rationalizing he'd done to assuage the guilt.

He remembered hearing that President Walsh had

flown to Los Angeles and had pledged to tour the entire city, using a sound truck to make a short speech every few blocks. Despite the incredibly tight security, three people had tried to kill the man while he carried out his pledge, one of the attacks coming much too close, the rifle shot wounding a Secret Service man just inches away from the president.

And finally, he remembered Terry ushering him into her apartment after saying goodbye to Dr. Wickshire and putting him to bed.

When had it all happened? How long ago? He seemed to have lost complete track of time.

He sat up in the bed and rubbed his eyes. His clothes were gone and so was his watch. He slowly got out of bed and shuffled into the bathroom. The cold shower brought him back to life but did nothing for the aching muscles. When he came out of the bathroom, Terry was seated on the edge of the bed, looking glorious in a dark green robe, smiling and pouring steaming hot coffee into two large mugs that rested on a wooden tray. Beside the mugs were toasted English muffins smothered in butter. The sight of the food made his mouth water.

He turned back to grab a towel, which he placed around his waist. Terry clucked her tongue disapprovingly.

"You took my clothes," he said.

"They needed cleaning," she answered, picking up his watch from the tray and handing it to him. He looked at it in astonishment. It was five minutes after noon. He'd slept for eighteen hours straight.

"I slept too long," he said, as he sipped the coffee and chewed on a muffin. He was ravenous.

"You were exhausted," she said. "And so you should be. You've been under unbelievable pressure with not much sleep for over a week. The human body has its limits, you know."

Indeed, he did know. Unconsciously, he massaged the scar on his chest.

"What's happening?" he asked.

She drank some coffee and said, "Well, as you know, Thursday night was the worst, what with the pitched battles in the streets all night long. Fires, gang fights . . . Then late yesterday, after Walsh arrived and started touring in that truck, things started to settle down. Either that, or they finally got enough troops into the city to restore order. Walsh seemed to be everywhere, talking to people, telling them that things were going to work out, that they had to work together. He did that all through the day and into the night.

"It seemed to work, because last night wasn't half as bad. This morning, things seem to be really coming together, although they're still having a terrible time with the traffic. So far, just under a million people have arrived at the evacuation center and, although it's a hell of a mess, it's gradually beginning to shape up. They say they expect to have everything pretty well organized in another two days."

Ted finished off one of the muffins and started on another. "I'm surprised the president is still alive," he said, between mouthfuls. "He'd been shot at three times by the time I fell asleep."

"The latest count is seven," she said. "Two Secret Service men were wounded and three innocent bystanders were killed, but he's out there again today."

Ted grimaced. "How many others?"

"You mustn't concern yourself with that," she said. "You had to do it, Ted."

His face tightened. "How many others?" he repeated.

She looked away. "Two hundred and thirty dead, and just over two thousand injured," she said, her voice soft and filled with sadness. Then she turned and smiled at him again. "But things have really slowed down. I think the major panic is over. It's not nearly as bad as Graves had predicted. Besides . . . you have to keep in mind the number of people that will be saved! That's what's important."

He stared into his coffee.

"Frank Leach called," she said, changing the subject. "He went to your office. I guess your secretary has quit. She left you a note and said she warned you. What was that about?"

The darkness left his face. "Oh . . . you remember the earthquake last week? Was it last week?"

She grinned. "Yes. It seems like a year, but it was just last week."

"Well . . . she said if there was another one, she'd go back home. I don't blame her. This one is enough to scare the hell out of anyone."

"Tommy called."

"Yes?"

"He said to tell you that they're hard at work at the site going over the data again. I guess Shubert is back there as well. He said that they've decided to increase the strength of the devices. He's not at all certain they won't trigger the quake, but they have no choice. He suggested we get out of the state as well, even though Menlo Park isn't in the actual evacuation area."

"He's still concerned about you."

Her gaze wavered. "Yes . . . but he also said that he recognized that there was something between us. He said he could see it in our faces. He wanted us both to know that he wishes us nothing but happiness."

"And how do you feel about that?"

Her eyes held his. "It doesn't matter what he thinks. Not really. I know I'm falling in love with you and have no desire to stop it from happening. I don't think I could stop it even if I wanted to."

He felt a strange twinge in his heart. Instantly, her face looked worried. "Am I being too aggressive

401

again?"

He took her hand in his and looked into her eyes. "Don't worry about that."

"But I do worry," she said. "I'm not normally like this. I blurt out things when I know I should keep quiet. God! I don't want to scare you away, Ted. And I'm afraid I will. Just forget what I say. I don't mean to put pressure on you. Not at all!"

He bent down and kissed her gently. As their lips parted, he said, "I'll let you know if you get out of hand. If it makes you feel better, I'm feeling what you're feeling. And I'm liking what I'm feeling."

"Really?"

By way of an answer, he lifted the tray and placed it on the floor. Then, he reached over and pulled her to his body, his lips covering her face with soft, gentle kisses.

He could feel her relax in his arms as her breathing quickened.

And then they were making love again, slowly, carefully, tenderly . . . until the passion consumed them both and the pace became urgent, demanding, both of them suddenly filled with the need to express their feelings in that magical, joyous blending of mind and body.

Later, he turned to her and said, "I think he's right."

"Who?"

"Tommy. I think we should get out of the state. Where would you like to go?"

"You'll come with me?"

He smiled at her. "Of course."

She thought about it for a moment and said, "I know this sounds silly, but I have a sister in Dallas I haven't seen for three years. It would be boring for you."

"No, it wouldn't. I'd like to meet her. Before we do that though, I'd like to take a look at some of the sights around here."

She looked at him in puzzlement. "Sights?"

"Yes," he said. "Seventeen Mile Drive, Yosemite
. . . We may never see them again if things don't work
out. They'll no longer exist."

The next day was Sunday. The quake predicted for
Hollister hit at precisely 2.36 P.M. It lasted seventeen
seconds and was rated as having a magnitude of 4.9.
Damage was slight.

If anyone had the slightest doubt that there might be
a flaw in the methodology developed by Vance Gifford
and Tommy Wilson, it should have been erased by that
quake.

But it wasn't.

Incredibly, six separate lawsuits were filed on the
Monday following the quake, representing a variety of
interests, five questioning the constitutionality of in-
voking martial law on the basis of mere predictions,
the other asking for a court order blocking the use of
nuclear devices.

Six judges ruled, independent of each other, that the
cases would be not be heard until after the twenty-
seventh. Those rulings brought immediate and not
unexpected appeals.

On Tuesday, the panic had almost completely sub-
sided. But the number of lawsuits increased. A total of
thirty-six suits were filed, twenty of them aimed at
preventing the nuclear devices from being detonated,
the rest aimed at rescinding the martial law order.
Governor Tasker, backed by President Walsh, proclaimed that both the civil and criminal courts systems
were to be shut down until June 1. The order applied
to both state and federal jurisdictions. It was determined that since evacuations were taking place, it was
impractical to allow the courts to remain open.

On Wednesday, the Supreme Court of the United States, by a vote of 9 to 0, ruled that the invocation of martial law was indeed constitutional, as was the order calling for the evacuation of southern California, rendering those suits moot. It refused to hear arguments on the question of detonating nuclear devices within the Los Angeles city limits. The press called it a major victory for the Walsh-Tasker forces, as they were now being called.

On Thursday, the first of eight nuclear devices was flown from Hanford, Washington to Los Angeles, and the installation of the device in one of the old oil wells commenced.

Through it all, President Walsh remained in southern California, acting somewhat like a cheerleader, urging, cajoling, pleading, thanking, praising . . . all on less than three hours of sleep a night. He seemed to be everywhere at once, giving support, making snap decisions, cutting red tape, unsnarling snags, spending hours on the phone with people located in cities all over the world, performing minor miracles hourly.

If his actions were a form of penance, it didn't matter. Results were what counted, and the results were there for all to see. Much like Churchill in the dark days of the London blitz, Byron Walsh was fast becoming a symbol of the moment, working tirelessly to encourage those affected, fighting hard to maintain some sort of order, dividing his time between those already in the evacuation complex and those still awaiting their turn to make the move.

As for Ted and Terry, they took the time to explore the natural wonders of north-central California, wandering through Carmel, Yosemite, and a host of other places that evoked a feeling of peace and natural order. They hoped they were not seeing these places for the last time.

They also took the time to explore the inner depths

of their own souls, coming to the realization that they were madly, passionately in love with one another, with hearts filled to bursting.

On the night before they were to leave by car for Dallas, they spent three hours in front of the television set, getting an update on the latest.

In a nutshell, it was working.

The evacuation center now held five and a half million people. Three million remained in various parts of southern California and they would be taken out in the next few days. Another two million people had already departed for other locations, to live with relatives or friends in other states. An additional million people already in the complex were making their own arrangements to move on as soon as possible. The city was flooded with troops, as was the evacuation area.

There were a host of problems, not the least among them being the large number of drug addicts and alcoholics who were having serious withdrawal problems while inside the confines of the evacuation complex. Everyone entering the camp had been thoroughly searched. Drugs and alcohol were banned. Special treatment areas were set up and therapy begun, but with privacy at a premium, the drug treatment center was fully exposed, its inhabitants looked upon as creatures in some zoo. The decision was finally made to move them all further inland.

There were other problems. Many had refused to leave their homes. While the emergency order called for the evacuation of all residents without exception, certain exceptions *were* being made, for no other reason other than the lack of time to resolve the issue.

The street gangs had been handled with dispatch. Thousands of youngsters had been rounded up by local law enforcement officials, placed into buses, and taken to a separate holding camp in Arizona.

But, all in all, it was working. Somehow, the common fear that most shared was the very thing that was drawing them together.

Despite the deprivations of the desert complex, a wide range of activities had been organized to keep people occupied. Many of those interned were busy helping erect temporary quarters for those who would follow. Thousands of tons of supplies were arriving daily, all of them needing to be sorted, catalogued and distributed.

Meals had to be prepared. Garbage details organized. Even latrines filled in and new ones dug. It was a perfect example of people cooperating with one another in the face of a common enemy. In this case, the enemy was an unseen, but well-understood natural phenomenon.

It was working.

There had been deaths. There had been injuries.

But Robert Graves had been wrong.

To the great relief of Byron Walsh and especially, Ted Kowalczyk, he had been very, very wrong.

The question that now remained was whether or not the quake could be successfully quelled.

In less than a week, they would know.

Chapter Thirty-eight

President Byron Walsh looked out the window of his trailer and shook his head in utter amazement.

The trailer was one of sixteen double-wides that had been positioned just yards from the intersection of the Hollywood and Ventura freeways. This particular intersection was probably the busiest in all of Los Angeles. At this hour, seven in the morning, the confluence of cars and trucks would normally come to a shuddering halt, the noise of them reverberating off the surrounding hills, the air fouled with their stink.

But today, aside from the frantic, last-minute activity attendant to a daring and possibly catastrophic attempt to circumvent the heretofore inexorable forces of nature, the freeways were empty.

Scientists and engineers were spread out over a two-mile-wide area. Security personnel flanked them on all sides. The trailer site was surrounded by additional

Army troops and law enforcement personnel protecting the president and the engineers inside the buildings. There was no one else.

The quietness of the place was almost eerie.

He could hear a sound that probably hadn't been heard at this particular spot for decades: the sound of birds as they warbled their songs. There were hundreds of them, some in flight, some standing stoically on concrete dividing barriers; others hopping defiantly along the highway itself, once dangerously off-limits, now, suddenly, a sanctuary of sorts.

Could birds think? he wondered. And if they could, what would they make of this?

A deserted city. An abandoned freeway system.

There was a strangeness about the scene that was chilling.

In just hours now, they would trigger the devices. Would they work? he wondered. No one really knew. They'd consulted graphs and charts and kept the computers running day and night, but in the end, they were really guessing. The computer programs could give them information. The decision had to be made by a human being.

And he'd made it.

Would all of this disappear? Or would there be a miracle?

As he continued to ponder the future, there was a knock at the door. Willard Coones opened the door a crack and stuck his head inside.

"Byron?"

Walsh turned and leaned against the wall.

"Yes?"

"Governor Tasker is here. He'd like a word with you before you go."

Walsh sighed and said, "Send him in."

A moment later, the tall, burly governor entered the room and closed the door behind him. Walsh nodded

408

and pointed to the window. "Strange, isn't it? The quiet. I never thought I'd see the day when . . ." He let the sentence trail off. "You wanted to see me?"

Tasker moved closer and stuck out his hand. "Mr. President, I know I gave you a pretty hard time when this first came to light."

"You had a right to."

A small smile played over Tasker's lips. "Maybe so," he said, "but I've watched you in action these past two weeks. I think you've done one hell of a job. Frankly, I don't think we could have pulled it off if you hadn't come out here and thrown yourself into this like you did."

Walsh shrugged and said, "You're being too kind, Governor. You spearheaded this operation. If it *is* successful, you can take full credit."

The president shook the governor's hand. The hand was warm and dry, the grip strong.

Tasker seemed uncomfortable. As he stood there, he kept shifting his weight from one foot to the other and seemed not to know what to do with his hands. "I'm not normally one to make mistakes in judgment," he said, "but I pegged you wrong. I realize now that you didn't have any idea as to what was going on. I'm sorry I accused you falsely."

Walsh waved a hand in the air and said, "No . . . you're wrong. I did know. Not until the last minute, but I knew. At the time I made that first announcement . . . I knew."

For a moment, his gaze left the governor and returned to the scene outside the window. Then he took a deep breath and gave the governor his full attention. "If I have any excuse it's that I was well and truly torn. At the outset, I had these so-called experts who had spent years analyzing these type of things. I had a cabinet that agreed with their findings. And then, after that newspaper story, all I could think

409

about was stopping the panic.

"I did what I thought was right at the time . . . but looking back . . . it all had to come out eventually. There are damn few secrets any more. I should have known that. I should have expected it. I should have relied on my own instincts. Had it not been for that clown who busted into the test site . . . Who knows?"

He sighed and said, "I don't deserve praise, Governor. To be perfectly candid, I feel ashamed."

"You shouldn't," Tasker said, quickly. "Given the circumstances, I think I would have reacted just as you did."

Walsh smiled weakly. "Well," he said, "it doesn't really matter much, does it? If these devices work, we'll be spared a disaster of inconceivable enormity. But even then, there will be those who question my judgment. I expect the courts will be years sorting all of this out, either way."

"Nevertheless," Tasker insisted, "I offer you my personal congratulations. I wanted you to know that *before* the devices are detonated."

"Thank you, Governor. I appreciate your comments very much."

"Good luck, Mr. President."

"Yes . . . you, too."

Governor Tasker turned and headed out of the room. A few seconds later, Willard Coones came back in and said, "We're ready, Byron. If you want to be in Washington when they trigger these things, we have to leave now."

Byron Walsh shoved his hands in his pockets and shook his head. "I'm staying here, Willard."

Coones's jaw dropped. "Byron! We went all over that! You're exposing yourself to unnecessary dangers for no good reason! You accomplish nothing by this action. Besides, you agreed that . . ."

The president held up a hand. His eyes became thin

slits. "I'm staying here, Willard."

They stared at each other for a moment and then Coones nodded and left the room.

Bill Price and Sam Steele were having another of their infamous meetings. Only this time, the atmosphere was decidedly different. For one thing, the meeting was being held in the editorial offices of the Kansas City *Guardian,* whose owners had gracefully arranged accommodations for the *Globe.* The Los Angeles newspaper had been publishing from this new location for the last ten days, distributing the bulk of their newspapers to those confined to the evacuation complex. Circulation had gone up one hundred thousand in the last three days alone and Sam Steele was no longer arguing with one William Price, master editor.

"Well, what do you think?" Sam asked, a broad smile on his face. "Will we have a newspaper to go back to or not?"

Price lit up a cigarette and inhaled deeply. The rules at the *Guardian* allowed smoking. For Price, it was heaven. He looked at the two headlines that had already been prepared, along with accompanying stories.

One read, "BOMBS FAIL!" in one hundred forty-four-point type. The other read, "L.A. SAVED!"

Both editions had been plated and were ready to go. There was nothing to do now but wait. And that's precisely what the two men were doing. Waiting.

"It's a real crap-shoot," Price said. "But if you'd like to make a small wager, I've got one for you."

"I'm listening," Sam said.

Price grinned at him and said, "I'll bet that it works and, in a few days, we'll all be back at work in our old building, cranking out the paper every day like normal."

"OK," Sam said, "I'll bet that it doesn't work. I figure the moment they hit that button, the whole city falls to the ground. Now . . . what's the action?"

Price pursed his lips and rubbed his eyes for a moment. Then he said, "If I win . . . you build me my own office where I can smoke any time I want. OK?"

Steele considered it for a moment and then nodded. "OK. Now, what if you lose?"

Price got up and headed toward the rest room. Over his shoulder, he said, "If I lose . . . I'll quit smoking." Then he laughed.

The devices were in position. Eight of them, one each in eight holes that varied in depth from one thousand yards to just over three miles.

They had been positioned according to the latest data that had been drawn from the probes in the wells immediately next to them. The data had been fed to a computer complex, analyzed, reanalyzed, and the final decision made. Now, just minutes away from the actual detonation, the tension was clearly evident on the faces of the men as they monitored the equipment or milled about one of the double-wide trailers that was being used as a command center. This was the room where the buttons would be pushed.

Tommy Wilson, his beard glistening with perspiration, removed his hard hat and sat in a corner of the room. Vance Gifford took a seat beside him.

The engineers looked over a bank of instruments that had been attached to one wall, checking and double-checking.

"All systems go," one of them called out.

"Ten minutes and counting," another barked.

Overhead, a single television camera, equipped with a wide-angle lens, took in the scene inside the building. The feed from that one camera was being fed to an uplink that sent the signal to a satellite stationed some twenty-two thousand miles above the earth. From there the signal was beamed back to a number of downlinks and then it was fed through a variety of other pieces of equipment, eventually ending up in the homes of an estimated one and a half billion people.

Someone had projected that fully half the population of the entire planet was watching this broadcast.

Jason Shubert approached the two men and descended to his haunches. "I just want you to know," he said, "that no matter what happens, you guys really did a hell of a job."

Tommy glared at him. "We're all pals now, is that it?"

Shubert looked hurt. "I'm just saying that . . ."

Wilson cut him off. "Save it! Just leave us alone."

Shubert rose and moved to the other side of the room. Tommy leaned back and said, "Bastard!"

Gifford nodded. "Did you hear that Walsh is still in his trailer? He refuses to leave."

"Good," Tommy said. "Maybe we'll all sink into a big crevice. At least we'll take the little prick with us."

"What are you so angry about?" Gifford asked.

Tommy stroked his beard and said, "Just this: if we had been allowed to operate in the open from the beginning, where do you think we'd be?"

"Well . . ." Gifford started to answer. Before he could finish, Tommy broke in. "I'll tell you," he said, his voice rising. "For one thing, we would have had months instead of weeks to prepare for this. We could have done a lot more testing to check out your theories. We'd be a hell of a lot more confident that this could work. In fact, I'd go so far as to say that we might not have needed to evacuate Los Angeles at all. It could have saved a lot of lives and billions of dollars."

Gifford shook his head. "You're dead wrong about

that, my friend."

Wilson seemed surprised that he was getting an argument. "Why?" he asked.

"You're forgetting about the lawsuits," Gifford said. "If this had been made public in the beginning, we wouldn't be here today. The entire operation would have been tied up in knots by every pressure group in the world. Nothing would have been accomplished. The only reason we're being allowed to make this attempt is because time was running out, so decisions were made on an emergency basis. If the politicians had been given time to really think about it . . ."

He shook his head and said, "As much as I hate to say it, you can thank God for Robert Graves. This was his idea from the beginning. As soon as he read that first report two years ago, he started the operation in Nevada. Without him and his ability to operate unfettered, this never would have happened.

"If this works," he continued, his eyes fixed on his associate, "Robert Graves is the one man who should be given the credit."

Tommy snorted. "You can't be serious!"

Gifford continued to stare at him as he said, "Think about it. I mean, really think about it."

They both lapsed into silence.

"Two minutes and counting!"

Ted Kowalczyk and Terry Wilson stared at the television set in the Dallas home of Terry's sister Maria.

The three of them were huddled together on the sofa, holding hands, not speaking, mesmerized by the actions being carried out half a country away.

Maria had a set of rosary beads in her hands and her mouth worked silently as she said the prayers.

"One minute and counting!"

Ted could feel his heart beating against his chest. In all his life, he'd never felt such tension. Even that terrible moment when he faced the woman with the gun in her hand had been less draining than this. That horror had taken place almost before he had time to think. This was different. He'd had much too much time to think. There were times when being unable to think was a blessing.

"Thirty seconds and counting!"

The plan called for the bombs to be detonated ten seconds apart from each other. There were eight in all. Seventy seconds of man-made violence that would either do nothing, or save billions of dollars in property damage . . . or possibly . . . create the very catastrophe they were attempting to prevent. If it worked, there would be many who would claim credit. If it failed, there would be a lesser number who'd be blamed. But standing above them all would be one Byron Walsh. He'd be the one to take the blame, deserved or not.

"Ten seconds and counting!"

He felt his lungs stop working. His mouth was dry, but the rest of his body was bathed in cold sweat.

The countdown continued until . . .

"Number One!" the man screamed.

The image on the television set shook as the first bomb detonated.

Men in white coveralls scanned hundreds of dials and computer screens, punching buttons and calling out numbers. The announcer, a man stationed some fifty miles from the actual scene, whispered, "The first bomb has been detonated . . ."

"Number Two!"

The image shook again.

"We have 3.5 on the surface!"

"Number Three!"

This time the camera shook so hard it was impossible to determine what was actually happening inside the trailer. A babble of voices continued to call out numbers and symbols that meant something to someone. To the announcer, they meant nothing. He was unable to say whether or not the project was succeeding or failing.

"Number Four!"

The camera shuddered once more . . . violently.

And then the television screen went blank.

Contact with the site had been lost.

Chapter Thirty-nine

Two minutes before zero hour, Willard Coones and Secret Service agent Roger O'Brien had finally prevailed upon President Walsh to leave the flimsy trailer. It was the worst possible place, they reasoned, for him to remain if something went wrong.

For hours, the president had argued that he did not want to be the focus of attention, insisting that he preferred to remain indoors and away from any media attention.

"Byron," Coones had said, once they were alone, "there is only one television camera, and it's inside the command center. There's only one pool reporter, and he's also inside the command center. So please don't persist in this ridiculous charade. What are you really trying to accomplish? Suicide? Are you hoping you'll be killed?"

"Of course not!" Walsh had snapped.

Exasperated, Coones had fired his last volley.

"You've always said that stupidity was preventable," Coones argued. "For you to remain in here is about as dumb as it gets. You've got enough image problems already. Why the hell make it worse?"

The statement had struck a nerve. Finally. So Walsh had moved outside and sat on the ground in an open space, surrounded by Secret Service agents and a few Army troops.

The city of Los Angeles had been successfully evacuated . . . to a point. They all knew that there were still tens of thousands who had refused to leave. It wasn't known how many of them would blame the president if there was a disaster, but those assigned the task of protecting him wanted to take no chances. So they surrounded him with a wall of humanity, their backs to him and Coones, as the two men sat on the ground and waited for the last few seconds to be counted off.

The countdown could be heard through a speaker that had been mounted to the outside wall of the command center. As the announcement was given that device number four had been detonated, the earth responded instantly.

The was a sudden jolt, then a violent vibration, followed by another jolt.

Immediately, the president was forced to assume a prone position and two burly agents placed their bodies over his. Flat on his stomach, Walsh looked back at the trailer he'd been using and his eyes widened in astonishment. It seemed to be afloat on a raging sea. It wallowed, creaking and groaning, as windows shattered, sending shards of glass descending to the ground like crystal snowflakes. The main entry door sprang open and slammed against the wall. A large section of the ceiling ripped away and crashed to the floor. Off to his left, some of the other trailers were suffering the same fate.

Conscious of the weight of the two men lying on top of him, he continued to observe, his emotions a mixture of terror and curiosity. Beneath him, the ground was alive. It was as though he was in Air Force One as it passed through some unseen turbulence. He was staring out at a land that seemed fluid, rolling and shaking, the movement causing great clouds of dust to rise into the tortured air. Almost directly in his line of sight, one of the wide, multi-lane overpass bridges began to disintegrate, and large chunks of concrete fell slowly to the highway below, seemingly in slow motion. He saw palm trees bending over so far their tops brushed the ground, then watched as they snapped back and momentarily exploded from the earth like failed rockets, their humble root structures no longer able to grasp the soil.

The noise was almost deafening. A dull, roaring sound that brought pain to his ears.

The dust was swirling now, blinding him, choking him, forcing him to grope helplessly for something with which to cover his face. But he couldn't move. The two agents seemed bent on shoving him into the ground.

The curiosity was gone. Terror ruled supreme. It had failed! The whole thing was a disaster! The ground was shaking uncontrollably, vibrating, heaving, threatening to open up and swallow them all!

It was happening! The effort a waste! California was in the process of being totally destroyed!

To his absolute horror, he felt his bladder release involuntarily.

Oh God! he thought to himself. They'll know! When they find my body, they'll know I pissed in my pants!

His chest was almost bursting as the fear began to

consume him and he screamed out in anguish.

The sound of the scream startled him . . . because he could hear it.

The quake had stopped.

It had, but only for a moment.

To his horror, he could feel it again.

Again he screamed. At least he thought he did. All he could hear was a roaring sound as though he was standing directly beside some massive jet engine at full throttle.

He couldn't see. He was unsure whether his eyelids were closed or open. He couldn't breathe, and he thought he was coughing, but he wasn't sure.

He knew he was dying.

And then . . . it was quiet again.

The noise had stopped, but the ground continued to move.

"It's over!"

He heard a voice. Coones's voice.

"Byron . . . it's over!"

He felt the weight lift from his back and hands were helping him to his feet. The fluid in his middle ear, still in motion, made him dizzy. It was impossible to stand. So he sat down again, his knees drawn up around his chin, his arms pulling them even tighter, as he tried to make sense of what had happened.

There had been a quake, that he knew.

He was still alive. For a moment, he considered whether or not he wanted to be. The dust still hovered above the surface of the earth, thick and opaque, preventing him from seeing what lay beyond. So he looked straight up.

The sky was a light yellow.

"Byron!

He turned to his right. It was then that he realized that his trailer had been completely destroyed. Where once there had been three large rooms, there was nothing but scrap lumber. And Willard Coones, bleeding from a cut on his face, was looking into his eyes, screaming at him, trying to get him to speak.

He coughed some more, then sneezed a few times. Willard was there with a handkerchief, cleaning his face like a mother might care for a child.

He wanted to vomit.

He bent over and retched. It seemed to make him feel better.

"Byron!"

Finally, he was able to answer. "I'm fine, Willard. Will you stop screaming in my damn ear?"

The face broke into a wide grin. "You had me going for a minute."

"I'm all right!" he repeated.

He was standing now, his face white from the shock, his hands trembling uncontrollably. Looking around, Byron Walsh observed, with some joy, that he was not the only one who had passed water.

He started to laugh as he pointed to the dampness evident on the trousers of Coones. Then Coones started to laugh.

They stopped laughing when they heard other voices. The dust was beginnng to settle and the voices were coming from just beyond their position.

Carefully, they picked their way through the rubble of smashed trailers and fallen trees until they were standing outside the command center. By some miracle, it was relatively intact. Now, as the dust settled even more, Walsh could see the extent of the damage in the immediate area. The overpass was destroyed and there were three visible cracks in one of the freeways, but another overpass seemed undamaged. Six of the trailers had been wrecked, and others showed some damage. Still others seemed completely undamaged.

Men and women were milling about and pointing to the southeast. Byron Walsh turned his head in the direction they were pointing.

And then he saw it.

The Los Angeles skyline. Tall buildings shimmering in the light . . . Still! Just as he remembered them. Intact!

And then he heard them cheering. They were cheering an earthquake! Were they mad?

There were millions of them. All gathered around the thousands of television sets that had been erected on tall poles throughout the evacuation complex. They had fallen into silence when the picture had disappeared and then, as they felt the earth begin to shake beneath them, they'd started to panic. But this was a panic that the troops had prepared for.

Immediately, automatic weapons were fired into the air and bullhorns were activated.

"Everyone lie on the ground! On the ground! Do it now!"

For a moment, the screams continued unabated and then more weapons were fired into the air.

The mass of humanity obeyed the orders and lay on the ground as it rumbled and shivered for what seemed like an eternity.

In fact, it was twenty-three seconds. Then, for a few seconds it stopped, only to begin anew, this time for sixteen seconds.

When it finally stopped for good, they looked around cautiously and then slowly got to their feet. Again, they gathered around the television sets. Television sets that broadcast no picture.

Suddenly, the screens were filled with a familiar

face. Peter Grace, anchorman for YBS news, appeared on the screen.

Ted Kowalczyk had stopped breathing the moment the television picture had been lost. His big hand squeezed Terry's so hard she cried out in pain.

Not able to tear his eyes away from the television set, he released the grip and mumbled, "I'm sorry."

"It's OK," she said.

And then they saw Peter Grace, as he sat at his New York news desk, his hand to his ear, a look of consternation on his face.

"We seem to have lost our signal," he said, expressing the obvious. "As soon as we can, we'll go back to Los Angeles and . . ." He pressed his ear as he heard something being fed to him audibly.

"Yes . . . we now have Jack Spencer, the pool reporter assigned to the . . . Jack! Can you hear me?"

The voice was coming over a telephone line that was static-filled. Even so, it was impossible to miss the jubilance in the reporter's voice.

"Yes, Peter. We're on a conference line here. I understand that the television signal has been lost, so this report is for all of you out there. I can report to you that it appears this most incredible experiment is a qualified success! We've experienced a rather sharp earthquake here and in a few moments, I will be able to give you a better idea of its magnitude, but in the meantime, I have beside me a man who is not only responsible for the development of the technology allowing this earthquake to be predicted, but is an integral part of the team working . . . I think he can give you a better idea . . . Vance! Vance Gifford! Would you tell a waiting world what had just happened?"

Ted heard the familiar voice of Gifford as he said, "Yes, I'll be happy to. All eight devices were detonated. The fourth device triggered an earthquake that was centered exactly where we expected it to be . . . a rather strong jolt, as a matter of fact. There has been some damage — that's evident — but I can tell you that it is minor in relative terms. We've all just come in after looking at the buildings in downtown Los Angeles and they're still standing."

There was the sound of cheers in the background.

"We won't know exactly how successful we've been for another seventy-two hours," Gifford continued, "but if our calculations are right, I think we may have succeeded in doing what we set out to do."

The reporter jumped in. "You had predicted that the quake would hit on the twenty-seventh or the twenty-eighth. Since today is the twenty-sixth, is that why you're saying you won't really know for another seventy-two hours?"

"Exactly," Gifford replied. "We know we managed to release some of the pressure by creating this slippage. However, until we've had time to examine all of the data still being entered into the computers, we won't really . . . Oh, they've just handed me some of the preliminary numbers here. The quake has been initially given a magnitude of 6.7 on the Richter scale. That's considered a strong earthquake. Then we had an immediate aftershock of 6.1. Both were caused by the devices, I'm sure. Again, we won't really know for a while, but at the moment, it looks very, very good."

"Thank you, Mr. Gifford. I'm sure we're all — Oh! Ladies and gentlemen, we've just been joined by President Walsh, who, I'm delighted to say, is looking just fine. He's covered in dust, as are most of us. I don't know — Mr. President! I'm on a line here to all of the networks. Is there anything you'd like to say?"

There was a pause and then they could hear the president as he took the microphone.

"Yes, thank you. To those of you listening, I'd just like to say that . . ."

In Dallas, Terry Wilson removed some tissues from her handbag and gently wiped away the tears that continued to stream down the face of Ted Kowalczyk.

Epilogue

Ted Kowalczyk rolled over on his back and stared at the now-familiar ceiling. He stretched and closed his eyes. As usual, Terry was up and about and the smell of the coffee brewing in the kitchen was wafting into the bedroom.

They'd been back in Menlo Park for two days now and he was getting anxious to get back to his own apartment. In another day, he'd be allowed to enter the city again, as his was the second last area to be reoccupied.

They'd set it up in the same order as the evacuation process. Those in areas that had been the first ones evacuated were the first to be allowed to return. Ted's area was scheduled for tomorrow.

The door to the bedroom opened and Terry entered, the wooden tray she carried holding mugs of coffee and plates of English muffins. She placed the tray on the bedside table and sat on the side of the bed.

"Good morning," he said.

"Good morning, yourself," she answered.

She removed the morning paper from the tray and handed it to him.

He opened the paper and leafed through it quickly. Nothing much had changed. They were still reporting on the quake and its aftermath, the newspaper filled with updated estimates of the damage, now listed as topping two billion, and more of the continuing dialogue as to whether or not the quake had been the result of the nuclear devices alone.

The debate that had started almost as soon as the shaking had stopped was now intensifying. Several hearings were scheduled and thousands of lawsuits were being filed. Scientists were lining up on both sides of the issue, their ranks almost evenly divided. As for the future of President Walsh, there was sharp division on that question as well. Some called him a hero. Others were much less kind.

Ted threw the paper on the floor in disgust.

"Idiots," he snarled. "Why is it that every jerk in the whole damn world feels free to second-guess somebody who just saved his life? They interview some clown who hasn't been out of his dusty office for ten years as though he were the ultimate authority!"

"Ted!"

He looked up at her. Her hair was glistening as it fell to her shoulders, and her eyes were tinged with anger. "I don't want to talk about it any more," she said. "I've heard enough to last me a lifetime. Can we talk about something else?"

He started to respond when the telephone rang. Terry picked it up, talked for a moment, and then handed the instrument to Ted. He cupped his hand over the mouthpiece and asked, "Who is it?"

"Somebody named Hughes," she said, "He asked for you."

Ted took his hand away and said, "Sam?"

"Yes. Ted! I got this number from your boss. I don't mean to bother you, but I've been away."

"Haven't we all."

Sam Hughes laughed. "I guess so. What I meant was, I was on vacation before all of this craziness and now that I'm back, I see there's a big parcel here that you mailed to me some time ago. The covering letter says I'm not to open the parcel unless I'm unable to locate you. Naturally, I'm a little mystified. What the hell's this all about?"

Ted felt the laughter well up in him. The report! It was the copy of Tommy's report he'd mailed to Sam Hughes weeks ago! The irony of it all made him double up with laughter. When he finally regained control of himself, he said, "Not to worry, Sam. You can throw it out. I'll fill you in when I see you in a few days."

"You sure?"

"Yeah, I'm sure, Sam."

"Okay, Ted. Whatever you say."

Terry took the receiver from his hand and replaced it in its cradle. "What was that all about?"

He shook his head. "Long story," he said. Then, "You said you wanted to talk about something else."

"Yes?"

"How about this? I get out of bed, get down on my knees and ask you to marry me. Is that something we could talk about?"

She rolled her eyes toward the ceiling. "Did anyone ever tell you that you aren't exactly the most romantic person on the face of the earth?"

He shook his head. "You have a suggestion?"

"Yes," she said. "You get showered and shaved.

Then you can come back here and make love to me. After that, you can get down on your knees and ask for my hand."

"And what will you say?"

Her lips were upon his, giving him his answer.

About The Author

HARRISON ARNSTON is the author of three previous novels, *The Warning, Death Shock,* and *Baxter's Choice.* Prior to becoming a professional writer, he was owner of his own automotive accessory manufacturing business that he founded in 1968. He lives in Florida with his attorney wife, Theresa.

THE PEOPLE BEHIND THE HEADLINES
FROM ZEBRA BOOKS!

PAT NIXON: THE UNTOLD STORY   (2300, $4.50)
by Julie Nixon Eisenhower

The phenomenal *New York Times* bestseller about the very private woman who was thrust into the international limelight during the most turbulent era in modern American history. A fascinating and touching portrait of a very special First Lady.

STOCKMAN: THE MAN, THE MYTH,
THE FUTURE   (2005, $4.50)
by Owen Ullmann

Brilliant, outspoken, and ambitious, former Management and Budget Director David Stockman was the youngest man to sit at the Cabinet in more than 160 years, becoming the best known member of the Reagan Administration next to the President himself. Here is the first complete, full-scale, no-holds-barred story of Ronald Reagan's most colorful and controversial advisor.

IACOCCA   (3018, $4.50)
by David Abodaher

He took a dying Chrysler Corporation and turned it around through sheer will power and determination, becoming a modern-day folk hero in the process. The remarkable and inspiring true story of a legend in his own time: Lee Iacocca.

STRANGER IN TWO WORLDS   (2112, $4.50)
by Jean Harris

For the first time, the woman convicted in the shooting death of Scarsdale Diet doctor Herman Tarnower tells her own story. Here is the powerful and compelling *New York Times* bestseller that tells the whole truth about the tragic love affair and its shocking aftermath.

Available wherever paperbacks are sold, or order direct from the Publisher. Send cover price plus 50¢ per copy for mailing and handling to Zebra Books, Dept. 2895, 475 Park Avenue South, New York, N.Y. 10016. Residents of New York, New Jersey and Pennsylvania must include sales tax. DO NOT SEND CASH.

THE ULTIMATE IN SPINE-TINGLING TERROR
FROM ZEBRA BOOKS!

TOY CEMETERY (2228, $3.95)
by William W. Johnstone
A young man is the inheritor of a magnificent doll collection. But an ancient, unspeakable evil lurks behind the vacant eyes and painted-on smiles of his deadly toys!

SMOKE (2255, $3.95)
by Ruby Jean Jensen
Seven-year-old Ellen was sure it was Aladdin's lamp that she had found at the local garage sale. And no power on earth would be able to stop the hideous terror unleashed when she rubbed the magic lamp to make the genie appear!

WITCH CHILD (2230, $3.95)
by Elizabeth Lloyd
The gruesome spectacle of Goody Glover's witch trial and hanging haunted the dreams of young Rachel Gray. But the dawn brought Rachel no relief when the terrified girl discovered that her innocent soul had been taken over by the malevolent sorceress' vengeful spirit!

HORROR MANSION (2210, $3.95)
by J.N. Williamson
It was a deadly roller coaster ride through a carnival of terror when a group of unsuspecting souls crossed the threshold into the old Minnifield place. For all those who entered its grisly chamber of horrors would never again be allowed to leave — not even in death!

NIGHT WHISPER (2901, $4.50)
by Patricia Wallace
Twenty-six years have passed since Paige Brown lost her parents in the bizarre Tranquility Murders. Now Paige has returned to her home town to discover that the bloody nightmare is far from over . . . it has only just begun!

SLEEP TIGHT (2121, $3.95)
by Matthew J. Costello
A rash of mysterious disappearances terrorized the citizens of Harley, New York. But the worst was yet to come. For the Tall Man had entered young Noah's dreams — to steal the little boy's soul and feed on his innocence!